ROSE CLARKE AND THE PURSUIT OF LEARNING

Rose Clarke and the Pursuit of Learning

Paul Ryley

First published in Great Britain in 2022

ISBN 978-1-3999-3697-2

Typeset in Goudy by Falcon Oast Graphic Art Ltd.
Printed and bound by ImprintDigital.com

1 3 5 7 9 10 8 6 4 2

CHAPTER 1

Friday May 20th 1803.

MISS ROSE CLARKE WAS BORED. True, she was attending one of the biggest, most glittering balls of the season, and she was wearing a handsome new pale green dress embroidered with Greek motifs in the very latest fashion, and her hair was a miracle of the arts of her maid, ringletted within an inch of its life, and set with tiny jewels – but she was bored. Well, not just bored, actually. Irritable would have to come in there somewhere; also frustrated, and tetchy; and were it not that ennui was so tiresome in others she would probably have had a dose of that too. What made it worse was that her cousin Louisa (just bowing to her partner at the beginning of this cotillion) was having the time of her life, while Rose stood at the side of the dancers, and felt, well, fed up.

It wasn't only that she hadn't been asked to dance very often. Well, she hadn't been asked, much, except for two invitations: one from her brother George (who didn't count) and the other from one of Louisa's hopeful hangers-on, who thought dancing with her might be a way of ingratiating himself with Louisa. In which he was right, because Louisa liked men who were kind-hearted. However, as Louisa's dance-card was already full for the rest of the evening, it wasn't going to do him much good. And he had been so tedious! Tedious and dull. And probably banal, drab and vapid, she thought, though that would have implied variety that just had not been there.

'Oh, good evening Lady Merton,' she said, as the countess drifted by with her empty-eyed daughter. What was her name? Araminta? Arabella? Arable farm?

'Good evening, Miss Clarke,' replied that lady, looking at her short-sightedly. 'Is it not the most wonderful ball?'

'It is remarkably resplendent,' she answered, curtseying a little deeper than was correct, as she had forgotten to do so when she first addressed the countess.

'To be sure.' The countess looked as if she was unsure whether resplendent was a real word. 'My Augusta has had six dances already, and it is only ten o'clock.'

'She must be most gratified.'

'It is such a comfort to me that she is so popular. All the young men are falling over themselves to converse with her.'

Rose was seized with a mischievous urge. 'I am delighted to hear she is so fond of conversation. Lady Augusta, what is your opinion of the recent declaration of war with France?'

'Oh! Miss Clarke! I scarcely know. I do not follow the newspapers, it is not really a suitable topic for a young lady. I prefer a good novel. Or of course, my embroidery.'

'Of course. I should not have asked.'

'Good evening, Miss Clarke,' and Lady Merton had sailed onwards, back ramrod straight and her face a mask, towing her daughter behind her, and leaving Rose to her introspection.

It was mainly that everyone here (those she had spoken to, that is, and by extension all the others, except her brother, of course) had nothing interesting to say. Or if they did, they perhaps thought there was a prohibition on expressing it. Some obscure rule of etiquette which forbade them from having an opinion not borrowed from someone else, who themselves had never considered whether it made sense. And nobody had read anything of import, either. After all, it *was* May 1803, and we *had* just declared war on Boney two days ago, and militia *were* being raised, but all people seemed to talk about here was which poor debutante was the most beautiful, or had the largest dowry, or looked the most likely to produce healthy male offspring for the continuation of a noble lineage. Not to mention the gossip, scandal and outright slander that passed for news about Miss this and Lord that; Lady the other and Mr what's his name (to whom she was not married); and last and not least, speculation about You-know-who and his latest sensational waistcoat. It was all *so* last-century.

It wasn't that she didn't enjoy wearing lovely dresses, or seeing the sparkle of jewellery in the candlelight. She could enjoy the music, too, and the spectacle of the opulence of the ballroom. Some of the men here were undoubtedly handsome and dashing, and she was not at all immune to the charm of a pair of well-formed calves in white silk stockings, or a broad set of shoulders filling a formal coat. Unfortunately when the calves or shoulders opened their mouth, as it were, her heart ceased to flutter, dampened by the cold shower of wearisome predictability.

Was it too much to ask for a man who had a brain, and had read something other than the General Stud Book? If he was good-looking too, that would be a bonus. Rose yearned to speak with a man whose conversation had actual content, for the exchange of ideas, for wit and banter. The women and girls were even worse, it seemed. Constrained by managing mothers and the expectations of society to be demure and biddable, to have accomplishments rather than knowledge and the ability to think, they seemed to be quite content to discuss ribbons and bonnets and dress embellishments, and who the latest unmarried viscount would be likely to set his sights on.

Stop it, she told herself firmly, you sound churlish and petulant, you are going to turn into a miserable and sour old maid, whom nobody wants to know. Just because you think the restrictions on what you can do as a gentle-born lady are ridiculous, and you long to be free of chaperones, and keeping an expression which gives nothing away, and never laughing out loud, and so on, it won't have any effect whatever on your situation. Smile, make it look as though you are not thinking any of this, and try and simper at the next gentleman who passes.

Fortunately for her, this resolve was not tested immediately, as the next gentleman that passed was Sir George Clarke, Bt, her older brother, come to seek her out to check she was enjoying herself. He was someone she could admire, and why was it that the other gentlemen could not hold a candle to him? He was not exactly handsome, to be sure, having a rather unremarkable set of features like her, and not exactly tall, being only her own height, about five feet seven, and not exactly radiating charisma, being rather conventional, but he did spend his time actually *doing* something, working for the Foreign Office, though he was forbidden from discussing with her what exactly it might be. Also, he had been to Cambridge University, and he knew things, and he thought about things, and he treated her as a person with intelligence, most of the time.

'How's my favourite baby sister?' he greeted her. 'Have you discerned the latest in hair-ribbons, and the most suitable eligible bachelor at whom you should set your cap yet?'

Rose glared at him briefly, then set her face into a simpering blankness. 'It is just *so* difficult to know, Sir George. There are too too many choices, where should a girl start?' she breathed, finishing off with an insincere giggle.

'Fed up?'

'To the back teeth, Doddie. Are there no men here you can introduce me to who you knew at Cambridge? No girls who can talk about non-haberdashery matters?'

'Don't call me that here, Rose, someone might hear. I *am* a very important man, you know.'

'Of course, my lord.' Rose gave him an exaggerated curtsey.

George scanned the room. 'I haven't seen anyone yet who might suit you. There's Edward Wharton, but . . .'

'Smells bad.'

'Unfortunate, but true. There's Peter Thomas?'

'Too Welsh.'

'You're probably right. How about John Terrier? He's at the Home Office.'

'I haven't had the pleasure. Who is he?'

'Ah, maybe not, after all.' George looked sheepish. 'Well, um,'

'Tell me!'

'He, ah, I heard that he, er, caught something unsavoury in, that is, from, a lady of the, um . . .'

'I see. Perhaps not Mr Terrier then.'

'The only other Cambridge man I've seen here is Lord Toby Pearce, he's the younger son of the marquess of Cranfield, but he was a pollman and I don't know how he even passed the Previous examination.'

'I could give him a try, if you think he might be interested to talk to me?'

'Hmm. Well . . . He is at least a tolerable dancer. Don't go away, I'll bring him over.'

Rose turned to check that her chaperone, Louisa's mother Mrs Naismith, was still happily chatting to the other matrons and spinsters, then looked with interest as George weaved his way through the crowd followed by a tall, good-looking man in a blue coat, whose beauty was only marred by an exceedingly ill-judged waistcoat of a cerise and navy lozenge pattern.

'May I present Lord Toby Pearce, Rose? Toby, Miss Rose Clarke, my sister.'

Rose curtsied, and Lord Toby kissed her gloved fingers.

'Delighted, I'm sure. George here says you are his favourite sister. Splendid!'

'He is too kind: I am his only sister,' Rose said dryly.

'So how can you be his favourite? Don't make much sense to me.'

Rose glanced at her brother, raised one eyebrow. George shrugged, ever so slightly.

'Anyway, hhrmm! I do believe the music is ending. Would you care for the next dance, Miss Clarke? Anything to oblige an old college chum.'

Rose hid her grimace at his unintentional rudeness and took his offered hand, following him onto the floor and passing Louisa as she did so.

'Good for you,' said Louisa as she bounced by, heading for the next lucky gentleman on her list. 'Nice calves.'

'Hmmm,' was all Rose could muster.

As they stood waiting for the set to begin, she thought she would break the ice. 'Tell me about your studies at Cambridge, Lord Toby. Which subjects did you concentrate on?'

'Studies? 'Pon my word, yes. Er, I did do some of those at least for a few weeks before the disputations: had to, don't you know, the old man hired a private tutor, had to grind away at Latin and Greek and the first bit of that Euclid fellow, interrupted the hunting season too. But it wasn't too bad really, only lasted a little while, soon picked up with the sporting set again.'

Rose hesitated. 'Did you not enjoy the opportunity to learn, then?'

'Learning? What's the use of that? All that arithmetic we had to do too: can hire a man to do the estate accounts, can't I? And I can't see what the use of algebra is to anybody. All those xs and ys. Bosh and flummery, if you ask me.'

Rose tried another tack. 'Lord Toby, what do you think about the war in Europe recommencing? Do you think we shall prevail?'

''Spect so: can't be trounced by frogs, can we? Why d'ye ask? Oh yes, I see, old George earns a crust at the Foreign Office, don't he?'

Rose was saved from answering this by the dance starting: conversation was made difficult by their repeated separations in the figures. Lord Toby did however dance beautifully, and was most courteous, except unwittingly. He complimented her dress, and her hair, and asked by whom she was being sponsored. Rose tried a little further questioning when she could, and managed to establish that Lord Toby had been a devotee of the dining table, the Wine Society, and the cheery conversation in the Fellows' Parlour of a Sunday evening over further wine ('Lost a packet to this fellow Young there, he had the most confounded luck with his bets'). But most especially, he had spent his time with horses: hunting in all weathers, trips to the Newmarket races and rides on the Gog Magogs when hunting was out of season.

At the end of the set they found themselves at the far end of the room.

'Been thinking 'bout what ye said, Miss. Bout Frenchies, I mean. And horses, of course. And George, don't ye know. Thought up a t'riffic wheeze.'

'Go on,' she replied, wondering what gem of intelligence he would disclose.

'Wouldn't mind myself being a kind of spy, y'know, dashing about on my best horse Alex, rescuing fair maidens from the guillotine. Well, chaps as well, I s'pose, but ladies preferred. I can see the news-sheets: "English aristo cheeks revolutionary ruffians and foils their plans." He looked ever so pleased with his idea.

Rose smiled faintly and held out her arm to be led back around the room. As they neared her chaperone, he asked her whether she liked hunting, or ever followed the hunt, rather.

'Alas, a ladies' saddle is not conducive to fast riding and to jumping,' she answered him, 'and I should not care to be a passive spectator in a carriage miles behind the action.'

'Too right. It's all about the thrill of setting yourself to jumps you can't be sure of making. Poor sort of thing to watch, I'll be bound. Well, cheerio, then,' and he was gone.

Rose turned to her brother, who had gamely awaited her return. 'I see what you meant, or hinted at, at any rate. What is a pollman?'

George sighed. 'Toby's a decent sort, but he doesn't have what you might call a brain. He was a fellow-commoner, that's a sort of excuse to pay more for tuition and have to attain less academically, as well as dining at High Table and various other perks. And a pollman is one of the hoi polloi, the peasants, who take the ordinary degree rather than honours, which is not what you might call an arduous test.'

'But I thought Cambridge was full of bright men, like you?'

'Sadly, no. You see, anyone can get in if he has a recommendation from an MA of Cambridge or Oxford, and the college Fellows have no duty to teach, so to avoid embarrassment all round the ordinary degrees are awarded for having very little knowledge.'

'You got honours, though? You were eleventh Wrangler, weren't you?'

'Well, yes, but I had to pay out a lot for private tuition, or I'd never have mastered the calculus and some of the harder parts of Newton.'

'Oh.'

'There are quite a lot of reading men there, but they're a bit thin on the ground here tonight. Shame, really, I'd love to help you out.'

'Lord Toby seemed to think you were some sort of spy. Are you?'

George snorted. 'Paperwork, that's mostly what I do. Paperwork. Carrying out instructions from my masters. And flattering people to try and get them to do what needs doing. Which they ought to do anyway.'

'Oh,' Rose said, disappointed.

'But now, if you don't mind, I see Warburton over there, I need to talk to him about some French matters. Hush hush, don't you know?'

'Very well. I shall fade into the wallpaper and wither away quietly.'

'Can't you talk to Louisa? She's alright, isn't she?'

'I would, if I could, but I can't, as she is tripping the light fantastic toe on a full-time basis.'

'Oh. I'm sorry. But I must dash. Later, perhaps?' and he slithered into the crowd and was gone.

'Rose, darling! It's been an age!' This gush came from directly behind her. Rose turned to behold Alicia Warren, who had graced Miss Snape's School for Ladies for two of the three years Rose had attended. She would have said, studied at the school, but she was averse to falsehood. After their father had died when she was fifteen, and George had succeeded to the baronetcy, she had persuaded him to let her go there rather than continue to depend on a series of unsatisfactory governesses.

'Isn't it thrilling?' Alicia expostulated. 'Harriet, you remember Harriet, she's about to be proposed to by Viscount Jersey!'

Rose did indeed remember Harriet Venables, she had been a feather-brained excrescence on the female gender. Blonde, dazzlingly beautiful in an ephemeral way, with violet eyes, long eyelashes and too much décolletage, she had few interests beyond men and fashion, dancing and the theatre.

'I am intrigued,' she responded. 'How are you privy to the viscount's intimate intentions?

'Everyone knows,' Alicia said dismissively. 'Well, nearly everyone.'

'I see. There must be some races of savage in the Indies ignorant of such matters, I imagine.'

'Pardon? No, of course, they would not know. They are savages, of course. But everyone who is anyone would know.'

'Does she love him?'

'I should not think so. But he has ten thousand a year, and she will be a viscountess!'

'Is she here?'

'Of course. Look, there she is, with the dowager viscountess, by the lemonade table.'

Rose craned her neck and could easily see her erstwhile schoolmate nodding and smiling at the older lady. It was one advantage of being tall. One of the few advantages, really. Men seemed to prefer petite ladies, with delicate small hands and feet, and pronounced figures. However, she stood as tall as many of them, her jawline was determined, her figure boyish, and her extremities more robust in size. At least she did not have red hair, or she would be completely out of the fashion, beyond the pale.

'Of course, he is at least forty-eight years old. And, shall I say, portly of stature. But these things are nothing, he is a fine catch.'

'Is he kind? Does he care for her?'

'I do not know. But he is likely to die soon, so that is all right.'

At this awkward juncture, Louisa skittered off the dance floor and grabbed Rose's arm. 'You must accompany me to the retiring room,' she beseeched. 'I am so in need of a rest.'

Rose made her apologies to Alicia and followed Louisa from the ballroom.

'You'll never guess,' she began, the moment they were clear of the crowd. 'Mr Rupert Bridewell is showing a definite interest in me. He somehow secured two dances on my card and spent them gazing soulfully into my eyes. I think he is smitten.'

'Mr Bridewell?' Rose pretended to run through a list in her mind's eye. 'He is the one with the wall-eye? No, the one with the stutter. I forget myself; of course, he is the pox-scarred gentleman with the club foot.'

'Stop bamming! He is new in town this week, you have not met him. He is charm itself, handsome, tolerably rich, at least according to the papers, and very keen on the management of his estates. Which are I think in Derbyshire.'

'Excellent. When shall I expect the wedding? I need time to decide on a dress.'

'Hush, silly! Now come on, I do actually need the retiring room, I drank too much lemonade earlier.'

After seeing to the demands of nature the two young women found an alcove, drew the curtain and sat down. Louisa had attended the school during Rose's last year there, in anticipation of their needing to make their debuts together. She was eighteen, one year Rose's junior, and while not precisely ingenious, she was quick-witted and sensible.

'What were you doing talking to Alicia Warren? I thought you detested her?'

'She took me by a sally from the rear. I was unprepared.' She drew a little closer to Louisa, and spoke in a hushed whisper. 'But I am now so excited, because she confided in me that Harriet, you remember Harriet Venables, who thought Boney was called that because he was thin, is absolutely certain to marry the obese and sickly Viscount

Jersey who is sure to snuff it within a month after the wedding, leaving her rich and happy.'

'Cat!'

Rose sat up again. 'I admit it. You know me too well. I do not know how I had survived this evening so far without this intelligence, though.'

'I am sorry for abandoning you, but I do love to dance.'

'I know.' Rose patted Louisa's hand. 'I know I'm rather captious, but I'm very happy for you to be enjoying yourself so much.'

'Oh I am! But what about you? I will have a disappointed partner left over, having left the ballroom for this rest. Would you like to have him for the next dance?'

'I don't see why not. I prefer cast-offs, really.'

'Oh, I'm sorry, I didn't mean . . .'

'I'm joking. Honestly, I'm joking. Anyway, your cast-offs are a better quality than most people's new gowns.'

'Are there really no men you like in all this crush? I saw you going to dance with one man who had legs to die for.'

'Nary a one. I did dance as you said, he was called Lord Toby Pearce, but he was too, um, too . . .'

'Say it!'

'I couldn't possibly. Well, all right. Too keen on his horses, whose intellect matched his more closely than mine did.'

'Now you are really a harpy.'

'I admit it; I am sorry; do my claws show beneath my gown?'

Louisa made to look, and shook her head. 'No, but your wings are deforming the line of the back of your dress.'

They giggled, and hearing the music drawing to a close, stood up, made for the ballroom again, and after a certain amount of negotiation, took once more to the floor.

Rose's second-hand partner, a Mr William Blackburn, hid his disappointment well, and was gallant. His dancing was adequate, though not as good as Lord Toby Pearce's, but his conversation was better. Also, and of equal importance with his intellect, he had glowing deep brown eyes and broad shoulders: she felt a fluttering in her belly which had nothing to do with his mind.

He was surprised at her asking about his opinion of the war, but made a few sensible observations, as much as could be expected in a reel with its constant separations. It seemed he was considering joining up, if he could persuade his father to buy him a commission, feeling that Napoleon's attitude especially in Italy and Switzerland meant it was only a matter of time before he set his sights on England.

After the set ended, he did not immediately leave her with her chaperone, but lingered for several minutes to talk, about the war, and about the plight of the *bourgeoisie* in revolutionary France, while Louisa skipped off with her next beau.

'It is refreshing to converse with a young lady on matters of importance,' he said. 'I only regret that I must leave for York first thing tomorrow from the Cross Keys in Wood-street, or I should call on you in the morning without doubt.'

Rose felt her heart sink. 'What business do you have in York, sir?'

'I must attend on my father, who is desirous of me taking up the family business, and convince him of the need for able men to come to the aid of their country. Fortunately his interests on the Continent mean that he might believe defeating the Little Corporal would be financially advantageous for him.'

'I should wish you success; but I would prefer it if you did not need to go. I should have looked forward to your visit tomorrow with great pleasure, sir.'

'And I too. I have very much enjoyed our conversation. Might you be free for another dance later? We could dance a second with propriety, I believe?'

Rose felt herself flushing, having briefly caught his eye as it swept over her figure. Her new dress required rather tight stays and her breathing heavily emphasised her . . . well, shape, such as it was. She showed him her empty dance card, and hoped he would think she was just hot with dancing. 'I could just squeeze you in, I believe.'

Mr Blackburn inscribed his name to a gavotte, and took his leave, as etiquette demanded. Rose looked after him as his exquisite back melded into the crowd, and sighed. He was the first attractive man who she could treat as an equal here, and he was leaving! Typical of her life and her luck. She needed to do something about her situation, or she would surely end up in Moorfields, in Bedlam, if it did not fall down first in disrepair.

'I am glad you have attracted another dance, my dear,' came Mrs Naismith's voice in her ear. 'I do not like to see you look sad.'

'I'm fine, Aunt,' she replied. 'It's just that, well, though Mr Blackburn was most interesting to talk to, I don't really feel this whole charade is me, somehow.'

'I know. I can see that. But what else is a young lady to do, but put herself onto the marriage market? It is not as if your brother is rich, nor we ourselves. We must persevere, and hide our frustrations, and take what pleasures we can from Society. Once you are married, if he is rich enough, you will be more free to do what you will.'

Rose sighed again. She hated that her happiness depended on the whims of men, who mostly judged her on her hips (narrow, not suggestive of fecundity) and breasts (almost nonexistent even in this dress, but ditto for producing heirs, not to mention more immediate interests) and her face (tolerable, but too squarely determined in the jaw, with an acute and perhaps sarcastic light in her eye which seemed to put most men off). It was not as if she didn't like the look of some of the other men here, for instance, there was one in the most impossibly tight pantaloons which left absolutely nothing to the imagination, but she didn't expect his brain would match his gorgeous rump.

She would dance again with the enticing Mr Blackburn, and wish he might not be leaving so soon; and stand around for most of the rest of the evening, trying not to look too much like a wallflower; and go home; and then try not to mind she had no suitors leave their card or flowers the next day, while Louisa had a cornucopia of blooms. In the meantime, had she seen some pastries on a table beyond the lemonade table? She was going to investigate.

It was much cooler away from the hundreds of candles which lit the ballroom, and after securing a bright pink confection which just begged her to eat it, she decided to wander along a few of the corridors and have a look at the house. Of course, she should not be doing so without a chaperone, but after all, it wasn't often she got to visit a mansion this size, into whose corridor her whole present residence would almost fit. It was peaceful, and besides she could eat her whatever-it-was without anyone telling her she would get fat.

She peeked into a large library, whose shelves were so neatly arranged with matching leather spines all of the same height, that nobody could ever take one out for fear of spoiling the symmetry. She found a gold and a silver drawing room, and a room full of portraits, though it was too dark to see anything of them. The next door opened to reveal a billiard table lit by a contrivance of suspended oil lamps, from which room she hastily withdrew as it was full of inebriated men discussing in detail and in somewhat colourful and biological language the physical merits of an unknown female.

Taking a moment to gather herself from this unexpected educational experience, Rose backed into a doorway and nervously smoothed her skirts while trying to decide if she ought to attempt to work out exactly what the men had been saying about which part of the lady's anatomy, and judged it was better left unconsidered. The door by which she stood was ajar, and she became aware that she could hear voices from within. Two voices, to be exact, a slightly deep female one, and a quiet male one which sounded awfully like . . . George, didn't it?

She couldn't hear the words they were saying, so she pushed the door a little more open and peered through the crack. There indeed was George, standing very close to a lady who held a piece of folded paper, it might be a letter; and she seemed to be teasing him with it, holding it out and then withdrawing it rapidly. She tilted her head up to George, and moved closer to him. He bent his head toward her. Rose forgot to breathe.

Was he going to kiss her? By her dress she was a married lady, or perhaps a widow. She was certainly over the age of thirty-five, and wealthy, to judge by her jewellery. Rose did not recognise her, but then she was not *au fait* with many of the upper reaches of the *ton*, generally only being invited to the smaller parties and balls, never before to something as grand as tonight's affair. George leaned in, and indeed there was no mistaking it. He was not just giving her a peck on the cheek either. The lady's arms went around his neck, and she even curled one leg around George's as she melted into his body, rubbing herself rhythmically against him. They embraced like this for she could not think how long, it seemed like minutes, and then as they reluctantly parted, she slipped the letter into his hand and then raised her arms to pat her hair. She was flushed from her face to her large bosom, and Rose suddenly realised she ought not to have been intruding on this, whatever it was. But her brother! What was he thinking of? And what was the letter?

In a turmoil, Rose backed out of the doorway and looked hastily up and down the corridor. There was nobody about, and she scuttled away, back to the ballroom, back to the crowds and noise and anonymity. Her hands were shaking, so she found a seat, and sat on them. George! Not George! He didn't do that sort of thing, did he? Did she not know him after all?

After a while her heart slowed back to its accustomed rate, and her breathing grew less ragged. She looked around, and spotted Louisa coming across to her. She must not seem at all ruffled, she must appear her normal self, she must ask after Louisa's partners, and be bright and cheerful. She could think about what she had seen later tonight, in bed.

CHAPTER 2

'I REALLY OUGHT TO TAKE you over and introduce you to our hostess,' came a voice in her ear. It was Mrs Naismith, sounding apologetic.

'Oh! Must you?' Rose tried to bring her mind back from ruminating on George's assignation.

'Of course, it is the polite thing. I'm sorry I did not present you earlier but there was such a crush, and we are only small fry compared to all the noblemen and women here.'

Rose stood, straightened her shoulders and tried to look demure. 'Very well, Aunt. Is Louisa joining us?'

'We shall catch her at the end of this figure, I think. It is nearly done.'

Rose followed her to the edge of the set, and stood with eyes downcast, practising what she had been taught at Miss Snape's about meeting important people. The ball was a birthday celebration for the Duchess of Swaffham, so she had to remember to say, Your Grace, and curtsey lower than normal, and not make eye contact beyond the first acknowledgement, and a host of other things that did not come at all naturally to her.

Aunt Naismith fixed Louisa with a beckoning eye as she pranced off the floor on the arm of a man in a scarlet uniform. She slipped out her hand and apologised to him, he bowed gallantly and departed. Louisa was flushed and glistening with perspiration, so her mother gave her her fan and told her to calm herself, explaining their object.

After a few minutes she declared herself satisfied with her daughter's appearance and the three of them set off around the room to where there was a short queue of guests by a small dais.

'Your Graces, may I present my daughter, Miss Naismith, and my niece, Miss Clarke? Louisa, Rose, the Duke and Duchess of Swaffham.'

'Your Graces.' The two girls curtsied in unison, heads bent, while the noble couple murmured something indistinguishable to them. They then looked up, expecting to move on, but the Duchess spoke. She had a normal kind of voice, not at all haughty.

'And this is my sister, Lady John Barnes. Cecilia; Miss Naismith, Miss Clarke.'

'Lady John.' They curtsied again, less deeply, and as they looked up Rose felt her heart jump into her throat. It was the woman! Her! She must keep calm, keep her face impassive, move on when Louisa did, and not show her confusion. She snatched another look at the lady, to be certain. Yes it was her, she still seemed a trifle bee-stung, or was that her imagination?

But who was this woman? She was a bit vague about titles, her father had only been created baronet a couple of years before he had died, and she had not paid too much attention to the etiquette lessons at school, never thinking she would need them overmuch. Lady John's husband would be Lord John Barnes, so, he must be some sort of younger son. Probably. She must ask Aunt Naismith. Once she could do so without seeming excessively interested. And what had George been doing with a duchess' sister? Apart from the obvious, that is. Oh, she didn't want to think about it, she really didn't. But she couldn't stop herself.

Lost in a whirl of thoughts, she found herself back at their spot by the side of the dancing floor, and being approached by Mr Blackburn.

'May I introduce my friend Mr Oliver James? We were at Cambridge together, and he knows few young ladies in London, so I thought I might presume?'

'Oh! Of course, Mr Blackburn. Delighted to meet you, Mr James,' she said automatically, holding out her hand for him to kiss and dropping the smallest of curtsies. Concentrate, girl, you have to concentrate.

Mr James appeared tongue-tied, so she took pity on him and asked, 'Which college did you attend, Mr James?'

'G-g-gonville and Caius,' replied the young man. 'F-from N-norfolk, y'see.'

Rose did not see at all, but let it go. 'Is Gonville where you were too, Mr Blackburn?'

'That's it. Except we refer to it as Caius, I'm afraid. Not a big college, nor a wealthy one, but good and central.'

'My brother was at Emmanuel. Might you have known him, Mr James? He is Mr George Clarke, or he was then.'

'N-never met any men from there, I don't think. I-I only just came down this year; is he newly graduated too?'

'No, he left about three years ago.'

'Mr James was a hard-reading man,' confided Mr Blackburn, 'and second Wrangler. That means he came second of everyone in the university this January in the Senate House exams.'

'I know about them: George was eleventh Wrangler in his year,' said Rose. 'How about yourself?'

'A mere Junior Optime, I'm afraid. I imagine you know what that means too?'

'At least you got the honours degree,' said Rose, sympathetically. 'And I expect you had more time for various amusements?'

'I did. Tried to get James here out on the river a few times but he stuck to his routine: study all morning, walk the Grantchester Grind as fast as possible in the afternoon, then study all evening.'

''S'not fair, Blackburn, I did take some time off!'

'Christmas Day, I grant you.'

'N-no!' Mr James looked hurt.

''I believe Mr Blackburn is teasing you, Mr James,' put in Rose, kindly. 'I expect you did many things other than study.'

'Well, chapel is compulsory of course, and I liked to attend the U-university sermon. And I tried to take t-tea in a chap's rooms at least once a week.'

'Mr James found mathematics as addictive as I find eating nuts,' said Mr Blackburn. He could not get enough of it.'

'Oh Mr James, I should *love* to study Mathematics. From the little I have seen in the annuals, you know them perhaps, the puzzles and rebuses and mathematical conundrums, it seems fascinating?'

'I did not think l-ladies were allowed to study Maths,' said Mr James. 'Or that they would be interested, beyond enough basic arithmetic to manage the household?'

'Regarding the majority, Mr James, I believe you are right. But I longed to learn something more of the subject, when I was at my school, where we mainly learnt deportment and sewing and arranging a table setting, and things of that ilk; and you are right, we were not allowed. But at least we had French, and Italian, and by diligent persuasion I was allowed to learn Latin, which was not difficult after mastering the two other languages, but sadly not Greek. And I was able to read many of the classical authors in translation in the holidays, and borrowed my brother's Euclid, but found it very difficult to make out, being written in an obscure manner.'

'I did not realise you were so passionate about learning, Rose,' said Louisa. 'I knew about the Latin, it was quite a *cause celebre*, but not about the rest. How odd of you to like Maths. I can hardly credit it.'

'For myself, on the contrary, I am impressed, Miss Clarke,' said Mr Blackburn. 'Many of my fellow students came up with almost no Latin and never having heard of Euclid. Not James, of course, he had already begun the Principia before he was sixteen.'

'No, Blackburn, I was fully seventeen. I began it in the summer before I started at college.'

'Nevertheless. I wish I had half your brain, James.'

'And I your ease of manner, B-blackburn.'

The next dance being announced, yet another handsome young

man claimed Louisa, and Rose followed Mr James onto the floor, where she rapidly discovered he was not a natural athlete. His expression was of the utmost concentration, and he seemed to be counting to himself throughout. She did her best to keep him to the rhythm, by gesture and word, and he appeared grateful rather than offended. It meant that she had few opportunities for further intercourse, except when they stood while other couples advanced down and up the set, but she discovered he had been offered a fellowship by his college and was intending to accept it, hoping to advance in his field enough to be offered a chair in due course, though he was doubtful of the honour coming his way as he had not the necessary influential friends.

He apologised for his dancing as they returned to the chaperones, saying that he was dreadfully short-sighted, which did not interfere with his reading, but made keeping track of the other dancers difficult. He also thanked Rose profusely for accepting his invitation, as he loved to dance, being fascinated by the patterns and permutations he could perceive in the movement of the individuals.

'May I ask you something?' he added, seeming about to take his leave. 'Um, I hope you do not find it, er, too peculiar. Did . . . did you perceive the music, as I did, to have been green? Like your dress, but a little darker?'

'Whatever do you mean?'

'Well, I d-don't usually mention it, but you seemed a sympathetic sort of person. Whenever I hear music, I see a colour. It depends on the key in which it is set: for example they are now playing a kind of pale blue.'

'How interesting. Fascinating, even. I do not see a colour, no: have you met any others who see as you do?'

He coloured slightly. 'Never a one. I would not like to mention it to most men, they would laugh at me. G-goodbye, Miss Clarke,' and he darted away into the crowd.

Mr Blackburn had stayed talking with Mrs Naismith and the other married ladies seated by the wall, but turned to her when he saw her abruptly abandoned, and invited her to join them.

'Thankyou for dancing with Mr James,' he said. 'He is extremely shy: I never knew him to be so free in his speech with a lady before.'

'College life will suit him, then. He said he would be taking up a fellowship soon.'

'Indeed, and you are right, it will suit admirably. Now, Mrs Cowper here – you know Mrs Cowper, I imagine? – tells me you are from Gloucestershire. That is where my parents used to live, before business took them to York.'

'Oh really? We have a small seat at Kilcott, near Hawkesbury, almost on the south border of the county, but my brother needs to reside in London, as he works in the Foreign Office.'

'A shame: I was hoping we might have some mutual acquaintances, but we came from the other extremity, in Tewkesbury, by the Severn.'

Rose discerned that Mr Blackburn was much taken by her, from his desire to establish such connections, and again wished the war would not deny her his company so soon, as he seemed a sensible and balanced fellow, and had praised her rather than been disconcerted when she had over-stepped herself with her enthusiasm for the pursuit of knowledge. She had not even been tempted to be sarcastic to him, as she was to most people.

They passed across a number of names of persons in their districts, but none was familiar to the other, and soon it was time for their gavotte. Rose thought Mr Blackburn looked very fine in this stately dance, and imagined how he might look in his red coat, with its buttons and braid, and sword at his side. She had at first thought him only moderately good-looking but now she was persuaded he was decidedly handsome. It was more his bearing and the light in his eye, she decided, than any true regularity of feature, but she found his physical presence quite unsettling. His manners were most attractive too: he asked her most politely about the rest of her family (father deceased four years since, and mother seven) and did not press her when she showed reluctance to talk about her twin brother.

He himself was the only child still living, and hoped this would not make his father too anxious for his survival to forbid his taking a commission.

'You see, I am not suited to a life in academia, like Mr James, nor am I one to relish the prospect of managing a business in the supply of the colonies like my father. I could not take orders and join the church, though the college has a number of livings in its gift. Also, I get terribly seasick, so the navy is not for me. It just leaves the army, which I am convinced will suit admirably. I am a fair shot, I ride well enough, and I am used to walking long distances. There was a craze when I was at Caius for taking enormous long walks and trying to beat others with the time taken. One man walked to London in twelve hours, and dined in Grosvenor Square, before returning the next day in only a little longer!'

'I like to shoot a pistol too,' said Rose, 'though I should not like to have Frenchmen shooting back at me.'

'Intriguing woman! Is there anything you cannot do?'

Rose blushed. 'Many, many things. I cannot draw or paint, though I have tried and tried; my piano playing sounds like a hurdy-gurdy turned by the monkey; but my other brother, not George, was very keen on pistol shooting, and I made him teach me how to steady it and how to aim. It is a most pleasing sensation to hit the target.'

'Do you also fence? Box? Play billiards like an expert?'

Rose remembered the scene in the billiard room earlier. 'Do not tease me, sir, please. I know that I am a lady, but I wish our opportunities were not so constrained, that is all.'

'I apologise. But I was not wishing to criticise you, rather to admire you for your aspiration.' He bowed, as the dance finished. 'It has been a great pleasure to meet you, madam, and I hope we can somehow become reacquainted again once I have finished with the Frenchies.'

'And I you, sir. Thankyou for the dances; and I wish you luck with your father.'

'Good evening.'

'What a most pleasant young man,' said Mrs Naismith. 'And so attentive to myself and my friends. He asked after all our families, and our health, and paid pretty compliments to each, without seeming ingratiating. His manner with Sir George, who chanced by while you were on the floor with Mr James, was also most affable, while still giving him the respect due to his title. He is sure to call upon you tomorrow, and I would welcome it heartily.'

Rose looked wistfully after him. 'He would, Aunt, I believe, were he not leaving for York on the early coach. He has a mind to join the Army, for the coming war with Napoleon. I admire him for it, but I wish he were not so admirable.'

'Oh dear. Well, what did you make of his friend, Mr James?'

'I liked him; but he would I fear be too studious even for my tastes, Aunt. He will marry a library somewhere, and add to its contents by writing volumes of new discoveries in mathematics.'

'Never mind, dear. There will be other balls, and soirees, and musicales, and I am sure with your advantages you will soon find someone who will make you happy.'

'And who has a fortune, of course, Aunt. Don't forget the fortune.'

'It is not correct to discuss money, dear. But I will not contradict you.'

'Now, tell me Aunt, if we are to continue to meet exalted persons I need to learn something of proper forms of address. When we were presented to the Duke and Duchess, we were also introduced to a Lady John Barnes. I could not make out who she must be. Clearly her husband would be a Lord John Barnes, but beyond that I am at a loss. Would he be a younger son?'

'Indeed he must be. With such a title his father could be a Duke or a Marquess: in fact he is the youngest son of the Marquess of Wisbech, and he has a small estate near King's Lynn, in the Fen country, as well as interests in the Indies and on the Continent.'

'How do you know such things?'

'About the titles, it is a matter of learning the correct forms, and you would do well to master them yourself, Miss, by reading useful, informative books rather than novels. About the estates, and such matters, well, we do not just sit here and discuss embroidery and recipes, you know. We are well-informed on all matters pertaining to our charges' interests. Reputations, incomes, who gambles unwisely, who is at loggerheads with whom, who has influence, all manner of like things.'

'May I ask something to test your fund of intelligence? For example, what is the *on-dit* about the Barnes?'

'He is not much liked in town; some say he has sympathies with Napoleon. She is reputed to be intelligent, and to wear more jewels than her husband's income might reasonably support. They are often apart, like this evening, but it is not apparent where he might go.'

'Aunt, you are amazing! Do you know everything?'

'No dear; but I can find out almost anything if I am given notice, and a round of tea parties and dinners where I can meet my friends.'

Rose went off to fetch some lemonade and wandered with it towards the terrace, thinking she might gather her thoughts, and wondering if it would be warm enough linger outside for a while. Now she knew who the mystery lady was, the whole thing made even less sense. What was George thinking of, embracing a married woman who was closely related to both a duke and a marquess? It did not seem like him. He was most proper, not to mention honourable. He would never do such a thing. But he had, her eyes had not lied.

She opened the French doors, and stepped into the cool of the evening. The stars were outshone by the candlelight where she was, so she walked a few paces from the house to see them better, and stopped by a low balustrade. The sounds of the ball were muted, she could see the shadowy garden below, the glories of the firmament above, and hear the light tinkle of a fountain: all this calmed her mood. After all, she didn't really know what George might get up to when he was in Town, he was a young man, and she had heard many stories of the cliques and coteries that men formed, and the antics they got up to especially when foxed, and their mistresses and Cyprians and so on. Still, George?

Her ears were assailed at this point by a squeal from one of the bushes in front of her, and a low-pitched curse, with an admonition to keep quiet. This was followed by a subdued giggle, by which Rose understood the lady to be not averse to whatever had occasioned the squeal. It however reminded her that it seemed to be only young ladies looking for husbands (and money) who were expected to have an unstained reputation and unsullied virginity, which was grossly unfair. If it got out that *she* had kissed a married man, or been misbehaving in a garden, she would be ostracised and have no suitors at all. Not that she had any anyway, but still.

It was too chilly this early in the season to stay out here long, so she turned for the house. As she reached to open the door a couple spilled out and nearly fell over her. The young woman was wearing virginal white, and the man, who clutched a bottle of champagne, looked no older than twenty, and they could not stop howling with laughter at some unknown eventuality, as they swayed off into the darkness clutching at each other for balance. How had they evaded the chaperones, she thought? And also, both, I would never wish to misbehave like that, and, I wish I could behave in such an untrammelled manner just occasionally.

Rose sadly re-entered the house and took her completely innocent lemonade glass back to the table. Almost immediately she was reunited with Louisa who had been deposited there by yet another beau. She was full of news of a new dance that some friend had come across on the continent called the waltz, in which couples dance in a kind of embrace, and which was thought scandalous by many. Rose tried to switch her mood to match her cousin's.

'You clasp hands, so;' enthused Louisa, 'the man puts his other hand on your back, just there, and you rest yours on his shoulder, and you rotate as you move, in triple time. The man must press his leg against yours as you move! It sounds dreamy.'

'Surely it will not be allowed in England? It would break all the bounds of propriety.'

Louisa's face fell. 'I expect you are right. Can you imagine the ladies of Almack's permitting unmarried women to snuggle close to men and not to be able to overhear what they are saying?'

'I cannot. Actually, are you not amazed as I am that those ladies allow both men and women to attend on the same evenings, so rigid are their rules?'

Louisa laughed, and put down her glass. 'Right, I will see you later; I have another engagement, with an elderly and gouty knight with whom I am very glad not to have to waltz. I bid you adieu.' And she was gone again, to throw herself into the jollification.

But Rose stayed where she was, and imagined revolving in the arms of Mr Blackburn, and talking with him uninterrupted, and looking up into his eyes, and seeing him appreciate her wit, and her mind. Not to mention, seeing him enjoy the closeness of her body, because for all her keenness on study, she was no Mr James, happy to embrace a life of celibacy.

CHAPTER 3

THE ARRANGEMENTS FOR LOUISA AND Rose to have a season had taken some ingenuity. Sir George had let his bachelor rooms, and combined with Mr Naismith to rent a small house just outside the most fashionable area, in Rupert-street, where he could reside with the two girls and Mrs Naismith, Mr Naismith remaining in his rectory in Cheshire. With such economies they could easily remain the whole season, and would be able to afford to do so the next year if it became necessary.

Sir George's country estate in Gloucestershire was moderate, but productive, and he employed a very capable steward to run it, which meant he only needed to reside there for a week or two at a time to superintend, perhaps four or five times a year. He would stay more, as he loved the countryside, but his work at the Foreign Office did not permit it. This was partly why after their father's death he had agreed for Rose to go away to school, as he could not spend the time with her he would wish, or supervise her and her brother adequately.

The three ladies had spent the morning in the drawing room receiving their calls - or rather, Louisa's calls. Rose had looked up the time of departure of the York Stage from the Cross Keys and sighed when she saw it was to depart at five-thirty am. At that hour Mr Blackburn would have not time even to arrange for his card to be sent round. Oh well!

Louisa had had seven callers, and by necessity Mrs Naismith had limited them to the correct fifteen minutes each. Only one seemed to have caught her eye enough for her to have wished he could have stayed longer, and she accompanied him to the door as he left with a coquettish fluttering of the eyelashes, much to Rose's chagrin. Mrs Naismith appeared to think such behaviour was acceptable, though, so she held her tongue.

The butler opened the door again around three o'clock. Eight callers! thought Rose. Can there be more? But the announcement was of "Mr Charles Clarke". Rose was both surprised and wary. They had not heard from her brother for over three months, and his re-appearance did not usually bode well. He had been asked to leave Shrewsbury school when he was sixteen, and his conduct had not improved since then.

'Morning, sister dear; Aunt; Louisa! Is my esteemed brother at home? Is there any food for the prodigal?'

'Good morning to you, Charles. This is a . . . surprise. Do sit down. I shall ring for some tea. And no, Sir George is of course in Whitehall at this time of day.' Louisa moved to the bell.

'Bit more than tea for me, if you would. I'm famished.'

'Naturally. May I ask, how did you find us here? We only made the arrangements after you left London somewhat precipitately in February to visit . . . Scotland, was it not?'

'Righto! Well, I'm a proper sleuthhound, I am. Called at old George's lodgings and got redirected, I did, by a queer bird who reeked of some sort of perfumed snuff, he could hardly speak for sneezing. Then it was a matter of a penny to an urchin, to set me right, and here I am.'

'And to what do we owe the pleasure?' asked Rose, raising her eyebrows.

'Ah! Well, the usual, I s'pose.'

'There are many, "usuals" with you, Charles.'

'Impecuneity?'

'Is that a word?'

'Dunno. Sounds like it should be. But I'm all out of blunt, at any rate. On the proverbial uppers. Skint.'

'And you've come to tap the fraternal purse?'

'You got it.'

'Well, I'm not sure you will be successful this time. Sir George is giving Louisa and me a season, so funds are not exactly begging to be spent on your roistering.'

'Roistering? How unkind, sister. Did we not once spend many months sharing the same maternal . . .'

'Thankyou, Charles,' interrupted Mrs Naismith. 'Not with ladies present.'

'Righto! But we twins should stick together, ought we not?'

'I am grateful that Rose does not stick too close to you, for the most part,' said Mrs Naismith, dryly.

'So, Charles,' put in Louisa, 'what did you do in Scotland?'

'Deuced cold country, Scotland. Well, I stayed with friends in Kincardineshire, where we rode a good deal, when the snow permitted, and skated when it didn't; and then we decamped to this fellow's castle in the middle of a place called the Great Glen, and did stag hunting. Beastly slow and cold business, that, crawling on your belly through scratchy heather and mud. But got a great taste for whisky, I did, warms a fellow up a treat. And they all went fishing too, but I can't be doing with sitting by what they call a loch up there, doing nothing. I like to be moving.'

'Sounds wonderful, though I expect a castle would be draughty?'

'Absolutely. Had to huddle over a fire of an evening, we did. Lots of blankets, all in checked patterns. Wonderful atmosphere, though, with the great blaze, and the cigars, and the whisky, and the bull. Got a trifle boisterous, mind, from time to time.'

'And why have you returned, Charles?'

Charles had the decency to look a little ashamed. 'Well, to be truthful, I perhaps outstayed my welcome a bit, seeing as I couldn't return the favours from the chaps who were putting me up. And then

I dropped a lot at vingt-et-un, and I was so cleaned out I had to cadge a lift with a fellow who was heading down South, and I'm camping out with another man over in Soho, but he can't keep me for more than a couple of days because his folks are due back on Tuesday.'

'Were there ladies present in your party, Charles?' Louisa asked, artlessly.

Charles glanced at Mrs Naismith, who shook her head. 'Can I give that one a miss, cousin? There was nobody there you would know.'

The tea and food arrived and Charles set to hungrily. Mrs Naismith asked Rose to take a turn around the room with her and asked what should be done with her brother. Rose thought it best to leave that to Sir George when he returned. There was certainly no room in their present house for him: Louisa and Rose were sharing a room as it was, let alone the effect it might have on the two girls' reputations if he were to stay and have his dubious friends to visit. Yet they could not cast him out. Sometimes it was better to leave such tricky decisions to a man.

The pile of sandwiches was almost gone when they had finished their discussion, and Charles looked up at them as they retook their seats. 'Trying to think what is to be done with me, eh? I'm a bad influence, eh? Still, Louisa here seems happy with my company.' Louisa blushed, and fiddled with her skirts.

'I am taking the girls for a stroll in St James' Park, Charles,' said Mrs Naismith. 'I believe Sir George should be home a little before five o'clock in time for dinner. I expect you can amuse yourself until then? I shall instruct the butler not to admit your friends until Sir George has authorised it.'

'Righto you are. I'll just pootle around, find something to amuse myself.'

The ladies left the room to change. On the threshold Mrs Naismith turned. 'You will find the spirits are all locked away, I should warn you. Sir George holds the only key. Farewell.'

At dinner, Charles was almost subdued. It seemed the interview with his brother had not gone well. Sir George was short with him, and interrupted two of his stories with a sharp "that will do, Charles" much to Louisa's disappointment. After they had finished, Sir George asked Rose to accompany him into the small library where there was his desk and a couple of leather chairs.

'I don't like to burden you, Rose,' he said, 'but I find myself quite at a loss about our brother. He cannot stay here, and indeed he would be better out of London in any case. I cannot take the time to go with him from Town, and supervise him, the War makes that quite impossible. I can keep him short of funds, but he seems to have an inordinate number of rich friends who lead him further astray every year, and he must be trespassing heavily on their good will. What can I do? You know him as well as I.'

'He took Papa's death very hard, you know he did, George. I miss him too, but it is different for a man, and Charles resented the way you had to take charge of him, having been previously a brother to compete with. I do not think he would respond well to your discipline now.'

'I should like to send him to Kilcott, away from the city, but I do not trust him alone there. There is only great-uncle Hugh, and he is so lost in his antiquarianism that he would be worse than useless. I wish I could set him to study, because he is nearly as intelligent as you, but I do not think he would take to it.'

Rose had been wondering about the very same problem on her walk in the park with her aunt and cousin, but had been distracted by three other issues: first, her dissatisfaction with the Season, and the type of people she had met; and second, her liking for Mr Blackburn, and his admiration for her wish to study, as well as for her person, both were pressing on her mind. There was also the matter of Sir George and Lady John Barnes, but that was too impossible of solution just now.

'I have an idea, George. I have only just thought of it, but it might work out. Let me see. Can you afford a tutor, for a few hours a week?'

'I could, readily. But why?'

'And would you allow me to study with Charles? Subjects suitable for a man, I mean: Mathematics, principally, and Greek?'

'What would people say?'

'We would be quietly rusticating at Kilcott: no-one would know except the tutors. You know how dull I have found the season, and how much I should like to learn. I could go with him to Kilcott, and keep a close eye on him, and report his conduct to you.'

'Why should Charles submit himself to such a regime? He never studied before.'

'I think he did, before Papa's death, you know. We had very good reports from his masters at Shrewsbury.'

'He will never agree to it.'

Rose rubbed her chin. 'What if you were to make his next allowance contingent on his reports? That he would not receive a penny unless he applied himself to my satisfaction?'

'Well . . .'

'Also, I think he would find it more tolerable if there was a time limit. It is now mid-May: how about three months? And we should not study all day, he can ride, and shoot, and fence perhaps – could we afford a fencing-master if he would like to learn? Though he might have to travel to Bath, or perhaps Bristol for tuition, I suppose.'

'It is certainly an idea. But are you sure you would not mind leaving London, and missing the balls and parties and so on? Not to mention being a kind of nursemaid to your brother?'

'The first I can very well do without; the second will be a challenge, but one I think I can meet. Besides, the prospects of Euclid and Leibnitz are a great incentive.'

'Liebnitz? What do you know of Liebnitz?'

'Aha, brother! You do not know me that well, do you?'

'It seems I do not.' He paused. 'What about Louisa?'

'Louisa will be fine, she has enough gentlemen to occupy her to not need me.'

'Well, I will give this matter some consideration, and speak with you again. What we spend on tutors we would save on your dresses, I suppose, at least.'

Rose punched him hard on the shoulder as she left. 'Be careful, brother. I will have you know that I am most economical in my wardrobe, thankyou very much.'

'Careful, sister, you strike like a man: that was no butterfly-kiss!'

Charles rolled up for breakfast looking mutinous. Sensibly, none of them bothered him until he had disposed of a good quantity of bacon and eggs and toast (with excessive amounts of jam), and coffee. Overnight, Rose's plan had seemed to her to have numerous benefits to herself, and she hoped to persuade Charles of its being far less onerous than perhaps George had painted it.

Once Charles' rate of munching had slowed, she risked addressing him. 'Did you sleep well, brother?' she enquired, with a sweet smile.

'Tolerably, I suppose,' he grumbled. 'Davis' bed is deuced hard, and the traffic very noisy where he is.'

'Have you considered George's offer?'

'Don't see I have much choice, do I? He said if I don't, he will not give me a penny of allowance, and I haven't a sixpence to scratch with, and I'm all out of credit with my friends. If I do, he will restore my stipend in three months. QED.'

'It won't be all bad, you know. I asked for the fencing-master for you: I thought you would like to learn?'

'Did you really? That would be capital. And some of the horses at Kilcott aren't half bad, I suppose.'

'And we will only sit with the tutors for a few hours each week. There will be plenty of time for other pursuits.'

'No visitors, George said. And he will write to the butler to tell him to keep the buttery locked. Wine strictly rationed, and no spirits. Deuced dull.'

'We can go on rides, and you will have trips to Bath.'

'Yes, but with you like a chaperone, I won't be able to have any fun.'

'It's only for three months.'

'What does he hope will happen in three months? I'm not likely to become all reformed and sensible, like an Evangelical, am I?'

'No, of course not. Which reminds me, George is expecting you to accompany us to church this morning. Part of the deal.'

'B--- and d---!'

Rose contented with raising her eyebrows at him, and grinning. 'Just don't let Aunt Naismith hear you say that, little brother.'

'None of the little, thankyou.'

'Well I am the elder, even if only by ten minutes, you know.'

'And you've never let me forget it, have you?'

'I don't believe I have.'

The ride to Gloucestershire in a hired carriage, arranged to start on Tuesday, was tedious and uncomfortable. Louisa had looked genuinely sorry at Rose's departure, but Rose was plotting some new ideas about exactly how she was going to spend the time with Charles. Her brother could be good fun, if he was not led away by his friends, and she had decided that rather than them simply learning from tutors the whole time, she would get him to teach her some other subjects, which might make him feel more important, and counterbalance her duties as guardian.

As she looked out of the window at the slowly-moving scenery, she checked that Charles was dozing and then reached into her pocket and pulled out a very grubby calling card which had arrived the previous day. Its condition was doubtless due to its having been in the grasp of an urchin who had taken almost three days to carry out his commission to find her. It bore the name of Mr Blackburn, with his address crossed out, and the brief salutation on the back: "I deeply regret not being able to call on you, and wish you luck with your dreams".

Rose reread the few words, and again checking that Charles' eyes were closed, allowed herself to picture Mr Blackburn, who must soon be reaching York, and thought about his coming interview with his father, and how he would look in his uniform, and whether she might see him again some day, and felt her cheeks warming. Then she sighed, and thought of Mr James, and smiled. What a contrast between them! And then of course, Lord Toby Pearce, he was something else altogether. How odd that they had all been to Cambridge, as had her brother too. It must be such an interesting place to be, quite apart from the teaching. Ancient and yet modern at once, she imagined. Full of nonsense and high jinks, but also of true learning. Old rituals and new discoveries. It sounded fascinating.

At the coaching inns, she enjoyed being the one to hold the purse, and to order the rooms and meals. Sir George of course could not entrust her brother with any money. In addition, he had given her a signet ring with which to seal any letters she sent so he would know they were truly from her, and she had it safe in her reticule. It was quite sensible: Charles was adept at forging her handwriting, and she was grateful for George's forethought.

For entertainment on the road, Charles was easily persuaded to tell her further tales of his time in Scotland, and more than hinted at the presence of a number of women of the town at the revels, which saddened her, and made her think again of Sir George and Lady John. At other times he slept, and she read a novel, finding the bumping of the carriage too distracting for working through her Aeneid.

At length they arrived at Kilcott, and were greeted by the familiar servants, who Rose was pleased to find had already received Sir George's letter of instructions, and who seemed genuinely pleased to see her, though with Charles they were more restrained. The housekeeper wanted to hear about her time in London, and the fashions, and it was so much more comfortable to be back among the sounds and sights of their country park. Charles headed straight for the stables, to renew his friendship with the horses, and presumably to try and subvert the head groom.

After changing, Rose thought she ought to go to the library and greet Great-uncle Hugh, who had not appeared as they entered the hall. Sure enough, he was oblivious to their coming, although the housekeeper had assured her that he had been told of it on three occasions. He barely looked up as she entered, but eventually responded to a question about the nature of his studies, which seemed to be related to the deciphering of the stele from Rosetta which had arrived in the British Museum the year before, after its capture from Napoleon's army. When Rose asked him a question about the nature of the script, he proudly showed her his copy of the print of the inscription, and pointed out the Greek characters, which Rose hoped soon to be able to read.

Rose left soon after this, impressing upon him that they should like him to join them at dinner, now they were back in residence, because Uncle Hugh normally only came to the dining room for breakfast, and the servants had to bring him food at other times to where he was working, and remind to eat it. Before she had left the room he was engrossed in his papers again, muttering to himself about cartouches, whatever they were, and a word which sounded to her like "demonic".

Sir George had clearly been busy with his letters. The day after their arrival, a greeting arrived from a retired schoolmaster who lived in Chipping Sodbury, who announced without preamble his engagement to teach Greek to them for an hour on Tuesdays and Fridays at 11am, beginning the next week. Then on Saturday morning, a gentleman rode up to visit to arrange mathematics instruction. It seemed that he had been one of the Fellows who had lectured Sir George at University, though he had been at another college, but he had had to resign his fellowship upon marriage, and instead received the living of Didmarton only three miles away. He had been intrigued by his former pupil Sir George's letter explaining how his sister wished to join in the lessons in Mathematics with Charles, and wanted to meet her for himself before agreeing to the plan.

This parson was a Mr Martin, a fairly young man, about thirty-five years old, in a sober set of clerical garments, but with a clear eye and a cheerful manner, and Rose took to him immediately. She outlined her plans, admitting she had so far had little chance to explore the subject, but found it immensely fascinating. Mr Martin admitted in his turn that he had been rather dubious of his teaching a lady, and was not sure it was quite proper. He apologised for this sentiment, but there it was. Rose, feeling it would smooth the path, said that his concern was of course understandable, but they were quite private out here in the country, were they not, and surely times were moving on now we were in the new century.

She had to fetch Charles from the breakfast room to meet his new tutor, and he appeared still munching toast, to her chagrin. Mr Martin sized up Charles with a glance.

'Sir, I detect that you are not entirely enamoured of this course of instruction sponsored by your brother, Sir George? That you might prefer to be out riding, or visiting friends, or at places of entertainment?'

'You have me precisely, Rector. Not a whit interested.'

'But you need to comply to have your allowance reinstated?'

'Indeed: more's the pity.'

'And your sister is your guarantor.'

'Aye.'

'And she is unlikely to be corruptible?'

Charles gave Mr Martin a rueful grin. 'As the Blessed Virgin, I should say.'

'So we have an understanding, you and I? I shall visit three times a week at the times I am accustomed to ride out in any case; that is to say on Mondays, Wednesdays and Fridays at nine o'clock sharp, and I will be sparing in the workload I set, if you will complete it satisfactorily. Otherwise, a more heavy target will be imposed. I am sure that your sister will aid you if you struggle for comprehension.'

'Steady on, sir! Rose here to aid me? 'Pon my word! To be outdone by a girl, it ain't to be countenanced.'

Mr Martin looked at Rose, and grinned. 'I now understand Sir

George's thinking. I believe we shall do famously. Do you have Euclid in the house?'

'We do: Playfair's translation, I saw it in the library.'

'Very good. I shall bring a second copy, so you may both have one.'

Charles perked up. 'I thought you were going to make us read it in Latin, like at school. That's something, at any case.'

'So you see, Charles,' said Rose once she had seen Mr Martin out, 'You will have plenty of time to ride and shoot and so on after Mr Martin's lessons, and on Tuesdays you may lie in until late. And once a week, perhaps on Thursdays, we will ride to Bath and you will see the fencing-master while I take the waters, or some such amusement.'

'Drink tea, you mean, and chat with the old ladies, I'll warrant.'

'You are correct, Charles, if not exactly tactful.'

'Hang on a second, won't you want to go by carriage?'

'If you recall, our carriage remained in London, for the use of Louisa and Aunt Naismith. But in any case, it would take too long, and I long to be free of restrictions.'

'Righto! So am I free until Monday morning?'

'Except for church on Sunday, yes Charles.'

'No way!'

'Charles!'

Charles saw her steely glare, and capitulated. 'Church, Sunday. Very well. I don't have to listen to the sermon, though, do I?'

Rose smiled to herself. 'No; just be sure not to snore.'

CHAPTER 4

ROSE WAS NERVOUSLY EXCITED WHEN the first lesson from Mr Martin was due, and could barely eat a single piece of toast for breakfast. What if she looked a fool? What if Charles was streets ahead of her with the *Elements*? What if Mr Martin decided he should not be teaching a girl a man's subject? She had put on her plainest gown, and plaited her hair so she could coil it out of the way on top of her head, and set out full inkwells and cleanly cut quills in the dining room. Charles was up and breakfasting: she had made sure the maids had called him in time. She had wrestled with the question of where to have the lessons all Sunday: the library was out of the question because of Uncle Hugh, but the old schoolroom would hold the wrong sort of memories for Charles, and she did not want to do anything that could put him off.

Mr Martin began by putting Charles as tutor, and asking him to explain Euclid's axioms and postulates to Rose. He stumbled considerably on this basic task, and Rose was gratified to see his cheeks colour somewhat as he did so. They then worked their way through the material at a fair rate, as she could see it was just formalised common sense, and Charles after his false start realised he could after all recall much of it from his schooldays, which cheered him immensely.

The hour was soon over, the reading set for the next lesson, and Mr Martin departed, declaring himself satisfied with his pupils' beginning.

'Well, Charles? Was that so bad?'

'He made it seem much less dreary than at school. No reciting in unison, and no switch on the knuckles, for a start.'

'And how do you think you will manage your set work?'

'Easy to be done in an hour or so, I think.'

'Good. Well then, what shall we do with the rest of the day?'

'*We*, sister?'

'Yes, "we". I had thought you might like to help me practise with pistols, like you did years ago.'

'Really? That would be sport. If I remember, you weren't half bad, for a girl.'

Rose wisely did not rise to this calumny, and contented herself with almost beating him on the first set of targets. He was better when they moved the targets further away, because her wrists seemed tired and she could not hold the pistol as firmly. She resolved to build up her strength, and wondered what exercises might achieve her aim.

Charles then announced his intention of going for a ride, and deciding he would be better let off the leash for a while, she contented herself with accompanying him to the stables, and asking him to tell her what he thought of the horses. He enjoyed showing off what knowledge he had, and she helped him saddle up his favourite. As she fastened the girth, and saw how plain the arrangement was compared to the awkwardness of the ladies' side saddle, she began to have the germ of an idea. Could she? What would Charles say? It would be only around the park and the common land, but it would be so much better. Maybe she would. In a day or two.

Apart from a brief reminder, she had no trouble getting Charles to look at his Euclid that evening. For herself she found that once she had completed the set task she could not stop, reading ahead several pages until she found two or three sentences she was unsure of, and a problem that did not seem to make sense. She made some notes so she could ask Mr Martin about them on Wednesday. Then there was Greek to prepare for, but on reflection she decided she ought to let her tutor set the agenda. The poor man might be troubled enough at teaching a girl, let alone having to hear her get ahead of herself.

Mr Fellowes was the antithesis of Mr Martin. He was about sixty, with copious white hair, and a rambling manner. He brought a text book for each of them and did not seem to take any notice of the fact Rose was a girl, rather launching straight into his lesson which he had obviously given many times. Fortunately he had assumed neither of them had any prior knowledge of the language, as was the case, and set them first to copying out the Greek alphabet in small and capital letters. Rose looked over at Charles, thinking he would cavil at this beginning, but he was surprisingly meek.

Next they had to transliterate a short passage; then there was an explanation of the way verbs conjugated, and then the present and imperfect tenses of the verb "to loose". It was all very old-fashioned, especially when Mr Fellowes asked them to recite the conjugations in unison. Charles kept a blank expression throughout, and Rose suspected something was Up.

After Mr Fellowes left, she pinned him down on this.

'You are plotting something,' she said, standing over him as he sat looking at his rather smudgy lettering.

'I? Or is it, Me?'

'I; as you very well know. Stop trying to distract me. Come on, out with it.'

Charles grinned. 'It's just that he reminds me so much of a beak we had at Shrewsbury. He was batty as a church steeple, and used to go off on long stories of when he was an advocate, and all the bizarre cases he was involved in. It meant we never got to do much Latin, which was alright, but then it was tricky the next year when we had to take the exams.'

'And . . .'

'Well, we might have played a few little jokes on him, I suppose. Not that I would repeat them with Mr Fellowes, mind, not with you watching. Not worth the candle.'

'Right. Not even worth half a tallow candle, I should say. Just make sure you remember that. Now, did you do your Mathematics for Mr Martin?'

'Yes, teacher.'

'Very good. Because I want you to teach me something else now, that I think you will be good at. I want to ride with a man's saddle. Those ladies' ones are dangerous if you get up any speed, and I would like to canter, and gallop, and learn to jump.'

Charles looked at her in some surprise. 'You aren't just a bluestocking, you're a daredevil, sister of mine. Well, well. And I thought you were all missish, and proper.'

'I am, when it is appropriate, and when I need to be, but we are in the country now, and I want to try new things. Will you teach me?'

'Surely. But you can't wear a dress, you'll need to, um . . .'

'Borrow some of your old breeches,' Rose finished his sentence. 'Yes I know, I've been thinking about it. There must be some which would fit me in a trunk somewhere. Come on, let's go and look.'

There were indeed some old nankeen breeches with a few grass stains on the seat which fitted her, more or less, being a little overgenerous in the waist, which was soon remedied with a length of string; and Rose was gratified to find some battered top boots too, far too small for Charles now, which fitted her well enough. She hesitated over what to wear on her upper half and decided she could keep her normal habit shirt, with her spencer, so as not to alarm the stable staff overmuch.

Once the matter of selection of a suitable saddle had been negotiated with the somewhat surprised groom, the two of them set off. Charles was an unexpectedly patient teacher. Though inclined to ask her to ask her to go too fast too soon, he was amenable to a request to hold back, and he had a very good eye for the faults in her seat. The Kilcott park was not large, but there was a good deal of secluded grassland round about, and they made steady progress without having to leap any hedges. Rose felt she had mastered the trot, and revelled in the greater control she had of her mount, feeling the mare respond to pressure from her legs as well as from the reins.

'That was wonderful, Charles. Thankyou, thankyou so much.'

'I had a good time too,' he replied. 'It's much more fun to ride with someone than on one's own. You're nearly up to cantering, I think. Not bad for a girl.'

'Next time,' said Rose, feeling a little stiff already in the legs. 'Next time.'

Thursday had been set for Charles to begin fencing, at a master in Bath, and Rose had been cudgelling her brains for a way of getting them both there without a slow and risky ride for her on her side-saddle. The problem was fortunately solved by the visit the next day, soon after Mr Martin had departed following his lesson, of a widowed neighbour and old friend who had heard they were back in residence, and called to offer greetings. Charles was keen to tell him how he was going to learn to fence, and was gratified to find that the master employed for him was not only well-known but well-regarded. It was a short step from here to the explanation of the difficulty, and its solution by the offer by their neighbour of the loan of his carriage, which turned out to be a phaeton.

'Mind how you drive, though,' he said, 'it is a tricky little number, prone to tip over if you corner too fast.'

Rose offered to pay him for the loan, particularly as they would want to borrow it every Thursday during the summer, but he waved away her pleadings.

'What are neighbours for?' he demurred. 'I can go everywhere I need on horseback: I only used my carriage today to give the pair the exercise. I'll send them over tomorrow at nine o'clock, will that be early enough for you?'

'You are too kind, sir,' said Rose. 'If there is any favour we can do you, please ask.'

As Rose sat by Charles the next day, high up in the light carriage, she could see how much he was enjoying driving this sporty vehicle.

He seemed not to be too put out by his enforced stay at the family seat, or even the study of Greek and mathematics so far, though to be fair Rose had spent far longer on preparation for yesterday's lesson than he had. Nonetheless, he had done what had been asked of him, and had shown he even remembered some of what he had learnt at school. It was the first time for some years that they had been together for any length of time, and she was remembering how they had got on so much better as children, before their father's death.

Rose was a little alarmed at the speed at which they were travelling, but said nothing, and tried not to flinch as they hit ruts, or tilted on bends, determined to allow Charles his head. Also, they would make much better time than she could have imagined, barring catastrophe, which would give her more hours to look around the city and investigate its shops, and so on.

Having arrived and left their borrowed conveyance at a convenient inn named the Three Tuns, she asked Charles to stay and take a cup of coffee with her before they separated, wishing to give him less time to get into trouble. Then, she delivered him to the fencing master's premises and set off to reacquaint herself with the sights.

Rose had not been in Bath for four or more years, and she enjoyed wandering in the May sunshine, looking at the varied hues of the golden stone of the buildings, and the colours of the ladies' dresses, and feeling excited by the bustle which had quite a different character from that of London, which always to her seemed to have an undercurrent of danger. She slipped into the Abbey for a few minutes and offered up a prayer for her supervision of Charles: however well it seemed to be going at present she knew it all might fall to pieces in a moment.

As she came out of the church she was hailed by a lady whom at first she did not recognise. As the lady came closer she turned over in her mind those whom she had known in Bath, but before she could retrieve any likely names the other lady spoke.

'Rose! It's Maria, you remember! It's been an age, but you haven't changed a bit. What are you doing here? Where is your maid?'

Rose was struck with a pang of guilt. She was out in town alone, which was highly improper for an unmarried woman, she had totally forgotten, having been chaperoning Charles for the last week; but on the other hand this was Bath, not London, manners were more relaxed here, and . . . well, it was still very bad form. But, Maria . . . Maria . . . oh yes! From Gloucester, she was the daughter of one of her late father's friends, wasn't she? And she certainly *had* changed. When they had last met she had been an awkward fourteen-year-old, with spots and no figure. Now she was lushly curved, with an ample bosom and a rather gaudy dress sense.

'I . . . I have come to Bath with my brother, I don't think you have ever met him. He is at the fencing-master's, and I am looking around until he is finished.'

'So you are unaccompanied.'

'I fear so. But we do not keep a lady's maid at Kilcott, and there would not be room in our borrowed phaeton in any case. I do not know what else I could do.'

'Well it is capital that I have met you then, because we can go around together. I am in Bath for the season, and my mother is taking the cure, but it is somewhat lonely when she is in the Pump Room and I do not wish to sit with all the old ladies and be bored.'

Rose groaned internally. She did not really want to saddle herself with Maria, who she now remembered was well-intentioned but tended to grate after a while, but being with her would avoid the censure that would undoubtedly soon come her way if she carried on promenading alone, and she did need to come to Bath with Charles, so needs must.

They walked along, past the Roman baths, stopping every so often to look in a shop window, and catching up with family news. Rose tried to keep explanations about Charles to a minimum, which was easy enough because Maria was able to converse without requiring much in the way of answers. She did tell her she would be in Bath every Thursday for the next few weeks, and Maria immediately undertook to meet her at the inn where they had left the horses, and spend the time of Charles' lesson with her.

Oh well, thought Rose, murmuring her thanks for the offer, I can put up with this for a couple of hours a week, I am sure. It will be character-building.

'Oh! I have just remembered,' exclaimed Maria. 'Next Thursday we are going to the theatre in Old Orchard-street for a matinee. It is the first Theatre Royal outside London, and it is ever so splendid. I shall have a new dress, and my maid has promised a whole new way to do my hair. I am so excited!'

'Well, perhaps we may not meet that week,' said Rose, 'I shall be fine on my own.'

'No, no, you must join us. It is a matinee as I said, it will start at one o'clock. It will fit in perfectly, I will ask mama to get you a ticket. Do say you will come, do!'

'I cannot trespass upon your mother's goodwill like this though, Maria.'

'I will ask her immediately. Come, the Pump Room is not far away.'

Rose found herself being led by the hand through the crowds at a rapid pace, and up the steps to the hallowed precincts where the healing waters were dispensed. There she was introduced to a lady whose only malady seemed to be that she was exceedingly fat, and found herself agreeing to the invitation to see the entertainment. It was only at this point that she realised Maria had not mentioned what was being performed. On reflection this did not surprise her, as Maria's chatter on the way had been all about the dress she was having made, and what the theatre looked like, and the sort of finery she would expect to see there, and the supreme comfort of the seating, and so on.

There was a clock in the Pump Room, and suddenly she noticed the time, and that she had engaged to be at the fencing rooms almost immediately. She took her leave hastily and hurried out, though Maria stuck with her and carried on talking as they hurried along the pavement, trailed still by her maid, who looked somewhat put out by their haste. In no time they were at the building where she had left Charles and she was able to say goodbye to Maria with no little relief. She entered the doorway and found Charles in the hall, just leaving, and looking hot.

'You have caught me,' he said guiltily.

'Yeeess?'

'I mean, Hallo, darling sister, of course.'

'And where were you going?'

'Only to wait for you outside.'

Rose frowned, and, stepping back outside, looked around her. Directly opposite was an alehouse, and she looked significantly back and forth between it and her brother.

'And how would you pay for your ale? I believe you told me you were lacking in sixpences, and all other forms of currency?'

Charles started to deny any intention of patronising such an establishment, and then when he saw Rose's disbelieving expression changed his story to plead a great thirst due to his exertions. 'I was intending to sit in the window, so I could look out for you, and when you arrived I felt sure you would settle my account.'

'You did, did you?'

Charles looked affronted. 'You would not? Heartless sister! You would see me cast into the debtor's prison?'

'Gladly, reprobate brother.'

Charles had the grace to look nervous, before Rose's face cracked and she doubled up with laughter, even thought they were in public.

'Come on, simpleton, let's go and have a drink and some lunch in the Three Tuns before we go home. I will buy you ale, but not too much, mind. I want the phaeton to arrive home with all four wheels intact.'

Over a light meal and a moderate amount of ale, Rose heard all about the fencing, how the rooms were called a salle, and the various swords that could be used, Charles having started with a foil, and the

French terms for all the positions, and the special clothing to protect the chest and arms, and especially the face, though he said the more expert fencers did not use the headpiece. He said that most of his friends had fenced, but he had missed out, and he was very glad now to have the opportunity.

Rose smiled to herself, and kept a close eye on his handling of the horses as they returned, and considered she was doing a fair job with him. She almost felt as if she liked him again, having previously become so distant.

So, they settled into a pattern. Greek and mathematics; riding and shooting; church on Sunday, and study (more than required in Rose's case, the minimum needed in Charles'); and within no time it was Thursday, and off again to Bath. Rose wondered when she was going to get Charles to show her how to handle the phaeton, as she had only before driven a heavy cart, but she thought she ought to leave it for now, until Charles was more blasé about his new, albeit borrowed, toy. She was surprised to find she was quite looking forward to meeting Maria, however silly she might be at times. She did miss female company, even though when she had it she often felt the urge to leave it behind her again.

After making arrangements for Charles to be given a meal at the Three Tuns following his lesson, and explaining about her appointment with Maria, and how she was not sure when she would be back, exactly, not knowing the nature of the play, or concert, or whatever it was, she went out to wait for her friend and waved to Charles as he strode off to the salle. Maria arrived in only a few minutes, and slipped her arm in Rose's as they walked towards the theatre, full of details about her dress, and its embellishments, and how this particular figuring of the ribbon at the waistline was the very latest thing from Paris, which Rose somewhat doubted, due to the war, but reined in the sarcastic comment which rose to her lips, indeed refrained from all comments other than admiring ones.

Arriving at the theatre and again meeting Mrs Thacker, Maria's mother, with one of her friends, Rose found herself catechised about her older brother and his current status. She was asked about George's work at the Foreign Office, and his day-to day activities, though she could only plead ignorance. Mrs Thacker seemed to think for some reason that with the war, he must be in charge of spying and secret missions. Then she moved on to how many balls and soirees he attended, and with whom he was intimate, gradually Rose realised she was being sounded out as to whether George was married, and what his income might amount to, with a view to his prospects towards Maria, in case she could engineer a meeting.

A bell rang, at last, and they went in. In the atrium, Rose discovered from the bills displayed that they were going to see "Twelfth Night" by Mr William Shakespeare, which she had not seen before, though she believed she might have read sections of it at school. Nonetheless she could not remember which one it was, except that it must be a comedy.

The auditorium was full, and hot. Mrs Thacker took up more than one seat, and Maria and Rose were rather squashed up, but Maria had the worse of it being next to her mother. The audience chatter died away as the candles were snuffed, and the play opened.

Maria seemed to be more interested in looking around at the audience, but Rose rapidly became immersed in the story. It seemed that the heroine Viola, having been rescued from a shipwreck, was extraordinarily easily able to disguise herself as a boy and fool everyone with her new identity, such that she could immediately get a job as a page with a powerful Duke. The Duke unaccountably was in love with Countess Olivia, who had shut herself away and would not see him, giving as a feeble excuse that she was mourning her brother, though he had died years ago. Rose thought this Olivia was a cunning vixen who really disliked the Duke but couldn't say so, much like she had been herself when trapped in the social round of the *ton* in London.

The plot seemed to get more and more implausible, as the Duke became inordinately fond of his new pageboy, and Olivia smitten with him (her) too. Rose got completely lost in the arguments between the maid, Malvolio, Sir Andrew and Sir Toby (though his name did remind her of her dance partner of the fortnight before, Lord Toby Pearce, and raised a wry smile). She then recognised the section where Malvolio appears in "yellow stockings cross-gartered" from her reading, and felt more comfortable at knowing where she was. Seeing the duel sparked off a thought that she ought to get Charles to teach her to fence, although she was sure she could make a better fist of it than the pathetic Viola even without any training.

After the interval things did not get much better. She almost snorted out loud when Olivia made love to Sebastian, thinking him the page, and they got married immediately. Whoever would do such a thing? How could Olivia not notice that Sebastian was not Viola? What a stupid play! The actress playing Viola had only pushed her hair into a cap and donned a page's tunic, so . . .! Words failed her.

The play wound on to its end. Everyone discovered who everyone else was and the Duke inexplicably wasn't at all concerned to have been in love with a boy, even if he did turn out to have been a girl all along. Everyone married everyone else without any proper banns or preparation, and Rose was left thinking that this Shakespeare chap had a better reputation than he deserved, although she did admit that some of his lines were very clever, and others extremely poetic.

As they left, she thanked Mrs Thacker profusely, and Maria whispered that she had not understood one word of the play but hadn't it been a *splendid* occasion? Making a promise to meet the next week at the same time she hurried back to the Three Tuns, and retrieved Charles, who had perhaps drunk more than she had hoped for, but not as much as she had feared. The phaeton did seem to swerve more than previously, but they reached home safely and she retired to her room and thought hard.

CHAPTER 5

AN IDEA WAS FORMING IN Rose's mind. It hadn't fully taken shape, but she was wondering. She had begun the shooting and riding lessons with Charles primarily to give him a sense of being important. Well, she had to admit, she had also wished to try them out for herself; but now she had enjoyed the activity so much she decided she wanted to add fencing and driving the phaeton to her repertoire. Also, she was getting on very well with the mathematics, and slowly getting the hang of the Greek, which just showed, didn't it?

Exactly what it showed she was not certain, except that it was ridiculous that ladies could not do these things, as if they were somehow incapable of them. She could do them, so why not all ladies? If they so desired, that was. She did admit many of her sex would not have the slightest interest in how to bisect an angle, or when to use the aorist and when the perfect tense, but *she* did, and it was unjust that she would normally be debarred from learning about such things.

They were making fine progress with Euclid, and on Friday after shooting with Charles (she had now moved up to a flintlock musket) and then riding, she raised the question of him teaching her fencing. She pointed out it would allow him to practise between lessons, and wondered if he might be able to borrow the equipment needed from Monsieur Gilles, his tutor. Charles seemed bemused by her interest in yet another physical activity, but promised to enquire on the next

Thursday visit. He disappeared to the stables, and she retired to the drawing room to rest.

This period of rustication was far better than the Season in London had been, to be sure. The only problem was, that it would end after three months, unless Charles reneged on the agreement, although she did not think he would, as he needed his allowance to be reinstated so he could again run with his fast friends, and besides, he was enjoying himself, liking his superior role as tutor to his sister, and tolerating the book-learning well enough, for fear of being outshone.

She had also dug out a copy of Shakespeare from the library and read through the text of the play she had just seen, wondering if she ought to become more knowledgeable about literature. It made a little more sense when she could read and reread the parts that confused her, but she still didn't like it much. It simply wasn't credible that Viola could so easily dissemble in boy's clothes, off the cuff, as it were, and be so convincing to both men and women; nor that her brother Sebastian should so easily pass for her that he could convince the love-smitten Olivia to marry him instantly. Even an idiot would realise that boy and girl twins could not be identical. There were . . . certain physical differences.

On the other hand . . . If one had time and energy to devote to it, it might be done. If she, Rose, would set her mind to it, she believed she could impersonate a man, she knew she could. And then . . . well, she might be able to engage in men's pursuits when she wanted to, and not just in the privacy of Kilcott. What freedom! She would not have to promenade in Bath accompanied by Maria; she could ride where she would; she could study what she wanted.

It was at this point that her brilliant idea came to her, springing fully-armed as Athena from the head of Zeus. She could go to Cambridge if she were a man, could she not? And learn far more there than she was doing at home with Charles, wonderful though it was? She would be able to experience the fun of living away from her family, and not being forever supervised and chaperoned if there was any society to kowtow to; to see how the other half lived! It was perfect!

Almost immediately she was struck with doubts. What would she do for clothing? And how would she live? And how to get in to the University in the first place? And then the practical everyday difficulties cause by the different anatomies of men and women, about which she was not fortunately as ignorant as some of the poor girls she had met in London. And her voice would give her away, surely. As would her complexion, milk-white from being secluded under her bonnet. Her lack of beard would be fair enough, as many young men did not grow facial hair until their twenties, and she could always claim to be younger than she was, perhaps sixteen. Men went up to Cambridge at that age, did they not?

But her fellow-students would realise she did not know the myriad of things a young man fresh from school would know. Ways of talking, slang expressions, how to drink, and smoke, and tell lewd jokes, for example. Her spirits dropped as fast as they had risen, faced by this mountain of problems. She sighed a great sigh. It had been such a wonderful prospect, too.

Rose stood up and began to pace. She was still wearing Charles' old breeches from her ride, and she looked down at herself, and paused by a long mirror. Her figure truly was negligible, and if the breeches were tailored a little better, no-one would be able to tell her legs were those of a female, would they? The boots covered half her limb, and the breeches were baggy, as was the fashion. She would not get away with close-fitting pantaloons, but her bottom was hardly full or round, as she had previously had occasion to bemoan, when men did not seem to be attracted to her as they were to her fuller-figured friends, such as Louisa.

She turned this way and that. Her narrow hips (narrow for a woman whose main job was to produce an heir, that is) now seemed providential; all that she needed was more muscle in her thighs, if she might be permitted to even think such a word. Hauling off her spencer, she critically examined her torso. She pressed her hands to flatten her bosom, which was already a bit of a non-event, and wondered. Men always wore a waistcoat, which would help to cover any binding she might use, as well as disguise her narrow waist, and she could have one cut longer than the current fashion. If she were to build up her shoulder and arm muscles too, she might do very nicely. She tried to imagine herself in a coat, perhaps not one that was cut away too much. It would disguise her hips very well, would it not? So after all, the ruse was worth considering, perhaps?

Rose tore herself away from the mirror and hurried upstairs to change into her dress before dinner. She needed to give her great idea time to settle, time to work itself out. There was no rush. A few days would not hurt. It might be possible after all. It might be, truly?

On Saturday, Rose began to make a list. She had to keep it folded up in her pocket, for fear of Charles coming across it, as she did not trust him to stay out of her chamber or her possessions. It had already been revised several times by bedtime that night, and she had carefully burnt the first drafts and crumbled the ash. She had been encouraged by seeing Uncle Hugh at dinner last evening, as he had been totally oblivious to her and Charles unless directly addressed, and she believed she could have sat down in a pierrot's costume without him noticing. Of course not all the Fellows would be like him, but she was willing to bet that some would be. Of more concern would be dons like Mr Martin, who was acute. She amused herself by considering that if Mr Martin was acute, Mr Fellowes must be obtuse, mathematically speaking, and ruefully decided she must be getting a mathematics mania.

So to the list. **One**, a suitable set of clothes, which posed its own set of difficulties, for how would she get a tailor to measure her and make such garments? **Two**, she would have to cut her hair to a man's style, but not until near the beginning of term, and she doubted she could do it herself. **Three**, she must build up her muscles further, and probably harden her hands, if she were going to pass off her body shape, however well-clothed. **Four**, she needed to acquire a more weathered complexion, which was tricky as she ought to stay pale until as late as possible. Hmmm.

Five, she had to be accepted by a college, and she feared she might have to let Sir George in on her plans, as how else might she be introduced to the Master? He would be most reluctant to enter into her deception she was sure, he was most upright. **Six**, her voice. She did not have a weak and fluttery, breathy kind of voice, but she knew she did not sound like Charles, for instance. **Seven**, habits, like drinking and smoking, and slang, and her knowledge of typical men's interests. She was markedly deficient here. **Eight**, the matter of having her own room, for she could not hope to conceal her bodily functions if she had to share. **Nine**, the matter of the college servants, for there must be some who attended to the rooms. Experience had taught her that it was impossible to fool servants for long. Would it mean bribery, or was there another way? This perhaps would be the most insuperable of the problems.

Nine items seemed quite a lot of obstacles, and she was sure she would think of others in due course. Sitting in the family pew in church on Sunday she found it impossible to concentrate on the service, but worried away at one problem after another. It was a good job, she thought, that I have always been tenacious, because another woman might just give up at this point. Yes, replied another part of her mind, but another woman would not have conceived such a hare-brained scheme.

Part of the solution came to her during the latter part of the sermon, where the curate was rambling on about the mission-field abroad and the lack of education of the savages. Rose was just thinking, I have enough Latin and French for the University; my Divinity knowledge is fair; and soon I will have Greek and Mathematics as good as most green lads; when she realised she could pretend to have been educated in another country!

Yes, that would help with many of the other awkward points, too! Her lack of the usual schoolboy experiences, whatever they were, her uneven learning of certain subjects, and the fact that no-one would know of her, and she would know none of their friends, or be familiar with the schools they had attended. So where should she decide to have been born? Not among savages, such as in the East Indies, or the Gold Coast. Not in India, she had no hope of getting such a tan as would be expected. Somewhere cool, and an English colony, but with not too-English habits. How about Nova Scotia, or New Brunswick, or Canada? That was ideal, she could have come from a remote area and been taught at home, which would excuse all sorts of inadequacies! She would have to read up about the country and settle on a place of origin, and hope nobody she met knew the district. She had heard that they spoke a lot of French in Canada too, which would mean different customs in itself. That would be fine.

Rose sang unusually lustily in the last hymn, feeling that she had begun to chip away at the heap of obstacles her glorious plan faced. If she was going to be a colonial returner, she would have been in an agricultural area, so she would know about working the land. That meant she ought to do some digging, to harden her hands and exercise her shoulders and arms, and being outside she would acquire something of a more believable complexion. It might work. She was on her way.

After two weeks, Rose and Charles had settled into a comfortable kind of relationship. She felt almost maternal towards him, but held back, as she could perceive he needed to boss her around somewhat, and show off his superior knowledge. He liked being her teacher in outdoor pursuits, and feeling he was one up on her. She had been able to compose a very favourable letter to Sir George after church (omitting his sleeping through most of the service they had just attended), and on the Thursday Charles had been able to borrow face masks and foils, together with a kind of padded jacket, for them to practise fencing at Kilcott. He said his teacher was pleased with his enthusiasm for the sport, and for his keenness to practise. Unfortunately he then expressed doubts as to whether Rose would make him a worthy opponent, which led to her threatening to run him through with her sword, jacket or no jacket, which amused him heartily.

'I do love it when you get in a snit, sister dear, it cheers me immensely,' he chuckled.

A few days after this Rose received a reply announcing George's plan to come and visit at the end of the month, to confer with his steward and to inspect the property, as well as see his brother and sister of course. This would only be a brief stay, as there was a mountain of work to do at the Ministry, and he would not be able to take the leisure to spend a week or more until mid-August when London had emptied itself as the great and the good departed for their country residences. Reading between the lines, Rose thought he wanted to check up on her, and see for himself whether Charles was behaving satisfactorily.

This news gave her to think hard about the best way of convincing Sir George to sponsor her for admission to a college. Many of her other obstacles she could see were surmountable but this one was well-nigh impossible without him. There must be a way, though! She was doing so well with her lessons, and developing a great thirst for understanding of all things mathematical. She *would* find a way to convince Sir George. She would!

The first upset to the smooth running of her plans came the following Thursday. As before, they had driven to Bath in the phaeton, and this time Rose had prevailed upon Charles to let her take the ribbons for part of the journey, and instruct her in the correct manner of controlling the pair. She found it harder than she had expected, which put Charles in a good mood when they separated at the Three Tuns, and he strutted off to the salle whistling. For her part she applied her mind to dealing with Maria's less than illuminating conversation, as they entered shops selling ribbons and embellishments, and others with wall papers and paint and house decorations, for as Maria said, 'One must keep up with all the latest fashions, mustn't one?'

On the other hand, it was quite pleasant to be with another woman for a change. Much as she liked masculine pursuits, she did enjoy the warmth and closeness that men friends, and especially a brother, did not provide. Maria introduced her to a number of acquaintances who they met along the pavements of the fashionable streets, girls Maria had met at the Assembly Rooms, or daughters of her mother's friends from the Pump Room, and Rose found she was getting interested in their tales of the gentlemen they had met, and the mishaps of their friends, and the mutual admiration of each others' gowns and so on. She decided that she had become rather snobbish about what interests were worthwhile, and realising she had enjoyed the girls' gossip, resolved to be more tolerant of the purely domestic. She did like that sort of thing, actually, but just chafed at being limited to *only* that sort of thing.

Also, she wondered from time to time about Mr Blackburn, and how he had fared with his father, and whether he had joined a regiment yet, and if so, whether he would be setting off to France, or some other theatre of war, and if he would be safe. She would have liked to look to see if he had been gazetted, but that newspaper did not reach them in rural Gloucestershire. His features were sadly less clear in her memory than they had been, after all she had only met him once, but he was the first man for whom she had formed any sort of liking in London, and who had seemed to like her.

It was on their return to the Three Tuns that she first realised all was not well. There was no sign of Charles, although she had arrived a little late, having been delayed by Maria deciding to haggle over the purchase of a new bonnet. Undismayed, she ordered a sandwich for them both, and sat down to wait. When having eaten her portion there was still no sign of him she grew alarmed. Asking the landlord to keep his meal, and to detain him if he did return, she set off for the salle, looking left and right as she went.

Upon entering at the door of the building, she was barred from going further by a kind of doorman, who informed her that ladies were not permitted to view the bouts. Rose swallowed her irritation and enquired if he knew whether Mr Charles Clarke was still in the building. The man informed her that he believed he had seen him depart in the company of other young men who appeared to be in high spirits over some triumph or other. He could not undertake to say where they might have gone. He was glad to have been able to oblige madam. He ushered her out.

Rose felt a cold sensation gripping her chest. Charles must surely have been enticed to a tavern and in spite of his lack of funds would have been plied with ale or worse, and might not appear for an age. She could not leave without him, and she did not want to stay on her own in the Three Tuns till he should appear. But Bath was full of alehouses and inns and such places, she had little hope of discovering him. Nonetheless she must try. Where should she start?

The alehouse opposite was moderately full, but revealed no Charles. She tried all the others in the street, attracting some raucous comments and whistles at one, and then turning the corner towards the Three Tuns, spied a place opposite from which was issuing a considerable volume of tuneless singing. Fearing she would find Charles here, totally incapable, she strode across and paused on the threshold to assess the situation. What relief! It was only some labourers who appeared to be celebrating somebody's birthday. Or possibly King George's birthday, held over from a week last Saturday, or any other excuse, she thought.

When by good fortune she did come across Charles, a further hundred yards down the street, the noise from the hostelry was considerably less, that is until she entered the room. The young bloods took one look at her and enquired of her how much? and which of them would she prefer? and other lewd suggestions of the same nature, accompanied by cheering. Holding her head high, she advanced towards her hapless brother, who had his head on the table and a half-empty tankard by his elbow.

'Charles! Wake up!'

He raised himself onto an elbow. 'I'm not asleep, I was just resting.

Been a hard morning.' His speech did not seem too slurred, but his eyes had not opened, and he hiccupped before slumping to the table once more.

'Gentlemen,' she addressed the party, 'I regret to interrupt your party but I must sadly remove my brother here, as he is wanted at home. No doubt you will be able to renew his acquaintance next week.'

One of the less inebriated men muttered something which might have been an apology, something about mistaking her for a doxy, sorry and all that, respect due to a man's sister, but she kept her mind on Charles and tried to haul him to his feet.

'Can't go till I've finished my beer. Mustn't waste it.' Charles tried to pull away from her.

Rose looked at his tankard, picked it up and drained it. It tasted foul. Banging it down on the table, and noting with pleasure the surprised expressions of a couple of the other young men, she wiped her mouth with her hand and said, 'No, it's empty, Charles. Come on.'

'Charles opened his eyes and looked at the pot. 'It is, you're right. That's strange. I'm sure it was full just now.' However, he got up and followed her more or less docilely out of the room, resting heavily on her shoulder.

Fortunately it was not far to their inn, where Rose deposited him in the stable before returning to settle up with the landlord. He was snoring by the time she returned but she was able to make sure the grooms hitched the horses to the carriage correctly, and was grateful she had studied how Charles had fastened the harness, before enlisting the grooms' help in getting Charles into the vehicle and settling him so he would not fall out.

She set off extremely cautiously, wary of the traffic coursing through the town, and mindful of the high spirits of the newly-fed horses and the lightness of the carriage. She hoped she had remembered the way correctly. Yes, there was the church with the funny tower; and there was the fountain, and the turn up the hill. They must go slowly here, the hill was steep and the road narrow. Good. There was the signpost for their route. She was set.

As she drove them home she wondered how Charles had got into this state in so little time. It must be less than two hours from when his lesson had ended to her finding him, so he must have drunk very quickly indeed. Or had they been playing some sort of drinking game? She had heard of such things, though no young lady ought to have been privy to those masculine matters. Unfortunately that was as far as her intelligence had gone. No matter. She would interrogate the reprobate later.

Charles did not make an appearance at dinner, which had had to be set back in any case because of their late arrival. Rose had the pleasure, if that was the right word, of conversing with Uncle Hugh, who was particularly animated because he believed he had made a breakthrough in the analysis of the Rosetta inscriptions, which he was anxious to communicate to collaborators. He kept slipping into Greek as he spoke, which confused poor Rose, who just recognised a word here and there, and he mentioned a whole series of names of scholars, the only one of which she registered was a Professor Porson of Cambridge, who seemed to have reconstructed the missing bottom right hand corner of the inscription, though how he could have done this Rose had no idea, since it was missing, naturally. He also seemed to be bemoaning the war principally for interrupting his correspondence with French scholars.

Was this really what scholarship was like? Would she be able to keep up with it? Was she being foolhardy even to try?

That evening Rose sought out Charles in his chamber. He looked a little under the weather, but was coherent. She established that he believed he had been duped by his friends into taking a quart of a beer called "Stingo" which was unknown to him, and downing it in one draught as celebration for his first victory in a fencing bout. He had responded to his success by calling for whisky for which he had acquired a taste in Scotland, and they all took a dram, as he called it. Well, maybe more than a dram, perhaps. Maybe three. And then feeling thirsty, he had begun a pint of small beer, which is how Rose had found him.

Rose surmised that this Stingo was somewhat stronger than Charles had been used to, and made a mental note to keep well away from it herself if she did pursue her enterprise of deceit. However, she decided the opportunity was too good to miss to tell Charles that when his head was more settled she wished him to teach her to drink, so that she might be forewarned about his likely misbehaviours in the future. Of course they would do it at Kilcott and not in a tavern, and she would give instructions to the butler about ordering in whisky and both ale and beer. Wine she knew they stocked, and there ought to be some brandy about, since there had been the pause in the hostilities with France until the recent resumption.

She pursued this line of discourse concerning various beverages for some minutes because she could see how adversely it was affecting Charles, who was too proud to tell her to stop. At length, she realised he was near to casting up his accounts, and she desisted, and handed him the chamber pot before withdrawing, waiting until she was outside the door before allowing herself to chuckle. Maybe he would be more careful in future. And maybe not.

CHAPTER 6

ROSE'S LIST HAD NOW ACQUIRED an order of sorts, indeed a prioritisation had taken place. The latest version read:

<u>Things being done</u>
1. Greek and Mathematics (tutors and private study)
2. Shooting, Riding, Driving, Fencing (Charles)

<u>Things to be done now</u>
1. Work in garden to strengthen muscles and tan skin (Me)
2. Learn to drink and smoke (Charles)
3. Learn to talk like a man (Charles – needs subterfuge)

<u>Things to be done when George is here</u>
1. Persuade him to get me into a college (How?)

<u>Things to be done later</u>
1. Arrange for suitable clothes
2. Arrange for hair cut
3. Work out how to deal with voiding and courses.
4. College servants?

She changed into her breeches and shirt after Friday's lessons and headed for the gardener's glasshouse. She had rehearsed a little speech which she hoped would stand up to his undoubted questions.

'Good morning Jenks,' she began when she saw him. 'I have come to ask you a favour.'

'Afternoon, Ma'am. Er, why are you . . .?' He began to comment, presumably, on her attire but thought better of it. 'What may I be doing for you?'

'I have been to consult an apothecary in Bath,' she said, 'concerning certain difficulties about which I will not explain, and he recommended a course of vigorous exercise for the shoulders and back. You may have noticed I have been riding a lot recently, but riding principally exercises the legs, and he suggested digging in the soil. Is there an area which needs cultivation? And could you supply me with a spade or shovel or whichever implement is suitable?'

Jenks looked suspicious. 'Are you sure, Ma'am? 'Tis not a usual occupation for a lady.'

'The apothecary was most insistent, Jenks. And as I have felt so much better for the riding, I am inclined to take his advice.'

'Hmm. Well, let me see.'

Rose could see Jenks was not convinced.

'There's a patch o' ground over behind the potting sheds there that's out of sight, if happen a visitor might arrive. I wouldn't want them to think we didn't be doing our jobs properly, like. You could do your digging there. It's heavy work, mind.'

'I don't mind that, Jenks. I don't mind that at all. What will you be growing there afterwards?'

'That'll be beetroot and some new sorts of carrot I've got in, from Holland. I thought I'd give them a try, for a late crop, like.'

'Thankyou, Jenks, I'm much obliged.'

'Let's be seeing about finding you a smallish spade then.' He set off towards his shed and Rose was sure she could hear him muttering to himself, something about 'Whatever will ladyships be getting into their heads next?'

Rose spent less time in the plot than she had anticipated. Jenks had been right, it was very heavy work, and her arms and shoulders and back ached after only a quarter hour, when she had turned over a tiny fraction of the ground. She looked at her hands, which had reddened and were getting a little sore, and stretched herself. She set to again, and discovered it was better to work at it steadily than to attack the soil like a whirlwind.

Nonetheless she had had enough well before an hour had passed. She replaced her spade in the shed, having cleaned it carefully, and thanked Jenks for his forbearance.

'I'll do some more tomorrow,' she told him, 'unless it is raining.'

She could see by his expression that he thought he had seen the back of her but this just hardened her resolve, and she walked, slightly stiffly, away, thinking a hot bath seemed like a good idea.

Saturday brought another letter from Sir George, intimating that he intended to ride down from London, expecting to arrive in the evening of Sunday week, and to depart on the Wednesday immediately following. That way he could meet both tutors, as well as consult with his steward. Rose wrote back straightaway imploring him not to hector Charles about his conduct as she was sure his relatively good behaviour was likely to deteriorate if pushed by a well-meaning elder brother, who to him would represent Authority and Disapproval (capitals).

Having sealed this missive she decided it was time for more digging. As she changed she wondered what Sir George would make of her new hobby, and thought she perhaps might conceal it from him at least for now, until she had raised the question of his arranging a college place for her, and determined his response. After all, she had carefully omitted mentioning Charles' little episode in the tavern in her news, and intended to reserve it in case she needed to use it as a lever against Charles at some future point.

Jenks as she anticipated was momentarily thrown when he came across her hard at work on her little patch of ground. He hid it well, but there had been a brief dropping of the jaw that she detected as he first came into view.

'Am I doing this correctly, Jenks?' she called across to him. 'Or ought it to be dug deeper?'

Jenks ambled over and surveyed her earth critically. ''Bout six inches is plenty, ma'am. That's heavy soil, there; I'll be mixing in some manure when you're done, I'm thinking.'

Rose had intended to think through her strategy with Sir George while doing her digging but found that the effort, and the concentration on getting the spade at just the right angle and so on, put it out of her mind. She was also disappointed that she had to stop to rest equally as often as the day before, and if anything felt more achy, but seeing Jenks wandering off to the glasshouses stiffened her resolve not to show weakness.

After an hour of this, and then a wash and changing into her day dress, she sought out the butler. He was as dubious concerning her trying out various drinks, as Jenks had been about her plan to dig the garden. It seemed it simply was not done for a lady, even if she was his employer and gave him his orders. In any case, he said, they only kept small ale in the house for the refreshment of the staff, both house servants and estate workers, and it would be a waste to get stronger brews in as most of each barrel would not be consumed. Now Rose had of course drunk small ale at times from when she was quite young, but she suspected the argument was simply the butler's way of saying that he strongly disapproved of her plan, and intended to block her wishes without direct disobedience. She decided to consult Charles on the matter.

Charles, fully recovered from his escapade, and expecting censure from his sister, was unsurprisingly very keen on yet another opportunity of showing off knowledge to his sister while imbibing a variety of brews.

'Why don't we walk down to the Prince of Wales in Hawkesbury,' he suggested. 'They have a good range of drink and we could ask for a private parlour to, um, be discreet.'

'Are you sure? It is very close at hand. I don't want to be a laughing stock in the district for 'Improper behaviour that does not become a lady', or some such.'

'Dinna fash ye'sel', as they say in Scotland. Look, I'll order the drinks, so no-one will know.'

'And you will remember I am not used to spirits or strong drink? No Stingo, Charles.'

Charles grimaced. 'No Stingo; righto. I think I'd give that one a miss anyway.'

They set off soon after. Hawkesbury was about two miles away and a pleasant walk along lanes which were only a little muddy in a few places. They were easily accommodated in a snug little room and Charles ordered (at Rose's insistence) half-pints, of four different ales and beers, which were set in front of them by a slightly puzzled-looking landlady.

'Old ale, bitter beer, pale ale, and stout porter,' she said, pointing. She paused, as if she were due an explanation.

'Mrs Potts, can you tell me which is the strongest?' asked Rose.

'The stout porter, for sure. Then the old ale; the other two are about the same.' Mrs Potts paused. 'Ma'am, I hope you don't mind me asking, but this,' she waved a hand at the four tankards,' is a little unusual. Can't I be getting a nice glass of lemonade or some such for yourself?'

'Thankyou Mrs Potts but no. It's a little experiment. It's a bit hard to explain. We'll call if we need anything. Thankyou.'

Mrs Potts left, and Charles looked at Rose. 'You've gone all pink,' he said.

'I have not.'

'You certainly have, sister. Bright pink. But to work. Where shall we start?'

'With the weakest, please. The pale ale?'

Charles stood, and ceremoniously handed her the pot. 'My lady,' he said, bowing.

Rose took a big draught, as she had seen men do. It didn't seem too bad, until she had swallowed it, when she was assaulted by an unpleasant – something. Ugh! How could men drink this? Small ale was pretty tasteless, but this . . .! She wanted to wash her mouth out.

'Did you not enjoy that, sister of mine?' said Charles, laughing at the face she was pulling. 'Have another swig.'

Rose looked at the mug in her hand. 'I couldn't!'

'A lot of chaps feel the same way the first time they try proper beers. You get used to it though,' he nodded sagely, 'and then you come to love it.' He took the ale from her and poured most of the rest of it down his throat. He made a grimace too. 'You might be right, you know. This one isn't much good, it might be off. Come on, try the bitter.'

The bitter produced a similar result for a different reason. It wasn't unpleasant in the same way but Rose just couldn't fathom why anyone would like to drink something so bitter. She liked savoury as much as sweet food, but this?

'Drink up, Rose. You need to judge the effect it has on you too.' Charles drank his portion and grinned at her, offering the tankard back to her to finish off. She screwed up her eyes and poured it down, then shuddered all over before clunking it onto the table, and emitting an unladylike belch.

'No wonder ladies don't drink beer,' she said. 'It gives one wind, too.'

'Try the old ale,' suggested Charles. 'It won't be so gassy.'

'Give me a minute, Charles. Remember, I'm not used to this.'

'Surely, dear sister. Take your time. We can tell a few jokes, can we not?'

'Jokes?'

'Certainly, jokes. Have you heard the one about the barmaid and the viscount and the broom handle?'

'Is that what you men do when you are drinking? Tell jokes?'

'Of course. And insult each other, and lay bets, and talk bollocks, of course.'

'I only asked you to teach me to drink, Charles. I shudder to think what the viscount got up to with the broom handle in your joke and I do not wish to find out.' She leant forward to try the next brew so as to close out the conversation.

'Spoilsport! Well, you see, this viscount was feeling a bit under the weather, and he decided to go to this pub with one of his friends. So the two of them walk into the bar, and . . .'

'Charles, No!'

The old ale seemed sweeter, more chewy and very slightly sticky, she thought. It was still thoroughly nasty, though. Also, she was starting to feel a little light-headed. That was ridiculous; she had only had just over half a pint. Charles looked as if he was about to recommence his joke.

'Charles, how much wine would be equivalent to a pint of this beer?' she said quickly, waving her pot in the air.

'That's not beer, it's ale,' said Charles. 'Beer has more hops in it, it's more bitter. But, um, about one large glass of wine to one pint of that old ale, I guess. Maybe a little more. Depends on the size of your wine glass.'

Rose put down the old ale and sniffed the fourth beer dubiously. 'This one's very black', she said. 'Why is that?'

Charles shrugged. 'Don't know. Sorry. Something to do with what they make it from, I suppose.'

Rose sipped the beer. Of the four it seemed the least obnoxious. Urged by Charles to try it properly, she took two large gulps. There. Done it.

Charles started chuckling again. 'So, which one shall we order another pint of for you?' he asked.

'We're done, aren't we?'

'No way. You drank far less than one pint. It can't have had any effect on you.'

Rose wasn't so sure of that. On the other hand, if she was going to be a man, she ought to learn to drink like one. She looked at the four pewter pots. Could she manage a whole pint? Which was the least revolting?

'I'll give that one a go,' she said, pointing to number four. 'The black one.'

'Righto. I'll go and bespeak two pints of stout porter then. I don't often drink it but I'll keep you company.'

Displaying unaccustomed tact, Charles waited in the bar for his order so Rose did not need to face Mrs Potts' gaze again. He set her drink down and took a chair opposite, lounging back and crossing one leg over the other as he raised his tankard.

Rose looked at him, and at her own pint. It seemed very large. However would she manage it? Whatever Charles said, she did feel rather odd. Also, she realised, she was going to have to learn to sit like a man, in postures that would be unthinkable for a woman. Also, to walk like one, and gesture like one. It was all getting very complicated. Well, here goes.

Seeing Charles had downed about one third of his pint in one swallow, she tried to copy him, but found herself choking, with beer running down her chin and onto her dress. It didn't help of course to see Charles laughing at her, and she thought of throwing the rest of her porter over him, but desisted. Drinking at a more sensible rate she got about two thirds of the way down the tankard before she got the urge to burp again.

'How do you manage not to belch, you men?' she asked.

'We don't try,' replied Charles happily. 'The louder the better, generally. Not to mention the bottom burps, of course.'

Rose tried out belching on purpose. She felt unnaturally elated when a loud and totally unladylike croak burst forth from her mouth, and she giggled.

'Like that?' she asked.

'Not bad for a girl, I suppose. Louder, really.'

Rose looked doubtfully into her drink. She felt very full of fluid. Still . . .

'Bottoms up,' she called out, and tipped the rest of the beer down her throat. It went down much more easily than the first slug had, really she must have relaxed a bit. Still she shuddered at the taste, but . . . She was nothing if not persistent, wasn't she?

'I'm persisiistent, aren't I?' she enquired of Charles. Very p . . . per . . .sistent.'

And a little tiddly,' said Charles. 'I think you've had enough, sister dear. Remember, the stout was the strongest one. Maybe not anywhere like as strong as that Stingo, mind, but strong enough.'

Rose looked at him sitting back in his chair, relaxed and grinning, and thought now would be a good time to learn to copy his posture. She tried to hitch up her right foot to set it on her left knee, but it caught on her underskirt and so she jerked it to try and free it from the cloth, lost her balance and fell off the bench onto the floor in a heap.

Charles just roared with laughter and she glared up at him from her supine posture with as much force as she could manage. Unfortunately it had no effect, and she struggled back to her bench as best she could before trying to tell him off.

'I can't be drunk on so little,' she complained, 'I've had two big glasses of wine at a dinner lots of times, and never felt like this.'

Charles tapped the side of his nose knowingly. 'Yes, sister dear, but did you not know that they always water the wine served to unmarried ladies, whereas we men get it full strength? Sometimes yours is only one-third wine.'

'So I have drunk about six big glasses of wine?'

'The beer hasn't harmed your arithmetic, has it? Five or six, yes.'

'Oops! Well, it's all in the cause of experience, anyway. And I can still speak properly as long as I don't try and say "persisistence", at least.'

'We'd better go home, I think. Can you stand up?'

'Of course,' said Rose indignantly, and swayed forward as if to get up. Nothing happened, though, and she swayed back again. 'Well, maybe I might need a little assistance, Charles. If you wouldn't mind.'

They proceeded out of the inn with Rose on Charles' arm, and walked fairly steadily along the road and onto the path into the countryside. Rose felt an unaccountable urge to giggle at everyday sights, and a strange sort of cheerfulness and freedom from care which was most pleasant.

About a mile along the way however, she was increasingly aware of the need to relieve herself, and it was certain that she would not make it home without accident. There was no alternative but to find a secluded copse and do her business as best she could with the aid of a tree for balance and a couple of false starts when she fell over while attempting to squat down. Maybe this drinking lark wasn't all that much fun after all?

On regaining the house she found she needed to visit the ladies' room again, and decided that beer would have to be a no-no for her deception, because she could not hope to conceal her visits to find relief from a crowd of men who would expect her to lower her fall front and perform as they did, and probably in front of them. What should she do? Well, first, she thought she had better go and have a lie down in her room, because she felt unaccountably tired.

Two hours later she awoke, feeling foolish. Fancy having such a nap in the middle of the day at her age! Anyone would think she was a valetudinarinan of fifty. She rose, straightened her somewhat crumpled dress, and sought out Charles.

'Apart from beer,' she began without preamble, the better to deflect any jocular comments from her brother about her reaction to two pints, 'What do you like to drink? Something with less volume, that is. That beer made me feel too full, and it tasted foul.'

'Whisky,' he responded immediately. 'I acquired quite a liking for it in Scotland. Why? Should we repeat our experiment forthwith?'

Rose grimaced. 'I think not, not quite yet. Perhaps tomorrow . . . but tomorrow is Sunday, and perhaps it would be better not to profane the Sabbath.'

'Besides,' put in Charles, 'I don't suppose there is any in the house, and I didn't see it in the tavern. We could buy some when we go to Bath,' he added, hopefully.

Rose considered. 'Very well,' she conceded. 'But I shall keep it under lock and key in my room, mind.'

'Spoilsport! And with me being so kind as to tutor you too.'

Rose scratched her nose, and cast her mind over her list. 'What we could do,' she said slowly, 'is see if George has any cigars in his study. I should like to try one, to see what you men like about them. I tried snuff a few times, but it made my nose run black and I hated that, but I never tried to smoke. Shall we go and see?'

Charles looked at her slightly oddly. 'Are you up to something, little sister? This is all most unusual for you.'

'Not at all,' Rose replied blithely, 'Except I have taken a fancy to enlarging my experience since we are out of the public gaze here, and I have an expert tutor to hand in my dear brother.' She tilted her head to one side and gave him a fatuous grin.

There was a good selection of tobacco in the study, and Charles lit a candle, showed Rose how to cut the business end of the cigar by the right amount, and how to light it. He struck a pose, and puffed away, trying to look sophisticated. She copied him as best she could with the smallest cheroot in the box, and leant forward to light it. Unfortunately her "expert" tutor had omitted to tell her to suck, rather than inhale, and with her first breath she fell into a paroxysm of coughing, reeling back into a chair and dropping the cigar onto the floor.

Fortunately it missed the Turkey rug, but still smouldered on the parquet, and Charles leapt forward to rescue it before it left a charred mark that would be noticed by Sir George, as well as by the servants. He kicked away the ash from where it lay, but there was definitely a black patch left in the wood. Ignoring his sister's distress and her streaming eyes, he tugged the rug over the mark to hide it, and then stood over her, grinning broadly.

'Told you girls can't smoke,' he gloated.

'No you didn't, pig!' croaked Rose between coughs. 'This is vile! How can you say you like it?'

'You aren't supposed to actually breathe the smoke in, sister, you just take it into your mouth. Like this.' He drew on his cigar and blew a dense cloud of smoke at her, setting her off coughing again.

'Horrid brother,' she expostulated, once she could speak, 'You might have warned me!'

'I'm glad I didn't,' he said, 'or I'd have missed a capital sight, you know. You do look funny.'

Rose stood up and punched him hard in the chest. 'I do not look funny, little brother, I am in acute distress. Now, give me that accursed weed and let me have another try.' She took the cheroot and very cautiously sucked a little smoke into her mouth, and immediately blew it out right in Charles' face. 'That's a bit better, I think,' and she took another few puffs. 'I can manage this,' she added, 'now what do I do with the ash on the end, I don't want to make a mess?'

Charles held out a dish into which he had knocked his own ash, and added that if there was a fireplace handy, some chaps used that. He explained it was a matter of pride to try and keep the longest tail of ash on the cigar, before it fell off, so often the floor was the place that received it, but that the servants would sweep it up in any case.

Rose tried some bigger mouthfuls of smoke, and walked over to the window to knock her ash outside.

'I'm starting to feel a little light-headed,' she reported. 'Is that normal?'

'S'right,' admitted Charles, 'you need to slow down a little, that's all.'

'I think I will, thankyou. You know, this doesn't taste of much,' she said, 'but I quite like the smell.'

'Some cigars are better than others,' Charles opined, like an experienced man of the world, 'but I don't expect George buys the good quality ones like Havanas, he's too economical.'

'It's easy to be extravagant when you don't have to balance the books,' retorted Rose, severely. 'Now, what to I do with the end?'

'Stub it out in the dish, and leave it,' said Charles. 'Want another?'

'No I do not,' Rose told him decidedly. 'I definitely do not.'

CHAPTER 7

ON SUNDAY MORNING ROSE WOKE with her mouth feeling like the inside of Charles' old top boots, but after washing her teeth thoroughly and seeing off a quantity of toast and eggs at the breakfast table she felt herself again. The next problem she had to face was how to get Charles to tutor her in the things men did when they were together, without arousing his suspicions any more than she had already. Also, she needed to practice sitting and moving like a man, which she could observe was immeasurably different from how she had been taught to behave by her mother, and then with more severity at Miss Snape's, but she felt she would not be able to perfect her attitudes unless she wore the proper masculine clothes, not to mention boots, all of which fitted her properly.

On the walk to church she carried her bonnet, so as to give her face longer in the sun, but tied it on when they approached the village so as not to arouse gossip. She spent the service watching the menfolk of the village, how they stood, and sat, and shuffled their feet, and fidgeted, and generally did everything but stay still, demure and self-contained, as she had had drummed into her that a lady must. The vicar's neckcloth gave her cause for thought: she would have to learn the different ways to tie a cravat; and then there was the matter of hairstyle, and how to eat and drink, and of how to address other men. She thought they tended to use plain surnames, or rude nicknames, but she wasn't sure how soon one could switch from formal to informal. It was bound to be different from how young women were expected to behave, and probably much freer.

Was her idea of impersonating a man just too preposterous to work after all? There was so much to know, and so much she wouldn't know that she didn't know, until she gave herself away inadvertently. Perhaps she should just give up the whole idea? She could enjoy this three months of learning, and then go back to being a dutiful girl, look for a husband, and try and acquire suitable accomplishments. Except that the piano and the drawing-book were already hopeless causes for her, and the embroidery-hoop held so little charm, though she was less clumsy with a needle than a brush. Singing? Well, she could hold a tune, but pretty airs were not her style, and she felt silly performing for a crowd of people who were essentially judging her for her looks and her docility, not her talent or the pleasure of the music.

There must be a way: she was after all persistent, as she had told Charles yesterday, and she took comfort in the Vicar's text for the day, "I can do all things through Christ which strengtheneth me". The service at length ended; she poked Charles to waken him, and as they left the church, she observed that she was quite as tall as most of the men there, though of course the gentry tended to be taller than the peasantry. So, she would not give up, but how could she dress up her idea of learning men's ways so that Charles would not catch on? He wasn't the most perspicacious of brothers, but even he would smell bad fish if she just sailed straight in.

Out again in the sunshine, the idea of dressing up her plans led to remembering the play she had attended with Maria, and then thinking about the whole business of costume and acting, and the memory of how in Shakespeare's time all the parts had been taken by men. Which led on to . . . well, what if Maria was to ask her to take part in some amateur theatricals, and then . . . it might have to be all women taking part, so she could be asked to play one of the male roles . . . and therefore . . . well, naturally she would have to practise for her part, and get some suitable clothing, wouldn't she?

Rose felt her heart begin to race with excitement. Now, she would have to work this one out carefully. How soon could she find out about this imaginary play? Thursday, at Bath? Or was there any prospect of learning of it sooner? Perhaps if she received a letter? Then she could begin tomorrow with her tuition from Charles. And which play would it be? Because Charles would surely want to hear her lines, to coach her in the way to say them, and the appropriate gestures, and so on. And she would need to work out where the supposed performance was to be held, and . . . but what if Charles asked Maria about the play? That would ruin her deception! But Charles thought Maria a silly twittering girl, didn't he? Or did he? Had he actually met her? She thought for a moment. No, she believed he had not. And there was no real reason for them to meet. But if they did, he would not want to talk to her, would he? Or did she know him well enough to know his taste in women? Oh dear, this duplicity was very complicated, wasn't it?

'Penny for your thoughts,' said Charles, as they left the village behind. 'Not that I have a penny, of course, thanks to old George.'

'Oh!' exclaimed Rose. 'I was miles away. What did you say? Oh yes, what was I thinking? Oh, nothing. Er, I mean, um, I was musing on the sermon, it was most stimulating. I don't think you heard much of it, did you?'

'Not a word, I'm glad to say, Rose. You are a funny stick, wanting to listen to that old hooey. Still everyone to his own, I suppose.'

Rose pulled at her ribbons and whipped off her bonnet. She turned her face to the sky and sighed. 'It is lovely not to have to hide from the sunshine, now we are in the country again.'

'You'd better be careful, or you'll be getting a tan, and then nobody will want to marry you, or at least nobody in London will.' He leaned closer. 'I think I can see a few freckles on your cheeks. Yes, definitely, and two on your nose.'

'If men can have freckles, or a tan, why can't ladies? It's not fair.'

'Surely. But that's how it is, I believe. Me, I wouldn't care two beans about a girl's complexion, I mean, I wouldn't want it all pock-marked or anything, but as for it being milky-white, I don't care. But they seem to in London, the little I've been out in the *ton*.'

'Well, I'm going to enjoy the sun, and I'm doing some more digging when I get back.'

'Digging? What do you mean?'

Rose jumped. She'd forgotten that she Charles hadn't been around when she had been in the garden. Subterfuge was very confusing. What could she say? Better go with what she had told Jenks.

'Oh, I consulted an apothecary in Bath when you were fencing and he told me I needed to build up the strength in my back and shoulders. Women's complaints, you know.'

'Right,' said Charles doubtfully. 'Seems odd if you ask me. But you know best.'

Rose had spent some time after her exercise, and an appointment to ride with Charles, and shooting practice, and then some Greek preparation, in forging a letter to herself so it appeared to come from Maria. It would be easy to pretend it had arrived with the other post, and she sealed it and hid it in her pocket. On Monday morning, however, after their Mathematics lesson, the footman came in with a letter for her, and she took it curiously, as it was clearly not addressed in her brother's handwriting, nor yet Louisa's, and who else would write to her?

Charles was lounging in the window-seat, gathering himself after his mental exertions, so she opened it circumspectly, and skipped to the end to read the valediction. It was from Mr Blackburn! She felt her colour rise, and so she slipped it into her pocket thinking she would read it in private, and made to get up.

'Who's your letter from, little sister?' called out Charles, teasingly. 'An admirer? Or just old skinflint George? No, you wouldn't hide that from me, you'd read out the admonitory bits aimed at me and feel superior, wouldn't you?'

'It is not from Sir George,' said Rose, thinking quickly. 'It's from my friend Maria in Bath, you know, the girl I went to the theatre with.' She reached into her pocket, broke the seal of the other letter before withdrawing it, and waved it at him. 'I was just going to read the rest of it in my room, but perhaps you'd like to hear what she has to say?'

'Hardly, I'm not likely to be interested in girls' talk, am I?'

'My dearest Rose,' she read out to Charles, teasingly. 'You'll never guess, truly you won't! After the play we went to see, my mother has decided that my friends and I need a project to amuse us and keep us from buying up the whole stock of the haberdashery shop, and has set her mind upon us performing a play!! Not anything as complicated as Shakespeare, of course, but still! We are to arrange for costumes, which will mean more trips to the shops of course, and we will have to design scenery and everything.'

'Please say you will be in it? It will be great fun, really it will. Now, we are all going to get together on Wednesday to decide on the actual play, that is, those of us who can meet up, of course, and on Thursday I can tell you which part you will have.'

'I think I'll go and have a look at my horse. He was starting to hint at a touch of lameness yesterday.' Charles got up, and headed for the door. 'You'll like that sort of nonsense, dressing up and acting silly with those girls, won't you? Leave me out of it!'

As he left, Rose smiled a self-satisfied smile to herself, and folded her letter. The ruse had gone better than she could have hoped. She could tell Charles what part she had been given later, and enlist his help in practising. But now for her other letter, the real one. Mr Blackburn indeed!

In the privacy of her bedroom, she shut the door firmly and sat by the window. She held the letter and noted her hand was trembling. Telling herself off for being silly, she opened it and began to read.

'Dear Miss Clarke,' it began, unexceptionably, 'I trust I may be permitted to write to you after so brief an acquaintance, but I have on several occasions thought about our meeting and rued the malchance that prevented me from paying you a call, or even discovering your address. This missive is precipitated by my meeting by chance with your brother Sir George, who kindly supplied me with details of your residence, and expressed himself happy for me to communicate with you.'

'Well, well,' she muttered to herself, and continued in thought: How has he met George, and, Do I really care for the idea that George will be vetting my gentleman friends? He writes very formally, does he not, and so he might, for he must be very unsure of my reaction to this letter.

She read on. It seemed that Mr Blackburn had after much discussion prevailed upon his father to sanction the purchase of a commission in the 51st Regiment, its being associated with the county of Yorkshire, at the rank of Lieutenant. It seemed that his parent had long debated whether he ought to enter his son for a more prestigious regiment, or at a higher rank, but the significant extra cost had dissuaded him. The only concession to pride he had made was to insist that Mr Blackburn was to be not a lowly ensign, as the higher rank demanded only a little more money, and carried much more dignity.

Rose smiled as she pictured the negotiations. Mr Blackburn would be conciliatory and concerned for his father's point of view, and hold his tongue when the issue was seen by his father as an investment and not a matter of conscience. No doubt he would have emphasised the arguments about the trade implications of Napoleon growing more powerful, and the prestige his father could claim if his son was an officer, and minimised the risks he might run. Mr Blackburn might not have performed as well in the Tripos exams as her brother, but he appeared to be his equal in subterfuge.

He was at present undergoing training at a camp not far from the village of Blackheath, and had met Sir George at a reception at the nearly-completed Somerset House, a very grand building. He was most gratified that Sir George remembered him, and had therefore presumed to ask if he may write to her. It seemed his duties were not yet determined upon, but he was likely to be in the country for some months, and if he were so fortunate as to have secured her favour, she could write if she desired care of the 51st regiment, 2nd battalion, Blackheath, and it ought to find him in due course.

That was all. Rose found herself unaccountably disappointed, though she could not tell why. After all, they had only met once, and he could have no certainty of her reaction to his writing. But still. She wished . . . she wished . . . she did not know what exactly she wished, but she had hoped for more, for more, well, personal information, or reflections upon their conversation, or something.

She refolded the letter and stowed it safely away again in her pocket. She would surely reply, but perhaps she would wait a while? Her heart seemed to be beating unaccountably quickly, and she found her hands were trembling slightly. Perhaps she ought to delay composing her response until her emotions had settled and she was feeling more level-headed. Perhaps she would make a start on her mathematics problems, that would be settling. Or would it be better to go and do something physical?

After a strenuous hour's digging Rose returned to her chamber and sat at her desk to compose a suitable reply. Her quill was cleanly cut, her ink to hand, her paper set just so – but she could not cause the words to spread freely across the sheet, beyond the date and the solitary address, "Kilcott, Gloucs".

What was all this? She who was usually fluent both in speech and even more in writing? She put her nib to the paper, but havered over whether to put, Dear, or My Dear, or just a plain, Mr Blackburn. A small blot leaked out from her pen, and she muttered under her breath, gathered her resolve, and wrote rapidly, "My dear Mr Blackburn, I was both surprised and pleased to receive your letter today, and can assure you that . . ." Then, pausing, she looked back and wondered if she were not being too forward, in putting "My dear" as well as "and pleased"; furthermore she could not think of what to write after "assure you that . . ." She stared at the pitiful line and after a few moments screwed up the sheet and threw it at the waste bin. Two seconds' reflection caused her to retrieve it and place it tidily on her desk for later burning, and she took another leaf of paper. Now, was this paper too expensive-seeming for such a letter? What would Mr Blackburn interpret from its quality? Would it be seen by his fellow officers and be the cause of innuendo and more?

Rose saw her hand was quivering, the remains of the feathers of her quill trembling in the air, and gave herself a mental shake. Come on girl, she admonished herself, stop making this letter out to be more important than it is! Just be yourself, be friendly and newsy and communicate that you would like to see him again if it were possible, and hope he might write again.

With this resolve she began once more. "Dear Mr Blackburn, I was very pleased to get your letter this morning and hope it is not too forward to reply immediately. In fact, I am quite cut off here in Gloucestershire, where I have returned with my brother, so any news from the outside world is most welcome. Of course I do like being at my home, but we get few visitors and apart from a weekly trip to Bath for my brother to take fencing lessons we rarely stray out of the grounds. I should love to hear about your doings with the regiment, and shall interrogate Sir George closely when he visits on Sunday about the Somerset House reception. He may have mentioned his planned trip to you when you met, and I am greatly looking forward to his appearance."

She paused, trying to think what might count as newsy chatter that she could fairly communicate, and eliminating her studies in Greek and mathematics, her experiments with drinking beer and smoking cigars, of digging, riding astride and fencing, of shooting and preparing for a complex deception in Cambridge, she was left with, "I have learnt to drive a phaeton with Charles, and while in Bath I have met up with an the daughter of an old friend of the family who took me to see a Shakespeare play whose plot I thought very unconvincing.

She has just invited me to take part in some amateur theatricals soon. Although I do not hold out great hopes for our efforts, it is something different to try. We are to make scenery and devise our own costumes, though I do not yet know who is to subject themselves to being our unfortunate audience." She wondered whether to mention Charles further, and contented herself with, "Charles would prefer to be out with his friends but Sir George feels he is better in the country for now, and I think he is bearing up under the restriction very well."

It all looked banal and boring. All the good bits had had to be censored. And, the most interesting part was a complete fabrication! Never mind, she could only work with what she had. For the rest, well, men always liked to talk about themselves and so she would ask him about the regiment and the training, and whether he was to leave for France soon, and then perhaps he would reply and give her more to talk about in the next letter.

Rose wrote carefully and she hoped, intelligently, for another two paragraphs, about the nature of his experiences in the military, and then wished him good fortune in his career. She signed her name, sanded the ink, folded the paper over and tucked the edges in, wrote the address on the outside, and sealed it. There, done. She would have liked to write a longer letter but any more would have made it seem laboured and artificial. Anyway, she did not know if she liked him that much, she had only had two dances after all, and . . . Well, she didn't know, really she didn't!

Rose pushed the letter deep into her pocket and stood up. She felt curiously unsettled, wobbly even, and she decided she must have overdone it with the digging, so she took herself off to her bed to lie down for an hour or so. That was only sensible, was it not?

As she lay, looking up at the moulded plasterwork of the ceiling, she found herself unaccountably picturing the Swaffham ball, with the couples skipping on the dance floor, but the figure of Mr Blackburn kept intruding on the picture and unsettling her. Really, it had been very kind of him to think of her and write, but it was she was sure merely politeness, triggered by his meeting her brother by chance. She should not put any weight on the letter, and she had replied promptly as was only polite, so she ought to think of something else so she might rest properly.

She turned her mind to the planned amateur theatricals, and what her next move should be in this subterfuge. She would be able to do nothing until Thursday, when she could pretend that Maria had told her of the play she had chosen, and perhaps given her a part to learn? Therefore, she would have to acquire a plausible script, although she doubted that Charles would want to look at it at all closely. He might go so far as to ask her the name of the play, though, and of course she would have to tell him about her part, as she would have been chosen to play a man, and therefore would have to acquire a male costume, and would need him to come with her to buy one.

So, which play should she choose? What would Maria and her friends choose? Surely they would not attempt a whole play? And it must be one which suited the temperaments and experiences of such girls. Perhaps one set in their world, in Bath? One of frivolity? A romantic froth? She turned over in her mind the few plays she had been able to see during her nineteen years, and then the others which she had read, or read of, in the absence of opportunity to visit the theatre often.

Well, how about Mr Sheridan's famous play, "The Rivals"? Or at least the first act. Of course, performing only one act would make nonsense of the story, but that would be quite like Maria. It was set in Bath, and she knew there was a copy in the library downstairs, and the first act was manageable for a group of novices, albeit they would mangle it beyond belief. Rose shook her head, for she had almost forgotten that this was a fiction of her own making, there would be no performance, no mangling. Nevertheless, surely this would be the ideal play.

She would play Captain Jack Absolute, of course. No, wait, she was but a new addition to Maria's group, and surely one of the others would be called upon to take the starring role? Not Captain Jack then, but his friend, what was his name, Faulkland. That would be better, no need to have military costume. And how would he dress? The play was about thirty years old, so the fashions would be a little dated, which meant she could have a frock coat (supposedly from Canada during her later deception) which would cover her form a little more than a modern cutaway.

As she pictured her costume, she found the image of Mr Blackburn, faultlessly groomed, appeared in the old-fashioned coat, rather than her own person. Shaking her head to dismiss the image, she tried to replace it with herself, but found that she could only see herself in a diaphanous gown standing very close to the man in the coat, as if they might be going to perform this new waltz that Louisa had told her about. His gloved hand rested on her back, and the other held hers, and . . . But she did not know how the dance was performed, and her illusion foundered at that point.

CHAPTER 8

THE FOLLOWING SUNDAY AFTERNOON PASSED in a turmoil of indecision for Rose. Should she play the demure little sister, and beg her brother to do what she wanted in the matter of a university education, to please her as no doubt he always wished to? She could employ flattery, and play on his goodwill for her guardianship of Charles. Or, conversely, should she demonstrate how far she had gone with her plans to impersonate a man, by dressing in her breeches and shocking him? Would it be better to approach him as soon as he had arrived and before he had become involved with his steward, or leave him to recover from the journey and relax a little? Should she talk to him while walking in the grounds, or in some private room in the house, perhaps his study? Or would that put him in a dominant position as the baronet, able to dictate whatever he wished?

And what real lever did she have to persuade him? If he were not swayed by a desire to further her happiness, then what more was there? Could she bargain with her supervision of Charles? Could he in fact afford the fees, even if he was prepared to countenance the deception? Would he value her having an education, as he had himself enjoyed, over her being married to some reasonably well-off suitor who would stabilise his finances?

She tried to distract her mind with the script of "The Rivals" but tossed it aside after ten fruitless minutes. She wondered if there might be any diversion in talking to Uncle Hugh about his inscriptions, and wandered towards the library, but unaccountably he was not there in his accustomed chair. Frustrated, she took a turn in the garden, and considered whether she could do any more digging, but decided not to in case George might unaccountably arrive early. She even toyed with the idea of getting out her paintbox and trying to capture the riot of colour spilling out of the flowerbeds, in spite of her lack of skill in drawing, but dismissed that plan as ridiculous.

Looking over her Greek was hopeless; even Euclid held no attraction. Charles had gone off on a ride somewhere distant, so she could not bait him. Eventually she settled in the parlour by her desk, with only a glance out of the window and down the carriage drive every four minutes or so, to check that Sir George had not come into sight. She set herself to write to sundry friends whom she had neglected of late. Louisa, of course. And Aunt Naismith, to be sure. These two were letters that needed to be written: she could compose them with hardly a thought, except to omit any hint about her plans for the autumn. Something about the weather; an observation about the difference in the air between the country and town; a few questions about the balls that had been attended; and in Louisa's letter at least a few sly comments about Mr Bridewell, and other young men to whom Louisa had referred in her last missive.

Her quill scratched across the paper purposefully, and, finishing, she wondered who next to address. She was discomforted to find that she had nobody else to whom she might reasonably write among her female acquaintance. Alicia and Harriet, from Miss Snape's, were out of the question. Lady Augusta similarly. And (consulting her meagre store of letters received since she had been here) she had been favoured with no-one else's attentions. Oh my! What did that imply about her?

The hour was still early, though. How about . . . No, she was abroad: Portugal, she thought. And . . . well, she had written to Mr Blackburn only a few days ago and writing again would look most odd. But . . . she might write to Mr James, might she not? After all, he was an academic, and not a suitor, so it would be proper. Also, it would be fun to think of how he might react to receiving a letter from a young lady, immured as he was in the enclave of Gonville and Caius. Yes, she would do it!

This was a harder epistle to compose, as she had only met the man on the one occasion and for even less time than Mr Blackburn, but she sucked her quill and bit her nails as she made the words come. He might like to know about her forays into Euclid, might he not? He might be entertained by her small knowledge of Greek, and so she constructed a line in that language (admittedly with recourse to the dictionary and the Grammar) and wrote it out with her best calligraphy. She told him about Charles' fencing, and her meeting with Maria, and the forthcoming play, forgetting until she had written about it that it was a fiction, and then not wanting to tear up the whole letter for the sake of removing it. She then thought he might be interested in Uncle Hugh's researches into Egyptology, so she added some of the little she had understood about the other two languages on the Stone, other than the Greek which had been translated some time ago.

By the time she had finished, the shadows had grown long on the lawn, and it was time to eat. After dinner she took a dilatory walk down the drive, and then found out Uncle Hugh (who had for some reason to do with his hieroglyphs been seeking inspiration earlier in the chicken sheds and the dovecotes) and was required on running him to earth to stay for nearly an hour listening to the latest theories from Professor this and Doctor that from one learned institution or another. At any rate, it passed the time, and before she knew it the sun had set and still there was no sign of George.

She only heard him come in when she had already half-undressed for bed. Judging that such a late hour would not be a good time to interview him, she retired, and lay awake staring at the ceiling for ages, trying to decide on her strategy.

The next day at breakfast she was all ready to take George aside once he appeared, when to her consternation, Mr Martin arrived to take their Maths lesson. She had totally forgotten about it in her nervousness about her great plan. Rapidly fetching her books and setting out their place in the dining room, she called for Charles and tried to focus on the day's theorems. For once, she could not see what Mr Martin was explaining, or at least, not so quickly as Charles, and she could see he was noticeably pleased by the eventuality.

Of course, once she had bid Mr Martin good day, and cleared away her papers, Sir George was nowhere to be found. The butler rather thought he had seen him leaving by the back door, and fancied he might be interrogating the head groom. He was not, however, in the stables; nor was he in the farm yard, nor yet in the corner from whence he was wont to survey the fields with his steward. Hot and frustrated, she stumped back to the house and at last almost ran into her brother as he came out of his study.

'George! Wherever have you been? I've been looking for you!'

'And I you, dear sister. I have several things to ask you.'

'And I you,' she replied, not liking the tone of his voice, but keeping to her plan.

'Shall we talk in my study?' her brother continued, turning without waiting for an answer.

Rose closed the door behind them and tried to read his expression. He did not look exactly cross, but there had been no fraternal embrace, nor did he offer her a seat. Grasping her courage, she walked to the most comfortable chair and planked herself down, lounging back in a somewhat unladylike manner.

'I have received some disquieting reports,' began George, 'concerning . . .'

'Oh, George, surely we should start with my report upon the progress of Charles?' she interrupted, hastily. 'Would that not be more opportune? It is all good news, I can say, and one should always begin with the good news, I am told?'

George looked at her, surprised, but inclined his head. 'Very well, sister,' he said.

'I can report that Charles has been, if not a model pupil, at least he has complied with every requirement that you set forth. He has attended all his classes in Greek and mathematics, and completed the tasks set in the lessons; and although neither Mr Fellowes nor Mr Martin would I think praise him for his application, nor his prowess, they have both said that they are well satisfied with his progress.' She thought a moment, and decided to add, 'I should also admit that I have also enjoyed the chance to study, and have been pleased that I have outstripped Charles in mathematics and kept ahead of him in Greek, which as his older twin I am sure you realise is important to me.'

George's face broke into a hint of a grin, before settling back into its stern expression.

'Also,' Rose hurried on, before George could start again on whatever had irked him, 'I have encouraged him to be active, not just in the trips to Bath for his fencing lessons, but also here, where we have been riding, and practising shooting and fencing.'

'We?' George's eyebrows frowned.

Rose sat up a little. 'Naturally, brother. You explained the need to supervise Charles closely, or at least as closely as he would tolerate, so I felt it necessary to take part in those activities myself. I must say, he seems to have quite taken to instructing me in the art of firing pistols and then the musket, and also I have taken the rôle of his opponent with the foil. I must say I have found that quite difficult; I have to admit that he is far superior to me in swordplay. Of course it helps that he is taller, but even so.'

George leaned forward. 'So, you have been doing these unladylike activities in order to keep Charles in check, have you? Perhaps I misjudged you, when I heard reports from the servants about, er, certain unusual practices?'

'Certainly, George. However, um, well, what else have you been told?'

'The patch of ground that has been dug over? The request to have strong drink brought into the buttery? The use of the man's saddle? The breeches?'

'Well,' temporised Rose, wondering if now was the time to plunge in, 'Yes, those things.' She sat up and leaned forward, mirroring her brother's posture. 'I have something to ask of you. I am not sure you will look favourably on it, but it is something I most passionately desire.'

'And I take it that this is not a new dress, or a repeat of your Season in London?' George observed, voice full of irony.

'Well, no. No, not that sort of thing at all.' This was going to be difficult, she thought. Here goes.

'As you know, I have not found the round of Society events much fun. In fact, I find the whole thing dull in the extreme, and I believe most of the gentlemen present at balls and so on find me, how shall I put it, unsuitable for their idea of a docile accomplished wife.'

'Fair enough,' George put in.

'Well, yes. Well spotted, dear brother. So, assisted by the need to rusticate Charles for a while, I have conceived a plan. A surprising plan, you may think. Perhaps a foolish plan, you may think. However I have been working towards it while also keeping Charles from mischief. Well, mostly from mischief: I must confess he was suborned by his fellow-fencers into an episode of drunkenness on one occasion, but I think that is not too bad for the time we have been here, and I was on hand to extricate him and return him home without mischance.'

She paused, and risked a look at George's face. He was looking expectant, and much less cross.

'Yes, well. So, . . .' it all had to come out in a rush, 'I wish to go to Cambridge to study. There, I have said it.'

'But you can have tutors here, surely?'

'No, you don't understand, I want to go to the University, to be an undergraduate there.'

George looked pityingly at her. 'I think you are forgetting your sex, dear sister. University is for men only.'

'Er, yes. Well, it is at the moment. I have, you know, read Mrs Wollstonecraft's book on the subject of the education of both sexes, and it seems that things may change. Perhaps, however, not for some years. But at present, I shall need to disguise myself as a man, and I have been working towards that end. However, I shall need your help and blessing in order to succeed in my subterfuge, and I here throw myself on your generosity.'

She looked up at George, not sure whether to expect an explosion or laughter from him. In fact he looked more startled than anything.

'So,' she continued, pulling out her list of tasks from her pocket, 'I have made a plan. I have completed the first elements of my preparatory education. I have the rudiments of shooting, riding, driving, and fencing in the style of a man. I already understand Latin, and now have enough Greek and mathematics not to cause suspicion, or at least I will have by the end of this summer. I have learnt about beer and shall shortly be moving on to whisky,'

'What!' interjected George. Rose! 'Think of the family name!'

'. . . and of course am now able to smoke cigars with the best.'

George stood up. Paced around. 'Rose, this is madness! You cannot be serious!'

'Quite serious, brother. But I need your help and blessing in order to secure a place, most readily no doubt at your own college, Emmanuel, and to procure a suitable set of clothes. I have, er, invented a play in which I am supposed to appear with my friend Maria and her friends, you remember her, she is the daughter of Mr Thacker of Gloucester? Hence Charles can help me acquire a man's long coat suitable for a supposed performance of Mr Sheridan's "The Rivals", and some other garments, but you could make the process much easier for me if you would.'

'No! Absolutely not!'

Rose quailed a little, inwardly, but persevered. 'I know from what you told me, that in order to be admitted to Emmanuel one only needs the simple recommendation of an MA of either university. That would be you, of course. Oh, and there would be the matter of fees, of course.

'No!'

'And, naturally, books, and so on.'

'No!'

'I think the most difficult thing would be to conceal the truth from the college servants, or at least the ones attending my room. Servants always know everything, as you realise.'

'NO!'

'I have decided that I am to be your distant cousin from Nova Scotia, Richard Cox by name, aged sixteen. This will explain my lack of beard, my lack of knowledge of those things which English boys learn about at school beyond the academic, and my different way of speaking, though I expect to soon learn the slang and mannerisms of my new friends.'

'You have gone out of your mind, Rose! This cannot happen. I forbid it. If, or rather when, you were discovered, it would cause an irreparable scandal.'

Rose stood up and faced him. 'I know you only want the best for me, brother, and truly, I want to do this. Look at my figure, or rather my lack of one. My height. Would you like to see me in breeches?'

George groaned. 'Rose!'

She fetched a taper from the mantelpiece and lit it from the fire. Going over to the box on his desk she took out two cigars and offered them to George. 'Would you clip them, or shall I?' When he didn't move she handed him the taper, expertly cut the ends of both cheroots, put both in turn to her mouth and lit them, and handed him one. 'I am very serious about this, you see, George. Smoking helps my voice deepen, too.' She puffed a mouthful of smoke at him and sat down, crossing her foot over the other knee as best she could in her dress.

George paced up and down, smoking his cigar, clearly dumbfounded by Rose's behaviour. He was the responsible brother, had been so since their father died, he had had to be sensible, curb his impulses to do anything outrageous. Charles on the other hand had done all the foolish things he might have done were circumstances different. But Rose! She was a girl, after all, a lady. Ladies did not do such things. He would tell her so, and that would finish it.

'Ladies do not do such things, Rose.'

Rose drew on her cigar, held the smoke, blew it out nonchalantly. 'They do in Mr Shakespeare's plays. All the time. And nobody seems to suspect a thing, even though they make no preparation for the pretence. I on the other hand shall be fully and meticulously prepared. For every eventuality.'

'But . . .'

I shall let you absorb this news, brother,' Rose got up and squashed out her cigar. 'It is a bit much for you to take in, but I am confident you will go along with my idea. You owe me, you know.'

She left the room, head held high, and waited until she was well away from the closed door before she allowed herself to indulge in a paroxysm of coughing. You need more practice with those cigars, she told herself when she had recovered.

Sir George it seemed had spent the rest of the morning with his steward, as she did not see him again until dinner. Rose had worked on her Euclid most of the time, but with periods considering how she might persuade George to back her plan. What did George value, what weakness could she work on? He did care for his sister and her happiness, to be sure, but he had said he was afraid of scandal. He wanted Charles to be kept from harm, so he owed her for the last five weeks, and for those to come. He was in a fairly public post, she knew, at the Foreign Office, and doubtless the recent declaration of war would have stressed him and increased his workload. He wouldn't have much time to spare, therefore.

The evening of the ball swam into her mind, connected somehow with thoughts of George's job at the Foreign Office. George looking smart in his evening wear; his various acquaintances from Cambridge; the Duke and Duchess . . . and then George with Lady John Barnes, the kiss, and the mysterious handing over of a letter. That would surely be a scandal if it got out? Not that she would ever tell anyone about her brother's dalliance? Would she?

He did not like scandal; and this was her secret knowledge; would she use it against him? Of course not. But . . . well, it was a lever. It was tantamount to blackmail, though. No, she couldn't possibly.

At dinner she was surprised to find George pouring her a glass of claret wine straight from the bottle. She immediately sensed a test. Raising it to her lips she took a small sip. It was most peculiar, but not unpleasant. The taste lingered after she had swallowed it, and seemed to stick to her cheeks and teeth. Now, how strong was it? The glasses were smaller than beer glasses so it must be much stronger. Of course, as she was from Nova Scotia she may never have tasted French wine, so she could plead ignorance. Except, Charles was there, looking surprised at his brother but pleased when he too had a glass poured for him.

'Jolly decent of you, bro. Rose here hasn't let me near the wine cellar since I've been at Kilcott.'

'Good for her. However, I am now here, so, tell me what you think of the wine. Rose first.'

Rose took another sip. 'It is very heavy, compared to the white wines I have been given at dinners and parties before. I am informed, though,' with a look at Charles, 'that ladies are usually given much-watered wine, so that this is a novelty to me. I think I could grow to like it, it is quite, um, sticky, I mean, it sticks to my teeth. And I think I can taste blackberries, or something like them.'

'Charles?'

'I usually drink port wine, brother; this is much less sweet. A difficult taste to like at first. It reminds me of a hot dry summer. If that doesn't sound silly.'

'Good. Rose, lets see how you manage after a glass or two.'

Rose gave him a meaningful look, and drained half her glass. 'I shall await results with interest,' she said. Privately, she decided to only drink two glasses at most, and to watch how her brothers reacted as much as they would watch her.

Within a few minutes she could feel a delicious lightness coming over her. She went to take another sip, but withdrew her hand at the last minute. No, she would not make a fool of herself in front of both men, she remembered the effect of the beer at the Prince of Wales, and so she decided she would keep the rest of this glass until they had eaten for at least fifteen minutes.

Charles drank more freely than she did. George finished his glass too and made to top up hers before refilling his and Charles', but she stopped him. 'Brother, I can decide for myself how much I wish to drink. You carry on. I am quite content.'

'Very well. I shall save a second glass for you.'

Rose enjoyed her meal and the skirmish with George. The wine grew on her; she kept to her plan and drank only another half glass in spite of George's teasing. Then when the dishes had been cleared away, port was served. This was a novelty for Rose, and she sipped her wine very cautiously. It was like molasses, like cordial. She did not trust George, she suspected this wine was much stronger, and left her glass unfinished.

George then asked for the cigars to be fetched from his study. He cut, and passed one to each of them and they lit in turn from a taper.

Charles was mystified. 'George, this is deucedly out of character for you! Not that I mind, I like a good cigar, but Rose?'

'It's alright, Charles, I have explained about our experiments to George.'

Charles sat back and blew out a cloud of smoke. 'Well, I shall enjoy it while it lasts, even if I don't understand it at all.'

George then proceeded to catechise Charles about his studies. He managed to do this without putting his brother's back up, for a change, and even seemed impressed with his recollection of the various parts of Euclid they had covered, and had him recite some Greek declensions and conjugations successfully.

'Excellent,' he concluded. 'I am well-disposed to reinstate your allowance once these three months are up, if this progress is maintained. Rose has given me good reports of you also, and I am most grateful to her.'

'I have enjoyed myself,' she said, 'and I think Charles has not found it too irksome?'

'Pretty decent, actually,' he replied, taking a puff of his cigar. 'Getting quite fair at fencing, beat one of the better men last week; having a fine time driving the phaeton, and riding.'

Sir George raised an interrogative eyebrow at Rose and she explained about their neighbour lending them his carriage, and how Charles had shown her how to handle it. She said that of course Charles was a better driver than she was, as he was a better rider and shot, and watched how pleased he looked out of the corner of her eye as she said it.

She felt she was handling the situation quite well. She reached for the remains of her port and finished it, feeling the silky sweetness as it descended her throat, and the slight acidity which balanced it, preventing it from being too cloying. She grinned at George, who had noticed her drinking, and leant over and refilled her glass before she could stop him.

Charles asked George about what was happening at the Foreign Office what with the War recommencing, which Rose thought was unusually tactful of him, and she listened as George talked about the meetings and the discussions and the preparations of the various regiments that had to be dispatched overseas in due course, and the state of the Navy, and Viscount Nelson's plans to safeguard the seas for British trade, and the reasons for the breakdown of the Peace of Amiens, and many other topics. She was particularly interested in his very circumspect descriptions of the secret activities of spies on both sides, and how vital military information needed to be both acquired about the enemy and safeguarded from him.

George clearly relished his role in organising his country's defence. Rose was reminded by this of Mr Blackburn, but she kept quiet, not wishing to give Charles a handle with which to tease her. Eventually George fell silent, and then stood up, asking Rose to come with him to his study, and tossing behind him the injunction, 'Oh, bring your port with you, if you would.'

CHAPTER 9

ROSE DID AS SHE WAS bidden, and took both the port and her cigar along with her after George. He closed his study door behind them, and sat himself down in his chair behind the desk.

'So, sister. I have to decide what am I to make of your, er, activities, these past weeks, having had a chance to consider them.'

'Make of them what you will, brother. But before we go further, may I ask you concerning Mr Blackburn? I had a most friendly letter from him, well, it was very correct, but it was most kind of him to think of writing to me with all the new activities he must be involved with. He said he had met you at a reception at Somerset House, and that you had given him my address and encouraged him to write.' She drew on her cigar, and sat in a chair to the side which made George twist round to look at her.

'Indeed I did, Rose. He seems to me a very fine gentleman, newly commissioned into the 51st regiment, and keen to serve his country. Also, unlike many of our officers, he is diligent in learning his role as a lieutenant and in getting to know his men. Am I to deduce that you liked him?'

'He certainly had more to recommend him than, er, your friend, Lord Toby. And while I also liked his friend Mr James, I think that I would find him, how shall I put it, less comfortable in Society, than Mr Blackburn.'

'Excellent. You could do worse than Mr Blackburn, Rose. Although,

I imagine he will be somewhat occupied for some considerable time to come with his military duties. However, I don't think it is letting out State secrets to say that it is likely we will not act in this War on land at least, unless or until Boney make a move, so he may be free to move in Society after some months. Would you like that?'

'Perhaps I should not answer that question, brother? Besides, it was I who asked you to tell me about Mr Blackburn.'

'Very well, but I cannot tell you much. The main part of his regiment is in India at Kandy; the complement is being increased from one to two battalions, and he is with the new recruits near Blackheath. He looks very well in his uniform, and I was able to introduce him to one or two more senior officers from other regiments who may be of aid to him in his career. That is all: I only spent about ten minutes with him, having many other gentlemen to see at the reception. Oh, no, one other thing, I almost forgot: he asked if it would be permissible to visit you in Gloucestershire, military duties permitting. I gave him my blessing: I hope I did right?'

Rose felt her colour rising, and tried to keep her mind on the matter in hand, and her feelings private. 'Thankyou, George. I am indebted to you. Now, if I may, I shall outline my plans in more detail, and explain the assistance which I hope you will give me.'

'As you have heard, I have prepared myself for the deception as well as I can in the short time I have had so far. This is the first time I have tried unwatered wine, and I think you can see that I can judge its effect on me so as not to become, er, careless in my behaviour.' She again pulled out her list of tasks for the accomplishment of her plan, and considered it.

'Firstly, please would you write to the Master of Emmanuel and request the admission of your young cousin from Nova Scotia to a position in the college. I leave it to you to decide at what rate I should live, but I would wish to live modestly, as long as I am able to have my own room. Lord Toby was a Fellow-Commoner, I believe; that is not for me. Equally I do not think I should flourish as a sizar, because waiting on others would give them too many opportunities to penetrate my disguise.'

'But . . .'

'Also, I throw myself on your expertise as to how to deal with the matter of the college servants, who would be bound to realise my sex, however easily I can deceive the other students and academics.' She consulted her notes again. 'Oh yes, and could you assist me in the procurement of men's clothing suitable for my supposed age and position? And I shall need a haircut, of course. However, I have a cunning plan, which is to have my beautiful tresses removed all of a piece, and a wig made so that I may return to my normal appearance in the vacations.'

'But . . .'

'As you can see, brother, I am most determined about this. I shall give you a written account of my past history in Nova Scotia to ensure you do not make any mistakes and arouse suspicion with the college. I have considered where we should buy the clothing, and I believe Bristol would be sufficiently far away for the transaction to be kept secret, especially as the clothes will ostensibly be for a part in a play. And then when I have one set it would be easy to have them copied without revealing for whom they are made.'

'But . . .'

'As for talking and moving like a man, I have been making a study of Charles' manner, and shall continue to observe your own patterns while you are here.'

'You shall do no such thing!'

'I am sure you will come to see the perfection of my plans in a short while, brother.'

'I surely shall not.'

'We shall see. I shall now depart and visit Uncle Hugh in the library, as I wish to enlarge my knowledge of the Rosetta hieroglyphs and what progress has been made on the translation, which I am sure will be most useful when I am resident in college.' She stubbed out her cigar, drained her port, and left, ignoring George's command to 'Wait right there,' and shut the door behind her.

Once out in the corridor she paused and shook herself, as if she couldn't quite believe she had said all that to George and then walked out on him. She set out with a resolute step for the library, in case George should take it upon himself to check up that she had actually sought out obscure information about ancient languages. It was going quite well, she thought: she hadn't had to threaten him with stopping supervising Charles, let alone revealing what she had seen at the Swaffham ball. But the news about Mr Blackburn's possible visit . . . She did not know how she felt about that at all!

On Tuesday George was out at dawn with his steward, visiting the tenants and noting repairs which need to be ordered for their cottages, and dealing with any problems they had which it was in his power to remedy (or so the butler told Rose at breakfast, in a tone which suggested that Sir George at least was comporting himself as a gentleman, even if his sister was, well, improper or worse). She noted his manner, and the way he raised one eyebrow, and resolved to practice this in her chamber in front of her glass, as a useful masculine style of put-down.

They were just putting their books away after Mr Fellowes' Greek lesson when Sir George appeared and took their tutor to his study to interrogate him about their progress. Before Rose could intercept him once he released the gentleman he was off again, calling over his shoulder that he would be back for dinner at five. Rose, put out, as she had worked out exactly what she was going to say to him this morning, stumped off, changed into her breeches and boots and went to do some digging.

She was cross with George, unreasonable though she knew it was, and so at lunch she asked Charles what he planned to do in the next few hours. Charles glumly said he supposed he ought to be working on his Greek, so that he could impress Sir George when he returned, but

Rose persuaded him without difficulty into a programme of riding, shooting and then fencing practice.

As she had anticipated, Sir George returned while they were engaged in duelling in the Gallery: or rather, Charles was tutoring Rose in the correct manner of performing the lunge, which she found bore painfully on muscles that were already sore from her earlier exertions, and gave Charles plenty of opportunity to criticise her posture. She stood up and imitated Charles' negligent stance, and enjoyed George's expression at seeing her in breeches and jacket. She grinned, and tried (unsuccessfully) raising an eyebrow at him.

'How is your sister's progress?' George asked.

Charles considered. 'Well,' he said reluctantly, 'not bad for a girl, I suppose. She is very aggressive. Lacking in refinement, but she is quite quick.'

'Yes,' Rose chipped in, 'I got three hits on you last time, didn't I?'

'You'd better get changed for dinner,' was all George could manage, before he strode off to his room.

Rose kept her counsel throughout dinner, making sure George didn't pour her more wine than she felt she could manage, and eating ravenously after her energetic afternoon. Once she had followed him to his study, she again interrupted his opening sentence by asking how the report from Mr Fellowes had been, which he had unaccountably failed to mention over dinner. It seemed that their tutor had given a very positive account, but she inferred that George did not wish to praise Charles too readily, nor admit that Rose was making fine progress.

Hence, sensing she was now once more on the front foot, Rose made her opening.

'I am sure that by now you will have come around to supporting your sister in her ambitions, dear brother? You have seen how I have applied myself to all details of its execution, and how confident I am of its success?'

'I must admit, you have been most assiduous, sister. But the fact remains, you are a woman, and such a course of action as you propose would be disastrous for my good name.'

Rose considered. Time to fire her first shot. 'You have discovered, have you not, how compliant Charles has been under my care with your plans? How he has applied himself to study, and to gentlemanly pursuits? It would be awkward for you if he were to return to London, and recommence his previous behaviour unsupervised, should I decide that I no longer wish to be his guardian?'

'He has no money to do such a thing.'

'Then his behaviour would be added to by the shame of his debts, Sir George.'

She stood with her arms folded, trying to look implacable. She watched George's expressions as they chased each other across his face.

'You would not do this to me,' he said finally.

'Are you sure? I am most strongly resolved in my plans, brother.'

'Hmmm.'

'It is the end of June, brother. I have three months to practise my deception, before term begins.'

'More, probably: lectures do not start before the division of term.'

'Come on, Doddie, you know you want to help your sister get what she wants. And you saw how unutterably dull I found the ball at Lady Swaffham's, and the soirées, and so on?'

'But . . .'

'Do you not think I cut a fine figure of a man in breeches with my hair tied back? A youthful man, at any rate?'

Reluctantly George agreed with this assessment.

'At least you can arrange for me to be fitted for a suit of men's clothes, on the pretext of my appearing in Maria's play? That at least you could do, without prejudice, as I am sure you have the contacts to arrange the tailoring more discreetly and effectively than I or Charles could. The play being Mr Sheridan's "The Rivals" is set thirty years ago, so I should require a frock coat, which is of course out of fashion here, but would represent well the fashions of the colonies, which must be behind London in modernity. Such a coat will conceal any extra breadth that might be perceived about my hips. And you already know that it is only artifice on the part of my dressmaker that gives me the illusion of having a bosom of any description.'

'Rose! Consider a brother's feelings in your descriptions!'

Rose ploughed on. 'So, do you know of a tailor who would make such a costume, in Bristol, or some other suitable place?'

'Well, er, yes, I do. In Bristol, as you say.'

'So?'

'I will consider it. No more.'

'Good. I will anticipate travelling there soon, with Charles of course, to be measured and so on. I know you will be too busy to accompany me; your work at the Foreign Office is very important.'

She reached over and took a cigar from the box on the desk. She noted George's pained expression as she cut it, took a taper and lit it. 'Want one, sir?' she said, as negligently as possible, in the way she had seen Charles speak.

'Certainly not!'

'Very well, have it your own way. They aren't half bad, these. But you could easily get better ones, you know.'

'A proper gentleman would take snuff, you know.'

'Possibly. But I am a provincial, you know, and prefer cigars.' She blew smoke in his general direction. 'Things are quite different over the water, you know. Lots of Frenchies around, at least those that pledged to the Crown back in the Seven Years War.'

'You really have been doing your homework, haven't you?'

Rose smiled, complacently. 'I have indeed, brother. I intend to leave nothing to chance. Remember, it would be my reputation as well as yours that would be at risk should I be discovered.'

'Indeed it would, and disastrously, I can foresee.'

'However, I have conceived an insurance policy should I be unmasked, as it were. I shall explain that the whole affair concerned a bet that you and I made with, well, someone of your choosing, that I could not pull off the deception for a year. I believe that such wagers are matters of honour, and would explain the situation to most gentlemen satisfactorily.'

Rose was rather pleased with this idea, which she had thought of while digging in the kitchen garden only that morning. George pursed his lips and hesitated to reply, as if he could see the logic of her statement. Rose wondered whether she should fire her last salvo while he was temporarily uncertain of his resolve. He would be leaving tomorrow morning, and such arguments would seem less forceful in a letter. Besides, she was reluctant to commit such intelligence to paper, as letters may go astray, or be read by others on arrival.

'Also, brother, I am in possession of a nugget of information which you might find quite embarrassing to have made public. I am unsure as to whether I would disclose it, but I might, if I am not happy with my situation.'

'Whatever might that be, Rose? Or should I say, Richard, was it?'

Rose swallowed. 'It concerns the passage of a letter between you and a certain lady, with whom you were entwined in considerable intimacy at the Swaffham ball.'

'What!!'

'I have put a name to the lady, a married lady, a titled lady. I do not wish to disclose any of this to anyone, and have so far kept it to myself, but it might slip out, if I was very distressed or unhappy or frustrated.'

'No!'

'Of course, I do not wish to publish this fact, I am after all your loyal sister, Doddie, but who knows what might happen if I am driven to it?'

Sir George looked apoplectic, so she considered it was time to withdraw. She stubbed out her cigar and marched off, as well as she could in her dress. As she closed the door behind her she shivered. She didn't like upsetting Doddie, he had always been good to her, and she still hadn't decided that she would ever use this information against him, it would be too awful, but perhaps it was alright to make him think that she might, she just might?

CHAPTER 10

BY THE END OF AUGUST Rose felt that nearly everything was in place. Charles had been reinstated with his allowance and had taken himself off to York, where he said there were several cronies whom he just must look up. The project of Maria's to produce Mr Sheridan's play had mysteriously been cancelled, but not before Rose had gone with Charles to Bristol, where Sir George had arranged for a discreet tailor and bootmaker he knew to outfit her, with the return visit for the final fitting leading her to take away just one set of clothes, the rest being sent by carrier to Sir George at his London address without Charles being any the wiser.

Moreover, once she had fetched the copy of "The Rivals" from the library she had been able to learn some of the lines belonging to Mr Faulkland, and persuade Charles to read out the other parts to coach her in the proper way to deliver her lines, as a man and a friend of Captain Jack, first in her working breeches and old boots, and then once her new clothes had arrived, in her full costume. Charles was most eager to criticise, enjoying pointing out fault after fault not so much in her speech but in her attitude. Rose had to bite her tongue often, as he was by no means an encouraging teacher, but she took what he said about how a man would react, and stand, and move, and gaze, and stored them away for her big performance. She also, now that she had had these many differences between the sexes pointed out to her, observed them for herself more readily in their tutors, in

Charles and in the people in Bath on their Thursday visits. With the information she spent many evenings practising masculine ways of behaviour in private in her room.

Sir George had arranged for the young Richard Cox to be admitted to Emmanuel College, to arrive in early October; and had made arrangements with one of the college servants who was heavily indebted to him for getting him and his wife out of a major difficulty with the authorities, to be responsible for Rose's stair and room, so as to avoid the risk of discovery by the other staff. She was to enter college as a pensioner, and was to have some private tuition in mathematics as George reluctantly admitted the teaching at college was often not all it should be.

All these things had been done, it is true, but the morning of Sir George's departure in June had been more than slightly fraught. He had joined them for breakfast, and remained almost silent, except for requests to pass cakes or chocolate, his face set in a frown, his occasional flashing looks at her hostile. He had spent a few minutes with Mr Martin before their lesson, and then departed without further comment. Rose had been a bag of nerves after he had gone, finding respite in her digging and riding, and then after Thursday's trip to Bath, in testing out the potency of the bottle of whisky Charles had purchased with her. Once she had learnt to sip it extremely slowly so it did not burn her throat unbearably as it had at first (to Charles' amusement) she had grown to like it, and greatly prefer it to beer, to be sure.

All these things necessary for her plan, then, had followed upon the arrival of a much-dreaded letter from Sir George on the Wednesday following his leaving Kilcott, a letter which Rose was sure would merely reiterate his refusal to countenance such a hare-brained scheme, in spite of all her clever persuasions. She held onto it for some minutes after its arrival, not daring to open it. Once she did she was so relieved she began to sob. Fortunately she had taken the precaution of removing herself from Charles' company, so she could avoid awkward and critical questions. It was a handsome letter, beginning, 'Dear Mr Richard Cox, I capitulate. I am persuaded that the subterfuge of a wager will reduce the ignominy of discovery, and I have enlisted the help of a friend at the Foreign Office as the supposed other party in the matter, without telling him the exact nature of the wager, you understand. However, the information that you hold concerning me is so sensitive that I beg of you not to reveal it to anyone (underlined in triple) not just for my sake but for your country's sake.'

It went on to say in very circumspect language, as letters can go astray or be read by others, that he was sure in any case that she would not betray his trust in her by revealing the "transaction", so he was doing this "unthinkable thing" for her purely as a devoted brother: as she had said, he did always want to do that which would make her happy. He then delineated the actions he had taken, the letters to the tailor and to the College Master, the visit to his old college servants, and so on. He would arrange for a discreet barber to visit her at his rooms, nearer the time, and a wigmaker to do the necessary following this. Rose danced a joyful little jig once she had finished, and then re-read it to make sure she had not been mistaken in its contents.

It was odd once Charles had left Kilcott. She had prevailed upon Sir George to continue the lessons in Greek and Mathematics even after his departure the previous week, but she missed chivvying Charles to do the work he had been set, and the trips to Bath, and driving the phaeton, and fencing practice with him. She even missed seeing Maria each week, which surprised her, though she found her friend's tearful farewells had been more than a trifle trying.

She could ride, though, at Kilcott, and shoot, but it was rather lonely. Even keeping in practice with the bottle of whisky which they had bought on the last visit to the fencing master, and smoking Sir George's cigars, wasn't the same on her own. The weather had been favourable, and she had managed to spend enough time outside without a bonnet and with sleeves rolled up, digging her patch of garden and walking in the estate, to render her face and arms more tanned than would be good manners in London, and (she hoped) believable for a lad from the colonies. She was surprised at how much muscle she had developed in her shoulders, and how much easier it was to do most outdoor pursuits than when she had started, without getting out of breath.

She had received two more letters from Mr Blackburn, one in mid-July and one soon after Charles had left. She had recognised his writing immediately on being handed the sheets, and felt an unaccustomed thrill at his thinking of her, and a surge of hope that he might be soon coming to visit. The letter opened with military matters, though: it seemed that he had been transferred from his duties at Blackheath to a different role in the Army. His battalion was being kept at readiness but not expecting to travel overseas at present. He was not at liberty to say what he was doing or where, but the Blackheath address would find him after only a brief delay. Unfortunately this meant that he would not be free for long enough to visit Gloucestershire, he was full of apologies. However, he was full of excitement in being able to serve his country, and wished she could be there so he could show her all the sights and people and places he was seeing, but it was all most secret. He had met Sir George again at a ball, he had been extremely courteous, and given him news of her and of Charles. He hoped they might meet again once her duties with Charles in Gloucestershire had finished, if he were free. He said some very complimentary things about her appearance and about her interest in study and current affairs, and that he had never met a woman quite like her.

She felt herself colouring when she had read this, in spite of the disappointment, and subsequently had dreamed of him on more than one night. He was in his red uniform, taking her in his arms at a ball, or riding through the woods here at Kilcott with her, or, oddly, confiding national secrets to her over a glass of whisky. She had woken from these dreams each time all stirred up, hot and bothered, and taken a bath in quite cold water as soon as the maid could bring it.

The second letter had been even more reticent about his military role, but he was full of warm regards for her and wondered if they might meet soon, as Sir George had said she was coming up to London in September for a short visit, and he hoped he might pay her a call if his duties allowed. This had led to a sudden fluttering in her breast as she read, and a recurrence of the dreams that night. Surely she could not feel this way towards a man whom she had only met once? Yet he was most interesting in his letters, and told her of various happenings in London, and inside information about events that had been in the newspapers whenever he could, and was generally as chatty as one could reasonably be on one side of a sheet of paper.

She had worn her new clothes in her room at every opportunity, partly so they would not appear too new, but also to get used to the different way they sat on her body, and how she could move in some ways more freely, and in others, less so. She managed to master the tying of a cravat, but disliked how it made her hold her head aloof. Bandaging her breasts flat was a simple matter, it hardly need doing. Her breeches were quite loose, but she experimented with ways of simulating a gentleman's . . . , well, his outline under them. Successfully she thought. And with the deepening of her voice with the cigar smoking (not too often, she really was not very keen) she felt ready. Ready, but extremely nervous, at the same time.

Three weeks later she was in the post-chaise for London, her trunks containing both dresses and her men's garb, her half-empty bottle of whisky and a few cigars, books of Greek grammar and Latin poetry, Playfair's Euclid and Newton's Principia. She hadn't dared open the latter, other than a quick squint at the title page, it looked intimidating and even though it was Motte's translation and not the original Latin version, she thought even having it in her possession was getting far too far ahead of herself. However, Uncle Hugh, who had looked it out for her when he heard that she was to continue her mathematical studies in London for a while, had insisted she took it, as he said, it was the greatest scientific book ever written. It had taxed her ingenuity to come up with a convincing explanation for him and the Kilcott staff as to where she would be for the next months, especially as she was not sure she would be home at Christmas, and this was the best she could do.

Uncle Hugh had also given her several letters to important men in London which he said he did not want to entrust to the post, letters with highly secret ideas about the decipherment of the hieroglyphs. She had promised him to deliver them at the first opportunity: he had impressed upon her that she must deliver them only into the gentlemen's hands, and not their servants or anyone else.

Sir George looked at the addresses on these bulky communications when she came round to his rooms from the hotel where she was staying (Mrs Naismith and Louisa having returned to Cheshire once the season was over) and recognised the name of one Dr Thomas Young of Welbeck-street as being that of an Emmanuel man, whom he had known slightly in his third year at college. He knew he was an immense intelligence, and had interests across the whole spectrum of learning as well as his regular profession as a doctor, but he had not heard that he was interested in Egyptology. He advised Rose that if she was permitted to see him, she should take the opportunity to converse a little on his current interests, as it was sure to be instructive.

Hence in her first week in London Rose spent some little time travelling with a maid from the hotel to several addresses of important people, finding them all well-disposed to her once she had explained her mission, and welcoming her in order to hear directly from her lips about Great-uncle Hugh's ideas. Fortunately she had spent some considerable time with him before leaving Kilcott, and could give a sensible account of his work.

Dr Young however proved elusive. She visited three times but found him out, either at the hospital wards, or the lecture rooms, or visiting a lady in Cavendish Square. She had plenty of other things to occupy her, not the least of which was packing her trunk for Cambridge, making sure to include only masculine items, nothing that could betray her, yet everything that she might need. She had made provision for managing her courses, which seemed to have become even lighter in the last couple of months, perhaps because of how anxious she had become once the reality of her adventure was upon her. She had practised restricting how much liquid she drank at times that might require her to use the gentlemen's room in a public place, rather than the pot in her own chamber or the privy which George told her was located near the pond in the college gardens.

Mr Blackburn had not appeared, sadly. He had however left his card at George's rooms, with brief scribbled apologies, and a hope that he might be free at the end of the week. She thought of him frequently as she was driven about the capital, wondering where he might be, and what he was doing. Then she would tell herself off, for making more of a passing acquaintanceship than was reasonable.

The point of no return was fast approaching: the haircut. Admittedly many ladies had previously worn wigs as a routine, and kept their heads shaven to combat headlice (ughh!) but these days, and for young girls, especially those on the marriage market, the fashion was for one's own long hair, naturally coloured, curled and dressed. If Mr Blackburn was to appear once she had had the deed done! She would have to pretend she was indisposed, and miss seeing him, there was no other way.

Then joy of joys! She was in her room at the late hour of four o'clock when his card was sent up by the hotel porter, and she rapidly made herself tidy and descended to meet him in the public salon. He was full of apologies for the hour of his visit, and his delay in coming to pay his respects, but he was the slave of his masters in the Army, and his time was never his own, and so on and so on.

'But you are here,' she said, curtseying demurely. 'Please, take a seat.'

She sat upright on the edge of the settle, making sure she didn't slip into the ways of her new role which she had been practising, and lounge about legs akimbo, by some unconscionable error. He was sadly not dressed in scarlet, but in a regular dark coat and buff breeches, with a plain and modest waistcoat. She thought he looked rather ill at ease, but it turned out that it was only his pressing engagements.

'I do apologise also that I can only stay for forty-five minutes: I am expected at the Admiralty and only found that I had this moment an hour ago. Your brother Sir George was so good as to tell me where you were staying. It is most rude of me, but I so wished to see you, if you will not think such an admission too forward.'

'No, sir, I do not. In fact,' she relaxed her posture a little, once she realised she was not going to misbehave by mistake, 'I am so pleased to see you that even a short time is wonderful. I have been sadly deprived of congenial company in Gloucestershire. And I have been most cheered by your letters.'

'Well that's all right then. I mean, I am most relieved, I was not sure how you might feel about my writing, or my coming today, in spite of your replying to me promptly.'

'Can you tell me anything more of your post in the Army?'

'I'm afraid I cannot. But I could tell you a little of the manoeuvres at Blackheath where I started out, if you like.'

'Please do.'

Mr Blackburn told her a few stories about the new recruits, and their unfamiliarity with Army discipline, mostly humorous, some funny at his own expense. She found him a most congenial companion. Then, after a tale about a drunken corporal finished, he asked her about her time in Gloucestershire, which gave her to hesitate.

She was able to describe some of her activities with George, and how pleased she had been to learn to drive the phaeton, and to ride out with Charles (omitting the matter of the man's saddle). She talked about how Charles had been making progress in fencing, and how he had explained about the skills required (omitting the part about practising with him). She told him about the lessons, and how much she had enjoyed the mathematics (omitting that she had a copy of the Principia in her luggage). It was quite a balancing act trying to be chatty and open while remembering what not to mention. On the other hand, no doubt Mr Blackburn must have been censoring his own activities and only telling certain stories that were not secret.

She asked him about his father, and about his earlier life, and in return explained about her own parents and how recently the family had been elevated to the baronetcy. She felt she was getting to know the man as well as the formal social facade, and was surprised at how easy it was to exchange confidences with him.

Only too soon, Mr Blackburn enquired about her future plans. She was a little nonplussed, she had been wondering what she could tell him as soon as his card had been brought to her. She decided on a straight falsehood.

I leave this hotel tomorrow, and return to Kilcott,' she told him. 'Sir George has been very good allowing me this visit, but we are not wealthy, and so I need to return home.'

'That is a shame and a great loss to me. I was hoping I might find occasion to pay you a longer call next week, or perhaps take you out for a drive. I am truly sorry to hear it.'

A church clock struck the three quarter hour outside and Mr Blackburn started, and rose, with further apologies. He promised to write again, and Rose had the quickness of mind to suggest he left his letters with Sir George if he was in London, to save her expense, as he would have to write letters to his steward, his housekeeper and to her, and he could enclose Mr Blackburn's epistle with them.

Mr Blackburn took his leave hurriedly, and left. Rose let out her breath with a sigh, and felt herself trembling. She told herself not to be silly. After all, he was only a man. An intelligent and funny man, yes, but a man who was so busy he was unavailable. As would she be from tomorrow. Good grief, the days were rushing on!

CHAPTER 11

GEORGE HAD ARRANGED FOR HER luggage to be moved to his rooms the next morning, and once it was taken away, she walked the short distance there in trepidation. He was waiting at the entrance, and took her up explaining how he had sent his valet on an errand that would keep him for some hours, and that the hairdresser had just arrived. He had explained to the man that she was to take a male part in some amateur theatricals, and she would subsequently adopt the coming fashion of the close-cropped ladies' style. Rose, or rather Richard, was to sleep in the truckle bed in George's room, for the next few nights until it was time for her to take the coach to Cambridge.

The hairdresser, a taciturn man, sat her down and surveyed her head silently from all sides. He felt her skull, lifted her long tresses to see her hairline, and hummed and hawed for a little while.

'May I suggest a Bedford crop, sir? I believe it would suit the lady better than a Titus or a Brutus, or any of the other fashionable styles. And also it would be easier to grow it out into a ladies' style in due course.'

'Very well, sir. Is that satisfactory to you, Rose?'

Rose nodded, folded her hands, and shut her eyes. She wanted this very much but it was still a wrench.

First the hairdresser tied her hair into bundles, and then cut it off so the hanks were as long as possible. He stored these away carefully and reassured her that they would make a fine wig, in case she was dissatisfied with the shorter style, until her own hair could regrow. Then he set to, to shape her into a young man of fashion.

Rose kept her eyes shut throughout, aware of the snick of the scissors, and the muffled exclamations from George, and the unfamiliar sensation of the air on her scalp. Eventually it was done. The hairdresser brought a glass and she was confronted with someone she hardly recognised. It was amazing. She didn't exactly look like a man, but she did look like a boy at the very least, and not at all like a lady of breeding.

'Will that be satisfactory, Sir?' said the hairdresser.

George didn't speak for a while. He like Rose was amazed at the transformation.

'Most satisfactory,' he managed eventually. 'tremendously satisfactory, sir.'

The hairdresser gathered up his equipment and Rose's hanks of hair and swept the floor tidily. He took his leave, nodding his thanks at receiving his fee and what looked to Rose like a large tip. The two of them looked at each other.

'For the first time, Rose, I begin to believe you might carry this off. If I didn't know, I would hardly recognise you. Your whole head is a different shape. The balance of your body is different, your shoulders seem broader, I don't know.'

'My shoulders are broader, brother, that's the hours I have spent digging in the kitchen garden. And wait till you see me in my coat and breeches!'

George of course had to leave soon after this for the Foreign Office, and needed some considerable reassurance that she would be able to manage for the rest of the day on her own, even once he had seen her in her new personality. He was a little reassured by how the shoulders of the coat altered her bearing, and the cut of its lower part and of the waistcoat concealed any broadness in her hips or narrowness of her waist. Rose had determined she would first test out her new character in public by simply taking a stroll around London, without having to speak to anyone or explain herself, and he left her to this programme, somewhat reluctantly.

She descended from the apartments carefully, wary of the steep stairs as her new boots were still a little stiff, and stepped out into the street. The day was sunny, but there was already a slight chill in the air, and she squinted slightly to see better what was in store for her. She set off, trying to walk as she had seen Charles do, loosely, negligently even, rather than holding herself elegantly contained; taking as long a stride as she could reasonably manage, instead of dainty ladylike steps. Her long boots were much more comfortable than the narrow half boots she had been used to; she held her shoulders back, and enjoyed the freedom to just wander without a chaperone. Every so often though she forgot, and checked behind to see that her maid was still with her, before remembering and cursing inwardly. Nobody took any notice of her, as she turned the corner into Piccadilly, and paused the better to view the thronging crowds.

She leaned against a wall on the street corner, ankles crossed, and watched how the other men comported themselves in the capital. She had of course observed the comings and goings of the world before many times, but it was quite different, somehow, looking at people in the guise of a man. She noted how nearly every man had a hat, but not all. She had presumably seen this before, but not noticed it, as it were, being expected to think only about ladies' fashions. She had not thought to provide herself with one, and made a mental note to ask George about the matter when she next saw him. The hats she could observe were mostly a kind of low-crowned top hat, or a military bicorn or busby, and some other clearly regimental hats she could not name.

One thing she noticed rapidly was how the gentlemen looked at the ladies. Having been taught to look demurely downwards when out in public, or at her companions, (and been frequently corrected at Miss Snape's for not complying, and for giggling) she had not had opportunity to see how a man would look a lady up and down in the street, appraisingly, and perhaps say something aside to his friends as a result. It was quite liberating to not have drawn the attention of anyone, and to be able to observe unrestrainedly. She saw how their gaze fixed on the ladies bosoms, and wondered what they really saw in them.

Rose set off again, crossing the road where it was less muddy, and making her way along towards the Green Park. She watched some liveried servants entering Burlington House, opposite; a trio of young men sauntering along, play-fighting from time to time; an older gentleman attended by a solicitous younger man; a man of the Law in his wig and gown; and tried to take in how they all moved and held themselves and how they treated any ladies that they came across.

At the Park she decided to walk as if she had urgent business at the Queen's House, so as to practise a rapid and determined gait, moving at a pace that no lady would ever consider proper. She saluted a small group of ladies she passed as she had seen other young men do, being pleased to see them turn to each other and whisper something, and smile.

In this way she passed some several hours, mostly looking, absorbing patterns of behaviour, and learning. She stayed within the area she had been told about when in Town for her Season, as being a reasonably safe area, although she had no large amount of money or valuables on her person should she be accosted by thieves. She bought a pasty from a street vendor, and sat on a bench to eat it. While there she practised looking appraisingly at young ladies, gazing at their bosoms and so on as young men did, and found it rather unnerving.

She was approached on one occasion for directions to St James' Palace by a gentleman and his wife, and was able to explain that she was newly arrived from Nova Scotia and was unfamiliar with the streets as yet, even though she knew in her real person perfectly well where it was located. She was unsure about her voice during this interaction, though the couple seemed to take her at face value, and decided after this minor success that she would risk going into a tobacco shop and purchasing some cigars.

This was quite an adventure for her, as ladies did not enter such places, which were reserved strictly for men. She entered the small and quite dark premises boldly, stood for a while letting her eyes adjust to the gloom, and waiting for other customers to be served. Having watched the two customers who were before her, she tried to copy their manner to the tradesman: their way of looking the man in the eye as they made their requests, and the matter of fact content of their demands. She decided to throw herself on the mercy of the tobacconist, explaining that she was a colonial who was unfamiliar with English practices, and ask him to recommend a small and mild cigar which she could purchase for occasional use.

She learnt that cigars were normally sold by the pound, that there were an unconscionable number of varieties, but that as she was a stranger he would sell her half a dozen as a trial. He offered her credit, but she explained that she was leaving town in a couple of days, and so she completed the transaction using coins from the pocket of her waistcoat, after briefly panicking when she could not find her (non-existent) reticule. Fortunately he did not see this mistake, being engaged in wrapping up her purchase at the time. She asked him to write the name of the variety on his card, so that she could return to his shop if they were satisfactory and purchase more.

Once out of the tobacconist's she hurried to a quiet area of a nearby square where she could stand out of view and collect herself. Her heart was pounding, to be sure, but she had the packet of cigars in the inner pocket of her long coat, and some change in her waistcoat, and the tradesman had addressed her as "Sir", and nobody else in the shop had paid her any attention. This was going to work! Probably? Yes, definitely.

The next day, having passed quite an uncomfortable night on the little bed in George's room, she discussed with George over breakfast what she might do that day. She had been introduced to his valet the previous evening in her guise as Richard Cox, a distant cousin from Nova Scotia. The servant was shared by Sir George with two other residents of the apartments, so she had not met him before, which made things easier. She explained that she was staying briefly with Sir George after arriving from the colonies, and before going up to Cambridge (which he knew, of course), and she had passed muster on that brief meeting. Rose took the precaution of being up and fully dressed before George called for the valet to assist him in dressing in the morning. However she had dared to enquire of the valet about methods of tying of a cravat fashionable in England, and had been shown one which was much more comfortable, not pushing her chin up so high, yet still quite acceptable in polite society.

George had insisted she spend several days in London in her masculine guise in order to practise in a situation where discovery would not be irremediable. He had spent some considerable time the previous evening catechising her about how she would behave in various social situations, and had been tolerably impressed at her answers, and her demonstrations of how she might walk, and stand, and generally comport herself. Hence he was grudgingly willing for her to attempt to deliver Uncle Hugh's letter to Dr Young once more, thinking that the servants would almost certainly not recognise her as the same young lady who had visited before, when she again presented Uncle Hugh's card. As a precaution he gave her his own card also, so that she could explain why Richard was delivering the package, and perhaps gain some connection with the scholar who had attended his college. Therefore George set off for his office accompanied by Richard matching him stride for stride, but they soon went their separate ways, and Richard made her way to Welbeck-street alone.

On this occasion the gentleman was at home and available. Richard presented both cards to the butler and was almost immediately shown in to his library where she received a most cordial welcome.

'Sir, I am most intrigued by your mission. You have a package for me?'

Richard held out the parcel. 'Indeed, sir. I am commissioned to give it into your own hands and none other. My relative Sir George Clarke asked me to bring it to you for him as he has business to attend to at the Foreign Office; I am staying with him for a few days before I go up to Emmanuel College to begin my studies.'

'Emmanuel is my own college, I was there almost two years.'

'And Sir George's too. He sends greetings, but believes you may not have known him personally: he only succeeded to the baronetcy four years ago, just as he was graduating, and he was a pensioner.'

'No, I do not think I know the name, though we must have been there at the same time. But Mr Hugh Clarke I do recognise. I have received letters from him before about the Rosetta inscriptions, but sadly have not found time to investigate them. I am greatly busy with my work lecturing for the Royal Institution and my researches on Optics. Do you know the content of his letter? It is very bulky.'

'No, sir, I do not, except that it is about the Rosetta Stele. Mr Hugh Clarke is I believe rather reticent about his researches except to trusted scholars, and in any case I have never met him, having only landed in England last week.'

'Have you indeed? And where have you come from?'

'Nova Scotia, sir, in America, from a small town some twenty miles from the port of Halifax.'

'I have no knowledge of that country beyond what I have read in the newspapers. Is it a prosperous place?'

'Indeed it is, sir. However it was considered by my family useful for me to come to England to study, and Sir George, being a distant relation, agreed to sponsor me for admission to the college. I leave in the next few days for Cambridge; I am greatly looking forward to it.'

'And so you might be, sir. Well, I attended the University only so I could receive a Cambridge degree to add to my qualifications from London, Edinburgh and Gottingen, so that I would be received by the College of Physicians. I found it a place of limited scholarship and passed much of my time alone, in reading and physical research, but I spent some time with the fellows of the college, and you must convey my warmest greetings in particular to the Master, Robert Cory.'

'I shall, sir. But, can you spare a few moments to tell me about your researches in Optics? I am afraid I have no knowledge of the subject as yet, but perhaps I may study it once I have mastered the rest of Euclid and begun the Principia?'

'Well, young man, I am pleased to hear of your desire for learning. However, if you as yet know nothing of the subject . . . well, let me just say this, that Newton, great man that he was, believed light to be made of corpuscles, in other words, minute particles, that convey the sensations of colour and brightness and so on. I have performed experiments which show that in contrast light must be a wave, like the ripples on the pond at Emmanuel when swans alight.'

He spoke further in this vein about his experiments with narrow beams of light, and the phenomenon of "interference", and how it related to waves, and many other things which he had discovered, to which Richard listened attentively, though without full understanding. She was fascinated.

'I think I follow you, sir. But this means you are saying that Newton, the great Newton, was wrong?'

'Sadly, in this regard, yes. He was the discoverer of many wonderful truths, but he was not infallible, and those who have treated him as unerring have perhaps even retarded scientific progress by doing so.'

'Can I learn about these things at Emmanuel?'

'I do not know. Teaching at Cambridge is sadly lacking. However, I suggest that once you have mastered some of the other works, Euclid as you say and the Principia, you should read Newton's Optics, and then seek out my researches in the philosophical journals. You seem a bright lad, but even so some of the ideas are quite complex, it may take some time, especially if you have to worry out the ideas without a knowledgeable tutor.'

'However, when you study Mr Newton's Optics, beware of the sections on light corpuscles: for example his explanation for why coloured rings appear if a very slightly convex lens is placed upon a flat glass and illuminated is sadly lacking.' Dr Young was clearly most enthused about this aspect of natural philosophy and expounded on it at some length.

'I am most grateful to you, sir, for being willing to spend time instructing me. I must not trespass on your hospitality any longer. I do hope the letter from Mr Hugh Clarke will be of interest, and even if you cannot spare time for investigation of the hieroglyphic inscriptions, Sir George tells me he would very much like a brief response from you about them, if you are able.'

'Certainly, lad. Well, I thank you for the package, and for your interest in my work, and I wish you all prosperity at Emmanuel. If I may give you one piece of advice: avoid the company of those fellow-commoners who spend their time gambling, drinking and whoring. They love to prey on the sizars and the pensioners to drag them down to their level, and to win money from them that they can ill afford. A nasty and parasitic species: though I myself was a fellow-commoner, being able to afford to pay for some privileges useful to me.'

'I shall definitely follow your advice. Goodbye, sir.'

Richard left, trembling slightly, more with excitement about the prospects of study than the exultation of not being recognised as a girl. Corpuscles of light, eh? Or rather, waves of light. It didn't make much sense, as yet, but in a few months . . .!

Richard sauntered along the street with a bounce in her step. She nodded politely to a pair of young ladies who smiled at her as she passed, thinking that she ought to have been wearing a hat so she could have raised it. She bought some food from a street vendor, and ate it with relish; she saw a man smoking a clay pipe and approached him to light a cigar from its bowl, which the man allowed with good grace; she admired the great buildings of the City as one from the provinces might be expected to do. All in all, she had a fine time, all the while observing, and noting, and at the same time keeping a weather eye open for pickpockets and ruffians, even in this civilised part of London.

She even went into a public house once she felt it was late enough in the afternoon, and ordered whisky. It was a large pub, and she was puzzled about the number of different bars in the same building: the lounge or saloon, the public, the tap room, the snug and so on. The landlord, once she had explained about her recent arrival from the colonies, was only too pleased to explain, and suggested the saloon or perhaps a lounge bar if there was one was the most appropriate for such a lad as he. Richard by now greatly needed the privy, and added the fact of the provision of this facility privately in pubs to her store of knowledge. She was very pleased with her idea to have chosen to be a colonial: it was becoming more and more useful. The whisky was fairly palatable; she had another for luck, and then made her way cheerfully back towards Sir George's lodgings for dinner.

A few further days passed in similar fashion, and then Richard had to make the final additions to her trunk (not including a hat, sadly, which she found she would need to order once at college) and then retire early in order to catch the coach to Cambridge, leaving at an unearthly hour from the Saracen's Head in Holborn. She was very grateful that Sir George had been able to accompany her, in order to ensure her luggage was loaded safely, smooth her arrival in college and generally prevent any mishap. Sir George for his part had an appointment to meet a colleague on Government business, and to take supper with the Master that evening. They were set, and soon it would be too late to go back.

CHAPTER 12

THE TRIP NORTH WAS UNCOMFORTABLE and slow, even though they had inside seats. The roads had not yet all been turned into mud by winter rains, but they still had several delays, to deal with difficulties at Ware and at Royston, when the wheels became stuck, and in Trumpington where a horse cast a shoe. Eventually late in the afternoon the dirty and broken-down houses of the poor appeared, and then the noble stonework of colleges. Richard found he was holding his breath, as he gazed out of the window, and wondered which building was which, and how his own college would compare with the others, and what his room would be like, and a myriad worries about how he would comport himself in a place so unfamiliar.

The coach turned down a narrow lane lined with both fine brick and stone buildings, and hovels of the poor, and stopped at its end in front of an imposing classical facade. Emmanuel College, at last! It seemed Sir George had made an arrangement with the driver to divert there before arriving at his goal, the Eagle and Child, for a consideration, for which Richard was most grateful.

The next hours were most confusing. Porters unloaded their luggage, greeted Sir George respectfully, and they were conducted through a fine stone court and a colonnade to a large garden containing a great pond and many fine trees, onto which faced a long building of warm red brick with pale stone quoins.

'This is your home in college, Richard' said George, 'commonly known as the New Building, or the Brick Building, whichever you will.'

'It doesn't look very new,' replied Richard seeing the Dutch gables, the worn brickwork, and the rather dilapidated staircase.

'New for Cambridge,' smiled George, 'Sixteen thirties, isn't it, Chapman?'

'Aye, 'bout that, sir,' replied the porter over his shoulder, manoeuvring the lower end of Richard's heavy box up the spiral of the stair. 'They say it was put up temporary-like, but it ain't fallen down yet, so why change it, I say.'

Richard's rooms were on the top floor, under the slope of the roof. He had a largish room with a fireplace, furnished with a desk, two armchairs and a small table, and a smaller bedroom off it. Windows gave onto the large garden with the pond on one side and a smaller area of greenery on the other, with many trees, which might have been an orchard.

'It looks splendid, Sir George,' he said, gazing around in pleasure at being finally arrived.

'You will need to order some more furniture,' said Sir George, 'the college only supplies the basics. I'll show you where you might find a reputable tradesman to fit you out. For instance, a bookcase would be handy, and a few more chairs. Maybe a rug or two, I remember these floor boards let all the draughts through, and Cambridge is a deuced cold place in winter.'

A third porter brought up Sir George's smaller bag, putting it with the other in the bedroom, and then they were left alone. Sir George handed the keys to Richard.

'All yours,' he said with a grin. 'I had this room five years ago. It has got a little more unkempt since then, but it's not bad. Out of the way, a bit. You are less likely to be bothered by Varmints up here.'

'Varmints?'

'Non-reading men who only want to have a good time: drinking, gambling, whoring, if I may say that to you, and fighting with the snobs.'

Richard must have looked puzzled again because he added, 'The townsmen, that is. Bargees, carters, that sort of fellow, they all seem quite keen on a bust-up if the numbers favour them. Now look, you unpack your box, I am going to pay my respects to the Master, and then I'll come back and show you around.'

'Yes, sir.'

Richard did as he was commanded, and soon had his limited array of clothes in the closet which was rather the worse for wear. The books had to be stacked on the desk with his quill and ink and some writing paper, his cigars and whisky on a shelf. He would need to buy a fair number of things to make the place habitable, it seemed. Glasses for the whisky, for a start.

All this took very little time, so he went to investigate the building. He seemed to have two doors, the one inside the other. There was an ordinary door inside, and a thick oaken one beyond it. The room opposite had both closed, there was no sound coming from it. In fact, the building was quiet as the grave. Was nobody else around?

He opened his windows, and leaned out to look at the gardens. They were well kept, there were ducks and other waterfowl on the ponds, and beyond the larger stretch of water there seemed to be a fence and a wall beyond which were further gardens.

He ventured to descend the stair, locking the inner door carefully behind him. All the other heavy doors were shut except one on the floor below. He reached the ground floor, and decided to go back up and risk seeing if the room with the open door was occupied. He hesitated outside, then knocked. No response. But was that the sound of movement within? It was. The door opened, and a face peered out. A young face, perhaps a lad of seventeen or eighteen?

'Good evening, sir. My name is Richard Cox, I am just arrived at college to begin my studies. May I have the honour of knowing your name, as we are to be neighbours? I am to live in the room above you.'

'Excellent! I am Edward Hever; I arrived yesterday, and the place is like a morgue and a graveyard. It seems nobody comes into residence until the last minute, when Term starts on the 10th of the month, so I am delighted to have a neighbour, indeed I am. May I ask where you are from?'

'From Nova Scotia, in America. I am glad to make your acquaintance, because so much in this country is unfamiliar to me.'

'We shall have to comprehend it together then. I am from Cumberland, from a town called Keswick. Do you know of it? It is so far north it is nearly another country.'

Richard shook his head. 'It is one of the many things I do not know, I am afraid.'

'Well, we're together, for I don't know anything of Nova Scotia.' He thought a moment. 'New Scotland? Is that it?'

'Yes, but not all of us are Scots. In the north of the colony many people are from there and from Ireland. I come from near the port of Halifax, however: we are mostly of English descent.'

Edward shook his head. 'I forget myself. Come into my keeping-room. I believe that's what they call it.' He opened the door wider and Richard followed him in.

The room was similar to his, but broader, being not under the sloping roof, and there were two doors on the far side. There was a dearth of furniture, like in his room, and a similar small pile of books on the table.

'I am to share this keeping-room with another sizar, I do not know who as yet. Are you a sizar too?'

'A pensioner, but a poor one. I hope to win a scholarship in due course, if I find my studies go well.'

'My father is a grocer, we have a large business in the town, we supply villages as far away as Troutbeck and Grange and Bassenthwaite. I hope to try for prizes myself if I can.'

'Mine is a man of business, he buys and sells, he imports goods, and trades with the natives for furs and hides, and for meat, and for beadwork and other artefacts which can be sold in England.' Richard thought it was a good job he had worked out his story carefully while still at Kilcott, it would never have done to have hesitated at this point.

'Can I offer you a drink? I have only a bottle of port wine, and no glasses, but I do have two tea bowls, if that would be satisfactory?'

'Surely.' Richard threw himself into one of the armchairs, and thanked his host for his drink. 'I think we must both go out tomorrow and make a number of purchases. Furniture, and glasses, and who knows what else. Books, perhaps later, once we have seen the college library, and spoken to our tutors?'

'A gown and a square?'

'Certainly.'

'Some low shoes, for I am told one may not dine in Hall in boots.'

'Indeed? Well, I have those already: have you made any purchases so far? What have you done today?'

'I have walked around the town, and tried to get my bearings. I have looked at the shops, and seen all manner of things which I would like to buy, had I the money. I have listened to the people, who talk very differently from those at home. It will take me a while to become accustomed to what they say: indeed I can't make out half of it.'

'I expect there will be many terms I don't understand either, that aren't in use over in my home country.'

They continued in this fashion for some time, Richard explaining about the situation in his country, and learning in return where exactly Keswick might be; hearing a little about his host's family, and a lot about the grandeur of the mountains which surrounded the town. He learnt a new word too, "sublime" as it applied to such natural marvels, and a great deal more than he wanted about Mr Wordsworth with whom it seemed the Hever family were most intimately acquainted, and also about Mr Southey and Mr Coleridge whom they also knew.

There was a banging about on the stair above them, and eventually Sir George knocked on the door, and was introduced by Richard to Edward. He said Richard had been invited with him to supper with the Master at eight o'clock, in the Lodge, and that the Master would be most interested to hear about conditions in Nova Scotia. He raised his eyebrows slightly at disclosing this intelligence, but Edward didn't seem to notice, being engaged in pouring port into a third tea bowl for his new guest.

Having engaged to meet with Mr Hever for breakfast in Richard's room the next morning, they departed for a tour of the town. Sir George had to first fetch his cap and gown for it was getting towards dusk, but he said Richard would not need them as he had not yet matriculated. Apparently this was a rather informal ceremony where the Registrary (a University Officer) visited the college and with the Master one's name was inscribed in the records upon certification of the candidate's present attainments, and the young man was formally admitted *in statu pupillari*.

Whilst robing in the room above, Sir George looked over his shoulder at Richard and asked, 'How do you find the college, Rose? Is the company to your liking?'

'Sir George!' he hissed, *sotto voce*. 'Not even in private, in this room! Who knows may overhear you? Always Richard, or you may give me away with a careless pronoun, or a gentlemanly action of deference.'

Sir George had the grace to look ashamed, and nodded in assent. They descended the stair and turned around the end of the building into the smaller garden. They crossed a little bridge over a culvert which Sir George explained supplied the water for the Great Pond, and originated from the ancient Hobson's Conduit. They walked through a kind of tunnel into Chapel Court and thence, with a greeting to the porter, into St Andrew's-street.

First they turned left, and walking barely a hundred yards reached the edge of town. Ahead of them was the Leys, an area of small fields giving on to a wild tract of boggy land over which Sir George said one could get a good few shots at snipe on the way to Grantchester, were one to be keen on fowling; but which was supposedly to be the site of a new college endowed by Sir George Downing, that had been debated for so many years that no-one believed it would ever be constructed, so much of the legacy having been eaten up by lawyers' bills. Just discernible against the setting sun were buildings which George identified as Pembroke and Peterhouse; Richard already felt his mind was full of new words and information.

Next they retraced their steps, and with the light fading made their way past Christ's, with the golden yales of Lady Margaret Beaufort over the gate; around the church of St Andrew to the cookshops of Petty Cury and thence to the Garden and Corn Markets, now empty of stalls; past the University Church to the splendour of the chapel of King's college, half-hidden behind broken-down houses but with its pinnacles silhouetted against the red of the sky.

There were almost no men around wearing gowns. Richard asked George why they had come up to Cambridge so early, and he replied it was so that he could accompany him, as he already had an important appointment made with his colleague for the next day, and otherwise he could not have been spared from the Foreign Office. 'Besides,' he added. This way you can get first pick of the second-hand furniture and be fully settled before the others descend on the place. You will be ahead of the game, which I always find an advantage.'

The oil lamps outside college gates and the better sort of houses were being lit as they walked down Trumpington-street, past the Black Bull, past Catharine Hall, past the gate of Corpus Christi, and thence to St Botolph's church close by Pembroke Hall. Even so Richard thought the street very dark and the side roads extremely gloomy compared to London, except where light spilled out of a tavern, or a church's windows glowed red or blue with candlelight filtered through the coloured glass. Bells rang the hour, some high and cracked-seeming, some sonorous, none in synchrony with any other. George told Richard he would need to be governed by his own chapel bell, for such things as chapel at seven in the morning, which was compulsory in Term, and for dinner at half past three, and lectures once they started after the division of Term.

'We have compassed almost the whole of the southern half of the town,' explained George, 'Cambridge is not such a large place, barely half a mile across and three-quarters from north to south.'

'I am totally lost,' said Richard, 'and as for the names of all those places you have told me . . .'

George laughed. 'In a couple of days, maybe a week, you will feel like a native, I guarantee you. However, I brought you round here at this time so I can point out to you some of the places that are best avoided after nightfall. Down this street, called Silver-street, lies the River Camus, or Cam. There is a large pool there full of barges, and above it the King's Mill. I suggest you avoid it after dark, but more so the street along here,' they walked a little way towards Pembroke, 'where the way is narrower, the lighting more insufficient, and the taverns more ribald. Unloading barges gives a man a great thirst and he becomes perhaps more prone to take exception to, well, to anything he sees, especially anything in a gown.'

Richard peered down the lane that led to the mill, and thought he could make out a few men moving around, but it was hard to see what they were doing.

'You see, I have agreed to you coming here to study, sir, but I still worry about you, as you are in my care. Mostly the town is safe in the daytime, and for a large group of gowned men even after dark, unless they go looking for trouble; but alone or in pairs, or if the man is less skilled in defending himself, not so much. I think I can trust you to keep yourself from harm?'

'Certainly, sir. I am not minded to become a target of ruffians.'

'Well, come down here. This is Pembroke-lane, it runs along the college boundary until the buildings give out, when it becomes quite open. You see how rough the surface is? It leads to the Beast market, and then becomes known as Bird-Bolt-lane, for reasons I have never discovered.'

They passed along a little way, noting the King's Ditch running on the side opposite to the college, and then the Botanic garden facing the fields.

'Do you recognise where you are yet?'

Richard looked around, trying to make out the building at the end of the road, or recognise any landmark he had seen before. 'No sir, I remember we saw some rough fields somewhere before, but I am at a loss.'

'That is Emmanuel directly ahead, the reflector casts the lamplight downwards so you cannot see the pediment of the entrance. And on your right are the fields of the Leys. But here, only two hundred yards from your college, is a favourite spot for gentlemen to make, shall we say, arrangements with ladies of the town once night has fallen.'

Richard took a few moments to sense the meaning that George was trying to convey. 'You are telling me, this is a rendezvous for prostitutes?' he hazarded.

'Indeed. I gather you are not as ignorant of the ways of men as some young la. . ., er, persons of my acquaintance, which in the circumstances is all to the good. I understand that the gentleman shows himself under the lamp over there, and soon whoever is available will come to him and, er, form a business arrangement. Once sufficient money has been provided they will disappear together into the Leys and, well, the lady will carry out her part of the bargain. I mention this to you only because I do not wish you to be taken unawares in this area so close to your college.'

Richard thought for a minute or two. 'So that is the Leys: I remember it now. What will happen to this trade when the college is built there, Lord Downing, I think you said had endowed it?'

'Not Lord: Sir George was but a baronet like me, I understand; but yes, that is where his college ought to be constructed, if it ever is. Interesting question. Would the trade continue, but within the precincts of the college, I wonder? Or would the college even take over the running of the trade? There have been stranger things known.'

Back in Richard's rooms they discussed their plans for the next day. Richard was keen that they took Edward around town with them after breakfast, so as to foster the friendship, and as both of them would be likely to need to buy or order the same sorts of items. They ran through what might be needed: clothing, shoes for Edward, furniture for the rooms, a gown and cap, and so on. George tried to tell Richard more about the town, and about the college, but he begged to be excused this, as his head was already full up, and he was very tired.

However he perked up at the supper with the Master. Dr Cory was most affable: he seemed a timid man, not prone to imposing his intellect on others, but keen to be informed. Richard did his best to tell him about the conditions in Nova Scotia, and about his voyage to Bristol, glad he had read up several volumes about the country and the ports while still at Kilcott. He explained that it was his great-grandfather who had emigrated in 1720, and that Sir George was thus only a very distant cousin, so it was most gracious of him to take the trouble to settle him into the college, and it was convenient that his arrival here coincided with Sir George's need to meet a certain gentleman in connection with his work.

'I hear there is a lot of French spoken in North America,' observed Dr Cory.

'*Évidemment, Monsieur le Maitre. Tout le monde faut le comprendre.*'

Just in time, Richard remembered to pass on greetings from Dr Young, explaining about delivering his cousin Hugh's letter. Dr Cory was most pleased to be saluted by his protégé, and Richard was able to explain about his work with the Royal Institution, and his continuing researches in optics. It seemed he had done himself a favour in Dr Cory's books by having met this scholar, which was all to the good.

The food was good: a cold meat pie with cheese and bread and tea; and Richard also took a little wine when it was offered. He was surprised how hungry he was, after all they had eaten dinner at one of the inns on the way. He learnt that supper was normally served in Hall in Term at nine, and one could choose to eat what one could pay for. Most reading men would be asleep by ten or eleven at the latest, in order to be up to get in some study before chapel and then breakfast. He also was told it would be convenient if he could matriculate the following afternoon while his sponsor was still here, together with Mr Hever, and that the Registrary would attend the Lodge after dinner, at about a half past four. And so to bed.

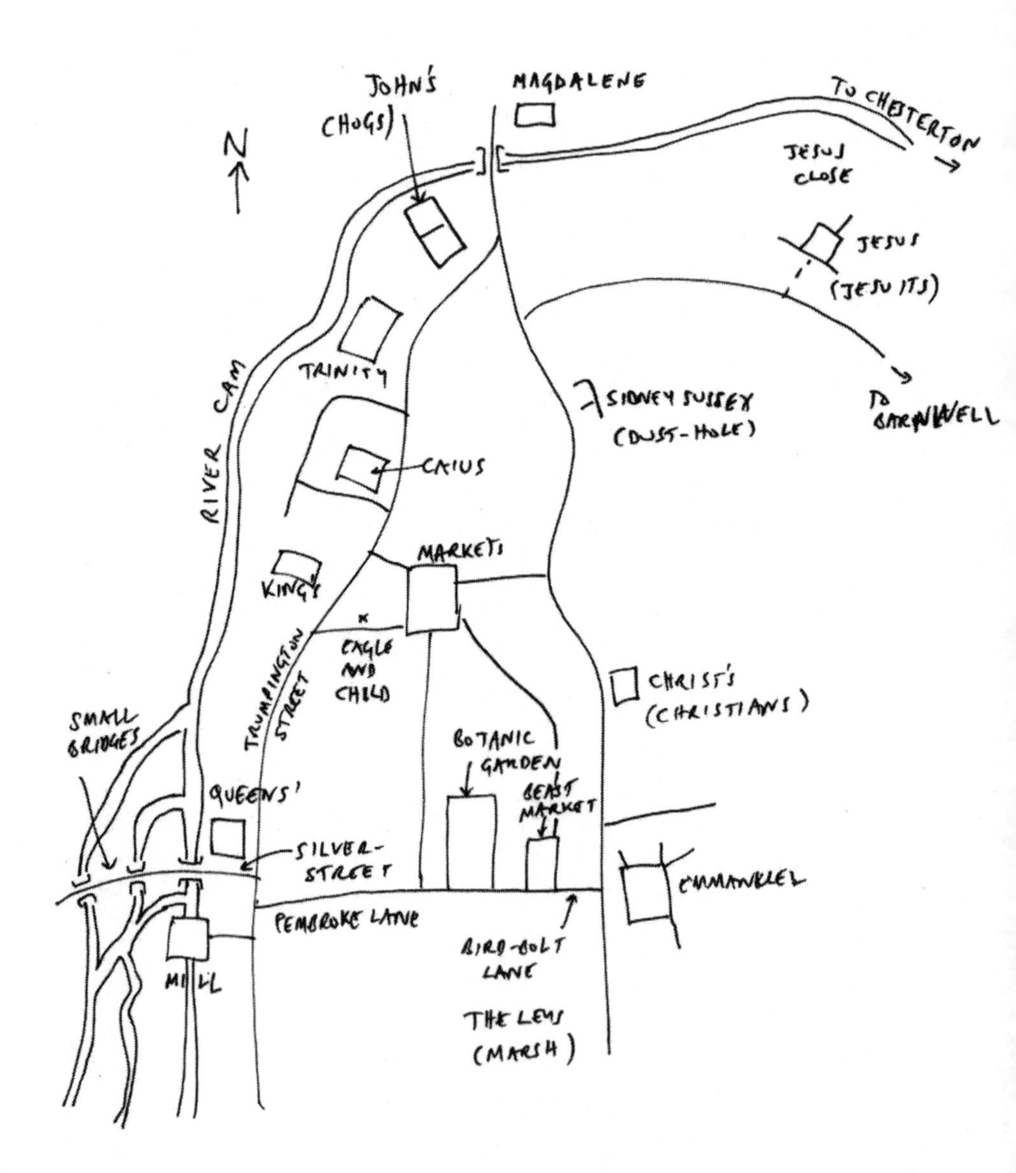

Edward Hever's sketch map of Cambridge.

Drawn to send to his parents, but he never got around to writing the covering letter.

CHAPTER 13

RICHARD WAS WONDERING IF HE was going to have to sleep in an armchair while George was with him, but it seemed George had secured the room opposite for the one night of his stay as its occupant was not due to come into residence just yet.

In the morning they were woken by the gyp at seven thirty, bringing tea, and washing water, then the bedmaker appeared at eight with breakfast consisting of rolls and butter with ham, and more tea. Richard had risen, made a sketchy sort of wash in his basin, and dressed immediately he had been called. He took a turn in the garden, where he found the privy, which was noisome in stench, but quite private at least.

Sir George was in Richard's room when he returned, chatting to the bedmaker about her family: who had got married, and how many grandchildren she had now; and the state of her bunions, and so on. She looked Richard up and down, and said,

'A fine young man you have there, Sir George. He can't be above sixteen, to my way of thinking?'

'You have it exactly, Mrs Fenn. And I am sure you will take great care of him, having regard to his youth.'

'That I will, sir. I am in your debt for ever, after what you did for me an' Fenn in front of the magistrate.'

'What's this, Sir George?' said Richard.

'Oh, it was nothing.'

'Nothing my arse, begging your pardon, sirs. Your cousin, sir, when he was still just a lad himself, stood up in court and talked an' talked until the lawyers didn't know which way to look. Me an' Fenn had been accused of . . . well, never mind what it was, because we never did it, but it was looking real bad for us. But Mr Clarke here, as he was then, begging your pardon, Sir George, he knew we was honest people, and he sailed right in an' gave us such a good character as I hardly knew it was us he were talking about. And then when he was questioned by the liar in the wig, what was his name, I forget, the lawyer, anyway, he arsked 'im when the crime was supposed to have been committed. An' then 'e told 'im straight that we couldn't possibly have done what we was accused of, because we had an alley-something.'

'An alibi,' put in Sir George.

'Right, one o' them. We was somewhere else at the time, and he was with us.'

'Not quite, Mrs Fenn, I said I had seen you both at my rooms at six o'clock that morning, and you hadn't the time to have got there from Histon after the, er, offence was said to have occurred.'

'Right you are, sir. Excepting we had an 'orse faster than the great Eclipse, you said, and exceptin' that we could ride 'im, which neither of us can ride anyway, which proved it. So there.' She folded her arms in satisfaction.

'Mr and Mrs Fenn were in danger of transportation to Australia, you see, and Mrs Fenn did not wish to travel by sea.'

'So, you're safe with Elsa, Mr Cox, and with Fenn, we'll see you right.' She nodded significantly.

There was a sound on the stair and Edward poked his head round the open door. 'I've brought up my breakfast things, is it alright to come in?'

He entered, while Sir George handed Mrs Fenn something as she left that clinked, and thanked her again for her help.

'So,' said Edward, with his mouth full of bread, 'can you tell me what the bedder and the gyp's duties are?'

'Well, it depends on your pocket,' began Sir George. 'Are you a fellow-commoner or a nobleman?'

Edward snorted. 'Josh me not, sir. A sizar, if you please. I am to help serve dinner on some afternoons, and run errands for fellow-commoners in part payment for my board and tuition.'

'Good man. Well, for all undergraduates they awaken you in time for chapel, and bring breakfast; but what they bring depends on your purse. They empty the chamber-pots, and see to the bed-linen, and take away your laundry to be washed, and clean the rooms, and bring coal, and tend the fires and light the lamps on the stairs and, well, for a consideration they will bring your other meals in your room, and get you anything you desire. Fenn is a mostly honest sort of gyp, not given to demanding perquisites above those which are basic, but some of the fellows know how to acquire absolutely anything or any person, legally or not, and have to be treated with respect on that account.'

'Perquisites?'

'Yes, they believe they deserve a share of the food, and all other supplies intended for the undergraduates. They refer to them as "perks" among themselves.'

'Are there very many gyps?'

'Enough. They each look after several rooms, or a staircase. There are more bedmakers than gyps. The Master told me that there are currently almost seventy undergraduates at the college, and the number seems to have been increasing gradually, especially among the fellow-commoners, as Emmanuel appears for some reason to have become fashionable among those who like a good time. It does not appear to have effected any improvement in its reputation for scholarship, though,' he added dryly.

'I intend to study hard and perhaps win an award or a scholarship, which will help my father considerably.'

'Well said. I hope you will encourage Richard to do the same. I hear he may be prone to idleness.'

Richard sat up, most put out, until he saw that Sir George was laughing at him. 'I believe Sir George did not win an award while he was at college,' he said aside to Edward.

'I did so. I won the prize for Greek verse in my second year, and was voted the most amiable quiz in the college by the Egotists Club.'

'Quiz? You, sir?' asked Edward.

'Yes, well, in Cambridge argot it means something different to the norm, it is an man considered eccentric because he has a reputation for reading and attending lectures, and who knows odd bits of useless information, and does not spend his time drinking or gaming. In short, a student who studies.'

Breakfast over, the three of them departed for a second, daylight, tour, this time of the Northern part of the town, as George wanted to make sure Richard began with a basic familiarity with the place, since he could not be around later to supervise him. Richard felt a bit put out about being nannied in this way but could not say anything in front of Edward, and also he could sympathise with George's anxieties about his safety to some extent. At the first college they encountered, George, with a grin, asked Richard if he could remember what the gilded beasts were over the gate. He could not, but Edward chipped in,

'This is Christ's college, and the undergraduates are known as Christians, and the beasts are yales, and they are imaginary fantastical beasts.'

'Indeed, Mr Hever. A sound knowledge.'

'I heard a man in cap and gown explaining this yesterday to a party of visitors who I believe might have been Chinese officials.'

'Chinese? I have never seen a Chinaman,' said Richard.

'There are very few who have voyaged so far as to come to England; I met one once at the Foreign Office and he was a most courteous man,' said Sir George.

'I had not seen one either, but I recognised their appearance from pictures in the books I have read.'

They went into a number of shops, looking for furniture, and glassware, and pictures to leaven the plainness of their walls, and all manner of other things which had not seemed necessary to Richard when planning his stay at the University. They stayed their hand from actually buying anything at the advice of Sir George, until they had compared prices and quality at other establishments.

Sir George pointed out Holy Trinity Church, the domain of Rev Charles Simeon, Fellow of King's and influential evangelical. Richard was somewhat reassured by seeing an obvious undergraduate arriving at the rather plain entrance to Sidney Sussex college with his parents, as he looked both shorter and younger than Richard believed he did himself. They passed Jesus-lane where unsurprisingly, Jesus college is to be found (whose inhabitants, Edward put in helpfully, are Jesuits); and walked as far as the Great Bridge over the river, seeing how the buildings rapidly turned into slums beyond Magdalene. George, and more particularly Edward, contributed innumerable fascinating nuggets of information which passed straight through Richard's head without finding lodgement.

Returning to St John's and turning into the lane which passed in front of its gate, Edward was pleased to recognise more yales, but was frustrated to be unable to recall what John's students were known as. Richard felt unaccountably cheerful at this deficiency. Sir George held his counsel on this one, and while Edward cudgelled his brains for the information, he took them for once inside a college: he chose Trinity presumably so they could be amazed by the immensity of its court, and impressed when he pointed out the rooms that Mr Newton had occupied, which was the most memorable point of the outing for Richard.

And so past Caius, and Clare, and Kings, and St Catharine's, and Queens', until both the lads were dizzy with trying to keep all the information in their heads. At length they stopped by the Mill Pool, somewhat less threatening than in the dusk, where Silver-street meets the Small Bridges, and gazed across the rather marshy land on its far bank to the small village of Newnham, and the wide country open in all other directions. They looked at the men unloading sacks from barges at the mill, and the foaming water coming from the wheel-race, and the wooden bridge just downstream from them at Queens' college, and the stream of people passing in both directions.

'So, do you think you will like this place?' asked Sir George.

'It is very flat,' observed Edward.

'It is very confusing,' added Richard.

'I think it is both of those things, but once you get to know people, and read widely so you spread out your range of knowledge, there is no place to beat it. There is no substitute for reading and learning in private, but then, finding so many like minds with whom you can discuss what you are learning about, well, that is truly wonderful.'

'Didn't you say it was dangerous to come to this part of town, Sir George?'

'Only after dark, when the men have been drinking.'

'Johnian Hogs!' burst out Edward, 'that's what they are!'

The others looked at him in puzzlement, then realised. He had been chewing over his memory to recall this fact for the last half an hour.

'Correct, sir; but beware where you say it: there are a number of hard-muscled men of the Blessed Evangelist's persuasion who are raised on dishing the snobs, and would break your head for saying so in their hearing.'

'My father had me read a book all about the University this summer, in preparation. I knew I knew it somewhere in here,' he tapped his forehead, 'in my head.'

Sir George made as to leave. 'I must depart to make my appointment with my colleague in Trinity,' he said. 'You two can find your way back to college?'

'Um . . .' said Richard.

'Certainly, sir,' asserted Edward. 'No problem.'

'Well, have a good look round, decide what you want and can afford, and make your purchases. If you do have need of guidance, we will meet at lunch in Hall at twelve.'

He walked away a few steps, then turned back. 'If you are a little, er, disoriented, you can go into any stationer's or bookseller's and buy a plan of the town. I found mine very useful when I was here. Goodbye.'

Edward turned to Richard. 'So where first, eh?'

'You decide. I'm quite turned around.'

They set off, Edward confidently leading them, aiming for a cheap furnisher's he had noted earlier. They passed two colleges, and then some houses, and then came to where there was a large house with grounds that did not at all resemble a college, opposite a building with bandaged persons sitting out in the warm sun, and others in bath chairs being moved around. Beyond them they saw only open, marshy ground.

'Er, is this right?' queried Richard. 'I don't recognise this bit.'

Edward looked puzzled. 'I'm sure I took the proper turn. I don't understand.'

'I think we should go back and get one of those maps Sir George talked about. I like a map anyway, I'm going to buy one.'

Edward looked a little mutinous but followed Richard back along the road. Soon they came to where they had left Silver-street, and, carrying on, found a stationer's who gladly provided them with the latest in town plans. Once they had the map the right way up, Richard saw the problem.

'Do you not learn your left and right up in Keswick?' he said. 'Look, here's where you went wrong, at the end of Silver-street.'

Edward didn't look at the map, but moved off in the opposite direction instead. 'Oh, there,' he said, 'King's Chapel. We couldn't see it from the other side of the road, that's what threw me.'

'Fair enough,' said Richard, pacifyingly, realising he'd been a bit sharp. 'Anyway, we're right now.'

They found the shop; Edward ordered four chairs and a bookcase to be delivered, but Richard thought he would wait and take Sir George's advice on the larger items. He did buy six small glasses and an old painting of a Dutch town which took his fancy, which was cheap because it was out of fashion and dirty, and the frame was damaged. Then Edward followed suit with four wine glasses. Returning towards college, they bought ink, and quills, and writing paper, and Edward got a few cushions in bright colours, three different shades of yellow and one Pomona green.

Sir George was already seated when they arrived at lunch. It seemed a very informal affair. Of course it was a light meal anyway, to stave off hunger until dinner, and there were no dons present, and only two or three undergraduates while they were at table. George had struck up a conversation with one of the other students, by name Will Peabody, who was in his second year, another pensioner. Richard and Edward were pleased to have someone else they could talk to, and a man of at least some experience.

Richard and Sir George left Edward and Will in conversation and departed to order Richard's furniture. Once that had been decided and paid for they acquired Richard's cap and gown, and he was measured for a low-crowned top hat. There were more men in the streets now who might be arriving undergraduates: bags were being unloaded from carriages, and porters hurrying back and forth. Sir George finally took Richard into a bank on the corner of Emmanuel-lane and St Andrew's-street and arranged for him to have access to money which he had deposited in an account in Richard's name. He felt very responsible all of a sudden, and decided there and then to spend as little as possible, excepting possibly on books.

Returning to his rooms before dinner, Richard was keen to show George his new painting which he had hung over the fireplace, there being already a convenient nail in that place. It was rather grubby, and the frame was certainly not what it might be, but he was pleased that George seemed to approve, and even gave him some ideas about how to clean it without causing damage.

It seemed odd to be dining so early, compared even to the hours they would keep at Kilcott, but as George said, the University is considerably behind the times in most things, so why not in the fashions of mealtimes? They sat in deference to Edward with the students, though Sir George was entitled to dine at High Table, and Richard for the most part kept quiet, the better to observe how the other young men spoke and dealt with each other, how they tore flesh off the joint and passed it along the table, and generally ate without so many manners as he was used to.

Then came their matriculation. This was performed in the Master's parlour, it mostly consisted of him signing the college's admission book and the Master certifying that the college had received payment for tuition for the term, and that his education so far had been certified by an MA (Sir George). There were two others besides himself and Edward being admitted, fellow-commoners by the looks of their gowns, who did not deign to talk with the lowly. Privately Richard thought they looked even younger and more nervous than Edward and himself, but he kept quiet. He nearly made a catastrophic mistake with his signature by starting to write "Rose" but at the last minute realising, and catching himself after only completing the "R". He made an excuse about the quill, and then produced the name "Richard Cox" in what he thought was a fair impression of masculine writing, so much more spiky than his normal rounded hand.

Immediately the ceremony was over Sir George said he had to depart to catch the evening mail coach for London, there being business that he could not avoid on the following day at the Foreign Office. Richard accompanied him to the Eagle and Child, where he said goodbye. Sir George looked rather worried about what he had started in train, and all the embarrassing consequences that might rebound upon him, but he said nothing to add to Richard's nervousness, and indeed once his bag had been taken into the inn, he set a hand on Richard's shoulder and said,

'You will do splendidly here, Richard. Be sure to write and tell me if there is anything on which you need advice; and if there is anything domestic, remember you can rely on Mrs Fenn. You understand?'

With that he disappeared into the inn. Richard felt excited more than scared, but then everything was so new and different, he might make a *faux pas* at any point. Good job he was a foreigner, that would cover up most mistakes. He hoped.

He wandered around town for quite a while, since it was still light, and several times pulled his map out of his pocket to work out where he was, and what such and such a college, or church, or imposing building might be. Several times he was pleased to recognise a landmark, or to see a shop that they had gone into before. He was still of course in his gown following his matriculation, and once somebody stopped to greet him having recognised it as from Emmanuel, before realising he was not the person he thought he was. However, the consequence of this was he now knew a third student from Emmanuel, even though only slightly, and he made sure to remember his name. John Wilks, a sizar in his second year. He repeated this to himself several times, to be sure.

Once back at his rooms, Richard lit a candle from a light that had been kindled on the stair, he assumed by the gyp Mr Fenn, pulled out his Euclid, and set to studying on the table by the window. Mr Martin had provided him with a plan to continue the progress he had made, explaining about the lack of supervision at the colleges especially in the first half of term, and so he read away, and worked problems, and made a note each time there was something he did not understand. He made certain to write his notes with a masculine hand, and several times practised his signature as Richard Cox, just to make sure he wouldn't slip up again.

The bell chimed for supper while he was still enthralled by a new concept, and he had to tear himself away, head full of definitions, propositions and proofs. He told Edward what he had been reading, and found Edward was ahead of him, having been studying Euclid for much longer. He heard a certain amount about prime numbers which seemed most interesting, and a great deal more about Edward's school and his tutors which was not.

In bed that night, Richard considered the day. Edward was alright, he supposed, but a bit inclined to pour out information without cause, and to use two long words when one short one would do. On the other hand, he had been quite rude to him about the left and right business, and Edward hadn't seemed to mind. Richard had noticed that men who liked each other were often rude in a way that girls would take huge offence at. Men were very odd.

CHAPTER 14

RICHARD TOOK HIS BREAKFAST IN Edward's room the next day, and afterwards, there being no academic demands on their time, they set out together to explore the town yet again. They met with another sizar who had arrived very late the previous evening, and had his room on the ground floor of their staircase, Abel Johnson, a man from Northamptonshire, and he joined with them on their expedition. Richard wanted to look inside the other colleges, to compare them with Emmanuel, but after the first three such visits the others tired of this, and insisted they instead looked around the shops which offered such a wide variety of goods that could not be found in their home towns.

Abel seemed quite a little older than they were, his shoulders were broader and his chin needed a shave. Richard thought he was quite handsome, and wondered if his mind would match his appearance. He seemed quiet, though, and diffident, but had a curious way of cocking his head to one side when he looked at the sights, and a gleam of humour in his eye. In particular he wanted to inspect the bootmakers' shops, explaining that his father had a boot manufactory in Northampton, and he hoped to take over running it one day, and also expand the business. Hence it was in his interests to keep abreast of the fashions and methods to be found in what he termed the "competition".

In the Garden market they came upon Will Peabody whom they

had met at lunch the previous day. He was engaged in buying carrots, and as he explained, trying to find celery, though it seemed it was slightly too early in the season for this. He said that nibbling at these vegetables in the raw state helped him concentrate on his books and saved him money in Hall. He also warned them that if they wanted to follow his lead, they must be careful to scrub vegetables thoroughly with clean water before eating, as they were usually grown using night soil as fertiliser.

'I've been wondering about that,' Richard put in, 'The privies stink terribly: aren't they cleansed at all?'

'They don't bother over the long vacation when there are so few people in college,' replied Will, 'except for the Master's private privy, that is. I expect the dung-man will be around tonight though, and most weeks after that. It's a lucrative trade, shit, you know. Not a pleasant one, but there's a good market for it. Watch where you tread tomorrow, until it has rained.'

'We're lucky in our house,' said Edward, 'the privies drop straight into the river, it is most convenient and agreeable.'

'Unless you live directly downstream,' said Abel 'then you curse the arrangement.'

'Imagine being married to the dung-man!' said Edward. 'His wife must keep a peg on her nose at all times.'

'Or make him live in the outhouse,' said Abel. 'How many children would he manage to father? Not many, I think.'

'If he did would they come out all shit-coloured?' said Edward, laughing at his own witticism.

Richard was most intrigued at the turn of this conversation. He couldn't imagine being a party to this sort of talk if he was a girl. Well, of course he was a girl really – but it was very confusing to think about it. He wasn't sure if he was repelled by the talk, or liked the freedom.

They left Will to his purchases and made their way towards the river. Richard persuaded them to enter Queens' college with him, the better to view its lovely bridge, first from upon the bridge itself and then from the far bank.

'I believe this is called the Mathematical Bridge,' said Edward.

'Surely all bridges are mathematical; at least, those which have not fallen down for want of proper design?' asked Abel.

'Well I read it in a most up-to-date guide book only published this year,' complained Edward.

Enquiry at the porters' lodge (by Abel, Edward being at the time in a sulk) revealed it was generally known as the Essex bridge after its builder. Edward grumbled on receipt of this intelligence, but consented to venture around to the first of the Small Bridges to get another view. From this vantage they watched as a barge came up the river, the horse wading along the riverbed ahead of its load, rather than on any kind of towpath.

'How singular,' observed Edward. 'Why do they proceed in this fashion, I wonder?'

Neither Richard nor Abel could explain it to him, and so he resolved to ask a bargee among those who were congregated on the quay near the Mill itself.

Passing by a whole series of taverns, as yet mostly empty, they made their way around to the wharf and Edward put the question. Richard hung back, remembering Sir George's warning, but the bargee Edward had picked seemed only too happy to explain, the while venting his feelings on the matter.

'Tis the blasted sodomites in them there colleges, that's what it is,' he expostulated.

'Won't bloody let us use the bank; say it spoils their view or some such crap. So we 'as to struggle up a half-assed path in the riverbed, which the 'orses 'ate, and we 'ate, just to please their lordships. Bastards.'

Edward thanked him profusely for this intelligence, and handed him a coin, which the man pocketed almost magically quickly. They walked back to Trumpington-street, and with Richard wishing to look inside Pembroke hall, they separated and plunged back into the town. Richard looked around the courts and admired Wren's chapel, then returned by Bird-Bolt-lane to Emmanuel, noting that the Beast market was engaged in selling animals at that hour, rather than ladies' virtue.

It was still early for lunch so he investigated the library, discovering from the librarian, a Mr Braun, that it had originally been the chapel, arranged for the puritan founders on a north-south line in defiance of convention, and that there was a reasonable, though not extensive, supply of books there which he might wish to read, including Newton's Optics. Mr Braun was working at his desk, and taking Richard for a sizar, asked if he would be interested in a post helping to catalogue some of the books, for a consideration. Richard was initially dubious about this, but then realised it would enable him to learn about old books and broaden his knowledge, and also meet people who came in to borrow volumes or seek information. He accepted on a basis of only a few hours per week, and left with the further realisation that here was an alternative place to study, when he became bored with sitting in his chamber. The wooden panelling, and the bookshelves, and the smell of leather were all peaceful and felt like the library at home, except for the absence of Uncle Hugh.

After a brief lunch, with no sign of Edward or Abel, he went back to his room to rest and to investigate the picture he had bought. It was very dirty, to be sure, both frame and canvas. He wondered again how best to clean it, though he had been advised on the matter by Sir George, and thought he would ask Mrs Fenn when he next saw her. He also felt he was missing out on physical exercise, and did not want to let his newly-acquired muscles fade away, and wondered what there was in Cambridge to keep him up to the mark. Could he risk fencing here, if it was available? A third issue was to find out how the teaching was organised. Surely there could not be nothing at all provided until next month? Did he have a tutor? And also, he needed to contact the private tutor who Sir George had engaged for him. He had an address, stored away in his box, but he thought George had said the tutor would contact him once term had started. Plenty to do, anyway.

Hearing a clanking sound on the stair, he looked out and found Mrs Fenn opening up the room opposite to prepare it for its occupant who was due to arrive the next day. He put the problem of the picture to her, and she took it to the light, the while tutting over it as being a "dirty ol' picksher, to be sure", and said she thought a bit of beeswax polish would make a heap of difference to the frame, and perhaps if Richard were to dab at the paint with a damp cloth it might get some of the dirt off without damaging the colours. She set it down and wiped her hands on her apron, and stumped off to fetch cloths and polish.

Richard started with the frame. Once he had wiped away the loose dirt with his damp cloth, he rubbed the polish in and found the wood lightened in colour quite markedly, as the cloth darkened. It didn't help repair where the corners were coming apart, but it did hide where the wood was chipped and broken, to some extent. Then with a new cloth he set to work on the painting itself. He dabbed very cautiously at first, constantly using a new clean bit of the cloth, until he was sure just how firmly the paint was attached. It was a long job, and by the time he was getting a crick in his neck as he bent over it, he had only done about a third of the surface. Still, it looked better already. He returned the polish to Mrs Fenn with thanks, and asked if he could keep the cloths for a while longer.

Feeling in need of a walk, he visited the porters' lodge and made acquaintance with all the men there. He knew it was essential to be on the right side of the servants in any establishment, so he was extremely polite, and complimentary about the college. He learnt that the name of his tutor would be posted on a certain noticeboard on Monday, when term started; that any post he might receive was kept in the Lodge, and he should call to enquire for it whenever he was passing: the costs would be added to his college bill. However there was a free service to take messages to any other college by University messenger, so he could make arrangements with friends from elsewhere readily. He had the wild idea of sending a note round to Mr James at Caius to suggest a visit, before realising he could not appear in his guise as Richard Cox to someone who had known him as Rose Clarke. Could he? After all, Mr James was very short sighted. No, of course he daren't risk it.

Just to be sure, he inspected the noticeboards situated in the screens passage, and noted where the academic instructions would be placed. He also found several useful lists, such as the times of the coaches to various places, and distances to the nearby villages. Inspecting the coach list, he was puzzled to discover that the night mail left the Eagle and Child at nine. Surely he had said his goodbyes to George there at a little after five? Why had he said he was in a hurry then? And what had he been doing in the next few hours that he didn't want Richard to know about?

Coming out of the Lodge he met Edward in the company of two men whom he had not met before. Both were newly arrived: one, a Mr James Smith, was to share Edward's rooms, and the other's name he did not catch, as Edward began talking about a coffee-house they had found, and the number of newspapers taken there, and the varieties of coffee beans stocked, and lots of other possibly fascinating information. The other man started to drift away towards the chapel, and Richard followed him, slightly reluctant to abandon his friend but wishing to avoid information overload.

'Fine sort of fellow, your friend Edward,' the man said, 'but a bit prone to overelaborate.'

'A bit,' agreed Richard. 'I think he is nervous being in this unfamiliar place, to be fair. I am, certainly. And you?'

'So-so,' he said. 'By the way, I am Peter Winton; and you?'

'Richard Cox, at your service, sir. Have you just arrived?'

'In a manner of speaking, yes. I live only a few miles away, in Milton, so I know the place well, but I am due to come into residence on Monday to begin my degree. Today I am a visitor, I am making arrangements to furnish my rooms and to ensure I have at least a half-honest gyp.'

'Where will you be living?'

'In this court, on that stair by the chapel, but facing the orchard.'

He indicated rooms which adjoined the Brick building. They continued into the garden, and set to walk around the pond.

'If I may say so, sir, you are a little older than some of those whom I have met so far,' ventured Richard.

'I am twenty-four, positively ancient I sometimes think. I was working in my father's business, and last year travelling around Europe partly to make new contacts for him, and partly to see the antiquities and so on. Mr Bonaparte having put a stop to such journeys this spring, I returned and decided that I would benefit from a period in the groves of academe. So here I am. My father told me I must come up as a fellow-commoner, but I do not wish to associate myself with that sort of idle fellow, so I am here as a scholar, hence the rooms.'

'Shall you be dining today, sir? It is almost time.'

'I think I will. And you?'

Richard explained his position. Wondering if this man would be knowledgeable about the system of education, he asked, 'Can you tell me how the teaching works here? All I have been told is that lectures do not start until next month, which seems very odd. What is the purpose of the first few weeks?'

'Good question. Well, for the non-reading men, it gives them longer to hunt and gamble and drink and make friends and spend their money. For those who wish to learn, it is a matter of trying to persuade the fellows to give some teaching, because nothing in the conditions of their fellowships allots them any duties whatsoever, except that the Master will appoint two of their number as tutors, to oversee the studies of the undergraduates. They do not even have to be resident in Cambridge, which is outrageous. However, even in the least studious college, there are usually some few who enjoy the contact with young minds, and will teach if they are asked. Mr

Griffith is one, he loves to talk; and Mr Watkinson. I do not know however who will be tutors this year.'

'I have a private tutor for mathematics.'

'Good man. Also, it seems that a lot of the teaching is done by discussion with your fellow-students. I am most keen to arrange such a group for Greek, especially for verse composition which interests me, and for the study of fossils, and for chemistry. That is, if anyone else wants such a discussion.'

'I would be most interested. However, I am only just started on Greek earlier this year, and know nothing of fossils or chemistry. Indeed, I am not sure exactly what chemistry might be.'

'The study of the nature of substances, and how they react with each other. For example, why do some things burn and others do not? The old theory of phlogiston being a component of all combustible substances has been utterly exploded by Mr Priestley and M Lavoisier, yet many still do not believe the evidence in front of them. And when they burn, what is the product so formed?'

The bell for dinner sounded, and the two of them separated to fetch gowns and change their boots. Such conversations continued with the enlarged number of undergraduates throughout dinner, and Richard felt so enthused by his new companions that he could hardly believe how he had survived in the round of balls and soirees and musicales of the season, with so little to stimulate him intellectually.

The college filled up very slowly on Saturday. Richard took tea with Edward and James in the room below, but mostly he read furiously, hoping to catch up a little on his Euclid and his Greek Grammar. On Sunday he decided to attend Mr Simeon's church of Holy Trinity, to broaden his experience with evangelical theology, and was much impressed with the lucidity with which the famous cleric spoke and his lack of arrogance. He was told by someone there that he would be expected to attend the University Sermon in St Mary's at least on certain Sundays during Term, or be subject to discipline from the college. He also discovered exactly what the "Grantchester Grind" was, in the company of Will Peabody and John Wilks, who showed him the various paths to and from the nearby village along each bank of the Cam between lunch and dinner, walking the route at a furious pace such that he arrived back at college panting for breath and sweating.

He learnt that there was indeed a fencing club at the university, and resolved to visit it when it opened in the next week, hoping to find someone else to go with, as it was a rather daunting prospect. He imagined the lordly fellow-commoners would make up much of the clientele, and he was not sure if he wanted to deal with their manners. He spent more time on cleaning his painting, and at length finished removing the surface dirt. He couldn't do much with the rather brown varnish, but it looked so much better now hanging on his wall. He wondered who might have painted it, and how old it was. Surely over a hundred years, he thought, considering the discolouration of the varnish? He took it over to the window and looked for a signature in the bottom corners, but there was none. Inspecting it closely, he noticed a woman's face peeking out of one of the windows he had not noticed before, and a cheeky little urchin teasing a cat just visible in a rear courtyard through its entrance alley. There was a wealth of detail in the execution: glints of sun off the wet roof tiles, slight irregularities of the cobbles, and so on. It was truly lovely.

While inspecting one of the walls, he found it. Not exactly a signature, more a puzzle. There was a capital M with a vertical line over it, and then the three letters "eer". Was it the artist? Why had he put his monogram, if that was what it was, there? Richard couldn't tell. Anyway, it didn't matter who had painted it, or when, or why: he just loved it.

Monday October the 10th was the beginning of Term. Nothing really happened, disappointingly, except that Mr Fenn woke him at six, in time for seven o'clock chapel, and the two tutors' names were posted on the board as promised, and one or two more students arrived. It seemed that the college numbered 69 undergraduates and 12 fellows plus the Master, but hardly half that number was in residence as yet. Will Peabody told Richard that some people dragged out their stay to four or five years, by not completing the terms of residence, and that this year there were only 15 new students enrolled. There was considerable laxity in ensuring people came up at the right time, especially the fellow-commoners, most of whom would only take the pass degree, which hardly took any study to succeed in. Emmanuel had no noblemen at present, but he said that these exalted ones just had to stay two years and then they left with a degree with no examination at all!

Seeing a Mr Griffith was allocated to him as tutor, Richard lost no time in presenting himself at his rooms. He went along with Abel Johnson, as Edward was allocated to the other tutor, a Dr Watkinson. He had the intention of asking him if he could see his way to give them some time to help deal with problems they might come across in their study, even before the formal lectures began. The problem turned out to be to stop the Fellow talking: it was most entertaining and not a little instructive, but it was hard to get a word in edgeways. Eventually, by dint of some careful flattery, and showing especial eagerness to learn in the areas which interested the don, they secured agreement that he would see them at eleven o'clock every Wednesday, to consider their progress in Greek, and also to point them toward further reading in Latin verse.

Richard thought he would then try his luck with the college chaplain. He had not been overly enthused by the compulsory early chapel service, at which most of the students were trying to sleep, and which none of the dons attended. However Rev Burton was surprised and pleased to have a keen applicant for instruction in theology. He recommended a book which the library held, and said he would see Richard once he had read it, the following week, and weekly after that if he so wished. If he could encourage anyone else to attend with him it would make for a more lively discussion.

Coming out into Chapel Court, he saw Peter Winton supervising the arrival of his luggage and its installation into his rooms. He was a very good-looking man, he thought, and being a little older, so much more . . . well, urbane, competent. Not perhaps as handsome as Abel Johnson, but actually very much more attractive. He felt a tingle in his belly, and then abruptly remembered that he was supposed to be a man at present, well, a boy really. This was going to be very confusing, being with these intelligent and attractive men, and having to stay in role as a boy, when his instincts pulled him in a quite different direction.

CHAPTER 15

BY THE END OF THE first week in November Richard was so settled he felt he had been at college for ever. He had written to Mr Blackburn early on (using George's address in London, naturally), and received an encouraging reply, but soon found the multitude of immediate interests pressed more on his mind. He had made huge progress with Euclid, firstly with the help of Edward, who proved very helpful in explaining the parts where Richard had become lost; and then with the tutor who Sir George had organised, who turned out to be a clergyman having the living of Grantchester, and whom they saw together on a Tuesday, halfway round the Grantchester Grind in the early afternoon. Rev Laughton had been a Fellow of Corpus Christi college until his marriage, whereupon he had been given the living, which was in the college's gift. He had known Sir George while both were students, though he was a few years older.

Richard had decided he would progress faster if he had his tutorials together with another student, as he had with Charles, and liked being able to help out Edward whose finances were quite tight. The only negative aspect of the arrangement was that he learnt all sorts of information he could well have done without on the walks there and back, such as how James Smith his roommate was also a grocer's son, from King's Lynn, which he described in great detail; and how he was only at college because his father insisted, though he could ill afford it, and had even less money than Edward, which was remarkable; but seemed to spend very little time in his room, which meant Edward had peace and quiet; and how James' best coat was still quite threadbare, and he had to do a lot of jobs in college for the fellow-commoners to make ends meet. It all felt like unwanted gossip, almost like being with a group of girls, except that he added in some local argot James had taught him from the sailors he had met, and mimicked James' strong accent most accurately.

With Mr Laughton's encouragement he had also read other mathematical books, especially about number theory, including Prime numbers, and the different ways numbers may be ordered, such as in Pascal's triangle, and Fibonacci's sequence, and many others which were a revelation to him. In their tutorials in college, he and Abel had made some progress with Greek, though Mr Griffith was inclined to stray off the point, but he pointed them in the way of some interesting texts and sorted out their tangles with poetic Latin idioms. The Fellow had also visited Greece some years previously and was able to describe some of the major monuments he had seen, which was fascinating, especially as he could show them etchings of some of the buildings, particularly in Athens, which he had bought while he was there.

Theological instruction had been rather disappointingly dry with Rev Burton, but Richard persevered, and had his horizons more interestingly stimulated by Sunday sermons from Rev Simeon at Holy Trinity, or in a completely different idiom at St Mary's. Moreover, he had joined with Peter Winton and a few other interested men for discussions on fossils, and on chemistry, but for the most part kept quietly at the edge of the circle, for want of knowledge.

And then this week the University lectures had begun. Richard had seen a long list posted on the college boards, and wondered how he could possibly get to all of them. Mr Griffith had however met with him at this point and directed him to some Mathematics, Latin and Greek instruction, and also agreed he could attend the Professor of Chemistry together with Edward's roommate James, leaving the other subjects till a later date. He found that lectures took place in the morning; some in college, some in other colleges and some in University rooms, which caused him confusion at first, having not read the notices about where to go sufficiently carefully. As a result he had now been to St Catharine Hall to hear about Homer, and was due in King's next week for Horace.

All told he had hardly a moment to spare. He now knew all eight other first year scholars, pensioners and sizars, the six fellow-commoners being prone to keep to their own kind; and several of the second year men. At table with them he would regularly be involved in discussions ranging from the nuances of Catullus' poetry to the somewhat subjective and usually salacious judgements of his friends on the merits of the young women who served in the coffee house opposite. He tentatively tried to voice an opinion on this latter topic once, but his view (about the cheeky eyes of one young lady) was rebutted by his friends in a jocular manner, on the basis of his being too young to need to shave yet.

Peter Winton had taken a particular interest in him, much as an older brother might, and had been the reason why he had elected to attend the Chemistry Professor. He often defended him when the others teased him for his youth, and his lack of general knowledge about English schools and schoolboy interests, such as was only natural in a man from the colonies. Richard himself was not always in need of defending by this paladin, and his sarcastic rejoinders often raised considerable merriment at the expense of his critics.

Hence Richard was pleased and flattered to be invited to a wine party at Caius by Peter, which was being hosted by a friend of his there. Pleased and flattered, but also a little nervous, as he had both heard of the drunken and riotous behaviour at such gatherings, and literally heard the same in the staircases of the Westmorland building of Emmanuel. Also, he did not think he could afford to purchase the several bottles that seemed *de rigeur* at such events, and then not consume them. Peter reassured him that this was an entirely different type of meeting: it was for reading men, or for those that studied at least somewhat.

Noone was required to drink more than he wished, and the expense was only for such drinks as one consumed. The form was that you put sixpence in a large jug for each glass you poured, which was easier than reckoning up later, as people's memories grew rather hazy after a while. The idea was to foster connections between people of different colleges, and generally to have a break from constant studies.

Hence after dinner on the Thursday in question, the two of them, with a fellow-commoner in his second year who Richard had not previously met called Robert Cork, sallied forth across town and found their hosts in a large set overlooking the Senate House, the Schools and University Library, and what Peter informed Richard was a detached part of King's college. He found this intelligence most confusing, and wondered if he would ever get the place straight in his mind, but still, he had only been here about six weeks.

There were already several people there when they arrived. Open bottles of wine were set out on a table, with a great many glasses of various styles. Somebody, who seemed to be the keeper of this room, explained that they had gone on a recce and collected them from various fellows' rooms for the purpose, but demmed if he could remember which had come from where, which was sure to cause a ruckus later. Richard timidly asked about the wine, and the man (whose name was Sterne) said it was deuced difficult to get in a decent claret these days, what with the blasted Boney and all that, most inconsiderate of him. 'Course college had a huge stash in their cellars, but he knew a man who knew a cove who could get this Portuguese stuff much cheaper than college would charge for the French, not sweet port wine, you understand, but regular wine from some other place there, not sure where it was. Not half bad, he said, try some.

Richard accepted a glass. He took a sip, it was not too different from claret, he thought, but less, er, what had Sir George told him it was called? Tannic, that was it. He thought he'd risk passing comment.

'It isn't half bad, as you say. Not quite as tannic as a claret from the Medoc,' he ventured.

'I like a man who knows his wines. I prefer the Graves myself, but some fine claret comes from Pauillac, I believe.'

This was more than Richard's knowledge encompassed, so he just nodded and took another drink. Fortunately Mr Sterne's attention was distracted by another thirsty man, so he dropped in his sixpence and melted to the back of the crowd, near a window.

'Don't think I've seen you before, sir?' said an extraordinarily tall man in a velvet waistcoat who was rather rubicund of face, and whose speech seemed a bit indistinct or mumbling. 'Faith, you must be a new bantling at the shrine of Camus?'

At first, Richard thought he must be a trifle disguised, given how he fidgeted and swayed, but then saw his eye was clear, and realised he was quite sober and just rather odd. 'Sir, Mr Richard Cox at your service. I fear I am not familiar with your cant, as I am but lately arrived from the colony of Nova Scotia.' Better speak quite formally to this man, until I get my range, he thought.

'Pardon, sir. I was but bamming you, you must have all of fourteen years?'

'Sixteen, sir. Sixteen. I am a new pensioner at Emmanuel. And your name?'

'Mr John Burgess, at your service. Trinity. Of similar standing, for the last three years. Sadly, I must face the Inquisition in January, over there.' He pointed vaguely at the fine marble building outside. 'I hope to avoid apostolic opprobrium but have no greater hope.'

'Sir?'

'You are green, are you not? An apostle is one of the lowest twelve names on the list of those proceeding to take their degree without honours. The most plebeian of *Hoi Polloi*. Such is the lot I trust I may escape.'

Richard set his head on one side and considered the man. 'You bam me again, I believe. However, I prefer to be green rather than red, I think.'

Another man leaned over and put in apropos of not much, 'The Burge is a certainty for the Senior Optimes, and a good each-way for the Wranglers,' and promptly vanished.

Mr Burgess laughed, and set his glass down unwisely near the edge of the windowsill. It toppled over and crashed into the court below. He ignored the calamity, merely exclaiming, 'A hit, a palpable hit! Green not red! I begin to like you lad. I confess, I have read the odd book now and then. If I have to. In between the necessary periods of testing the college's cellars, of course. La, I believe Trinity stocks enough claret to last us even if this war carries on until the next century. Possibly why I appear to fly my colours at all times like a shrinking bit of muslin.'

Richard thought hard about this speech, and decided he was trying to insult young women who blushed. Perhaps. Anyway, it deserved a rejoinder.

'I prefer to observe the pure virtue shown by the modesty of maidens to the vices of a man who dips deep, sir.'

'Ha! Well said. Best not to get bosky when you are such a pretty lad, anyway. There are those who might take advantage, you know.'

'I have no intention of becoming incapable, you will be pleased to hear. And though young I believe I can hold my own in a fight. Do you fence, sir?'

'Not my game, lad.'

'Well, I have dispatched several men taller than me at the salle this term already, and laid a fair blow on a velvet-gowned man who fell against me in far too pressing a manner in the street one evening. He spent a while not just in the arms of Morpheus but in the gutter. Not a clean gutter, I think, but I did not examine it closely.'

'I will remember it.' He turned away, grinning, to speak to another man, and Richard took another sip of his wine, while noticing how fast his heart was beating. He had never thought of himself as pretty when he was a girl, but maybe he was rather too fine-featured as a boy? He would have to watch out and be sure to be robust in personality even if not in looks, so that nobody might suspect him.

'Not a bad crush, eh?' came a voice in his ear. It was Peter Winton, looking out to see he was at ease, as usual. 'I see you have met our Mr

Burgess, a man whose fame is widespread even among those such as I who merely have lived near Cambridge, and not before been up at the university.'

'I have indeed. A most curious gentleman.'

'Highly intelligent beneath that bumbling facade he affects. Did he boast of how much wine he drinks?'

'He did.'

'Well, it is only half true. He enjoys pretending to be drunk so that his friends drink more than they can hold, and then he may more readily relieve them of their blunt at piquet or pharo or vingt-et-un. Now, let me introduce you to another man I know from my time in my father's business, he is at Caius here, his name is Joshua Little.'

Richard moved around in the room from one conversation to another. He kept a sharp eye on how much he was drinking, and how the time was passing, and after a while judged it reasonable to spend another sixpence on refilling his glass. He was surprised to see someone in a gown which proclaimed him a Fellow, and more surprised when the man spoke to him, and after asking what he thought of the wine, talked for quite some little time about the history of Caius college, and its buildings, once he found Richard was both ignorant of his surroundings and interested in them. Richard made an effort to remember his name, as befitted being condescended to by a Senior Member; it was Oscar Seligman, which was most unusual. The don explained it was of German origin, though his family had been in England for years.

He came across Robert Cork again, with whom he had walked to the party, and found him very affable and unpretentious for a fellow-commoner. He was another man who had travelled widely on the Continent, in the long vacation after his first year in Cambridge, during the brief peace that had existed following the Treaty of Amiens. He seemed to think that Bonaparte coming to power was an improvement on the various Revolutionary councils and the Terror, and that he was likely to restore the balance of power in Europe, which might lead to a longer-lasting peace than there had been for decades. Richard became even more aware of all the things which he did not know in the course of listening to him, and felt a little disconsolate for a while.

After an hour or so, someone fetched a violin, and began playing songs on it, in which a few of the men joined. After the first few such arias, the music became more boisterous, and soon there was a rendition of a ballad which Richard thought must have been called "The Plenipotentiary" from the repetition of this phrase with each verse. It was a bit hard to make out most of the words, but the inferences he could make from the ones he could hear, and from the singers' gestures, was that it was singularly bawdy.

He was standing by the door while this epic was being performed – it appeared to have an infinite series of verses – and was startled by a loud rapping and the door being opened suddenly. There right in front of him was a man in a Fellow's gown, peering short-sightedly at the crowd and banging his stick on the floor. It was Mr James! Richard shrank back out of sight behind the opened door, and tried to be invisible.

There was a momentary lull in the music at the incursion, and Mr James tried to speak. 'I r-really must protest at the level of noise, sirs,' he said. 'Think of those who are trying to w-work in this place of learning. Think of those attending chapel. K-kindly cease the playing of your instrument and desist from rendering that appalling song. Thankyou.'

He made a dignified departure, and after a brief pause, the singing began anew, though just possibly at a diminished volume. Richard admired Mr James for his bravery in confronting his crowd, timid as he was by nature, and hampered by his stutter and his poor sight. He hoped he had not been seen, and was certain he had not been recognised. So Mr James was now a Fellow, as he had hoped. He must surely be in his true home here. He remembered Mr James' confidence to himself when he was still Rose, at the ball in London, and wondered what colour he would have perceived the singing to be, how the key would have appeared to him. No doubt blue, he thought, smiling to himself. Bright unabashed blue.

It was hard to have much of a conversation with all the noise of the singing, and so some of the men spilled out onto the landing, including Richard, and continued talking as if nothing was unusual. After about ten minutes a large gentleman with the appearance of a pugilist but the dress of a college porter climbed the stairs, worked his way past them, and entered the room. The music abruptly stopped, and the man back came out holding on to the instrument and its bow.

'You can have it back in a week's time once you apologise to Mr James,' he said over his shoulder. 'And any more disturbance and it'll be fines for the lot of you.'

The party broke up soon after, as it was getting towards dusk, and most had not their gowns with them. Threading their way through the narrow streets Peter half-apologised for the party being more raucous than he had anticipated.

'Don't worry about that, Peter. I had a most interesting time. That man Burgess now. He must be at least six foot four, he's a giant.'

'Six five, I am informed. He strikes his head on the beams even if he hasn't been drinking. I hear you gave him as good as you got, anyway?'

'How do you know?'

'I just know things,' he said mysteriously. 'No, actually, Cork overheard you and told me. You have a keen observing eye, and a fine line in sarcasm.'

'Thanks. I spoke to a lot of other people too, it was most stimulating. You seem to know many men already for someone who has only been up as long as I have: do you know who that don was that came in to tell them to stop singing?'

'No, I don't. Quite assertive for such a little person, wasn't he?'

'I thought so. And he followed up his protest by instructing the porter. I admired him.'

Their own porter was just lighting the oil lamp over the college entrance as they returned. 'No gowns, gentlemen? Five minutes later and you'd have been in the book, you know.'

They passed inside. 'He's a good sort, Cobb,' said Peter. Always gives you a bit of slack on the rules. Don't abuse it though, he'll have to report you if it's flagrant. More than his job is worth, you see.'

'I don't intend to be a reprobate, you know. But I had forgotten all about my gown, to be fair.'

'Sir! Mr Cox, sir!' The call came from the porters' lodge. Richard turned around.

'There's a letter for you, sir.'

Richard was a bit surprised. Could it be from Sir George? But he had only written two days ago. Curious, he retraced his steps and collected the letter. It had come by the university messenger. Odd. He put it in his pocket to read it in his room.

Once upstairs with his Horace, he took out the letter and opened it. It contained only one line, and no signature. It simply said, "Fibonacci to 13". How odd. He turned it over but there was nothing else on it. Just the address, Mr R Cox, Emmanuel.

What to make of it? He had no idea. It was good quality paper, and a full sheet for such a small message. Anyway, he had Horace to wrestle with, with the possibility of a prize for a Latin verse composition in his style, and the lecture next week to be prepared for. Maybe tomorrow would bring some fresh ideas about it. He slipped it into the back of Horace and forgot it.

The following day brought a change in his routine. Peter Winton caught him after chapel and asked him if he would be willing to substitute in a boating party after lunch. They had a four-oar booked but one of their number had taken to his bed with a fever. He explained the outing was principally for exercise, their group having found walking the same old routes had quickly palled.

Richard professed himself completely a novice at anything to do with water, but his objections were brushed aside as Peter said none of them had as yet any degree of mastery of the oar. Therefore after a quick meal, the two of them marched rapidly to the river above the sluice by Jesus Green, where a boat lay waiting for them. It was a broad and sturdily built craft, and three other fellows were already there putting the oars in their places and seeing to the steering-lines. Peter showed him how to enter the boat without oversetting it, and Richard settled himself in the seat in the bows, laying his coat on the thwart beside him as instructed, and removing his cravat.

Rowing was a very new form of exercise for Richard. It seemed to mainly tire the lower back and the arms, in a way like his digging had done, but again unlike it. The main problem at first though was for the four of them to keep in time, as each seemed to have a different idea of the rate at which they should row. The boat rocked and twisted in its course, until the man sitting in the stern with the rudder took charge.

'Halt, the lot of you! Now look, think about what we practised last time. Guy, you are the stroke. You set the timing, you must keep your movements regular as a pendulum, and not too fast. The rest of you, you have to measure yourselves by Guy. Lean forward when he does, dip your blades with him, and pull with his strength. Do you hear me?'

There was a mumble of assent from all of them. Guy took off his waistcoat, as did one of the others, but Richard did not feel he could risk this degree of exposure.

'Right! Get set . . . Row!'

This time they all came forward as one, and the oars bit, and the boat began to move in a much more orderly fashion. Guy, at stroke, seemed to have a little difficulty in keeping regular, so the steersman began to count a loud and regular rhythm. 'One, and, two, and, three,' and so on. The banks started to slip past at a steady rate. Once or twice someone missed the water with their oar, and cursed; then while they were steering to avoid a barge and its tow-rope the man in front of (or was it behind? thought Richard) Guy missed his stroke so energetically that he fell off his seat and tumbled backwards into the bottom of the boat, to much laughter from the others.

They made their way somewhat erratically past Midsummer Common, by the village of Barnwell, and then round several bends until Chesterton village came into view – or at least did if Richard twisted around to look where they were heading, which nearly caused him to fall off his seat also. Stopping for a while so they could rest, Peter explained that there was a great fair on Midsummer Common, opened with pomp and ceremony by the university officers in June, and also one on Stourbridge Green just a little further along the river, in the middle of September, which had reputedly been the largest in Europe, but was now declining somewhat. It seemed to Richard that everyone was able to inform him at every opportunity of facts which somehow he felt he ought already to know, but he was always deficient.

Richard's hands were getting a little sore, as his calluses from the digging had softened in the weeks since he had left Kilcott, and he was hot, and his muscles ached. Nonetheless, he thought he was getting the hang of staying in rhythm, and pulling the oar smoothly throughout the stroke, and was keen to continue when the question was raised. They set off again, and as the houses of Chesterton slipped by, and gave way to fields, they stopped by two pink-washed cottages, at the beginning of a straight section of river Peter told him was called the Long Reach.

Time was getting on, and so they turned the boat, which involved the two on one side rowing backwards and the others forwards, which Richard found very confusing, and it led to his oar hopping out of its place (which he learnt was known as a rullock) and out of his control. Eventually they got themselves straight, and set off to return. They had two narrow shaves with barges that the steersman did not see until rather late, and their timing got rather ragged as they tired, but eventually they fetched up at the bank by the sluice and clambered out. Carefully, as the steersman told them, having disembarked first to steady the boat. This was not entirely heeded by Guy in the stern, who almost missed his footing and stepped between boat and bank, but recovered in time.

Richard ached all over. His shirt was soaked with sweat under his waistcoat, and his stockings were falling down. Even so he felt elated at his achievement, at having held his own with these new acquaintances.

'Peter, would you and your friend care to come to Jesus for dinner?' asked Guy, as he handed the boat back into the care of the waterman and paid for its hire. 'It's much nearer than Emmanuel, and I bet you need a drink like I do.'

'Fine idea, Guy. Is the plan agreeable to you, Richard?'

'Certainly,' said Richard, keen to see inside another college. 'Though I might need a bath chair to get even that far.'

They made their way slowly and haltingly over Jesus Green and around the ditch which protected Jesus Close, to the lane which led to the college entrance, called confusingly, The Chimney. Richard discovered that the steersman was known as the cox, that oars could be called blades, that he had rowed bow-side, and although he was in the bow the other man two in front (or behind?) him was also bow-side, though nearer the stern. He learnt the names of the other two men, also from Jesus, and promptly forgot them, and discovered that this was only their third outing in the four-oar, though one of them had sculled before.

'Skulled?' he asked, puzzled.

'Sculling,' said Rob, who had rowed at number three, the other man on bow-side (Richard thought he had got that right). 'It means having two oars, one in each hand, it is hard, because you have no cox; I hit the bank several times when I tried it.'

'Oh, I see.'

They repaired to Guy's rooms via the Buttery, which produced a tankard of ale for all of them. Richard was dubious about this, but felt he could not refuse. Also, he was parched with breathing through his mouth during his exertions. Guy had a beautifully-furnished keeping-room, with several prints of classical scenes on the walls, comfortable chairs, and dark red rugs on the floor. The sun shone in at an angle on the fireplace, and lit up two engraved silver cups and a small terracotta vase on the mantel. It was homely, and snug. Richard sipped his ale, tried to relax his aching muscles into the armchair, and examined the blisters on his hands.

'Thanks for filling in for us,' said Rob, 'our fourth man is half dead with fever. He fell in the Cam after an altercation with a bargee, and swallowed far too much before they fished him out. We're going to visit him in Magdalene after dinner, but they say he's in a bad way of it.'

'Yes,' said the cox, whose name Richard couldn't recall, 'Father Camus is horrid around the Great Bridge, full of rats, and rubbish thrown in by the Hogs upstream.'

The ale was not at all bad, thought Richard, not too bitter, and much needed. He tried to copy the others in their manner of drinking, and felt the ale couldn't be too strong, as they were swallowing it at such a rate. He kept to a slower pace, but wondered how he would manage the volume of fluid in a strange college whose facilities he did not know.

The others began discussing horses, and hunting, and Richard wondered what sort of men these were. Peter knew them, so he supposed they were all right kinds of fellows, and he noticed that Guy had a bookcase full of volumes, and there was a pile of papers and books on the desk, so he probably was a reading man. Knowing nothing about hunting, he kept quiet and listened, and soon the dinner bell was heard and the five of them levered themselves upright, and made across to the Hall. He had not finished his ale, but Guy told him to bring it with him, and finish it at table. He disappeared into a room on the staircase as they went down, and came out with two gowns for them to wear, saying their owners would not miss them as they were out somewhere in the vicinity of St Neot's engaged in wildfowling.

In Hall, he followed his hosts, and found himself seated at High Table. He must have looked a little nervous at the prospect, because

Peter leaned over and told him quietly that his hosts would be paying for the meal, they were not short of resources, and just to enjoy himself. Evidently these men were fellow-commoners, he surmised, but awfully decent sorts. He looked around, and saw only two men who might be Fellows, one of whom stood up at a signal from the butler, whereupon the whole company rose, and a Latin grace was declaimed at speed, very similar to the one at Emmanuel as far as he could tell.

The food was markedly better than he ate at the lower tables at Emmanuel. He was offered wine, but declined, sticking with the remains of his ale. And was he hungry? He devoured the pigeon and the salt beef, and took an extra helping of pickled beetroot, and of bread and butter. He even accepted a small tankard of ale, once his original one had emptied, and found his aches were receding pleasantly.

The conversation turned first on horseflesh, and then on the war, where Richard felt able to contribute a little, having had the intelligence from Mr Blackburn about the 51st regiment, in what now seemed to be another life entirely. Then it turned to matters of Guy's estates, and how several of his tenants had joined the army, and the problems that caused. Gradually he realised that these men were not just fellow-commoners, but that they were exceedingly wealthy and probably of noble birth. He felt a little intimidated, but then realised he had rowed with them on equal terms, so even though he was only the sister (brother?) of a baronet, he could be their equal in other ways too. It was a reassuring thought.

CHAPTER 16

THE FOLLOWING MONDAY RICHARD ATTENDED his lecture in King's on Horace. He was surprised that the lecturer was the same man as the one who had lectured on Homer the previous week in St Catharine's, and took note of the his name. It was one Richard Porson: the name seemed strangely familiar somehow. He found the manner of his talking most pleasing, and made a number of notes, as well as taking down a short list of books that might be deemed useful to consult in writing poetry for the forthcoming prize that he was thinking of entering. Professor Porson seemed remarkably well-versed in a number of languages besides the classical, and in ancient history, especially that of Egypt, to which he referred often when talking about the antecedents of Horace's poetry, and Richard suddenly remembered it was Uncle Hugh who had talked about him, he was the man who had restored the broken segment of the Greek text on the Rosetta Stone. He was truly moving in exalted circles.

As the lecture drew to a close, he noticed a large and shambling man making his way out on the other side of the room. Surely that was Mr Burgess, whom he had met at Caius? He hurried around to greet him, but he found him deep in conversation with Robert Cork, the fellow-commoner who had come with him and Peter to the wine party, and he didn't like to interrupt.

Since he was there, he decided to look inside King's enormous chapel. This was far larger than the rest of the college put together, he thought, and once inside, he marvelled for many minutes at the stonework, the windows, and the sounds of the organ which it seemed someone was practising. Seeing a noticeboard, he discovered one could attend sung services here on a daily basis, and resolved to attend evensong as soon as might be convenient.

A voice behind him addressed him as he looked up again at the fan vaulting of the roof.

'I say, it's young Richard, isn't it? You helped us out in the four-oar on Friday.'

It was Guy. 'Sorry I was miles away, looking at this ceiling. Isn't it amazing?'

'Darn right it is. Well, it's a good chance I spotted you coming into this place, see, we're short again for the boat, and Tom at Magdalene is worse if anything, they're almost despairing of him, but there's nothing we can do, so, we thought we shouldn't cancel the trips just because he might be on his last legs. Any hope of you joining us again today?'

Richard looked at Guy. He was wearing a full-sleeved gown that was quite different from his own, and carrying a top hat, not a square. 'Guy, are you a nobleman?' he asked, diffidently.

'Well, yes, I confess it, but you don't have to bother about all that nonsense here. We all have two arms and two legs, don't you know?'

'I ought to know, though, didn't I? I mean, to avoid saying the wrong thing?'

'I don't see you making any howlers here in the University, but, well, I suppose I am officially Viscount Guy Beauchamp of Knotton, since the pater shuffled off this mortal thingummy. Now forget you knew that. Guy to you, my lad. So, can you join us?'

'Certainly. At the same time?'

''S'right. Rob and Charlie are booked, and Peter, he's very reliable, salt of the earth. Are your blisters healing? We'll give you a few more today, I'll be bound.'

'See you then.'

Richard caught Peter at lunchtime and catechised him about his new friends. It seemed he had been boating with half the stud book. Rob was Lord Robert Dumas, youngest son of a marquess; and Charlie the Honourable Charles French, second son of a baron. Oh well. Peter said they were all sound men, and some of the few of their type that bothered to study. Charlie was coxing them because he had a game back, from a fall out hunting last winter with the Quorn, which hadn't recovered properly.

It felt much more normal the following day to be walking with Edward to Grantchester for his maths tutorial with Mr Laughton, and sitting with the sizars and pensioners in hall, and bantering with James Smith over his alleged lack of knowledge, or with Will Peabody about his prowess with the ladies, or implying to the others that Abel had disgusting personal habits. Not that the Jesuits had made him feel out of place, far from it, it was just a bit of a shock to discover their status when he had had them down as well-off sons of financiers or business men of some type. He had heard that Tom's parents had been called to see him, as he was going down hill rapidly, and they turned out to be the Earl and Countess of Netherby, according to Peter. The world was a complicated place, and dangerous even for the privileged.

'How come you know all these titled folk,' he asked Peter on the way out of Hall, 'I mean, you are just ordinary, aren't you? Or are you secretly the Duke of, I don't know, Cambridge or something?'

'Not me,' Peter laughed. 'Like I said, I'm from Milton, my dad is in business, but I have travelled a fair bit, wars permitting, and so I've met a lot of folk. Also, we supply a number of great houses, so, it follows I know the owners. Now sorry, I have to go, I need to see a man about a dog.'

'What?' but he was gone. Richard went back to his room to wrestle with square roots.

❋

Cambridge was getting colder. An icy wind blew from the east, and the rooms especially in the Brick Building were chilly even with their fires burning. Fewer people played bowls on the grass in the garden by the pond, and Richard wore his gown most of the time, simply for a bit of extra warmth. He bought woollen gloves and a scarf, and had his new hat on his head whenever he was out and an academic cap was not required.

He went boating about twice a week with the Jesuits, and was saddened to hear that Tom had died from his fever following his immersion in the river, though he had never met him. He did attend the sung evensong at King's as he had resolved, and finding it magical and uplifting, decided to go again some time, if only he could fit it in among all the other activities. It was difficult, what with invitations to the coffee houses, and the taverns, and to men's rooms for tea or wine, and so many books that he simply must read. Not to mention the few hours a week he spent in the library, dealing with the book cataloguing, and issuing loans.

It was while he was doing this job one Monday evening that he came upon a most mysterious piece of paper. It was inside a copy of a book on chemistry, dealing with the varieties of combustion. He tried to discover who had borrowed the book previously but it seemed that no record was kept of this once the book had been returned by the reader, the slips being consigned to the fire.

It was a single sheet, covered in writing, all in normal sentences which made no sense whatsoever. It looked like a passage of poetry, or possibly prose, but the meaning did not follow logically. It read:

VLF
My eager eye too long strained my nerve.
None could overset his experiences.
We vie, none can persuade me of them.
Physical inquiries are not scrambled.
Diets of off beans.
We will fight his enemies, rout some . . .

It tailed off with a trail of ink across the page as if the writer had barely the strength to finish it. Richard stared at it. Who could have written it? There was nothing on the rear side such as an address, though it looked as if it had been folded; no recognisable signature, salutation or any such thing. Had one of the other undergraduates lost his mind? He had heard of such a thing, from Will Peabody, who said that one of the pensioners in his year had had to be admitted to a madhouse, having become convinced that all the food in the college was tainted with arsenic so that he would not eat it, and that the Master was able to listen in to everything he said through an apparatus which he kept in the Lodge, so that he refused to speak except outside the precincts of Emmanuel.

On the other hand, the writing was careful and well-formed, it did not look like ravings of a madman, other than the trailing-off. Whatever could it be? Mr Braun was approaching him looking as if he wanted an errand run, so he slipped the paper into his coat and looked attentive.

Back in his room he looked at it again. He held it to the light, and saw a faint watermark. It looked a little like a trefoil. The paper was of good quality, stiff, and undamaged. What did it remind him of? Was it the nonsense written on it? No, not that. The paper? Maybe. Where he had found it? Not quite . . . and then he had it. He had found it in a book and he had put that other odd piece of paper in his Horace. He looked in his bookcase for it, and then remembered it was in the pile of papers where he had been trying to compose a poem for the competition.

There it was. And it looked the same sort of paper, and . . . yes it had the same watermark. So what did that mean? It was all very secretive, it was an enigma! (He liked that word, he had recently learnt it in regard of the Riddle of the Sphinx). So, does it mean the words have a hidden meaning? Like, a sort of code or cipher? And, was "Fibonacci to 13" the key in some way? Who could he ask about it? Well, Sir George, he supposed, or maybe Peter Winton, he liked puzzles; and if he could but approach him, Mr James might be a useful person; or even Uncle Hugh. On the other hand, it would be much more fun to try and work it out for himself, unassisted.

He had a tutorial with Mr Laughton to prepare for, this being Monday evening, so he decided to put the papers away together in his Horace, where noone would come across them, and deal with them afresh after dinner tomorrow. Perhaps sleeping on the problem would help him decide where to start. Meanwhile, he needed to look at Pythagorean triples, and then see if he could find out about Fermat's conjecture, which Mr Laughton was going to discuss with them.

The next morning, sadly, he had had no breakthroughs in his dreams. At the tutorial, after the review of the problems which they had worked, and discussion of the difficulties they had encountered, Mr Laughton brought them as anticipated on to Fermat's conjecture, sometimes called his Last Theorem. He showed them his copy of Diophantus's Arithmetica, in which Pierre de Fermat's assertion that he had discovered a proof that there are no equivalents for Pythagorean Triples for powers greater than two, was printed. He talked about the efforts that had been made to rediscover a proof, and the very partial successes (for a few small numbers such as 4 and 3) that had followed, explaining that this sort of thing was what drove mathematicians on, the knowledge that there ought to be a way of proving or discovering something, and that just perhaps they themselves might find it. Clearly he found mathematics absorbing and exciting, just as Richard did.

Richard asked Mr Laughton if mathematicians were interested in codes too, and he told him that there was a whole field called cryptography, which could be very mathematical, looking to produce systems designed to prevent an enemy from finding out vital information. There were basic letter substitution codes, ways of mixing up letters, distributing the letters among a jumble of other ones, and numerous others, but they would have to wait until they had completed Euclid, and probably until after they were well into the Principia too, because ideas had to be built the one upon the other.

On the way back to college he was unusually silent, which led Edward to ask if he was upset about the rebuff.

'Not at all, I am merely thinking about what we learned today; and wondering if I could ever aspire to prove M Fermat's theorem some day.'

'I just want to pass the Previous Exam, the Little-go. I don't really care about cube powers and so on for themselves.'

'That's fine, you're going to work in your father's business, aren't you? But some people devote their lives to it, like Mr James at . . .' Too late, he remembered he was not supposed to know Mr James, only Rose knew him, and he was Richard.

'Who?'

'Oh,' he temporised, 'um, this don, er, well, you know the wine party I went to with Winton, the one in Caius, I told you about that terribly tall man I met there? Well, he was the don who came and broke it up, someone told me his name, and how he worked all day in his room, only emerging for a quick walk round the grounds once or twice a week. He's doing something to do with, er, what was it? Developing Newton's fluxions, I think.'

'Hum Drum,' responded Edward.

'Pardon?'

'I heard the phrase in the Blue Boar, and I liked it. I think it means, boring and tedious, at least I hope it means that.'

'Sounds all right, well, except that I think fluxions will be fascinating once we get to them.' Richard hoped he had covered up satisfactorily: he thought he had, Edward had not the most inquisitive nature.

After Hall he set to with his new idea. First, he set out Fibonacci's sequence: 1, 1, 2, 3, 5, 8, 13. Then he tried to apply it to the message, if that is what it was, taking the letters in their places according to the rule. Nothing came of it. Then he tried it without the first number 1, reasoning that having two letters clearly written together would make the code too obvious. Nothing. Then he tried it using the Fibonacci numbers as the spaces to jump before the next signifier. Nothing again. This code business (even assuming it was a code) was pretty hard, also the letters seemed to jump around and several times he made a mistake in counting them.

Perhaps the thing to do was to write out the message in a strict array so it was easier to mark where he got up to? He fetched a fresh piece of paper and began to copy it out. As he did this, he realised that the VLF at the top would make a bizarre word by any method, it would have to begin VF. . . or VL. . . which was not possible. So then, what was this VLF at the top? Was it part of the message? If he left that out . . . He tried again, taking the letters in their places. No go. Then the sequence as letter jumps, which made it . . .

M – E – E – T – T – E – N – . . . It was making some sense, at least. He pressed on. He got lost when he had taken the thirteenth letter after the previous one, but realised he just had to start again with 1, 2, 3 and so on. Eventually, after a couple more mistakes, he had a message:

Meettennovsevenpmcaiuscoffeehouse

And with spaces put in: Meet Ten Nov seven pm Caius coffee house.

He had it! But, who was it for, and what was the meeting about, and why was it in that book, and why had he been sent the key to the cipher? And today was the fifteenth: so the tenth was last Thursday, so he had missed whatever it was.

And what should he do now? Apart from dancing a little jig at his success, that was, which he did very quietly, in case anyone should come up and ask what he was doing, and see his papers, and need an explanation.

He couldn't think of anything practical to do really, but he did think he ought to go and look into the coffee house opposite Caius, if only to examine the stable after the horse had departed. So, should he go now? It had grown dark while he had been puzzling the message out, and he had never been in there, and it would be much better to go with someone, especially walking across town at this hour.

Who though? Edward, or Abel, or Edward's roommate James Smith, though he didn't know him so well. On balance, Edward, he thought. He might welcome a trip out. Perhaps they should go at seven, just because . . . He would check the chapel clock, and then go and ask Edward a little before the hour.

As they walked up Trumpington-street Edward (who had had no objections at all to being disturbed) asked him again why they were trailing all this way when there was a perfectly reasonable coffee shop right opposite college.

'I said, I just fancied a change,' Richard said. Thinking he needed a bit more of a convincing reason, he cast around in his mind for an idea. 'Well, alright, I wasn't going to say, but this man I met in a lecture at King's said there was, er, a fine tempting armful serving there, and I wanted to go and have a quiz at her.'

'That's not like you, Rich. You don't normally go for the apple dumpling shop.'

'What? Where do you get these expressions from, Edward? Apple dumplings?'

'Yes, well,' he gestured around his chest, 'You know, the, er, lady-bumps.'

'Oh, I see. Well, he didn't say anything about her figure, he just said she was lovely to look at. Anyway, she might not be working this evening, I don't know, but I had had enough of irrational numbers and I wanted a break from reading.'

'Fair enough.' They had reached the shop and so entered. It was only about a third full. Richard chose a table in a rear corner where he could see the rest of the room, and they ordered chocolate, reasoning that coffee was too enlivening for the hour. Their serving-woman could not be any stretch of language be called Lovely to look at, being of a certain age and, well . . .

'Her apple dumplings fly below her waist,' murmured Edward to Richard once she had gone, and indeed they did.

Edward kept turning around to look for any of the other staff who might be more suitable targets for lust, but Richard kept still, leaning back a little into the shadows while looking to see if there might be areas of the shop where secrets might safely be discussed, such as in a snug in a tavern. There was what looked like a curtained booth near the back on the other side, which he thought of going to look into. While he watched, a youngish lady emerged, looking a little coloured up, and very pleased at something. She disappeared to the back of the house. Shortly after a gentleman emerged, still buttoning his fall. Richard looked away, not exactly shocked, more disapproving, and sad for the woman who was selling herself this way.

Their chocolate arrived, with a different waitress, thin and angular, and also past her prime. 'Not much luck so far,' said Edward, 'unless your friend meant the doxy that just left.'

'I don't think so,' said Richard. 'He definitely said, one of the servers.'

At that point there was a commotion at the door. Five men seemed to be trying to enter at the same time, indulging in an orgy of shoving and jostling and name-calling, all in what appeared to be good or even high spirits. Eventually they all tumbled in, and headed for a table by the window, calling for coffee and cards. They appeared to be young bucks, not of the University; or at least, none was wearing a gown, and by their spurs, they may have been out hunting. On the other hand, Richard had noticed that many men wore spurs to be in the fashion, rather than out of need.

One of them appeared to be the butt of several jokes, and was looking rather put-upon. He had his back to them, but there was something about the line of his shoulders . . . As he half-turned to look towards the counter, he suddenly realised. It was Charles! What was his brother doing here? And what was he to do?

Richard was filled with panic. He could not risk Charles seeing him, he would recognise Rose immediately in spite of her masculine clothes. Also, he felt sisterly concern for the poor lad, he wanted to rescue him from his tormentors, and he could do nothing. And there was Edward, already wondering why he had been brought here, even he would get suspicious if they suddenly upped and left.

He moved the candle on their table further forward, hoping the light would prevent anyone seeing his face behind it. Then he picked up a newspaper which was lying discarded on the bench by him, and lifted it as if to read.

'What are you looking at?' demanded Edward.

'I just wondered if there was anything interesting about the war,' Richard temporised. 'Why, did you want to have some scintillating conversation from me? I could tell you about irrational numbers if you like, that's all I have in my head at present.'

'Thanks,' said Edward, with heavy irony. 'I'll just cut my throat first, if you don't mind.'

Richard pretended to read the paper, thinking as fast as his wits would allow in their jangled state. He glanced up, saw the swells were milling around the table arguing as to who would sit where for their card game. It looked like Charles was going to be directly opposite, facing them. Time for action.

'Edward, how do you fancy having a look inside that alcove?' he asked, pointing. 'I wondered if it might be a good place for us to, er, organise some sort of get-together, sort of, private, you know.'

'What, you mean the two of us together with one public ledger? Bit of a challenge, eh?'

Richard had no idea what he was talking about, but rose and made for the closed curtain clutching his chocolate while Charles' attention was still focussed on the argument about table position. Edward followed, slowly, still looking around for the supposed lovely waitress.

Behind the curtain it was rather stuffy. There was a table and a couple of chairs, but also a couch which though it may have been put there for sitting on, had clearly been moved back for other purposes. There was a small window, which Richard opened, and although the candles flickered the air grew fresher.

'Finely appointed, I should say,' said Edward. 'Will you organise the Covent Garden Nun or do I have to?'

'What? Edward, I can't make you out. What are, what did you say, the nun, and the ledger?'

'Ladies of easy virtue, my lad. Doxies, whores.'

'I don't get you.'

'Public Ledger, open to all parties; Covent Garden Nun, an area of low repute, where there used to be a religious house and where many still attend to worship.'

'No, you Noddy! Not that sort of meeting. Oaf: I meant a quiet place where we could play cards for small stakes, as befits our impecuneity, or discuss topics of interest, or some such.'

'Oh. Well, maybe it's as well. Don't suppose you are up to it,' he nodded significantly.

'I expect not. After all, I am only sixteen. And you, are you a man of much experience, or is it all flim-flam?'

'Well, that would be telling.'

'That's a no, then. I thought not. Still it's no bad thing. Be a shame to go home at Christmas to your parents with the pox.'

'I'm not going home, it's too far, and too expensive on the coach.'

For a moment, Richard had the urge to invite him back with him for the festivities. Then he remembered. That would be impossible. He didn't know where he was spending the season himself yet, but it probably would be at Kilcott. No, impossible.

'So, what are you doing?'

'Staying in college, and doing some jobs to earn my keep, that's what. Mr Watkinson wants me to reorganise his books, and sort out his papers. I don't know if you've seen his rooms, but they're piled up to head height in places. There will be a few others of us around, so it won't be totally dull.'

Richard pulled his attention back to their predicament. Well, his predicament, really. From the sounds outside Charles and his friends were going to be there for hours. Snatches of speech came through to them: something about the races tomorrow; a demand for more coffee; a snatch that sounded like "apple dumplings" (!); complaints about how sticky the cards were.

Both of them had finished their chocolate. He gave a coin to Edward and asked him to pay, while he visited the necessary room. He was hoping there would be another door to the outside from there, to avoid going past the lads at the front. Edward got up and left, while he made sure he hadn't left anything behind. His newspaper had fallen under the table, so he stretched down to pick it up, scrabbling a bit under the seat. Deciding that the shop wouldn't miss it, it was three days old anyway, he stuffed it in his coat. Then, making sure his face was to the back of the room, he slipped out and headed for where he hoped was the passage.

As he turned into it, there was a loud Psst! from Edward. 'Is that who your friend meant?' he whispered, loudly.

There was a new girl coming out of the kitchen wiping her hands on a cloth. She certainly was not "of a certain age", not was she lacking in comeliness. Why now, thought Richard, just when we were about to escape?

He risked a glance. She was heading for the group by the window. Perhaps their attention would be taken by her, and they wouldn't see him standing in the shadows? Edward though was moving towards Charles and his friends. Good grief! What was he to do? The only thing was to leave, pretend to go to the necessary room, and then get out of the back if he could. And hope Edward came out eventually.

Luck was on his side. There was a door to the street. He went outside, walked down the lane back to Trumpington-street, and stood himself in a shop doorway opposite, in a position where he could see Edward leave the coffee shop, but he hoped, not be seen by those inside. His inside was churning, and he actually did need the privy, but there was no chance for now. He hoped Edward would get a move on.

Was he getting too entrenched in his role as Richard? He had actually found that young waiting-woman attractive. She had a great figure; Edward would probably have an argot word for it. Feeling this made him feel weird, unsettled. But then he had found several of the men he had met in the last few weeks attractive too. That had caused its own problems, remembering to behave properly, as a man. He had nearly slipped up a couple of times, to be fair. Meeting Mr Blackburn when he was Rose had been much simpler, well, more straightforward. Except that on the first occasion he went off to join the army immediately, and then when Rose met him in the hotel she was off to change into a boy the next day and she couldn't tell him anything important. So it was complicated in another way. Life: really, it was all most complex, puzzling. And now she was thinking like Edward, using two words when one would have done.

And here in the university there was so much more choice of men. Well, a lot of them were boys, or overgrown boys, really. Peter Winton, now, he was grown up, he was the sort of man she could . . . Better not go there. Any more than she ought to think of the boating men, all titled or related to titles. Not really accessible to a sister of a baronet, except in romantic novels. Even less so to a lad from the colonies with no connections of any note. And of course they wouldn't think of her (?him) in that way. She (he?) hadn't foreseen this when she planned her deception. He couldn't even keep track of his pronouns. Better stop thinking about Rose or you'll make some silly mistake.

At last, there was Edward at the threshold. He waved to someone inside, the windows were steamed up so he couldn't see whom. He waited until Edward had crossed the road, then headed towards him.

'Where've you been?' said Edward.

'I was waiting for you out here, like I said.'

'Well, you missed out big time. I attached myself to that group of lushey lads, so I could get a good look at her, well, charms. Your friend wasn't mistaken. She was a right good bit of muslin. I got a fair squint down her dress, too. I think she saw me, and she smiled.'

'They have to keep the customers happy, I suppose,' said Richard, somewhat waspishly.

Edward didn't seem to notice. 'And those hunting boys, they were a fine crew. Been making their way down from York towards Newmarket, as far as I could tell stopping at every tavern on the Great North Road. Lost a packet on the St Leger in September, and holed up at someone's pater's estate to recuperate for a while. Spot of hunting, spot of shooting. Off to Newmarket next, I think. Might have got that bit wrong. Anyway, a fun crowd. And good cover for me to look the wench over. She left: I left. So, back to irrational numbers for you?'

'Better had. I feel in the mood for them after this break,' he lied.

CHAPTER 17

UNSURPRISINGLY RICHARD COULDN'T CONCENTRATE ON his Maths or his Greek when he got back to his room. Edward talking about women in that way: well, he was used to it in a big group but this was more personal, more demeaning. Then there was seeing Charles: that was a close run thing. And thinking the maidservant attractive, and thinking about those other men, and Mr Blackburn, well, he would be churned up with that on its own. All together, it was far too disturbing to know what to do with himself.

Too early to go to bed; didn't want any supper after the chocolate; what then? He decided he'd look over the newspaper he'd picked up. Arranging the candle for best light he lay on the sofa and pulled it out of his pocket. A piece of paper fell on the floor. He picked it up, and was going to put it on the table when he saw what was written on it.

Intelligence from rgts
Information about pts
Responsible officers and degree of loyalty
Agents in post
Supplies of pdr and storage
Dates and times
Cipher for next month: π to 6sf

He dropped the newspaper and stared at the other. Sitting up and lifting it to the candlelight he recognised the trefoil watermark. Hurriedly he got up and found the other papers from his Horace. They matched exactly. So what on earth was going on? Had it been inside the newspaper, or had he picked it up from the floor inside the booth when he was scrabbling around? Who had been meeting, and what were they meeting about? If they had met on the tenth, how did the paper come to be still under the couch today? Surely the coffee house must sweep up every day or two at least? And what did the abbreviations mean?

He went to his desk and set out the papers. They seemed to be in the same writing, a rather careless hand. “Officers” made him think of the Army. So, was “rgts”, regiments? And “pdr”, powder? This looked like notes from the leader of the group to remind him what they had to discuss at the meeting. If so, they were very amateur, leaving such things lying around. The same went for the coded message in the chemistry book here in Emmanuel. Was there someone at this college involved in this, well, secret group? And why had he of all people been sent the cipher for the following message? Messages, probably.

He looked again at the briefest message. “Fibonacci to 13”. It didn’t tell him any more than it already had. He turned it over. Inspected the address: “Mr R Cox, Emmanuel College”. That was him, or at least his alias. He looked again, the last letter, “x” was quite scruffy, as if it had been crossed more than once. In fact, it looked a bit like it was a badly formed “k” with something run into it. Could it be “rk”? Which would mean, it was meant for Mr R Cork? Robert Cork? Whom he knew, if only slightly.

An idea came into his mind. Mr Cork had his rooms on this very staircase, on the first floor, on the opposite side to him. And many people were careless about locking their doors, in fact most people didn’t bother at all, as the porters kept undesirables out of college, and the bedders were always in and out of the rooms in any case. Could he go and have a look round his set while he was out? It was rather underhand, but if these people were gathering intelligence about regiments and powder supplies, it might be something very wrong that was going on, and the right people ought to be told about it.

Also it could be dangerous for him, if Robert returned while he was looking. Unless he had an excuse for being in his room, perhaps? Such as, well, he could be looking to borrow a book, maybe? He could look to see which books Robert had out when he was next on library duty, and then he would know to ask for one Robert actually had.

Whom could he tell? And what could he tell them at this stage? It all must look a bit thin so far, these cryptic messages, and the meeting (or meetings) at the coffee house. It would be better if he could find out a bit more before thinking whom to tell. Well, he could let George know, he supposed, he worked in the Foreign Office, but he was a long way off in London. Also, he would quite like to show George that he wasn't the little sister any more, he was an independent person. He'd think about this one.

Lying in bed that night he wondered how he could find out when Robert was going to be definitely elsewhere. And of course it would have to be at a time when the bedders and gyp were off duty. And his door would need to be unlocked. Richard didn't think he had the skills with picklocks that would be needed even on such a simple lock as these doors sported. Also, of course, he had no picklocks, and no idea where he would get them anyway.

On Wednesday morning he couldn't wait for his next duty, but slipped into the library after chapel and looked through the borrowing slips. Yes, there was a suitable book lent out to R Cork: Lavoisier's *Traité Élémentaire de Chimie.* He would say he had something from a lecture he wanted to look up. If he were spotted in Robert's room. Which he hoped he wouldn't be.

Then, how would he know when the room would be empty? What did Robert do during the day? He didn't think he was much of a reading man, apart from his interest in chemistry, but beyond that, he was ignorant. He didn't like to ask the porters, it would look odd. Besides, they might tell Robert that Richard had been asking after him. Who would know? Well, Peter might. He had seemed quite friendly with him. As he was with an inordinate amount of people for someone who had only just come up. He had a lecture to attend in the Schools, so he couldn't do anything for now. Later, though, if his nerve held.

Happily Peter Winton was at the lecture, it being on Greek verse, and he said he believed Robert went out for long solitary rides most days that he wasn't hunting or taking his gun out with his friends. He had seen him go off on one this morning, in fact. Why did Richard want to know?

'Oh, nothing really. I just thought, he lives on my staircase but I never see him around. I know he dines at High Table, but he is often not there either. I just wondered, that's all.' It didn't sound too convincing, but it was the best he could do.

'Friendly warning, though, Richard. I wouldn't think he was a very good person for you to get to know too well. There's just something about him, a feeling I have.'

'Oh. Well, thanks, but I wasn't thinking of it, it was just curiosity.'

'Good.'

Richard took himself back across town rapidly, and after jettisoning his gown in his room, and making sure Mrs Fenn had gone for the morning (no bucket on the stairs, the mop and broom cupboard locked) he steeled himself for his act of burglary. Assuming the door was unlocked. He half hoped it wouldn't be, if he were honest with himself. It wasn't the sort of thing he did, and Rose would have been shocked at it if she hadn't already got used to so many other things that would previously have shocked her during this term.

Descending the stairs quietly he paused on the first floor landing. Everything was quiet except his heartbeat. He listened with his ear to the door, tried the handle with clammy hands. It opened; he slid inside, and shut it behind him carefully and silently.

The room was as big as the set that Edward and James shared, and much more luxuriously furnished. There was no sign of a desk, just settles and armchairs and a table covered in a luxurious Persian rug in the old-fashioned style, and hunting pictures on the wall. There were boots with spurs, and several whips, and a hat he supposed was a hunting tile. Also a well-stocked drinks tray and glasses that matched, unlike his and Edward's. It came to him that he wasn't sure what he was looking for, really. Just something that might be a clue. Papers, perhaps?

He looked into one of the two rooms beyond the keeping-room: it was a bedroom with the bed neatly made and nothing out of place. He left it undisturbed, and went into the other, which rather that another bed as in Edward's set, contained a magnificent desk, several bookcases, and two large mirrored sconces on the wall to illuminate reading. The bookcases were not very full, but there were some volumes piled on the desk. He quickly looked through those, checking for papers that might have been slipped into them, but they were all clear. Chemistry titles, including the Lavoisier he had found on the lending slips, as well as Boyle; some mathematics, Euclid and a couple of others; and some classical texts. It looked like Robert was intending to learn enough for an honours degree, even if not exerting himself to excellence given how much of a sporting man he was. After all, he would have the Little-go next term, he would need to pass that even for an ordinary degree.

Papers. Where were papers? There were no more on the desk. What about the drawers? No luck. The pigeon-holes? No. Richard cast around, looked for places that might conceal a sheet of guilty secrets. He looked in all the bookshelves, and then, returning to the dresser in the keeping-room, opened its drawers too. And then he saw a corner of a sheet protruding from under the tray on which stood a crystal decanter. Lifting the tray carefully he drew it out. It was covered with the same meaningless drivel as the other one! Huzza!

He set the tray down carefully, and considered the paper. He needed to decode it, and so he would have to copy it. It would be far safer to do so in his own room. He slipped it in his coat, and left, as silently as he could, relieved at being out of the zone of risk.

Hands trembling he took quill and ink and copied the strange lines as quickly and carefully as he could. Leaving the paper to dry on his desk he again put the original in his pocket and tiptoed down the stairs. Just as he was approaching Cork's room, a voice hailed him.

'What-ho, Richard!' It was Edward, returning from his tutorial with Mr Watkinson, together with James Smith. 'Not deep in Euclid, you brainy cove?'

'Sorry, can't stop, have an urgent appointment with the Spice Islands,' he said as he pushed past his friend.

'Sorry?'

Over his shoulder Richard called back, 'The privy! Don't say I know some argot you don't?' and hurried across the grass holding his tummy for effect.

After a suitable interval enthroned over the pit, Richard returned, cautiously. He entered the staircase, ascended one floor. No sounds. He listened at Cork's door, entered, replaced the sheet as accurately as he could where he had found it, and left, heart hammering again. Then, banging up the rest of the stairs he pounded on Edward's door and barged in without invitation.

Only James was at home, he told him Edward had gone straight out again. Puzzled, Richard carried on up the stairs and found Edward in his room by his desk, looking at his transcription of the note! He had forgotten to lock his door in his haste to return the paper.

'What's this old fustian?' asked Edward, almost accusingly.

'Oh, that.' Richard thought furiously. 'Oh, it's just maths nonsense I found in an old number theory book.'

'You're bamming me. Come on, the ink was barely dry when I came in.'

'Anyway, what are you doing in my room?'

'Why not, we're Trojans together, aren't we?'

'Well, yes, but that paper's private.'

'So why does it start off with "Vive La France?"'

'It doesn't.'

'That's what VLF means, you natural. From the revolution, you know. Had you heard there was one going on over there?'

'Duh!'

'So, come on, what is it?'

'I can't tell you.'

'Are you a revolutionary? Sent over by the Acadians to plot against us? Planning to set up a guillotine in Chapel Court?'

Looking at Edward's face, a mixture of disappointment and frustration, Richard gave in. 'Well, I'll tell you, but you can't let on to a soul. Promise?'

'On Holy Water,' he said, grabbing Richard's whisky bottle.

'Well it's like this.' Richard explained about the other papers, and how he had gone looking for clues in Cork's room, and showed Edward how the sheets had the same trefoil watermark, and the one he had replaced had had the same. He told him about finding the list of items of business in the coffee house, and how he was wondering what to do next.

'Obvious, cub. Translate the new message.' Edward looked excited now.

Richard set to with the first six significant figures of Pi, 314159, with Edward leaning over his shoulder and hindering him with helpful suggestions. In spite of this he soon had the message unravelled. The original nonsense:

> VLF
> Pi now can define real numeral, or rad. give to centre marks.
> Aspic tanks of the finest low musts, less can their ninth four earn laying down fifth setting.

became "Powder arrives Pink Houses Thur. night", after only a few false transcriptions. He sat back and looked at it. 'Powder must be gunpowder,' he observed.

'Well it's obvious what to do now,' said Edward.

'Is it?'

''Course. We go and hide by the crib and watch the stuff getting delivered, to make sure of our facts. Then we go to the powers and authorities.' He paused. 'Well, that's as long as we can find out where the pink houses are by tomorrow. Could be anywhere.'

'On the river,' said Richard, feeling pleased with himself. 'Just past the end of Chesterton village. I've seen them when I've been out boating with those Jesuits and Peter Winton. Anyway, what do you mean, "we"?'

'I'm in on this with you now. What a lark!'

Richard wasn't so sure. This was his puzzle. He had wanted to solve it all by himself. But, whatever he may have been thinking earlier, and however scared he had been of searching Cork's room for clues, this was a whole new lay, and a queer one at that. He wasn't at all keen on going on his own, at night, to spy on the writers of these messages. It felt very unsafe, dangerous in the extreme. He didn't want to tell Edward that, though. He had a thought.

'Who are the, er, powers and authorities in this case, do you think?'

'Ah. Yes. Well, not the Master, naturally. Or our tutors, or, well, any of the Fellows, they'd be hopeless. And Cambridge doesn't have anything like the Bow Street Runners in London. You have me there.'

'Who could we ask about it, I mean, who would know who to tell?'

'Nescio.'

'Who's he?'

'I thought you knew Latin? It means, I don't know; or, in Cambridge anyway, any sort of negative. Or so I read in my guidebook. I quite like sounding classical at times, you see.'

'Sorry, I wasn't concentrating properly. Yes, I mean, no, I mean, I don't know either.' He bit his lip. 'If we go out at night we'll be in the porters' book, and in trouble with our tutors.'

'No problem. A man showed me a good bit of wall with a few bricks loose at the end of the Close, we can get out and back in there. It'll be dark, we'll be fine.'

'And think how risky it would be going all that way at night. We might be caught by the proctors without our gowns.'

'Not if we go across Jesus Green and across the sluice there.'

'And I've heard Chesterton's a rough place.'

'Not as bad as Barnwell, though. Some of the men go and play billiards in Chesterton, I've heard. They say it's alright there. Are you chicken-hearted, then?'

'Well, yes, a bit. I mean, these men might be desperados.'

'I thought you said they were University people?'

'Well, I thought so, but they could have, what so you call them, accomplices. I mean, who's going to be bringing the gunpowder to the Pink Houses? It would probably be coming by river, so, um, would it be on a barge? Which would mean bargees, I don't fancy meeting them at night.'

'We would be in hiding, though.'

'Umm . . .'

'Come on, it's too good a chance to miss out on.'

Richard screwed up his courage. A real man would have done this without shrinking, but he was, well, when it came down to it, a girl. A girl who felt vulnerable and always thought of all the things that could go wrong in advance, to make sure she was prepared. He had planned his impersonation so carefully he had believed it would work, and it had, but he couldn't know all the things that might happen on this escapade, he couldn't plan for them. Still, he had to do it, he couldn't back out now.

'All right then. I'm on. What time do you think we should set out?

'The message said, Thursday night, didn't it? So that could be any time after dark. Which is about five o'clock. So, we had better leave about five, because they'll want to be sure it's fully black before they do whatever they are doing, but if the powder is coming by barge they won't want to be too late because of leading the horse along the towpath. Unless there's a moon? Is there one? I haven't noticed.'

'Nor me. I have an almanac, though.'

After consulting the tables they determined the moon would be only a couple of days from new, so it would be very dark. Also the weather of late had been overcast, but they thought it would be a bad idea to take any sort of light.

Richard looked at Edward. 'If we left a bit earlier, we could get there in the dusk, and we could go out of college the regular way, and not have to sign the book, and then we wouldn't have to risk the wall twice, and, well, if we got it all done early, I mean before ten, we could just come in by the Lodge.'

'Yes, but we wouldn't have our gowns. You're not thinking of doing all this in academical dress, are you?'

'No, I forgot.'

'But you're right, we ought to get there in the light so we can see where we're going. Should we do a reconnaissance before? Like today?'

'No, I don't want to do that, we'll just go tomorrow. Just remember, don't tell anyone else about this business, not any of your friends, not James, nobody. Got it?'

'On Holy Water,' he repeated, taking the whisky bottle again and this time having a swig from it. 'This stuff is disgusting, Cox. Why do you drink it?'

There was quite a bit more of this on and off over the rest of that day, whenever he and Edward were together and not overheard. Richard was reassured to some degree by having Edward come with him, but he still didn't know who they were going to tell about whatever they found. Then a little before supper time he had an idea, and cursed himself for not thinking of it before. He could write to Sir George, could he not? He would know, he worked for the Foreign Office, and if this had something to do with France, he would want to be informed. He probably knew people in Cambridge who were involved with the government in some way. In fact, what had he been doing in the hours between saying goodbye and the night coach leaving from the Eagle and Child? Perhaps he was having secret meetings about government business? After all, he didn't really know what George did all day in his job. Maybe he was some kind of spy? Also, he had had a meeting with someone in Trinity earlier on the same day. Was he involved in the same business?

He wrote a short letter, keeping to the main facts:

> I have come across several coded messages which I have been able to translate. It seems there is a group of men who meet and plan something to do with France, as their communications begin "VLF" for "Vive La France". They talk of intelligence about regiments, and information about "pts" which item I have not understood. Also, there is to be a delivery of powder, we think this must be gunpowder. I am going to watch the house where the powder is to arrive with Edward Hever, but we will need to inform someone in authority once we know the identity of more of the group. Do you have any contacts here? Please let me know as soon as possible because it may be important.

Sanding it, he addressed it to Sir George at the Foreign Office, Whitehall, hoping he might receive it there sooner than if it was sent to his apartment. He took it to the porters' lodge and asked how he might dispatch it urgently. Mr Chapman offered to have it taken round to the Eagle and Child to catch the evening mail. Sir George might get it tomorrow, with luck.

On Thursday he found it hard to concentrate on his Mathematics, although there was a lecture in college on parallelepipeds which ought to have been fascinating but somehow he kept losing the thread. He went for a walk around town, just to clear his head, but found he kept overthinking the whole business. For a start, just who might be in the gang, if that is what it was? Robert Cork, obviously, he must be in on it. He was quite friendly with John Burgess, he'd seen them talking at least twice, he might be involved. What about Peter Winton? He seemed to know far more people than he ought to for a new student, and he knew Cork and Burgess, in fact he'd met both of them at the party Peter had invited him to. And then after that? He couldn't think of anyone else that seemed suspicious, but then, if you were plotting, you would take care not to seem suspicious, wouldn't you?

And then, he kept running over the way they would go to Chesterton, and how they might hide, and what he would do if they had to stay out all night, would he get too cold, and how would he answer calls of nature with Edward at his elbow, and how would they find their way back in the dark, and hundreds of other such worries.

In amongst the fruitless churning he did have one useful idea. How about they left college in gowns, and hid them somewhere in case they could return before ten, and then they could just walk into college before the gate was locked, and nobody would know where they had been. And if they were as late as midnight, they could ring to be let in, and it wouldn't be too bad for their record as a first occasion of lateness.

As he wandered around, he passed Sidney Sussex college, and was irritated to recall that Edward had told him it was known as the Dust-hole. He kind of liked Edward, but he was also irritated by him, by his endless recital of information he found interesting, but at the moment by his barging in on his secret. He was surprised to have a thought that what he needed at the moment was the company of some females, girls he could just talk with about this plan, but also about feminine trivia, to feel he belonged here. It was all very well indulging his urges for knowledge, but he wasn't cut out for a pure and monastic academia, not like Mr James. He wanted, he wished for, well . . . if only he could be here as a girl, on equal terms with the men, and able to be friends with both sexes. Still, that was never going to happen.

He turned into Green-street and looked in a few shops to divert his mind, forgetting himself for a moment and examining the ribbons in a haberdasher's window until a group of town girls coming out of the shop giggled at him as they passed. He muttered something about "having to get something for my sister's birthday", and hurried away. As he came into Trumpington-street and turned towards the older buildings of Caius he saw a man in a gown heading into the college by the gate opposite St Michael's church. He only saw him for a moment but he became unaccountably convinced it was Mr Blackburn. He had the same bearing, and was of a like height, with hair as far as he could see of a similar colour. What was he doing in Cambridge? Should he go and look for him, or ask the porter if he was indeed in college?

In a moment he had discounted those ideas. He was Richard, after all, and even after their two brief meetings Mr Blackburn would be bound to recognise him. Or recognise Rose, anyway. Whatever. He'd better just go back to Emmanuel and have a bite to eat, and get stuck into his chemistry book, before dinner.

Nonetheless he couldn't resist pausing at the gate and looking into the garden beyond in case the man had lingered. No such luck, but he thought he saw his black silhouette vanishing through an archway. He sighed.

CHAPTER 18

BY FOUR O'CLOCK RICHARD WAS as ready as he ever would be. He had avoided drinking too much since returning to college, and had made sure he was wearing his blue worsted stockings which would be less conspicuous that the white ones. He had his scarf and gloves, and his hat, and some bread in his pocket in case of hunger. Also, a lead pencil and some paper in case they needed to make notes of what they found. And, hidden away in his waistcoat, a small flask of his whisky in case he needed to boost his courage or warm his inner man. But where was Edward? He had said four, hadn't he? Straight after dinner?

Edward came sailing into his room about a quarter after four, looking carefree. 'Shall we be off?' he said, and turned on his heel and left without waiting for an answer. Richard picked up his gown and followed, glad that at least Edward had agreed to his plan about hiding the academicals outside for later retrieval.

Richard looked, but Edward didn't seem to be carrying anything useful with him, as he was. Then, after they had gone through the gates and out of sight of the porters, he showed him a tinderbox and a candle. Richard cursed under his breath for not having thought of this, except, he supposed, that as he didn't have such a useful object in his possession, he couldn't have brought it. Oh well.

They went by Emmanuel-lane to Christ's pieces, where they hid their gowns in a dense bush. Richard was surprised and pleased to find Edward had scouted this place earlier. Then, over Jesus Green to cross the river over the weir, which Richard found quite scary, and next a short walk across the fields to the Chesterton road. Edward had wanted to go by the towing path, which was a shorter and simpler route, but Richard reasoned that it was possible that the Pink Houses would have some occupant looking out at the river for the delivery of the powder, and would observe them arriving so openly.

As they entered the village it was already quite dark, and very few houses had any light above their doors, except the taverns which were just setting their wicks in order and kindling a welcoming flame as they passed. There was a faint gleam from the church over towards the river, and a few house windows glowing dully, but as they passed through to the end of the village it was almost black night apart from a feeble lightening of the sky fading in the west behind them.

Richard hadn't counted on this. He wasn't sure which way to go, and it was difficult to stay on the road, being unable to see its edge, but Edward confidently led them on, taking the right hand turn when one offered, and pointing out in a low voice that he could now see a hint of open water across a small field, so they must be nearly there.

The road was now little more than a muddy track full of stones, which it was easy to trip on. It bent a little to the right, and then they saw up ahead a glimmer of yellow light, as if from a tallow candle, faintly outlining a small window. Surely this must be their goal? Edward held out an arm to check Richard, and then they moved forward more slowly close together, trying as best they could to stay silent.

Gradually they worked their way forward to the broken-down boundary of the property, and halted under some stunted trees to consider where best to site themselves to observe events. Edward wanted to be close enough to overhear anything said in the houses, but Richard thought they ought to keep their distance, and just be near enough to the river to watch the arrival of any barge or other craft, which would surely carry lights for the unloading.

In the end they found, mostly by touch, a place where the boundary fence met the towing path hedge, which was overgrown and fairly sheltered by overhanging branches. It was damp, to be sure, and the ground was cold, but they could see after a fashion towards the house, whose river frontage was in darkness, and rather better towards the river. There was even a small pile of logs to sit on, and so they settled down to wait.

It seemed Edward was not very good at doing nothing. Richard felt him fidgeting almost as soon as they had sat down. Within a few minutes he was on his feet again, and peering out into the blackness. Every movement made a rustling sound, which Richard feared would be overheard, and he tugged on Edward's sleeve to keep still, but to little effect. After only fifteen or so minutes Edward whispered that he was going to creep across the grass to the lit window and see what he could see or hear. Richard tried to hold him back but he was gone, cracking a few twigs on his way out of their den.

Without his warm presence Richard started to feel that the night was even blacker than before, the screen of branches more inadequate, and that his breathing and even his heartbeat must be audible to anyone who might chance near. He took out his flask and sipped, cautiously. The whisky burned and warmed him all down his gullet, and he replaced the cap and put the flask away deep inside his clothes. He wound his scarf around his neck and put his gloves on, even though it was not all that cold as yet. He waited.

Chesterton church clock struck the half hour. Nothing. He rubbed his arms together to raise a little warmth, stretched out one leg to relieve its position. Felt a need to relieve himself, which was ridiculous as he had only visited the privy immediately after Hall, and not drunk anything since lunchtime. Waited.

Just when he was fearing that Edward had been caught by whoever was in the house and imprisoned, he returned. He hardly knew he was coming until a branch, ever so slightly darker against the sky, moved, and some leaves crackled.

'There are two people in that back room,' he whispered. 'One looks like a countrywoman, she might be the woman of the house, and the other is a gentleman of some sort, he has a cutaway coat and polished boots, but I couldn't see his face, he had his back to me. They aren't doing anything much, she is sewing or something by the light of a smoky candle, and he is lounging back in a chair and smoking a cigar. They seem to be waiting. That's all. The man did say something to the woman from time to time, but I couldn't quite hear what. She shook her head, and seemed to tell him to just have patience, or not to fret, that kind of thing.'

'Did the man have a hat?' asked Richard, thinking of Robert Cork and his hunting gear.

'Couldn't see one. But he'd likely have left it in the hall, if he did.'

They settled down again to wait. At least, Richard did, comforted by feeling the warmth of Edward's body next to his. Edward of course kept shifting position, wriggling, making small noises in his throat. At one point he got up to relieve himself just behind their perch, which Richard found somewhat disconcerting. Nonetheless he was so glad that he hadn't had to keep this vigil on his own. He didn't like to think what he would have done, even if he had dared to set out to keep watch. He might have turned back at the edge of Chesterton village, before he even got to the area of danger, or turned tail once he saw the lights of this house. Maybe men did have some qualities that were better than women's, even if women were far superior in most ways? Including sitting still, she thought, as Edward got up again to stretch himself.

At least, if there was a gentleman waiting inside the house, the delivery ought to be coming fairly soon. Also, if it was coming by river, as seemed most likely, due to the position of the house, the bargees wouldn't want to make too much distance after nightfall because of the horses. She hoped.

The clock struck six. They waited.

If they had to stay out past ten o'clock, he thought, and had to scale the wall, how am I going to avoid Edward touching me too intimately as we help each other over? Because, if he grabs my bottom to shove me up, or we come together on top of the wall, or he catches me as I land on the other side, he will feel that my body is not of the same quality as a man's, even though I do have muscles, and quite thick layers of clothing. He might feel I am softer, and more pliant, and then what would I do? I'm sure he couldn't keep my secret for an hour, he's just not capable of it, and it would make him lose his mind to be around a boy who was really a girl and stay natural.

'Edward,' he whispered, 'how long do you think we should wait, if nothing happens?'

'Quiet,' he hissed. 'I think I can hear something.'

Richard strained his ears. There was a faint clinking, as of metal on metal. Or was there? It seemed to come and go. And was that a muffled thudding, or just his imagination?

'I think I can hear a barge,' Edward breathed. 'Or a horse, at any rate.'

Minute by minute they became more sure of the sounds. Then, someone's voice, cursing by the tone. A plashing of water, a creaking of wood. 'What should we do?' asked Richard.

'Nothing, chucklehead, just wait.' Edward got up and moved a little to the river side of their hideout, peering through the gap in the branches. Richard strained his ears.

As the barge approached he began to see a light on the river. He could smell the horse, a dusty, musty but distinctly horsy smell of hay and sunshine mixed with sweat. He could hear the heavy hooves on the muddy towpath. He even thought he could sense the men working the great boat, leading the horse, steering into the bank right by them. He almost stopped breathing, fearing giving his presence away.

Someone opened the garden gate, a shadow slid past their hide, then there was a quiet knock on the door away to their left. Men were grunting, lifting, rolling heavy somethings off the boat along a plank, as far as he could see by the light that spilled from the hold. He tried to count the somethings, he thought there were six, they might be barrels of some sort. Nobody spoke, except odd words of warning, of command to lift, or catch hold, or move along.

Someone was coming out of the house, carrying a lantern. It seemed to be the man in the cutaway, his face was yellow in the lamplight. Richard couldn't quite see him, the bushes were in the way. He tried to move but Edward's body blocked him, and he didn't want to risk moving away and breaking twigs.

'You're late' said the man from the house.

'Trouble with the lock-keeper at Baits-bite, didn't want to let us through after dark,' said someone in rough tones.

'Well, at least you're here. Do you have the goods?'

'Right you are, Mr Cork. Six barrels of . . . flour, as ordered,'

'No names,' the man hissed. 'If your men don't know things they can't tell them.'

'Right you are,' he repeated.

The gentleman seemed to lean over the first barrel, tug at something, take a pinch of the contents, taste it. 'Seems pukkah,' he said. 'I'd better check the others, we don't want to make, shall we say, tasteless bread, do we?'

'You're the boss, mister.'

The man moved along the cargo, checking its contents. Apparently satisfied, he stood back and the bargees rolled the barrels up the path and lifted them into the house. There was a clinking as of coins, many coins, being handed over. Richard tried to work out where the barrels were being stored, but all the curtains on this side were drawn. The men left the house, the gentleman said a brief thanks, and closed the door behind him. On the bank, more bumps and bangs, but little talk, then the horse moved on, rope sliding over grass and flopping into the water; a creak as it took the strain, and the dark bulk of the barge slipped away into the night, faint gleams from its lights reflecting off the water.

Richard let himself breathe again more freely. He found he was rigid with tension, he tried to relax his muscles, drop his shoulders. So it was true, there *was* something serious going on, and Robert Cork was involved up to his neck.

Edward beside him was shifting his post, pressing against him. He stumbled against a low branch, caught hold of Richard by the shoulders. Richard immediately felt anxious of discovery, but also felt something he couldn't identify at the physical contact.

'That was a bit of a squib,' he stated, 'not a lot of action. Do you think we should try and get into the house?'

'No!' squeaked Richard. 'Don't even think of it. We have to get away quietly and, um, tell someone who knows what to do about these things.'

'That Cork fellow will be going back to town soon, I imagine. Should we wait and follow him?'

'We'd be sure to be seen. There aren't many people out at this hour, especially university types, in Chesterton at any rate.'

'We could see where he goes. He might be going to report to his superior.'

'He'll probably be going back to his room on our stair.'

Just then a side door opened. A figure was briefly silhouetted against the light within, and then it came out, carrying a lantern. Before they could do anything, it had gone behind the house, and then reappeared in brief flickers as the man walked away along the track towards Chesterton.

'Well, that settles it. We're too late to follow him.'

'You're right, for once. So, do we go? Can we go along the towing path? It'd be a lot easier.'

'We might be seen by the men in that barge. It must have moored somewhere along the river, we'd have to pass it.'

'Good point. Did you get its name? I saw it was a King's Lynn boat, and the name was Prince something.'

'No, I'm sorry, I was concentrating on the man from the house. Cork, that is.'

'You'll never make a spy.'

Richard felt hurt. He said nothing, but followed Edward out of the thicket and across the field to the road just along from the house. It had been his discovery after all, and he hadn't wanted to bring Edward really. And they had discovered quite a lot tonight, actually. They just had to find someone to tell. They walked in silence.

'Hey, look,' whispered Edward after a while. Across this little field: there's a barge, it's all on its own, not tied up in a group like they usually are. I'm going to have a look.'

He set off the short distance to the river, and Richard reluctantly followed. Even though his eyes were fully adjusted to the dark, he couldn't see where Edward had gone, and he stumbled on the uneven surface. Eventually, close by the hedge, he heard the sound of breathing.

'Edward?'

'Quiet. I'm trying to see the boat's name.'

Richard moved to one side, and peered through the hedge. He couldn't see anything useful, just a vague shape, with a couple of small lit windows at the rear. Edward seemed to be trying to slip through the hedge, he held out an arm to stop him but it was too late. He'd gone. Richard didn't know what to do. He stayed stock still, and prayed.

A few moments later Edward was back. 'Black Prince, it is. Worth finding that out. And it looks as if this road joins the towing path in a bit, by a tavern, so we could get back on the riverbank and miss out Chesterton.'

They worked their way around, and sure enough came out on the towing path by the Pike and Eel inn. They marched rapidly along the path, found the sluice, and crossed back into Cambridge. With every step Richard felt less nervous, and once they had retrieved their gowns and were strolling nonchalantly (he hoped) along Emmanuel-lane, he started to feel elated. They had done it.

CHAPTER 19

NO SOONER THAN THEY HAD entered Emmanuel than Richard stopped, causing Edward who was eyeing a woman in the street to bump into him.

'What'you doing? Keep moving.'

'I've had a thought'

'Not really?'

'Mr Cork will have likely come back along the road and over the Great Bridge. Yes?'

'Maybe. I s'pose.'

'So, it's only, what,' he squinted at the clock across the court, 'eight o'clock, nearly, we came back a shorter way, so he might not have got to town yet. We could go and hang around on Bridge-street and see if he comes by, and then we could follow him to see where he goes.'

'I thought we'd finished with all this?'

'Well, we could leave it. But I want to see who else is in the gang, and I'd rather go with someone.' He had a thought. 'We could wait for them in the Pickerel or one of the other inns along there.'

'Now you're talking.'

Keeping a close look out in case they passed Cork on the way, they found themselves settled in the Pickerel Inn just over the bridge, with a good view of the roadway. It was dark, to be sure, but there were lights over the inn and over Magdalene opposite, and even some in the street itself, obviously new. Richard perched on a high stool by the window, eyes fixed on the passers-by, while Edward reluctantly fetched the drinks. Even though Richard had provided the blunt he looked as though he felt he oughtn't to be doing this, somehow.

Edward took a loud slurp of his ale and looked condescendingly at Richard's whisky. 'You want a proper drink, you do,' he asserted. You're not Scots, anyhow.'

'I like it, thanks. It's the water of life, so they say.'

'Not much water in it, I'd be bound. Too fiery for me.'

Richard was sure they would only have just reached the junction of Bridge-street and Trumpington-street in time to see Cork returning, and hoped they hadn't been too late. If they hadn't missed him, he ought to be along pretty soon. Well within an hour. So, if he hadn't come past by nine, they'd go back to college, and he might even be able to read a bit of his Horace before bed.

Once Edward had finished his pint he looked at Richard's glass in disgust. It was still barely touched. 'What's wrong? Don't you like your firewater?'

'It's fine. Quite good in fact. Why don't you try some?'

Edward took a cautious sip. He coughed, banged the glass down, coughed some more. 'Must have gone down the wrong way,' he said once he could speak. 'I'm getting more beer. Want another?'

'Not yet.' Richard was abstracted, most of his mind was on the road.

When Edward returned with his drink he brought with him several men whom he introduced as Trusty Trouts that he knew from somewhere or other that Richard didn't take in. Either way, they seemed to be mostly drinking friends, and although they had sizars' gowns they seemed fairly free with their spending on ale. Richard had long given up on remembering Edward's new argot that he was always picking up, so he avoided asking about the Trouts and just kept his eye on the roadway, and sipped his whisky.

It was not until Edward and his crowd had gone for a further refill that he saw him. Cork, ambling along, looking just as though he had been for a short stroll, not like a man who had walked all the way from beyond Chesterton. He had laid aside his lantern and acquired a gown somewhere. Perhaps he had stopped in a tavern in Chesterton or nearby in Castle End for the purpose. That would explain why he had taken so long. Richard tossed back the remains of his glass and was off. Edward he left to it, he was far too involved with the other men.

Cork was easy to follow. He went slowly, he didn't look around, he gave a perfect impression of an undergraduate returning from a soiree of some sort in a chap's rooms, taking a constitutional before bedtime. He turned off Bridge-street by the Round church, passed John's without a glance. Would he be going to Trinity, or maybe to Caius? For a moment he stopped by All Saints' church, and Richard shrank into the shadows beyond the yales of John's entrance, but it seemed he had only been spoken to by an acquaintance, because he then crossed the street and passed under the Great Gate.

Trinity? Did that mean he was going to see Mr Burgess? Richard followed, keeping what he thought was a safe distance, trying to look as if he too was simply going to visit a friend for supper. Cork crossed Great Court, and entered a staircase. Hurrying a little, Richard reached the stair in time to hear that he was still ascending. That ruled out the ground floor rooms, at any rate. He did not wish to follow his quarry up the stair, but he had his pencil and paper, and he could note down the names of the men who resided here, painted upon the jamb with their room numbers. He could just about make them out in the light of the lamp above the door. Preston, Telmann, Hope, Price, Surtees, Noakes. There, it was one of these.

He stepped back into the court, and looked up. Most of the windows showed lights through their curtains, but some did not. That eliminated Preston and Telmann; also Surtees. So, his man must be Hope or Price or Noakes. Satisfied for now, he decided he ought to return to Emmanuel. After all, it was now a quarter before ten. He hurried out of Great Court, through the town, and soon was passing under the classical pediment of his alma mater before the chapel clock struck the hour. He was home, safe and considerably better informed about this conspiracy, whatever it was.

Friday was very busy. Before chapel Richard had some maths to read, then after breakfast he had a lecture to attend in college, then another in the Botanic gardens down Bird-Bolt-lane, (as he had decided not to only attend those professors designated by his tutor). Then at the lunch hour there was an extra tutorial with Mr Laughton to fit in, which he had requested on Tuesday to deal with some problems he had with conic sections. At least the four-oar wasn't due out today.

On this occasion his visit was without Edward as it was essentially a problem session, and by the time he returned he had of course missed lunch and was hungry for dinner. He spent most of the walk to and from Grantchester worrying about communicating his intelligence about the conspirators, and wondering if Sit George would have got his letter yet. It was only when he returned to college that he realised he hadn't seen Edward all day.

He was however present at dinner, unreasonably still nursing a sore head, and full of self-pity. It seemed that the Trusty Trouts, ie his good friends, had moved on from the Pickerel to the Cock and Magpie further down Bridge-street, and thence by an avian association to the Eagle and Child in St Bene't-street. He had tried to climb into college by the wall he had told Richard about previously, but found it too difficult with his level of disguisement, and he had had to knock up the porter and be noted in the late book, else he would have spent a most chilly night in the fields behind the college. He only picked at his meal, which was understandable given his greenish colour.

It was at this point that Peter Winton came into Hall, somewhat late, looking apologetically up to High Table, relieved to see only two Fellows present yet again, together with the Master. He slid onto the bench besides Richard and started to help himself to the meats and pies.

'Can I have a word with you after Hall,' he said in a low voice. It's quite important.

'Surely. Do you need me to help you with your Greek?'

'If you want to make a cake of yourself, lad. No, listen, it really is important. I have had a letter from Sir George Clarke, your sponsor.'

'Sir George?'

'The same. He tells me, well, it had better wait until we are private, I believe.'

'Absolutely. Sir George, wrote to *you*?'

'You catch on fast, Richard. Now eat your dinner; I'm starving. The news can wait for a few minutes.'

Richard couldn't think what could have occasioned George writing to Peter. He didn't know him, for a start. Or did he? All sorts of wild ideas flew around in his head. He was about to be turned out of college for some infraction of rules of which he was unaware. He had been discovered to be a girl by some unknown person, and George wanted him away before there was a general scandal. George was in difficulties himself, and he needed help from his sister; or finances demanded his education came to a halt. Or maybe it was just Charles getting into trouble again? In which case, he would have written to Richard himself surely?

The tart he had selected suddenly seemed tasteless, and he laid it aside. On an impulse he stole a draught from Abel's wineglass which stood conveniently nearby, and felt better for the opprobrium which followed, and his own retort. He toyed with some bread while Peter finished his meal, and then followed him closely out of Hall and across the court to Peter's rooms.

'What's up?' he asked as soon as the door was closed.

'Can I offer you a glass of wine? I'm having one.'

'No, tell me, what is it?'

Peter went over to the table and poured himself a glass. 'Sure?'

'Oh, alright. Just, what is it?' he repeated.

'I think I ought to sport my oak, just in case,' Peter said, going over to the entry and closing both doors. Next, he shut one window which stood a little ajar, and checked in his bedroom and his study for unauthorised visitors. He sat in an armchair and pulled a letter from his pocket.

'First, to show my *bona fides*, I have here your own letter to Sir George, which he enclosed with his, for my information and to reassure you.' He passed over the sheet to Richard. Yes, that was what he had written, what, less than two days before.

'Second, have a look at this letter. You recognise your cousin's hand and signature?'

'That is Sir George, without a doubt.' Often had Rose teased him about the way he formed his letters, the odd sort of "e" like a Greek epsilon, and the slanting verticals.

'Now, do you know where your cousin Sir George works?'

'The Foreign Office, I believe. That is why I wrote to him.'

'And what he does there?'

'Not really. Not at all, in fact. He has not spoken of it.'

Peter consulted the letter in his hand, as if to finally make up his mind. 'He works in the intelligence section. As do I. In fact, we are, to put it succinctly, Intelligencers. Of a sort.'

'Spies?'

'We prefer to call ourselves intelligencers, but, we find out information prejudicial to His Majesty's interests and then try and negate the work of his enemies. So, yes, spies.'

Richard was more than a little surprised. Relieved that he was not in trouble or any such, but . . .

'But you're an undergraduate like me?'

'I am; though I was perhaps not entirely truthful when I gave you my past history. Although I did work for a while in my father's business, for most of the time my travels have been on behalf of King George. It was considered advisable that I came to Cambridge to investigate reports of enemy activity within the university, and where better to be than hidden in plain sight in a college?'

'So that is why you know so many people here. I had been wondering.'

Peter smiled. 'Well, actually, it isn't my job. I just, well, have had quite a sociable life in many different fields. For example, Guy and his friends from Jesus, I knew because our families have connections by marriage; and thank you by the way for helping us out in the boat, you seem a very competent oar.'

Richard murmured something or other deprecating, but he was pleased. 'Well, what do you want of me?'

'Firstly, can you tell me everything that you have discovered so far about this, shall we say, conspiracy?'

Richard thought. It didn't seem much, when it was all boiled down.

'Well, first I found this message in a book I was dealing with in the library. No, wait, the first thing was a letter addressed to me, which I only realised much later had actually been sent to Robert Cork, but the address had been written very badly, and the porter had thought it said Cox not Cork. It read, "Fibonacci to 13". Then when I got the message in the book, I thought about codes, and after a while, I managed to decipher it. It made arrangements for a meeting in Caius coffee house at seven o'clock on the tenth, which date had already passed. Nevertheless I went to see over the place with Edward Hever, and accidentally picked up a sheet of paper written in plain English which looked like a list of items to be discussed at a meeting. But the meeting advised in the coded message had happened five days previous, so I could only imagine there had been another meeting after that, in the same place.'

'And, what next?' He thought. 'Oh yes, then I, er, investigated Mr Cork's rooms while he was out on a ride, and found another cipher letter. Fortunately the paper from the coffee house had the new key to the month's cipher, which was Pi to six significant figures, and I found that there was to be a delivery of powder to the Pink Houses, you know, the ones on the river just before the Long Reach.'

Peter tapped the letter. 'Yes, Sir George particularly implored me to prevent you from going, because of the danger. However, . . . I see by your expression that I am too late. You have been already, have you not?'

'You are very perspicacious, Peter. Yes, Hever and I went last night. Well, he knew nothing about the business until Wednesday, but he entered my room and saw my copy of the coded message and so I had to tell him about it. To be fair, I was very glad of his company last night, it was coal-black and I would have felt most unsafe on my own.'

'And?'

'Not so much. We saw Robert Cork receive six barrels of what we imagine to be gunpowder – though they referred to it as flour – and, well, actually, I couldn't have sworn to his appearance, but the bargee addressed him as Mr Cork. Anyway, the barge was the Black Prince out of King's Lynn, and it moored afterwards by the Pike and Eel.'

Peter made a note. 'Go on.'

'They stored the barrels in the pink house, the one nearer to Chesterton, and, um, what else? There was a countrywoman there, I think she must live in the house. And, oh yes, later that evening I waited for Cork to come by at the Great Bridge, and followed him, he went into Trinity and . . .' He paused as Peter had drawn a sudden breath.

'Go on.'

'Well, I thought he might be going to Burgess' rooms, but he didn't, he went up a staircase belonging to,' he fished out his list, 'Hope, Price and Noakes. There were other names on the jamb, but only these ones had their lights lit. Well, there were others on the ground floor, but I heard Cork's steps going up so it couldn't be them.'

'You've done excellently. And you haven't been suspected? By Cork, or anyone?'

'I don't think so. Certainly not at the Pink Houses, and I don't believe Cork saw me following him, it was very dark, and I kept my distance. Nobody takes much notice of a boy, anyway, even if he is in a gown. And I was very careful to replace the paper in his room exactly as I had found it, same way round and everything.'

Peter leaned back in his chair. 'So, we know that Robert Cork is in it. I had wondered, partly because he seems very sympathetic to Mr Bonaparte's regime. That's why I took him to that Caius wine party, because I knew Mr Burgess would be there, and I wanted to see if they already knew each other. Which they did. And it seems you too suspected Mr Burgess?'

'Well, sort of. At the party, I didn't much like him. I saw him talking to Cork outside the King's lecture room a while later. And I had a bad feeling about him, I couldn't say what.'

'Ah. Yes. Well, I know nothing for certain, but it is said, and by quite reliable people, that Mr Burgess is rather too interested in young boys for it to be entirely, er, wholesome.'

Richard puzzled over this for a few seconds. What did Peter mean? Then it clicked. 'Do you mean like the Greeks? "A woman for duty, a man for pleasure . . ."'

'Quite, quite.'

'I thought that was just the ancients.'

'Sadly, no. It is also quite modern, too.'

Richard readjusted his views about the dangers of being in male company somewhat, and thought that Sir George would not wholly approve of his having read such texts, but, that was what giving a classical education did for a man. Or a girl, for that matter. But not actually being a young boy, he had felt the whatever-it-was rather differently when he was talking with Burgess. It had still been disconcerting, though.

'However, we have no evidence against him, not to do with this French business, at any rate,' Peter went on. 'Is there any more?'

'I can't think of any.' He had a disquieting thought. 'Did Sir George tell you about me coming up to college, right from the beginning?'

'Yes he did. He was quite concerned about how you might cope. And, if you won't be too offended, he asked me to keep a friendly eye on you, from a suitable distance.'

'Did he say why?' Was his secret shared with anyone but George?

'Just that you were very young, and from a long way away, and not used to English customs. But I must say you have acquitted yourself splendidly for a first term here, he needn't have worried.'

Richard pulled a face. Interfering older brothers! Next time he saw George he'd . . .

He dragged himself back to the present. 'So, what shall I do now, where do we proceed next with the investigation?'

'For you, it is at an end. These men may be desperate, and it is no business for a young boy to be mixed up in. Leave it to those whose job it is.'

'But I want to help.'

Peter smiled. 'I'm sure you do. But you have done your part for your country. Obviously if you come across any more messages you must tell me immediately. But no creeping around people's rooms, or following men through the streets, or any of that, please. I wouldn't want to face Sir George if you got hurt.'

Richard must have looked crestfallen, because he added, 'Don't look downhearted, I'll let Sir George know what a sterling job you have done.'

'What about Edward? Hever, you know.'

'If you wouldn't mind, could you just tell him you found someone to inform of your discoveries, and that who it is has to stay secret?'

'Won't he suspect you, having seen us leave Hall together?'

'Seeing his hangover, he will likely not be in top form mentally, but if he asks, you could say we were talking about the Greek poetry prize if you like.'

'Latin. Horace,' said Richard mechanically. 'Oh well, it was great while it lasted, I suppose.' He looked up. 'Can you tell me what you are going to be doing next at all, or is that secret too?'

'Well, obviously we need to keep an eye on the gunpowder at the Pink Houses, but we had better not act unless they try and move it. I'll depute a man to watch there, covertly. Also, in that agenda you found, "information about pts" refers to ports, I am sure. So we need to see if that King 's Lynn barge is connected with anyone we have information about. I'll be getting another man on to that when we have finished, he looks just like a regular bargee, swears like one too. Oh, and by the way, could I have the actual messages, we might be able to see something in them you didn't.'

Richard remembered. 'They all had a trefoil watermark in the paper.'

'Did they now? That could be very useful. It makes me think of Trinity, you know.'

'I see. I'm not sure these men are much more than amateurs, you know. They seem to have made a lot of mistakes, leaving papers around.'

'Let us hope so. But they could be just as dangerous, you know, as regular intelligence men.'

'What else are you going to be doing?'

Peter paused. 'I'm not sure I ought to tell you this, but, well, we don't know much about who else is in the group, or how to infiltrate it. There is a big Winter Ball happening at Trumpington Hall on the 9th December given by Mr Francis Pemberton, and his cousin Christopher Pemberton who manages the estates. Francis was at this college a few years ago, your cousin Sir George might have known him. The idea is that because Mr Pemberton is involved with the Cambridgeshire militia, and has invited a lot of military men, as well as friends and acquaintances from Emmanuel and other colleges, on top of the usual important people from the county, it is an ideal opportunity for us to observe connections between people who we didn't previously know were intimate.'

'Mr Pemberton himself and his family are above suspicion, because, well, I won't explain, but we have ways of finding out things about people if we have to. We had to investigate them before we made any plans about keeping an eye on the guests, naturally we would need his cooperation. We believe that this group or gang of French sympathisers will use the ball to make contacts, sound people out, or even to murder some of our top military men, which would severely hamper our War effort. We have to be on our guard against explosives; but also pistols, swords, all sorts of overt weapons, because many men will be in uniform, of course. Also, we need to have eyes and ears everywhere, to notice things that aren't quite, well, quite as they should be.'

Richard's eyes were wide. 'It sounds terribly complicated.'

'Yes, and terribly dangerous. You see why I don't want a young lad involved? We had thought of getting Mr Pemberton to call the ball off, but it is too good an opportunity to miss. We need to get inside this ring and their plans, and here is our opportunity. We will have plenty of men around the building, and men on the dance floor, and others circulating generally. We'll get them, don't you worry. And your lead about Cork is going to be invaluable. I bet he's on the list of guests, Mr Pemberton provided me with a copy.'

'Oh, well. You'd better come and collect the papers, the messages I mean.'

CHAPTER 20

RICHARD FELT HUM DRUM FOR the next couple of days. As predicted, Edward didn't enquire too hard about what he'd done with the information they'd gathered, and didn't even mention Peter Winton. Sunday morning at Holy Trinity gave him a lift, though, Mr Simeon's exposition of Paul's letter to the Romans making the old words have life and relevance. He chatted to some of the Queensmen there, sometimes laughed at for their evangelical leanings, but found them a sensible and thoughtful bunch, and men who took religion seriously, without being serious or dull. The service was certainly more stimulating than morning chapel, though that was partly due to the early hour.

It felt a bit odd going on the river on the Monday with the Jesuits, Peter sitting in front of him at two-oar, and wondering if the others were involved with the Foreign Office too, and what might be happening about the plotters. It felt odder walking to Grantchester with Edward on Tuesday and avoiding talking about their escapade. By Wednesday he felt he had to talk to Peter about it all again, if only to be told nothing.

He caught up with him after dinner and invited him to his room for a glass of whisky. Men always seemed more amenable after a little slug, he had found. Once they were settled in the (not very comfortable) chairs, he first enquired how he liked his drink, and how he was in himself, and how his studies were going, and then dropped the question.

'How is your investigation going, Peter?'

Peter didn't say anything for a while, just sipped his whisky and frowned. Perhaps he was thinking whether he could tell him anything, Richard thought.

Eventually he said, 'Not so well, actually. My man couldn't get anything from the bargees, the Black Prince is just a regular on the King's Lynn to Cambridge run, this time she was carrying coals which had come on coasters from Newcastle. And the kegs of powder have stayed put, no action there at all. Cork, well, it's hard to keep track of an undergraduate, as you probably know. He's off on one horse or another most days, and we can't readily follow him. He may be just taking exercise or he may be going to Army camps and collecting information. Of course, the information has to be got out of the country, but we are of course watching all the ports. Mostly the south coast and the Thames estuary, but Norfolk and Suffolk too.'

'Not so good,' sympathised Richard.

'Not so good.'

'And the Ball?'

'Not so good either. The problem is, the enemy, if I may call them that, no doubt know many or most of our agents, at least the ones who wouldn't look out of place at a ball, the gentry, I mean. The men outside aren't a problem, they will be there to keep people safe from a frontal assault, if you understand me. But it's information we need. We want someone in the ballroom who can listen and ask questions without being regarded. Someone invisible, perhaps. Someone nobody would suspect. None of our men is invisible unfortunately, and all of them might be suspected. It's a real conundrum.'

Suddenly, Richard had his Great Idea. It was on a par with Rose's idea about coming up to Cambridge, which had started this whole thing. It was still just a brilliant possibility, a cunning plan, but he needed to think about it. And discuss it with Sir George, of course. He didn't feel he could act on his own in this.

'Are you feeling yourself?' asked Peter. 'You look a bit flushed up.'

'I'm fine. Something you just said about being invisible gave me a great idea for my Latin poem, the Horace one, the one for the prize,' he lied. 'I need to get it down on paper before I forget it. Do you mind? You've finished your drink, haven't you?'

He saw Peter to the door, then settled at his desk for verisimilitude. Just as well, because Peter put his head back into the room and told him he could give him updates from time to time, if he liked, since he had been so helpful with the messages.

He thanked him, and then when he had gone, thought furiously. Who does noone take account of at a ball, in terms of serious matters? The women, of course, particularly the unmarried girls. Their job is to look beautiful, and be compliant, and listen to the men talk, and agree with them, and dance when asked, and hope to attract a man who needs a wife. Nobody thinks of them as having discernment or brains, indeed brains are positively discouraged in a wife.

So, he could go to the ball disguised as a girl, couldn't he? Well, really, he could undisguise himself from being a man, in fact. He did have more muscles now than was usual for a girl, but he could wear a dress with more fabric around the shoulder. His hands were callused from the rowing, but he would be wearing gloves. His face was tanned, but less so now it was winter, and he would wear makeup, which would make it paler, and probably rouge too, to alter the shape of his face in case anyone from the university might think they recognised him.

He had left his girls' clothes in London, but George could send them up by carrier. He would wear the lower-cut gown, the violet one, with tighter stays, as he wanted to attract the men, so they would talk with him, which would be out of character, but he could do it for the sake of his country. He wondered if that would make anything out of his bosom, after it had spent so long confined. He would try. A bit of uplift might do wonders.

Hmmm. This would take planning. Not just getting the clothes, but the persuading of George. How would he change identities? He couldn't very well arrive at a ball as Richard, and then go into a back room and come out as Rose. Also he would need an invitation, and someone to go with, unmarried girls always needed a chaperone and often an escort too, and he would have to arrive by carriage, so, he would need an accomplice.

Who was in charge of this business? Was it Peter? It didn't seem likely, not a thing of this importance. He was too young, probably. But he did seem quite high up in the ranks of the intelligencers, as far as Richard could tell. No matter, the first thing was to enquire of George.

He settled down to compose his letter. He would have to be quite circumspect in what he said, in case of the letter being intercepted. However, he would also need to put his request quite clearly and if possible forcefully. This meant a number of false starts, and crossings out, and rewriting, but eventually he burnt all the drafts in the fire and reread what he hoped was a final version.

Dear Sir George

I have been talking to your colleague here about the French matter. It seems that although the information I had found out is most useful, it is not enough to achieve the aims of your organisation. He says there is to be a ball at Trumpington Hall in honour of the county militia, given by a Mr Francis Pemberton, whom you may recall from your time at this college. He says it would be advantageous if an agent who is not likely to be suspected were present to observe and ask questions.

I would like to be that person. I could disguise myself as a girl and then be in a position where noone would suspect me. I think I would carry this impersonation off very well. If you agree would you please forward the box left at your apartment by carrier. Ensure it contains the violet gown, and the heavier stays, and all the trinkets of jewellery and the slippers and stockings. Most importantly, do not omit the wig which was made in September. Also you will need to purchase white face paint and rouge and a kohl stick, perhaps

> you have a lady friend who could assist you if you might find this shopping embarrassing, as I cannot readily do this myself. Please avoid the kind of rouge made from vermilion, I am told it is most poisonous.
>
> It seems to me that this lark cannot occur without the cooperation of your colleague here, who would then be party to our secret. I am prepared for this disclosure, in the interests of our country, and also am fully aware of the dangers of this course of action both in the attendance at the ball and for my continued residence in this place. Please could you reply as soon as you have considered my request. I trust you will see its advantages far outweigh its disadvantages.
>
> Yours, Richard

He read it once more, thinking that at least he had not revealed Peter's identity, but he had had to compromise his own secret, at least partly, and he had needed to be quite specific about the ball. He folded, tucked in and sealed the letter, addressed it to Sir George at Whitehall, and after checking with the porters as to the best way to get it to London immediately, took it to the receiving office himself and handed it in, being assured it would catch the evening coach and be delivered the next morning.

All he could do now was wait. Sir George, he knew, would immediately say no to his plan. He would want to protect his little sister, naturally. However, once he had considered the matter, Richard was sure he would see its advantages, and change his mind. He hoped. If he did not, then his next step would be to put his plan to Peter Winton, which of course would mean revealing his secret. This would only be worthwhile if Peter were to think his idea feasible, and then be willing to persuade Sir George.

In the meantime, he had better get on with his Horace ode, it would look rum if he had not made progress on it if Peter were to ask. Anyway, he need to get it in by the end of term, he wanted to win the prize. Could he really get in a bit about invisibility? What was the Latin word for invisible? He reached for his dictionary.

On Thursday he went to a mathematics lecture at the Schools and on his way back saw Mr Burgess outside the gates of Caius deep in conversation with a man he thought he recognised. His back was towards Richard, but as he spoke he gesticulated in a familiar way, and once he had walked on a few more steps he could see part of the side of the man's face. It was Mr James! The last person he would have thought would be intimate with Mr Burgess! Whatever could they be talking about?

This set his mind racing again, and he had a sudden urge to go and visit Trinity, to see the staircase on which lived Hope, Price and Noakes. What he hoped to achieve he did not know, and before he had gone very far along Trumpington-street towards the college he stopped, stood for while in thought, then turned on his heel and headed back to Emmanuel. He could only look at their names on the door-jamb, and anyway he had plenty of reading to do, and a supervision in college on the Trojan wars, and he was due in the four-oar too. Oh well.

There was no message from Sir George on Friday, which was the earliest he could have expected one; he hadn't really hoped it would come so soon, but he needed to know his response, he was on thorns. At least Peter had told him that Cork was indeed on the guest list when they were walking back to college after boating the day before. Somehow though he managed to finish his Horace poem, and hand it in for the prize, and he had also been able to concentrate quite well on a lecture about explosives given by the Professor of Chemistry, at which he noticed Cork was also present.

Saturday arrived without anything in the morning post either, when he checked after chapel. He thought the porters would wonder what he was expecting, the number of times he had enquired at the lodge. Edward banged on his door at breakfast time and demanded to know what had happened to the gunpowder consignment.

He had to lie and say he had heard no more, and then partly out of contrition and partly because he felt so unsettled, he suggested they went and called on a few fellows at other colleges, for a change of scenery.

Edward was only too glad of an excuse to leave off reading for a while, though he did seem a bit disconcerted when he heard Richard had already handed in his poem, as if he hadn't even started his own submission. They managed to look up three or four men at Caius, who gave them tea, and told them the gossip, and recounted a few wild tales, some of which might even have been true, and then, feeling they perhaps ought to do a little work, returned to college in a much better frame of mind.

Richard opened his door intending to sit down with his Euclid until lunch, and stopped on the threshold as if shot when he saw George sitting there in his armchair with a newspaper as if he was in his own morning-room.

'George! What are you doing here? How did you get in?'

George set his paper down, put his hands behind his head, and grinned at him. 'You need a haircut, lad. You're starting to look like a girl.'

Richard pushed the door to behind him. 'Hush, walls have ears.'

'It's good to see you, really it is. I was very impressed with what Winton told me you had found out about the codes and so on. Is your college work going as well? And your painting has come up really nicely. Good job.'

Richard was slightly nonplussed by the rapid change of subjects. 'The painting, oh yes, I call it my Meer, I found a sort of monogram on it, I love it. But what else did you say?'

'College work going well?'

'College work? Hmm. Surely you know? I would expect nothing less of you than that you have suborned one of the Fellows to spy for you and report on my reading?'

'Now, now! I am sorry about Winton, but well, I do feel responsible for you, you know. I felt I had to have a backup in case there were any problems, and I was far away. You're not a bad younger, er, brother, truth be told.'

'Cousin. Keep your mind on the job'

'Cousin. Right. I didn't tell him about our other secret, though, you know.'

'I worked that one out for myself. Thankyou. I thought he might come to suspect since we go boating together, and I have to take off my coat, but if he does he has been very discreet. But anyway, again, why are you here? And, how did you get in?'

'Key from the porter. And, you wrote to me. Do you remember?'

Richard threw a cushion at him. 'Duh!'

'And I thought it was a bit complicated to thrash out in epistolary fashion, so as I had to come up here anyway some time to deal with this ball business, I thought I'd come sooner rather than later, and have it out with you face to face.'

Richard's face fell. 'So, you are totally against my idea,' he said. 'I knew you would be.'

'Well, not exactly. I don't know if you've realised just how important this whole thing is, the Cambridge group I mean, but we need to break it up as soon as we can, and we're taking suggestions from monkeys as to how to do it at the moment. No, no,' he added, seeing Richard starting to bridle, 'your idea is very very good, I didn't mean you were a monkey, I just meant we were desperate. So, against all my instincts as an elder, er cousin, I think we have to see if it would work out. There have been female spies before, of course, but not I think at a Cambridgeshire ball. And more often than not they are, shall we say, ladies of dubious reputation, who hear secrets whispered into the pillows of the victim. I am hoping that is not part of your plan?'

Richard looked at him with one of those looks that say, Watch it brother, before I brain you with a beetle.

George hurried on. 'So, as I was saying, um, what was I saying?'

'Just be careful, cousin, I have grown considerably in strength in the last months. You were pontificating about, "Against my instincts . . ."'

'Oh yes, um, I just need to know, well, lots of things. So, do you realise you could be killed if the gang find out?'

'I do.' He rolled his eyes.

'Or, much more likely, that you are discovered to be leading a double life and your career at Emmanuel will come to an abrupt end?'

'I do.'

He sighed. 'I thought you would. That's what has been worrying me most. I'm quite happy to take risks myself for my country but I recoil from sending a girl to do the same, especially . . .'

'Surely, you wouldn't be human if you didn't. Also, if I were to be unmasked, it would exonerate you from your deception in having me admitted here under false pretences. You would simply say you did it for the sake of espionage.'

'That's a point. Though, you know the real reason I agreed to your request to come here?'

'Lady John Barnes?' he said, grinning at the memory.

'Not really. I didn't think you would carry out your threat, not knowing how harmful it would be. No, it was mostly, that, well, you know I came into the baronetcy when I was about to graduate?'

'Mmm.'

'So I need to be careful of my position, what with my job and everything. And before that, father was unwell, and I had to take responsibility for a lot of things while I was still a student? Well, part of me wished I could have been wild, or a bit wild at any rate, like Charles, you see, and so your masquerade was a way of me having a bit of a fling through you. Do you understand? Do you mind?'

Richard nodded, slowly. 'I think I do. Understand, I mean.'

George sat back in his chair. 'Now, do you think you can impersonate a girl convincingly? Wait, I'm not being facetious. You will have to wear the wig we had made, and have some excuse for why you are wearing it. You will have to be a somewhat different sort of girl from your natural self, if you are to dance with enough of the men we want to know about to be useful.'

'Hence why I requested the more robust stays, the rouge, and so on. I had thought of all this: it will be a trial, but I shall imagine I am Alicia or Harriet, you know them, I was at school with them; or Lady Augusta, or any of countless other, er, eligible girls, and simper with the best of them. I shall wear the violet dress without a fichu and heroically expose what little bosom I can muster, for the sake of England.'

'Also, you will probably meet some men from the University that you have met as Richard. You will need to convince them you are Rose, not Richard, however similar you may look. If you want to return to your studies, that is.'

'Yes, I see. In spite of the rouge and so on, I might be likely to relate to them as I have done as a boy, because I have been so used to it for these last weeks.'

'Quite.'

Richard was struck with the irony of having to be careful that he behaved at all times as a girl, when he actually *was* a girl. That he would perhaps greet Edward, say, with a slap on the shoulder and a rude comment about his spots or his ugly face, as he had been accustomed to. He chuckled a little to himself at the image, the while noting it as a serious matter. He might have to practise, to relearn ladylike manners. How odd.

'Also, you will have to decide on your name. It would make undesirable connections in our enemies' minds if they thought Rose was related to me. You could still be Rose, but not Clarke.'

Richard thought a moment. 'I shall be Rose Carbery, I think. It sounds quite elegant.' He then backtracked. 'Wait on. If I am not Clarke, then people who have known me as Rose Clarke will know there is something suspicious. There are bound to be people who have met me in London at a ball or soiree or musicale or some such, at an event of such size.'

'Good point. Hmm. I think then that you must take your own

name. I of course shall not be at the festivities. It would be too obvious. I shall however be . . . shall we say, around and about.'

'Who will be there, in public view, then?'

'Peter Winton, for one. He and two others are in charge of the arrangements in Cambridge. You know, he at least is going to have to know your secret.'

Richard grimaced. 'I know. It is going to make boating with him awkward. He will have an urge to be gentlemanly, and that would be disastrous.'

'Oh I don't know. Winton has worked as a diplomat: he is very used to dissembling for his country. Shall we meet him?'

CHAPTER 21

PETER WINTON HAD JUST SENT for lunch to be brought to his room when they knocked, and so he called down the stairs to his gyp to fetch two more portions. While they waited for it to arrive he poured them each a glass of wine, and told Sir George how well Richard had handled his oar in their boat, and how he got on famously with the Jesuits, who tended to move in a fairly highflown set normally, and how impressed he was that a lad of only sixteen handled some of the discussions they had had in the various groups that they both attended, and so on.

The food arrived, the oak was sported, and then he sat down and looked at them expectantly. Sir George and Richard looked at each other. Where to start?

Richard finished his mouthful of bread and began. 'You know you said to me that you wanted someone at the Pemberton Ball who was invisible? Well, we have an answer to your conundrum.'

'Really? Who?' He turned to Sir George. 'Do we have an agent that is not known to any of the Frenchies?'

George coughed. 'Well, yes, in a manner of speaking.' He looked at Richard, the hint of a smile on his face.

'You see, Peter, I am not, well, I'm not really from Nova Scotia. Never been near the place, in fact.' He cleared his throat. 'And I'm not sixteen, I'm nineteen, nearly twenty. And . . . I'm not George's cousin, either. I am his sister.'

He waited, and watched the different expressions which chased across Peter's face. There was a certain amount of surprise, to be sure, but also a kind of relaxation, as if some realisation had taken place.

'I see. This explains a few things, things that have puzzled me.'

'Such as?'

'Well, your face, your skin: I have been thinking you must be younger than sixteen, but lads often lie about their age when they are to spend time with older men. On the other hand, you pull a pretty oar for a child, but I did wonder why you never took off your waistcoat even when you were very hot. And then there's how I . . . No, I'll leave that one.' He looked quite uncomfortable.

Sir George tipped his head on one side seeing this, and said, 'He does make a very attractive boy, doesn't he? Even I think so, and I'm his brother. I mean, her brother. You wait till you see him as a girl, though. Rose is lovely.'

'No I'm not,' Richard brushed off the compliment. 'Not in Society, noone thinks twice about me.'

'Maybe,' said George, 'but you have the light of intelligence in your eyes. Puts off the Nick Ninnies. Attracts the cognoscenti.'

'Cognoscenti?'

'Those in the know, those of taste and refinement.'

'I'll try that one on Edward, bet he doesn't know it. And I take it the Nick Ninnies are the simpletons? He won't know that one either, I'll be bound.'

'Indeed. Now, Peter, we need to know if you think Richard, I mean Rose, here, would be helpful to your plans.'

'It's too risky. He could, I mean she, could be in real danger. No, I can't countenance it. I can't guarantee her safety.'

'Stay with Richard, and he and his, please Peter. Otherwise you'll give me away when you don't mean to. And I do know about the risks. And am quite prepared to take them.'

'I still must say no, George. Really I must. It's, well, it's unprecedented.'

'So it is. That's why it's a great idea. You know, when I got Richard's letter I reacted like you. More so, he's my sister. But after a while, I realised that it's our best hope. He can circulate among everyone and talk to them about who is who, which men they know and what they are like without arousing suspicion, they will all think he is simply finding out who might make a good husband, someone he may set his cap at. Do you have a better plan? Or any other plan at all?'

'Er, well, um . . .'

'So no. I thought so. Well, we'll leave you now to digest this, and perhaps we'll see you at dinner. Would you care to join us at High Table? I'd quite like a word with Dr Cory about one or two things.'

Richard drained his glass. 'You know, I have been successfully masquerading as a boy for the past two months. I ought to be able to impersonate a girl, I think.'

They left Peter to his conflicted loyalties, and went off for a walk. Since it was fine, they took the route over the Leys towards Grantchester where they would not be overheard.

'I'm going to have to do a lot of homework before this ball, you know. I shall have to have the guest list, and learn all the names you are interested in, and how they are connected, and all the *on dit* about them. Won't leave much time for study. Good job I've got the Horace ode in.'

'Horace?'

'Yes, the Latin verse composition. Can't have you being the only one with a classical prize from Cambridge.'

'Oh, so it's a competition, is it?'

'Naturally. I intend to be higher than eleventh among the wranglers, too.'

'You and whose brains?'

'Huh! For that, you can tell me whether Lady John Barnes will be there. I expect she will be. And tell me all about it.'

'Ah. Yes.' He paused for a moment. 'This is going to be more embarrassing than I would like. Still . . . Lady John is not on our payroll, exactly, but she carries out commissions for her husband, such as the delivery of letters. However, she and he are not quite, er compatible, shall I say, and so she exacts payment for services commissioned by him in, how shall I say, er, a physical form.' He had the grace to blush. 'What you saw was my receiving a letter from an agent in France that Lord John had passed on. It is quite helpful that he and I never meet, to keep his involvement secret.'

'Not compatible? You mean they live separate lives?'

'Not at all. Er, let me just say, oh, I shouldn't be telling you this,'

'Yes you must, I need to know about everyone I shall be meeting.'

'You're right. It's just that unmarried girls . . . well, anyway, Lady John has a much higher, er, interest in marital relations than Lord John. In fact, than nearly any man I have ever met. She is, most keen on intimacy. Not that I have . . . well, not more than you have seen, anyway, I hasten to add. But she . . .'

'. . . has rumpled the sheets with many a fine gentleman?'

'Indeed. Where do you get such phrases?'

'Mostly from Edward Hever. He has added to his book knowledge about Cambridge an encyclopaedic array of slang, argot and cant. If he applied himself to Mathematics as well as he does to increasing his vocabulary he would be sure to be Senior Wrangler.'

'Yes. Well.' He turned away, coughed. 'Moving on. Lord John will be elsewhere. Possibly in France, I believe.'

'Are any of the people I have mentioned in my letters in your employ? Or suspected?'

'Let me see. Viscount Beauchamp, no, Charles French, not as far as I know, Lord Robert Dumas, no, in spite of the name.'

Richard nodded after a slight pause. 'Oh yes, Guy, Charlie and Rob. You have been paying attention.'

'It is my job, you see. Now who else. Mr Burgess of Trinity, not sure, definitely a possible suspect if I can put it that way. We haven't made any progress on which of those three men you discovered Cork visiting at Trinity, I believe. Cork, confirmed to be in the gang. Mr

Sterne of Caius, hmmm, could be a suspect. As could Dr Seligman of Caius, the don. Have you met other people I have not heard about?'

'There's all my friends at Emmanuel.'

'Edward, Abel, James, Will, John, Luke, George, Hugh, to name but some. None has aroused suspicion as yet, I believe. That does not mean they have been exonerated of involvement, however.'

'You certainly do have a good memory; but I know lots of other men.'

'Any that have taken your eye, in your other person?'

'It is most odd, being with men as a man. I see them quite differently. So, no, to your question. Also, I have acquired a certain, shall we say insight, into how men tick.'

'Moving swiftly on, once more. Peter, once he agrees to your plan, will of course supply you with the guest list and answer any questions you have. I hope your memory is up to the task.'

'I shall ensure it is. If I can get the hang of the Optative mood of irregular verbs in Greek, I can surely learn a few names.'

'Good. Now, let us turn back towards town along Trumpington-street here, I have a man I must see in Peterhouse.'

'About a dog?'

'About a whole pack of hounds, I suspect. You will be able to make your way back to college when we part? I shall see you at dinner. High table, remember, Peter too. At my expense, of course.'

Sir George's conversation with Dr Cory at dinner seemed to be all about the extent to which members of the college were studying Political History, and whether it was being taught along with the more ordinary elements of the curriculum. As far as Richard could ascertain, one of the Fellows and three third year students attended a discussion group in Trinity with the Professor of Modern History, Mr Smyth. He wasn't sure what this had to do with anything, so he kept quiet and concentrated on enjoying the better-quality food and wine.

Peter too had been almost silent at dinner. On the way across the court to their rooms, Sir George having stayed with the Fellows in the Combination Room for more wine and dessert, he handed Richard a set of papers, saying quietly that he had, as Sir George had envisaged, seen there was no other course for them to take, so against his better judgement, here was the list they had talked about. 'Take a look and then you can ask me about it,' he finished off rather tersely, and didn't look at all happy about it. Whether it was at being out-flanked by the facts, or just a reluctance to involve an amateur, and a girl at that, Richard couldn't tell.

Once in his room Richard spread the pages on his desk. There were hundreds of names, not all of them would accept, or even if they did, actually arrive for the festivities, but it made a huge task. Peter had annotated it here and there, using red ink, to indicate what the person's connection with the Pembertons might be, for example University, County, Local, London, School (Mr Pemberton had been at Eton), Business; and then a number of others, particularly of women who were there to even up the numbers, Fellows being of course unmarried and students all male. Well, thought Richard, mostly male.

He saw Mr Laughton, his maths tutor, on the list as Local, being the vicar of the adjoining parish; Lady John Barnes down as London, with her husband, both marked with an X. Burgess, Sterne; and also Guy, Charlie and Rob were there among the University contingent together with Noakes and Price from Trinity who had featured when he had followed Cork. Cork himself was also there, as he had been told.

From Emmanuel there was Dr Cory and both the tutors, Griffith and Watkinson, as well as some names of Fellows he was not familiar with, perhaps they had left between Pemberton's time and now? Also some names who were noted as friends from student days, including one Sir George Clarke, also marked with an X.

It was all a bit overwhelming. Richard thought he'd give Peter a chance to regroup, and settle his surprise about his being Rose, and then go and have a chat with him about the list. Maybe around seven o'clock, when he usually found he needed a break from reading anyway. He needed to be clear about this whole thing, after all it was less than two weeks away.

He had been working on his Euclid for an hour or more when George reappeared, pronouncing himself very pleased with what he had learned from Dr Cory and another of the fellows, a Mr Jukes. He wouldn't say any more about this, but asked how Richard had got on with the guest list that he could see on the desk.

'Just had a first look, George, felt I ought to leave Peter to recover from the shock before going through it with him.'

'Tactful,' said George.

'But since you're here, you could tell me about Pemberton. You were in his year here, weren't you?'

'I was. We weren't close friends but I did ride out with him a few times, and for a while we were both in the University Militia.'

'Really? I've seen them doing sham battles on Parker's Piece. Never felt the urge to join.'

'No? Good: better to read your books. Sorry, I'm sounding like a protective older brother again. Anyway, I left after a few months, too many drills for me. But that's how I got into the Foreign Office, I met some officers who pointed me at the right people, and then I went to London for an interview, and had a job waiting when I graduated. Good thing too, as father didn't leave our finances in terribly good order when he died.'

'Really?'

'Sorry to say it, but yes. The actual estate was running quite well, because we had such an excellent steward, but there were a lot of debts.' He stopped, clearly embarrassed yet again.

'Gambling debts?'

'Mmm. And, er, Cyprians, I am sorry to say, after our mother died.'

'Oh dear.'

'You see, you being a boy at the moment makes so many things different, Rose. I would never have burdened you with these things normally. I don't know why I told you anyway, really.'

Richard smiled. 'Perhaps I'm more grown up than I was, even if I do look fourteen?'

'You know, you are.' He shook his head as if to clear it. 'I never thought you coming up here would make so much so difference.'

'Anyway,' he continued, 'Pemberton doesn't normally live at Trumpington, his cousin Christopher has been doing, but there is a rumour that Francis may be coming back and basing himself there. Christopher manages the estates; I've rather lost touch with what Francis has been doing since he went down.'

He pointed to another pair of names. 'Look, here are the Swaffhams who gave that last ball you went to before you took Charles off my hands. And Warburton, he was at that crush too. He's a colleague at the Foreign Office, good man. Was at Oxford though: Christ Church. Seems to have recovered from that error of judgement now.'

George stayed around Cambridge until he caught the Sunday evening mail coach back to London, promising to send on Richard's box with all the things he might need for his role as soon as he arrived. Peter, once Richard had been rude to him, and punched him hard on the shoulder for a sarcastic comment about his lack of beard, and helped himself to his wine without asking, seemed able to go back to accepting Richard as a boy, even when they were talking about their plans.

The matter of the carriage and their arrival was no problem: Peter and his mother and sister would be leaving from his home in Milton in their coach, so there would be room for one more, and he would have a chaperone. He would arrange for Richard to get to his house, and transform himself in private, and then Rose would have the services of their lady's maid for adjustments and coiffure and so on. It might be a little awkward to hide this switch from the other servants, but he would think of a way round it.

He had overnight leave from college to attend the ball, and he would ensure Richard also was excused. He had arranged for Richard to meet his father, to discuss a possible role in the family business once he had graduated, he said. No matter that his father was at the present time in Barbados, it would pass muster in college. Assuming all went well, Richard could reappear in the morning after Rose had said goodbye to her hostess, and return to college before lunch on Saturday. It would be better if his mother was not involved in the deception, and he would try and ensure she was not. As for how he would explain Rose's connexion to them, he had not worked that out. 'A mere detail, Richard,' he assured him. 'Leave it to me.'

Richard worked hard on the list, memorising names, trying to imagine what they might look like. At least he knew some of them already. As for the University men, Peter made sure he took Richard along to various parties and meetings where they might be, and pointed them out surreptitiously; and suggested he go to lectures he would not otherwise have patronised to learn the appearance of some of the professors, such as Drs Jowett, Hailstone and Wollaston, as a result of which he became enthused to learn more about fossils and minerals, and about experimental philosophy, but much less keen on learning any law.

It was going to be tricky being at the ball and possibly meeting people he knew as a man, especially Guy and his friends. He didn't think any of the other people who knew him well were going, but these three were a problem. He might have to keep an eye open and avoid them, somehow.

At times, he wished he had another girl to talk all this over with. It was quite lonely, planning attendance at a ball and having nobody to talk dresses and ribbons and hairstyles. Surely, it was too much when that was all girls could discuss, but from time to time, he wanted some frippery. Still, Peter had a sister, perhaps there would be time before they left to make friends?

The time at Emmanuel had been rushing by as it was, it seemed hardly a moment since he had arrived, but it was speeding up still further as the ball approached. There was Latin and Greek and Mathematics and Chemistry and Theology to study; tutorials to carry on attending, lectures to hear, and, just as important, ballocks to talk with his friends over a coffee in the Emmanuel coffee house opposite college, or in a tavern over a whisky (beer for the others, they still thought him odd for drinking spirits), or at a wine party in someone's rooms. There was boating, and walks to Grantchester, and Dr Simeon's sermons, and practical jokes to pull off, and all manner of other activities, it was amazing it all fitted in. All this and the preparation for his big night to add to it.

The box of clothes arrived, and Richard made sure to keep it locked at all times except when he was inspecting the contents. Sir George had sent a variety of cosmetics: he wondered who had assisted him in making the purchases, and smiled to himself at the thought of his having to ask a lady to help him shop. The wig was very fine, and fitted his head well. He remembered with gratitude the care which the hairdresser had taken in measuring his head in all directions. Of course it was somewhat itchy, and somewhat hot, but needs must, and all that rubric. He did not have a mirror beyond the windowpane, but he thought with a little artifice by a good lady's maid it shouldn't be too obvious that it was not his own hair. Well, it was his own hair, actually; but it should pass muster unless anyone got too close. He did need to have a story ready in case anyone was impertinent enough to ask why he wore such an old-fashioned thing as a wig, though. His own hair had grown somewhat, but it had been cropped so short back at the end of September that it would not show past the artificial coiffure he thought.

One exciting addition to the guest list that Peter told him about on the Tuesday before the ball was Dr Thomas Young. He had been at Emmanuel at the same time as Francis Pemberton, but had not for some reason been included before. Richard was quite excited that he might see the great man again; he had discovered he had been known at college as "Phenomenon Young" (intelligence as always from Edward, who loved anything quirky) and had learnt of several of his habits when up, such as winning numerous bets in the Combination

Room after dinner, and never attending any medical teaching in the course of his residence to obtain his medical degree (having completed his studies elsewhere previously).

He saw Mr Laughton for his tutorial on the Tuesday, and wondered as he watched him how likely it was he would be recognised. Mr Laughton tended to look into his books, or stare out of the window when he taught them; he seemed quite shy, or at least wary of eye contact. All to the good.

He saw Mr Griffith for his college tutorial on the Wednesday, and wondered if he might be involved with the plot. He had travelled widely on the continent, to be sure. It wasn't very nice suspecting persons who might be wholly innocent, he was glad he did not do this job all the time. He watched Dr Cory at dinner, and wondered why Sir George had been taking to him about Modern History. He read his list of guests and wondered which of those at Peterhouse had been the object of George's visit the other day. He hadn't told him, and Peter didn't seem to know. On Thursday they went out boating, and he worried whether the Jesuits would rumble him when dressed as Rose. And then it was Friday. Time to act.

CHAPTER 22

THE PORTERS CARRIED RICHARD'S BOX down his stair and loaded it onto Peter's carriage on St Andrew's-street. He settled himself inside, and Peter joined him.

'*Alea iacta est*,' he said as they moved off.

'Almost,' said Peter. 'You could still back out now, if you liked. I'm still worried about your safety. You'll be talking to some pretty desperate men, if we can carry out our plans.'

'Yes, what exactly are your plans?'

'Right. Well, you are going to be going as my sister's friend, all she will know is that I need her to introduce you to anyone and everyone she and my mother know. The fact that you are Sir George's sister is not published; but it is not secret either. Your line is that you and Julia, that's my sister, met at a musicale in London and you are visiting her in Milton. Hence, when the ball invitation arrived, you were included, as young girls are most useful to balance the numbers, since Mr Pemberton's acquaintances are mostly men and he is unmarried.'

'I see.'

'Julia will also introduce you to a number of men, some of them my agents, so that they in turn may introduce you to their friends, or rather, to the men that they think may be involved in the plot. I should expect you will be invited to dance every figure, as a result, and this will of course make you prominent and noticed. This is my worry.'

'It will be a novelty for me. Mostly at balls I dance with one or two men only.'

'You know the names in which we are interested: you will be able to put faces to the names very soon. More importantly, you may be able to make connections to other gentlemen we have not thought about, and I trust your memory is in order, because you will not readily be able to make notes.'

'You forget my dance card and pencil, Peter. I shall write on its back surface.'

'Excellent. Now, you must keep these observations to yourself until we return to Milton, we could so easily be overheard at Trumpington Hall. I shall point out my colleagues Mr Plant and Mr Graham as soon as we arrive, so you could attract their attention in case of need. They are local men, invited on their own merits as far as the other guests know.'

'Thankyou, Mr Winton. I must practise calling you Mr Winton, else I shall forget.'

The coach rumbled over the Great Bridge and turned onto Chesterton-lane. Richard watched Cambridge disappear behind him.

'So, Mr Winton, when we arrive at your house, how shall we proceed?'

'The coach will take us to a side door and we will ascend to your room privately. I think it would be best if you were to change into a day dress and assume your role as Rose immediately, because then you can meet my mother and sister, and get to know Julia in particular, so the relationship will seem realistic.'

'Will you send the maid to dress my hair and assist me?'

'Yes, once you have divested yourself of your men's clothes, and locked them away out of sight. The fewer people who know . . .'

'. . . the fewer can tell secrets, yes, I agree.'

'Have you an explanation for why your hair is so short? I am not an expert in such matters but it seems to me that very few ladies under thirty would wear a wig of any sort these days.'

'You are correct. I was sadly caught in a candle flame in the summer and though I was able to plunge my head into a basin of water to extinguish the blaze, the only option was to shave my head both to enable the injury to be treated, and as my own tresses were quite ruined. My scalp has fully recovered, but my hair has not as yet regrown. Will that pass muster?'

'Sounds gruesome.'

'It was terrifying. I still shudder at the recollection.'

'Now, what subjects interest Julia? At what is she accomplished?'

'She plays the pianoforte very well. And sings most beautifully. She speaks French, and I expect she embroiders, as all ladies do.'

'Not I. I am less clumsy with a needle than a set of ivory keys, but I do not relish the diversion. Does she take part in outdoor activities? Read widely? Attend concerts?'

Peter shook his head. I am most ignorant of these. I have not been at home for some time now, and I have paid too little attention to her. She is aged eighteen, and I have not spent time with her for the last four years.'

'Very well. We shall gossip about how her brother has neglected her, as a beginning. And enumerate your deficiencies, Mr Winton. That will serve splendidly. And your mother?'

Peter's eyes softened. 'She is top-notch,' he said. 'A real trouper. Anything you want, she will find for you.'

'Is she *au fait* with the *on-dit* in this locality?'

'Indubitably. She knows everything. And can hold a secret like the vaults of the Bank of England.'

'We shall get on famously, then.'

As arranged, the coach avoided the main drive of the Wintons' mansion entirely and pulled up without fanfare at a door opposite the stables. Peter and Richard ascended a back stair and went into a cabinet to look at Peter's father's curios, while the coachman followed with Richard's box, put it in a bedroom and departed. Once he had gone they left the collection of native garments and Richard entered his room. After looking briefly at the view, he unlocked the box.

'I shall send the maid up in, how long? Five minutes?'

'You jest, sir. May I ring for her, once I am partially ready?'

'Certainly. Here is the pull. I will await you in the morning room, the maid will show you.'

'Don't expect promptitude from me. I shall need to get used to my dresses again, and remember how to walk and sit. I might be some time.'

An hour and a quarter later, Rose descended the grand stair, stepping elegantly, holding herself erect, and wondering whether her bosom was showing enough, or too much. She was of course not yet in her evening gown, but she thought she ought to practise having a décolletage, which was normally alien to her, even in her day dress. Stairs were much easier as a man, she thought, she wouldn't have had to worry about catching her heel on her hem, or her slipper falling off.

It did feel nice to be wearing a dress again, though. She liked the freedom, without her neck held by a cravat, and her shoulders held back by a coat. On the other hand it was odd to not be wearing unmentionables, and have her bottom bare to the air. Why had ladies no such garment, she wondered? It had never occurred to her before she had become Richard.

Mr Winton stood as she entered the morning room and introduced her to his mother and sister. He looked very fine, she thought: she was surprised by how differently she saw him now she had changed into a dress. She had made sure she observed his face closely as she came in, and was rewarded with a whole raft of expressions in sequence. Wariness, certainly. Admiration, possibly. Shock, a little. And a soupçon of discomfiture, definitely. It was a good thing she had spent so much time standing around at social events, watching, because she was quite good at reading faces. She had forgotten how differently men and women looked at others. Men rarely noticed things, they were too busy doing and moving.

Mr Winton stepped back and she spoke with Mrs Winton for a while, as was polite, explaining she was the sister of a friend of Peter, and how grateful she was to be able to go to the ball with them as her brother was unable to attend. She said that Mr Winton had insisted she told people she was a longstanding friend of Miss Winton, which certainly made it easier to explain her presence at the ball in the absence of her brother, and how she was so grateful for this, and she hoped that she and Miss Winton would soon in fact become friends. Mrs Winton's eye flicked to her son, and it was quite clear that she swallowed none of this farrago, but she inclined her head, and suggested Rose and Julia take a turn around the room to get acquainted.

Julia was a sweet girl, and most pleased to have someone to travel to the ball with, although as she said, she hoped she would meet numbers of her friends there, and would be ravished to introduce Miss Clarke to them all. Rose enquired about her family, and learned there was a younger sister of twelve, and a much older brother who had been killed in the French wars six years ago. Rose was shocked that Peter had never mentioned him. It explained perhaps why he had entered the intelligence services, instead of going to University at the usual time.

It was not long before they were on first name terms, as was necessary in any case for the deception, but Rose quickly warmed to Julia who was unaffected and clearly devoted to her brother. She sat by her when lunch was announced, and having made sure to find out the time of dinner first, ate more than she would have at college, as the Wintons kept the modern meal hour of five o'clock.

From time to time she had a worrying thought: were her shoulder muscles too prominent, did she sit correctly, was she too forward in conversation? It was surprisingly difficult to shake off the last two months of behaviour, for example she kept wanting to lean back on the settle and cross her legs, and at lunch she nearly commented on her wine being watery, before she recalled the convention. At least she wouldn't have to restrict how much fluid she drank today, to avoid embarrassment with the chamber pot in her male guise.

After lunch she heard Julia play the pianoforte, and sing, and agreed with Peter she had a lovely voice, while privately being a little jealous of her abilities. On the other hand, she thought, Julia probably doesn't know anything about, say, William Smith and his geological researches, or the wave theory of light. She then told herself off for being cattish, and asked her what books she read, being gratified to hear she had a fairly wide range of interests, and hearing of several novels she herself might like to look at over the vacation for relief from study. Julia regretted they could not take a turn at archery together, the weather being inclement, because she found it so enjoyable, which further recommended her to Rose.

The two girls agreed a story together about where they had met, and how often they saw each other, and how long Rose had been at Milton, and Rose learnt the names of some friends that would not be at the ball, so as to appear convincing. Julia did seem a little suspicious as to why she was being so thorough, but Rose felt she had to be prepared, as so much rested on her meticulousness.

Julia was well-informed about the course of the war, although little directly involving England had occurred so far. She knew about the arguments over Malta, and Cape Colony, and Sicily, and how vital the Royal Navy had become. Rose was impressed. She tried to get Julia to tell her about her brother's neglect of her, but she got nowhere. Julia seemed to think he was a paragon, which gave Rose to think of how she saw him herself.

Peter was indeed a very attractive man, and had brains. He was hard-working in two spheres at once, being a reading man at college and also carrying on his intelligence job. Also, he was present, whereas she had not seen Mr Blackburn for two months. She did not know how she felt about Mr Blackburn now she had met so many other men and spent far more time with them, and being with Peter, no, Mr Winton, was going to be most confusing when she turned back into Richard.

Dinner was served and eaten, and then the two girls retired upstairs to change and to prepare. Rose admired Julia's white gown, with its classical motifs and modest neckline and wished she had Julia's bosom for the evening; Julia was envious of Rose's violet dress and its décolletage, and helped her to tighten her stays to make the most of her limited assets. The maid did wonders with her hair, arranging the ringlets and curls so it was difficult to tell it was a wig, and embellishing it with tiny star-shaped pins. Makeup had to come next, just a light layer of whitening to the face, and a hint of rouge to cheeks and lips, really she could not countenance any more, already she felt she looked like a doll. Julia assured her that in the ballroom it would be much less garish, and to be supportive applied some to her own lips and puckered to assess the effect.

With a sense of being carried along on a great wave of inevitability Rose boarded the carriage and settled herself opposite Mr Winton, who looked splendid in a silver and black waistcoat under his cutaway, and the tightest of pantaloons, with gleaming Hessian boots. Mrs Winton signalled to the groom, the harness creaked and jingled, and they were off, the horses' breath steaming in the cold air.

It was most odd to drive down Trumpington-street in a carriage, in a dress, past Trinity and Caius and King's; to pass by people, some in academicals, who seemed to belong to another world which Rose had abruptly forsaken. She felt her stomach clenching as they left the houses behind them and headed into the country between the hospital and the grand house she had seen when she first explored with Edward, which Mr Winton now informed her was one of the properties of Mr Christopher Pemberton.

All too soon they joined the queue of carriages on the drive; they were disembarking, they were mounting the steps to the front door, they were handing in their cloaks and changing their footwear, and going forward to be announced. The curtain was rising: the performance was beginning.

'Mrs Winton, Mr Winton, Miss Winton, Miss Clarke,' called out the servant at the entrance to the ballroom. Immediately Julia spotted one of her friends and tugged Rose with her to introduce her. Before she knew it she was amidst a whole crowd of young women, all chattering and comparing dresses and ribbons and slippers and so on, and talking about who they might dance with, and who they had seen already, and which man they admired most, and she felt both curiously at home in this female embrace, and at the same time completely detached from the scrimmage.

Mr Winton approached her and introduced a man called Warburton, who promptly took her onto the floor for a reel. She recalled him as a colleague of Sir George, and he made sure she knew he was a person to rely on in case of need. Once the dance was finished and he returned her to Julia's side, she introduced her to two other gentlemen, Mr Plant and Mr Graham, Winton's colleagues in Cambridge, whom she danced with in turn, feeling she was being unnecessarily protected by Winton, and having her loyalties rather broadcast to the room. Feeling she had neglected Julia's friends shamefully, she was conducted by the second man, Philip Graham, back to the group, and found Julia and all the others were already booked for two or more dances themselves. So much for altruism.

She took herself off to the lemonade table to catch her breath, and observe the room. It was already half full, although the Winton party had arrived at the earliest polite moment, for obvious reasons. She needed to identify the people Mr Winton had labelled as possibles as soon as she could, and try and get into conversation with them. So far, none of those she might recognise had arrived, and Winton would doubtless come to her once any she did not know came into the room.

As she scanned the ballroom, she became aware of a familiar slightly hunched back nearby. She moved a few steps to get a better look. It was Mr James, looking somewhat uncomfortable.

'Mr James! How pleasant to see you here. If you recall, we met at Lord Swaffham's ball in London in the spring.'

'Eh? Oh, um, d-did we? I am afraid my eyesight is not what it might be, M-miss . . . ?'

'Rose Clarke. You were hoping for a fellowship at Caius at the time, and you told me that you saw music in colours.'

'D-did I really? I did, now I remember. Yes, they are p-playing in a shade of mauve at present, and I have indeed accepted a fellowship, I am researching the uses of the square root of minus one and studying complex numbers.'

Rose was most intrigued, but remembering she was supposed to be a lady ignorant of mathematics, and invisible, said, 'Mr James, how interesting, but would you care to ask me to dance? I know it is not usual for the lady to make the invitation, but I recall you are of a retiring nature.'

'Indeed I am, Miss Clarke. But I should be glad to take you onto the f-floor, if you wish.'

They danced a gavotte, Rose recalling how methodically Mr James counted the steps, and how intent he seemed, to the exclusion of conversation.

'Do you have friends here?' she asked, once they had taken refuge by the matrons. I should not like to abandon you, but I must meet with several other gentlemen who have claims upon me.'

'Oh yes, Miss, I do. I came with William.' He looked around short-sightedly as if his friend might appear from nowhere.

'William?'

'Certainly, he introduced us in London. Mr B-blackburn, you danced with him.'

Mr Blackburn! Why was he here? He was not on the guest list, and for that matter neither was Mr James. What should she do? But Mr James was still speaking.

'He had an invitation very late, and he asked if I would come with him. He is always keen to get me out of college, and he said that a man I knew from Trinity would be here, a Mr B-burgess, but I have not seen him.'

Mr Burgess? Surely Mr James could not be mixed up with the conspiracy? Or was he playing a very deep game, as someone who could not be suspected?

'It is still early, Mr James, and there is a fair queue of carriages waiting in the drive.'

'Of course. Also, I believe there are one or two men from my college who should be here, a Mr Sterne, who is a very good mathematician, but inclined to be rowdy, and Dr Seligman of course, he is a sound man. But I must not detain you, M-miss, you will have dances to dance, and suitors to meet, I have no doubt. I shall go and look for my friends.'

CHAPTER 23

ROSE RETURNED TO MRS WINTON'S seat and made sure she was not lacking in refreshments, and then focussed on her task. She watched the people arriving, trying to work out who was who, and how they all fitted together. There was Mr Burgess, unmistakeable by his height, greeting Mr James, and entering into conversation with him; there were the Duke and Duchess of Swaffham surrounded by their orbiting satellites; and Mr Laughton, talking to another man in clerical garb whom she did not know. She had a thought.

'Mrs Winton, are you acquainted with many of the people here?'

'I am, dear, or most of them. since they are local worthies for the most part.'

'I am anxious to know who some of them are. Who is that talking to Mr Laughton by the statue of Venus?'

'That is the vicar of Trumpington Mr Heckford, and see, they are being joined by Mr Hailstone of Trinity college, the Professor of Geology. He has a great interest in the village, and some say he may become vicar once Mr Heckford is gone.'

Rose recognised the Professor from his lecture, and realised she had a gold mine here. Mrs Winton was not in any way ignorant of her son's occupation or his interests, though she did not allude to them. She catechised her about a number of other persons, and made mental notes as to whom to observe and what they might be interested in.

'Is there anyone you would particularly like to dance with, dear? I could introduce you if you like?'

Rose thought. It might be helpful to talk to the geology professor, as he was at Trinity, and ask if he was aware of any of his students being here. At her suggestion, Mrs Winton towed her across the room, cut Mr Hailstone out of the group he had joined, consisting of several learned-looking gentlemen, and addressed him forthrightly.

'John, this is a ball: you need to attend to the ladies, not talk rocks with your fusty friends. Come, I have a visitor at Milton, Miss Clarke, you would do much better to dance with her. Miss Clarke, Mr Hailstone.'

Rose dropped a middling-sized curtsey, as befitted a Professor of a certain age. He was a well-set up man in his forties, and he grinned at Mrs Winton.

'Does Miss Clarke have a liking for fossils?'

'Come on John, you are not that old. Take her onto the floor.'

Mr Hailstone inclined his head. 'Delighted. Miss Clarke?'

They had to wait a few moments for the next dance to begin. Rose enquired which college he was at, and then whether there were any others from Trinity at the dance. He explained that Trinity was a large college and he did not know most of the students.

'Except, Miss Clarke, you may well have noticed Mr Burgess there yourself, he is so recognisable by his great height. I do not care for the man, but he is said to be a very able mathematician. Also, there are some undergraduates whose faces I recognise from dining in Hall, but do not know their names for the most part. Ah, now, see that man at the end of this set, that is Noakes, he is a Trinity man.'

Rose gazed up at his face while trying to memorise Noakes' appearance out of the corner of her eye. 'It must be so interesting to be able to study at Cambridge.'

'Hmm, well, maybe. It seems most of the University does not share your view, Miss. Do you have an interest in minerals and fossils? Or,' inclining his head towards Mr Noakes, 'perhaps more of an interest in younger specimens?'

'Sir! I do find minerals interesting, but I have little knowledge. I have seen specimens of gemstones in gentlemen's curio collections, and the names seem most complicated.'

'It is a very young science, and there is hardly anything about it as yet that we understand. However, that means there is much to discover. Not just which rocks are suitable for jewellery, but how they are formed, and how old they are, and so on. Also, why certain creatures are only found in certain types of rock, in certain strata, and how they appear to become more complex as you move through the strata. But I apologise, I must be boring you. Let us dance.'

The next figure was beginning, and they took their places. Rose bit back what she wanted to say, which was to tell him she was anything but bored, and to ask him to say much more about the rocks; and instead smiled at him, while noting that Mr Hailstone nodded to a couple of gentlemen in the set; how Mr Burgess was now with Mr Sterne, and how others had arranged themselves in groups around the walls. It was slow work, trying to see the patterns of people's interactions, the while keeping from tripping up in the dance, and conversing with her partner, but it was exciting. Also, she had never had so many dances as at this ball, it was exhilarating to be in demand.

After the set Mr Hailstone, with a rather sardonic grin, took her over to Mr Noakes and introduced her, saying 'Miss Clarke tells me she is most interested in fossils, but I divined she may have other preferences,' which made Rose blush. Mr Noakes gallantly took her out onto the floor and she realised why Mr Hailstone had pushed her at him: he was most handsome and debonair, he was tall and elegant, and he spoke with a hint of an accent. She felt his voice was caressing her, and she tingled in her spine at its sound. She asked him about where he came from.

'Yes, Miss Clarke, you are perceptive. My mother was French, and we lived in Paris until the Revolution. After some time my father felt the city was not safe for us, and so we departed for London. I was aged nine.'

'How interesting. Do you still have friends back in France? How have they fared under Napoleon?' She gazed up at him, while plucking at the neckline of her dress.

'Very few, Miss Clarke. It has not been possible to keep in touch, because of the war. Also, my mother tells me some of her friends have been executed, and others who joined the revolutionaries have fallen from grace and also lost their lives. It was a most dangerous time, the Terror. But Napoleon seems to have restored peace and order, and has galvanised the country to become great again after the excesses of the Bourbons.'

Rose remembered she had to seem ignorant of politics. 'How sad, Mr Noakes, to lose so many friends in that way. But Mr Bonaparte has been very good for the people, you say?'

'Indeed. He is a great man. He has restored much territory that France had lost, and given the country back its pride.'

'That is marvellous to hear. And what do you think will come of these changes?'

'I foresee peace in Europe, which has not been the case for years. But, Miss Clarke, what of you? Where do you come from?'

Rose explained her visit, and her friendship with Julia, and decided she had to risk a probing question. She patted her hair, and smiled again, and said,

'It is so interesting to meet such clever men as you who are at the University, Mr Noakes. One of my relatives was recently at Emmanuel. Do you know any men at that college?'

'Trinity is such a large college, Miss Clarke, that one can find all the society one needs within its walls. And I am only in my second year. When was your relative at Emmanuel?'

'Oh, I am not sure. Quite recently, I think.'

'And his name?'

Rose was having trouble keeping up with her inventions. 'Oh, yes, he is, um, John Clarke, that's right, but I think he must have left before you started. Silly me!'

'I don't recall any Clarkes there. I do know one fellow I suppose, he was at school with me, Robert Cork. But that's all.'

'I see. And do you attend many balls, Mr Noakes? This one is so exciting, so many important people are here.' Rose wanted to take the conversation away from Emmanuel now she had the link.

'Not so many, I'm afraid. I'm lucky to have been invited to this one, but it seems Mr Pemberton wanted to have a wide range of guests, so he asked some of his college friends to each pick out a couple of likely men to come. There are Dukes and Duchesses here, and little old me, a poor sizar with few prospects.'

'Surely not, Mr Noakes. You have so many things to recommend you.' She turned her head away, coyly.

Fortunately the dance finished at this juncture, as she was finding it increasingly difficult to play the *ingénue* without giggling at herself. Mr Noakes led her back to Mrs Winton, and she curtseyed again to him before he left her.

The ballroom was filling up. Peter – Mr Winton (she really must remember to keep to his proper title now she was Rose) – came over and pointed out several people whose names she had learned, and she tried to hold them all in her head. She made a few notes on the back of her dance card, but it was much better to keep them in her mind.

Then, trying to keep the excitement out of her voice and manner, she tried to tell him of what she had just learned from Mr Noakes, but he hushed her, and drew her aside into a place where they could not be overheard. Then she explained that he was a sizar invited to the ball *via* Mr Hailstone, and therefore might be in need of money, that he had French sympathies, and that he knew Mr Cork. Returning to the ballroom she then spent a little time with Mrs Winton and the other matrons, so as not to appear to be too noticeable, to give anyone who had noticed her talking with Noakes or for that matter

Mr Winton time to forget her apparent interest. All the while, though, she was keeping half an eye on the rest of the room, just in case.

There was Guy, or perhaps she ought to try and remember his proper title, um, yes, Viscount Beauchamp. And he was with Charlie. Charlie was . . .. and she nearly missed what Mrs Winton had said, for trying to recall his title.

'Sorry, Mrs Winton, I'm afraid I was distracted by those handsome young men over there,' she temporised.

Mrs Winton gave her a knowing look, and offered to introduce her to them once she had found out who they were. Rose couldn't risk actually dancing with one of the Jesuits, it would be far too close an inspection to survive, so she said that Mrs Winton was too kind, but it would be too embarrassing, so please, no. And all the while she was remembering Charlie was the Honourable Charles French, and that he had a bad back, from a fall from a horse, but she didn't know this as Rose. Naturally.

She needed a drink. Not lemonade, but a proper drink. Unfortunately she had seen no whisky and she couldn't possibly have had any if there were any. Which there wasn't.

'Would you like me to fetch you a glass of wine, Mrs Winton? And your friends?'

Mrs Winton winked at her. 'That would be most acceptable, Rose. Three glasses, I think?'

Rose managed to have the wine poured for her from the bottle and not from the jug which stood on the table, explaining that these drinks were for her chaperones, and found a tray for the five glasses she had requested, and took them across to the ladies. She took a deep draught of her own glass before she arrived, once she had found a ledge to set her tray down on, and tried to relax her shoulders.

While she was contemplating a second perhaps more ladylike sip, she saw him. Mr Blackburn, in scarlet, with his sword by his side, looking so amazingly handsome she forgot Mr Noakes' charms, and Mr Winton's attractions, and went all wobbly inside. It might not sound terribly elegant, but that was what she felt. She had forgotten that he was going to be here, since Mr James had told her, what with all the thinking about the suspects and looking for who knew whom. She quickly swallowed the rest of her wine, set the empty glass down and scuttled off to the matrons before he saw her.

Mrs Winton received the tray and having passed wine to her friends, took her own glass, leaned over to Rose and murmured, 'A very fine figure of a man, that officer. Would you like me to keep your second glass until you have spoken with him?'

'I, er, Mrs Winton, you have very good eyesight.'

'I wasn't born yesterday, my dear. Whatever is going on between you and Peter I don't want to know; I am sure it is most proper, but it is exercising you considerably this evening. However, I see you are also clearly quite taken by that officer. What is his name?'

'Mr Blackburn, madam. I met him at a ball in London in the spring, and once more in September.'

'Should I attract his attention?'

'That would be most desirable if I were not, um, engaged on the business you have discerned but do not need to know about. If that is satisfactory with you?'

'Certainly. What do you intend to do now?'

Rose thought. 'Well, would you take a turn around the room with me? I should like to see who else I might wish to talk with.'

They set off in a most leisurely fashion, Mrs Winton pausing to greet every acquaintance, which gave Rose time to look around and notice for instance that Mr Noakes was now in conversation with a lordly-looking gentleman of middle age, whom she did not recognise, and also a young man whose back was to them. They were in an alcove off the main room, where they would not be overheard, but they only stayed together for a few seconds and then separated. She tried to make a mental image of the younger man's coat and his calves, and the older man's face, but her memory was getting very full.

Also, she was worrying about Mr Blackburn. Was he here because he was involved with the conspiracy somehow? Why was he not on the guest list? And there was Mr Burgess talking to Mr James and Mr Sterne: what was going on there? Not to mention that she needed to avoid the Jesuit oarsmen, and keep her eye on Mr Hailstone, and see if anyone approached Mr Price, the other man on Noakes' staircase who was on the guest list, once she had identified him.

As they circulated there was a slight commotion as a group of men carrying something heavy tried to make their way through the crowd. It was a huge cake, or sugar confection, done in the style of a mediaeval castle, with candles on the turrets and a tall flagpole in the centre, placed upon a huge mirror. The buzz of rumour around it vouchsafed that it was a tribute to the Cambridgeshire militia in whose honour the ball was being held, and the candles were to be lit at supper when all were assembled.

Everyone wanted to get a closer look, as it was so finely constructed, and detailed. Rose held back, and instead kept her eyes on those who did not crowd round, seeing their expressions and reactions to its arrival. Most people were agog at the excitement, but a few held aloof. Interestingly, one of these was the lordly-looking man she had noticed with Noakes. What could this mean?

The cake was placed on a space hastily cleared in the supper-room, and someone rang a bell for silence. The accompanying card was read out: "To the members of our brave County Militia, wishing you every good fortune in our struggle against tyranny. For best effect please dim the lighting once supper is announced, and light the candles and flagpole. Best wishes, your friends at the University."

Rose first tried Mrs Winton's fund of knowledge to identify the lordly-seeming man; then, having drawn a blank, and trying to keep the man in sight, searched for Winton, or Plant, or Graham, or anyone who might know him. For some reason they had all disappeared. Even Mr Blackburn was nowhere to be seen. Supper was being announced, and the guests were flocking to the supper room. Pride of place was given to the militia officers, who stood around the table in their dress uniforms looking splendid, and to the nobles present. The colonel of the regiment stepped forward with a lighted taper. Servants snuffed out some of the candles around the walls, and carried candlestands from the room. A hush fell on the crowd, broken only by some muffled shouts from outside, and heavy thuds as if there was a fracas going on.

Just then, Rose noticed James Smith on a kind of balcony which overlooked the room. He was the room mate of Edward Hever, he lived just below Rose in the Brick Building. What was he doing here? He wasn't on the guest list. And his coat was familiar. It had a narrow tarnished-silver trimming, just like that man talking to Noakes and the older man had. He had a kind of excited grin on his face, not a look of enjoyment, but a look of dreadful anticipation. She had seen that expression before. When would it have been? She had it: he looked just like her brother Charles just before he perpetrated some disastrous practical joke on her or George.

What could it mean? And where were all George's colleagues? Were they outside fighting? She couldn't see anything through the windows: the candles reflected from them too brightly. She moved closer to the supper tables, shoving her way through the crowd, using her elbows, ignoring the cries of perturbation from the onlookers. The colonel was making a speech, thanking Mr Pemberton for his hospitality, thanking his brother-officers for their support in raising the company, thanking the guests for their good wishes. He was going on a bit, to be fair, milking the moment, but that suited Rose. She had begun to have an idea about the cake. Surely they wouldn't do anything so amateurish? But then, they did seem to be rank amateurs, and if she didn't do something about it, their plan might well work.

Finally she forced her way to the front of the crowd. The colonel was just lowering his taper to the first candle. Rose suddenly decided. If she was wrong, then so be it. She threw herself forward, grabbed the taper from the man's hand, flung it to the floor and ground it out. Cries of outrage followed. Hands reached out to seize her. Twisting away, she grabbed a sword from one of the officers and slashed at the cake. One turret fell off, then another. She hacked at the base of the flagpole, before she was dragged away.

'Look at the cake!' she yelled. 'Since when was a cake made on a base of iron? Taste what is below the flagpole!'

The colonel paused in his pursuit of her. He looked at the ruin of the cake, at the base now revealed by the collapse of the sugar paste. He leant forward, licked a finger, reached out a hand. He touched the small hole that had been where the flagpole was sited, tasted his finger.

'Gunpowder!' he announced, in a stentorian voice. 'Gunpowder!'

CHAPTER 24

THERE WAS A RIPPLE OF shock in the crowd, a crescendo of talk, rising in note, panicky. But Rose relaxed slightly. The hands that held her loosened, and she gave over the sword to the nearest officer. Panting, she stepped forward slightly. She was going to need a very good cover story now. And she had no time to think one up. It had better be the truth, then. Or as much of the truth as she could reveal.

She curtseyed to the colonel. 'Sir,' she said, 'would you examine the cake again, more thoroughly?'

The colonel took out his sword, cut away the rest of the sugar paste, to reveal a squat, grey, iron box with a small aperture at the top. Rose picked up the flagpole from the floor and handed it to him silently. He examined it, peeled away the covering, smelled it.

'A fuse. A long, fast-burning fuse. Whatever next?'

'Sir, I think you will find that iron casing is packed full of gunpowder, like a giant grenade. If you had lit the flagpole we would all have been blown to bits. Sir.'

The colonel had gone rather pale. He looked at the fuse in his hand, at the cake, at Rose. 'But, how . . . ; I mean, how did you know?'

Rose leaned forward close to his ear. 'Sir, if you would be so good, can I have one of my colleagues explain later? I would prefer not to be known publicly. Perhaps you might escort me to a private room? And ask Mrs Winton my chaperone to come and join us?'

The colonel harrumphed a little at this, but soon agreed. He sent one of his men to find Mrs Winton, and took Rose and his host to a morning-room quite out of the way. The three of them stood awkwardly for a while, until Mrs Winton arrived, and then they sat down. Rose reached for Mrs Winton's hand because she had begun to shake all over.

She raised her head. 'Sir, and I would be glad if you told absolutely nobody about this, I can tell you that I am assisting the Foreign Office in uncovering a group of traitors working for France. Mr Pemberton here knows, I believe, of my colleague Mr Peter Winton, as he has had dealings with him in the making of arrangements for tonight?'

'Correct,' was Mr Pemberton's only contribution to the discussion.

'I do not know where my colleagues are at present, but I suspect they may have been lured outside by an attack designed as a feint, and engaged in a fight so that none of them would be near the cake when it was to be lit.'

She paused, trying to collect herself, and stop her voice from trembling. Mrs Winton squeezed her hand. 'You are doing so well, Rose,' she said, comfortingly.

'Anyway, I hope they will have seen the ruffians off,' she continued, wiping a tear from her eye, 'but I thought I was the only one here inside, so I had to do what I could. Please, don't tell anyone anything, Colonel. Obviously, you will have to deal with the bomb, I mean the cake, and so on, but could you tell people, I don't know, something that doesn't focus on me?'

'But you saved us all. You should be honoured.'

'Please, no. I need to stay unknown.' The colonel still looked unconvinced. What could she say? 'Colonel, I am . . .'

In that moment, Rose realised that what she was really, was a spy. Maybe a fairly untrained one, but a spy nonetheless. And she needed to continue her education if she was going to be truly effective, and for that she needed anonymity. What should she say next?

Suddenly the door burst open and Winton hurtled in looking

dishevelled and with his face streaked with blood, closely followed by . . . Mr Blackburn? His coat was cut about, and his face filthy.

'What happened? I could only get a garbled story out there of a bomb? And a girl saving everyone?' Peter Winton looked beside himself.

Rose looked up at the two men, and started to speak. Her voice didn't seem to be working, though, and she burst into tears and buried her head in Mrs Winton's bosom.

'There, there, dear. I'll tell them.' Then to her son and Mr Blackburn. 'Rose here realised the cake that was delivered to celebrate the militia's efforts was a bomb, and stopped the colonel from lighting the fuse, and we are all safe and nobody is hurt. Except maybe you two. What have you been doing?'

'I'm fine, mother. Just a few scratches. We were called out to deal with a gang of ruffians who were about to break in and cause mayhem, and it took us a while to send them about their business. I'm not sure about all the others, but William and I are fine.'

'Plant got a ball in his arm, but he's being looked after,' said Mr Blackburn. 'Graham was knocked out, but he's coming round. I didn't see the rest, the outside men I mean. But, Rose, I mean, Miss Clarke, what are you doing here?'

Rose lifted her head. 'It's a long story,' she said, wearily. 'Can it wait? I take it your secret job is with the Foreign Office? That you're, um, working alongside Mr Winton?'

Blackburn looked at Winton, who nodded. 'Got it in one. I always said you were a bright girl, didn't I?'

Everything took a long time to arrange after this, but eventually Rose found herself in the Wintons' carriage heading back to Milton. It seemed that the ball had restarted once the debris of the cake had been cleared, and the supper table relaid. Everyone was having a fine old time rehashing the horrors that never had been. Rose fell asleep against Mrs Winton soon after they left, and missed most of the trip. Julia apparently wanted all the details, but her brother told her she was not to ask, and not to badger Rose for them either. It took some persuading by her mother, but she eventually agreed.

In the morning, Rose sat up in bed to find she had a pair of visitors, Mrs Winton and Peter, bringing her breakfast on a tray.

'I'm only here for propriety, dear,' Mrs Winton said. 'I shan't hear anything.' She sat herself by the window and took out some embroidery.

Peter sat awkwardly on a chair a safe distance away as Rose tackled her coffee and cakes. 'Do you feel up to going back to er, town?' he asked, eventually. 'I mean, you seemed all in yesterday. Perhaps you ought to rest here for a few days?'

Rose grinned brightly at him. 'I'm fine now,' she said. 'I know, you think a man wouldn't have burst into tears, and maybe he wouldn't, but I'm a girl, and we work differently.' She glanced over at Mrs Winton. 'Anyway, I don't want to miss Mr Spurgeon on Sunday, nor, er, well, any of the things I have been doing.'

'So,' Peter looked up at her cautiously, 'shall you leave here as you came?'

'Indubitably. Just give me a while to get this breakfast eaten and do a little washing and rearrange my outfits, and I'll be ready to get back.'

There was quite a little argy-bargy before Peter conceded defeat, and Mrs Winton took him away promising to explain to Julia why Rose had had to leave so early without saying goodbye. Soon Richard reappeared in his previous incarnation, and taking the same back stair as before, was whisked into the carriage heading into Cambridge.

As they could not be overheard within the carriage Richard explained what he hadn't felt able to say in front of Mrs Winton. 'You see, I need to go back to Cambridge and to the lectures and reading and so on. I'll need to be fully educated if I'm to be a full-time spy.'

'What!'

Rose smiled sympathetically at him. 'Did your fight harm your hearing? I said, I want my degree if I'm going to work for the Foreign Office.'

Winton was shocked into silence for a while, so tactfully Richard left it for a while, until they were entering Chesterton.

'There is just one other thing,' he said. 'Mr Blackburn, what exactly is his job?'

Winton still looked grumpy. 'I'm not sure I can tell you. Maybe I should let him do it.'

'Might be tricky. Remember, I'm now Richard again.'

'Oh yes, so you are. And he doesn't need to know about your disguise. Does he?'

'Absolutely not. Please don't tell him about me. And obviously I can't meet him, not as Richard.' As she said this he had a sudden trembling again, wishing that things were different, and he could just have him call on her, no, on him, and send flowers, and all those normal everyday kinds of things.

'I see. Well, he is developing a new kind of post for himself, a sort of liaison man between the Army and the Foreign Office. He hears about unrest in the ranks, and anyone seen taking too close an interest in our troops, or officers who seem potentially disloyal, and tells us: we let him know anything that concerns the Army that we find out from our intelligence men. Is that enough?'

'That will do fine. I expect you'll tell me more once you know about the rest of the gang.'

'Maybe. Maybe not. Need to know, you see. Now, what have we learned? That somebody was able to sneak some of the gunpowder out of the Pink House without our man noticing; and that they have some other base where they can prepare their equipment, meaning the cake bomb. Have you discovered anyone who is involved that we didn't know about?'

'Not for sure. Mr Noakes, of Trinity, seems likely to be the man Cork visited after we watched the gunpowder being delivered, but I don't know for definite. It still could be Hope or Price: I didn't find out what Price looks like, and Hope wasn't on the guest list. Professor Hailstone invited Noakes to the ball, but there doesn't seem anything to connect him otherwise. Noakes was talking to an older man I didn't know, together with a younger one, who I think, but I'm not certain, is James Smith who shares with Edward Hever on my stair, just before the, um, bomb business.'

'What about Burgess?'

'He talked with Mr James, Fellow of Caius, whom I met in London before, and who is so unworldly I find it hard to believe he is involved, except inadvertently; and with Mr Sterne of the same college, who hosted the wine party you took me too. Mr Hailstone knew him, but I expect everyone does, because of his height.'

'Not a very good feature for a conspirator to have, unless he uses it as an enormous bluff, perhaps. Now, what did the older man look like? The one with Noakes and, did you say, Smith?'

'Yes, I saw them together quite briefly, and the older man seemed less activated by the commotion around the cake being lit than the other guests. Well, he was about forty-five, perhaps, a little portly but only slightly so, he had dark hair in the Brutus style, quite long on top, an inconspicuous waistcoat, a quite unmemorable face . . . really he was quite unremarkable.'

'Yes, could be a lot of people, I think.'

'Your mother didn't know him, because I asked her.'

'Well, that lets out about two thirds of the company, she is an encyclopaedia of connections.'

The carriage rumbled over the Great Bridge, and headed down past Sidney Sussex towards Emmanuel. Richard leaned back away from the window and set himself mentally to recommence his role as a boy in college, after this brief day of being Rose. He would have to make sure he behaved towards Peter as a fellow-undergraduate now, not as an unmarried lady out in Society, nor yet as an intelligencer. He hoped Peter would remember his pronouns, and not be too diffident about his language and conversational topics, and all the other things that might give him away.

'Hope you had a good time meeting my father, Richard,' said Peter as they drew up. Maybe you'll take up a job with him in three years or so?'

Richard shook his head. What was he saying? Oh yes, his cover story. 'He was most friendly, Peter. I might well do that.'

They separated in Chapel Court, Peter heading for his own staircase while Richard followed the groom carrying his box up to his room. At the top of the stair he was surprised to find the groom entering the room before him. The door was unlocked, open even! He bumped into the man on the threshold.

'Sir, looks like you've had a burglar,' said the groom.

Richard wriggled past him. The room was in disorder. Papers were strewn about, his glasses smashed, books everywhere. In the bedroom, all his clothes were out of the closet, and the bed overturned. Someone had been looking for something. But they could not have found anything, for he had given all his papers over to Peter Winton, and burnt all the sheets on which he had worked out the codes.

He came back out into the keeping-room, where the groom was still standing holding his box, looking shocked. 'Would you mind putting my box in the bedroom, please,' he ordered, and stood, dismayed, surveying the mess. Then he noticed: his painting, his Meer, had been pulled off the wall and cut to pieces! He felt a chilling grip around his heart, tears began to prick his eyes. How could they do this to him? What evil men would destroy his favourite possession? And why would they want to?

The groom coughed behind him. 'Shall I send up your gyp to clear up this mess, sir?'

Richard blinked back his tears. It was all very well saying it was fashionable for men to cry but he couldn't risk it, not in his position. 'I don't know. Wait a moment. No, I think we should leave it until . . . I want to fetch someone to look at it first, thankyou.'

He saw the man out, and then decided. He had better fetch Peter Winton first, he would know what to do. And together they would be better able to catch the criminal. And if he got his hands on them, well, they had better be strong and capable or else he'd tear them to bits. His poor painting!

CHAPTER 25

PETER SURVEYED THE SCENE OF devastation with him. 'Have you touched anything?' he asked.

'Nothing. I came straight to you. Well, I locked the door after me, it had been left open when we got back. And the groom put my box in the bedroom.'

'Are you sure you locked it yesterday?'

'Absolutely. What do you take me for?'

'Good. So, what do you think they were looking for?'

'I suppose, any papers, anything to link me to the gang.'

'And were there any?'

'No, none at all. You took them away, remember?'

'That's right. And my things are quite safe. How about letters? For example, from Sir George to you?'

Richard looked embarrassed. 'I only had a couple, I keep them in my coat, it makes me feel better, somehow. Silly, isn't it?'

'Not at all. This, er, masquerade of yours must be rather hard work, quite draining, I should think. Having to remember all the time how to behave, and so on. Without any mistakes that I have noticed. And it turns out very fortuitous, they can't link you to the Foreign Office that way.'

Richard gave him a grateful but rather wan smile. 'Sir George got in because the porters gave him a key, they know he is my sponsor. How did the burglars enter?'

'We can check with the porter, but I expect it was skeleton keys.' He examined the lock on the door. 'Yes, see here, some fresh fine scratches on the plate, around the keyhole, quite different from the marks of keys. A careless use of the picks, as one might expect from these men.'

Peter looked carefully around the room, picking up occasional items, inspecting Richard's books, feet occasionally crunching on broken glass. He straightened up after looking under an armchair. 'Here's your whisky bottle, lad. Rolled out of their way, I'll be bound, or they might have taken it with them. Take it, you might need it. They were definitely looking for papers: see how the spines of all the books have been bent back.'

'What about my painting? Why would they destroy that?'

'I expect they were looking for anything hidden between the canvas and the backing. Ideal hiding place, if you don't know that every burglar knows about it.'

'I'm going to kill them for that. I loved that painting.'

'Hang on, lad, I don't want you putting yourself in danger.'

'Like I wasn't in danger at the ball, when the colonel was about to light the fuse of the bomb?'

'Good point. Sorry.'

'So what next? I'm going to ask the porter if anyone asked for a key to my room, in case they tried that before picklocks.'

'Just a moment, before you rush off. First, when would this have been done?'

'How do you mean?'

'Well, your bedder would have come in to clean this morning, and the gyp to set the fire, even though you were away overnight. Yes?'

'I see. And they would have noticed the mess, and the open door.'

'Correct.'

'Well, they both officially go off duty at ten, though Mr Fenn isn't on this stair after nine, he does the next staircase too. Mrs Fenn starts at the top with me and the man opposite, she's done on this floor about eight thirty.'

'Maybe, but she'd be sure to notice someone trashing your room, it would make a fair bit of noise.'

'Of course. Well, she generally slips off for a pipe of tobacco a little after nine thirty, she goes to see her friend in one of the houses at the end of the Close.'

'And we got here about eleven. Hmm, he was cutting it fine. Which means that rather than searching here yesterday, he was compelled to wait until this morning. Which implies he was probably unaware you were out of college yesterday until it was too late, and he was engaged in the evening. But, I should say, he was almost certainly of this college. Possibly he even lives on this stair.'

'Why?'

'Knowing the movements of the bedders, and so on, and being able to observe who had gone out this morning. Also, how would he know of your connection to our group? Have you told anyone?'

'Nobody at all. I mean, nobody except Hever, of course. He knows about the Pink Houses business, and the codes, and Cork being involved, but nothing else.'

'What did you tell him you were doing yesterday?'

'I didn't mention I would be away.'

'Could he have told anyone?'

'Well, I made it very clear that this was all completely secret, but, he does like to talk, and he might have said something to someone after a few beers, I suppose.'

'I think our next move is to find Mr Hever and ask him a few questions. Well, actually, you had better ask him the questions, so that my identity is still secret.'

'I will. So, first I will go and check with the porters whether anyone asked for a key for my room in the last day or two; and I can get them to tell Mrs Fenn about the mess, so she can clear up my room. Also, I can ask if they know where Edward is, and then give him the third degree.'

'Good. I will be in my room until dinner, let me know how you progress. I have to write some reports.'

'That's a thought. How is it that your rooms have not been searched? I'm sure the plotters must know you are an agent of the King.'

'I had one of Mr Bramah's Challenge Locks fitted to my oak when I moved in. It is said to be unpickable, and nobody has as yet claimed the £200 reward for solving it. I always sport the oak when I go out for any reason. It is a most solid piece of wood. My strongbox has a similar lock, and it is secured to the floor in my study. I have learnt caution over the last few years. I am only sorry I did not think you too would be a target in college.'

Richard was impressed with his precautions. 'How could you have known I might be vulnerable? Noone knew of my discoveries. Except Edward, of course.'

The porter expressed shock and outrage that anyone could have burgled Richard's room, and agreed it must have been someone from within college, as no visitors had come into college this morning, and nobody had asked for a key since Sir George two weeks ago. He promised to alert Richard's gyp and bedder to make good the damage, and said that he rather thought Mr Hever had gone out of college about nine o'clock in the company of his room mate Mr Smith.

Richard reported all this to Peter, and then decided he had better have a little lunch, if it had not all been cleared away. Nobody there had seen Edward that morning, though only a few of the undergraduates were lingering in Hall over an argument about prizefighters. Neither Cork nor Smith was there: he wondered about whether to go and ask James Smith if he had seen Edward. He still wasn't sure about him: he had certainly been watching the cake from the balcony with that awful expression, and he hadn't appeared on the guest list, and he might well have been the man talking to Noakes and the older man, but could he really be fully involved? He thought he ought to at least go and visit him, the porter had said he had gone out of college with Edward this morning.

There was no reply to his knock on Smith and Hever's room. That was nothing too strange: it was the hour for physical exercise, perhaps they were both out walking or some such. He tried the handle: it was locked. He did not have the skill or the tools to enter, and judged it would be a bad idea anyway. He carried on up to his room and found Mrs Fenn just finishing up stacking the books on his desk.

'Thankyou very much for this, Mrs Fenn. I'm sorry for the mess: as you see I had an unwelcome visitor.'

'It's something awful, sir. And your poor picture, I knows you was real fond of it, I've put the pieces by, but I don't think you could do anything with it, it's so cut about, like.'

'No, thankyou, Mrs Fenn, could you just throw it away please. It's beyond saving.'

'Right you are, sir. And I've swep' up all that nasty glass on the floor, you won't be cutting yourself now. An' hung your things up in the closet, best I could. Made the bed; I think that's all tidy and shipshape now.'

'Thankyou again. I must say, it was quite a shock to find it like that.'

'It was all straight at ten o'clock, sir, because I got behind with my other gentlemen and didn't leave the staircase till then, you know.'

'That's most useful to know. I got back into college at eleven, so whoever did it must have been quite quick about it.'

'Right you are, sir. Do you have any idea who might'a done it?'

'We think it must have been someone from in college. Were the other men in their rooms on this stair this morning?'

Mrs Fenn thought. 'Mr Dillard opposite was out, I think he said he was going to Ely for summat; Mr Hever went out with Mr Smith about nine; Mr Jones and Mr Bugden facing them were both in, because I had to clean around them, but they went out before I left.' She paused, scratched her chin. 'Mr Cork was in. He slept in late, he wasn't up until just before I went, he'd been at some ball or other last night, he said. And what about Mr Bedford and Mr Archer beside him? I don't rightly recall.'

'I think I heard they were going hunting?'

'That's right, of course they was, Fenn had to clean their boots last night, they'd got muddy with Friday's hunt. So that's them, they was out too. Seems like there was nobody around this morning, doesn't it? Now, Mr Johnson was here, he was reading some book or other, but Mr Yaxley who rooms with him was, let me see, he . . . I don't rightly know about him. And Mr Beeching is the last one, he isn't in residence, his father took ill, he had to go home to see him. That's your lot.'

'You're a marvel, Mrs Fenn. Thankyou again, and I think I'll call on Mr Johnson and see if he heard anything.'

'Right you are, sir. Well, I'll be off, if there's nothing else?'

'That's all, Mrs Fenn. Goodbye.'

Abel Johnson said he had been reading Xenophon all morning and finding it hard going. He vaguely thought there might have been some noise at some point, but he hadn't paid it any attention as he had to finish a long section before a tutorial on Monday, and he had had pages and pages to go still. Yaxley had gone to fish first thing, somewhere over towards St Neots he rather thought. Sorry he couldn't help any more. But by the way, did Richard have any idea about this bit of his text that didn't seem to make any sense?

Richard did his best with the awkward construction but had to admit he was no better than Abel at untangling it. He decided he would probably meet Edward at dinner, so he might as well get his books and clothes in the right order, and then cast an eye over his Euclid until that time.

Dinner came: no Edward. Also, no Cork, and no Smith. Richard's suspicions were increasing, and he followed Peter out and told him what he had found out.

'I think, you know, that Edward might have been lured out of college by Smith and then something nasty might have happened to him. And that would leave Cork free to search my room. As far as I can find out, the only other person on the staircase after ten o'clock was Abel Johnson, and he is on the ground floor, so he wouldn't have heard much.'

'Surely you're going too far? I mean, Edward isn't a target for them, is he?'

'I don't know. But it isn't like him to be out of college all day, or especially to miss dinner. He likes his food. I'm just worried about him.'

'Well, I'm not sure what we could do. None of my men knows what he looks like, so we can't really keep a look out for him, and also we're a bit short-handed, because Plant and Graham are out of action for now, after the mill last night.'

'We have to do something.'

'He'll turn up soon. He's probably gone off with some crony on an escapade, or he's drinking in a tavern, or something.'

'At nine o'clock in the morning?'

'He's a young man, young men do all sorts of mutton-headed things, you know.'

'Yes, but . . .'

'Look, if he hasn't turned up by tomorrow morning, we will hunt for him, but we need to leave it for now. I have to go and report to my superiors. I'll be at Peterhouse, but I ought to be back before nine if you need me.'

Back in his room, Richard couldn't settle to his Euclid. Edward was in danger, he was sure of it. He didn't know how he knew, he just did. He had to go and find him, even though it was getting late, and already it was nearly dark.

He decided. He put on his gown and his hat, and locked his door carefully behind him. The gown was an awkwardness, but he didn't want to be progged if he was searching around town after dark. He could always hide it in the bush he and Edward had used if he needed to go further out, like to the river.

That was it, the river! Somehow, Edward had been taken to the river, probably onto the Black Prince, and was being held there. He was sure of it. He didn't know how he knew it, but he did. He couldn't tell Peter his ideas, he would think it was some girlish fantasy, and anyway he had gone off to Peterhouse, he didn't know where he could find him there.

He set off, wishing he had Edward's tinderbox and a lantern. Annoyingly the moon hadn't risen, and anyway it was nearly new moon time, so it wouldn't be of much help when it did. He made his way first rather nervously along Pembroke-lane to the Mill Pool, and cautiously looked for moored barges, watching out for unfriendly bargees who might take the presence of academicals as a challenge to their manhood. There were no boats at all lying there: perhaps it was because tomorrow was Sunday, or something?

Next, he cut through Queens'-lane to Trumpington-street, knowing that the colleges didn't allow barges to moor on their hallowed grounds. He hurried along, impelled with a sense of dread for his friend, passing Caius, worrying about Mr James and his links with Mr Burgess, and passing Trinity, half-expecting Mr Noakes to jump out of the Great Gate and accost him.

The river by the Great Bridge was busy with boats. It was hard to make out their names in the poor light. He toyed with the idea of asking one of the men if they had seen the barge he was looking for, but decided it would lead to too many questions and possibly alert the gang to his search. Instead, he worked his way slowly along the towpath, scrutinising each boat as he passed, and doing his best to see the names of the ones moored opposite. He did have some idea about the general shape of his quarry, it was a full-length boat, narrow, with a tarred canvas covering the cargo, and a short stubby chimney at the back end

Richard felt most uncomfortable doing this search in his gown, and at the first opportunity, when he got to Monk's Corner and felt he would not be observed by any university official, took it off and tied it around his waist under his coat. It was awkward and bulky there, and as soon as he crossed the King's Ditch and got to Jesus Green he stuffed it into a convenient bush, marking the place carefully so he could retrieve it.

There seemed to be no end to the barges. Every so often there would be a gap, but then another little cluster of boats, as if the bargees huddled together for warmth or protection. On and on he trudged, crossing the river when the towing path did, and keeping a wary eye out for any hostile-looking groups of men. It was much worse than when he and Edward had walked to the Pink Houses: for a start he was alone, but also he would need somehow to rescue Edward if he found him, and he had no idea how he might do this.

Past the lights of Barnwell on his right he walked, until the shape of Chesterton's church spire appeared dimly against the sky. There were no boats now, and he thought he would have to turn back in failure. He was cold too, without his gown wrapped around him, and he wished he had brought his scarf and gloves, but he had gone out in such a hurry. Maybe he would just go as far as the Pike and Eel, where the Black Prince had been moored before. If he didn't find it by then he would have to return to college and reconsider.

There it was! Moored all alone, unlike the other barges, the Black Prince lay about fifty yards before the tavern, showing a light at her stern, with sounds of men talking coming from inside. Richard crept up, holding his breath, and looked for somewhere to hide in the undergrowth beside the towpath. He crouched down and listened. He couldn't make out any words but it seemed there was an argument going on.

What should he do? All he could do, really, was wait, and listen, and hope. And pray, he thought. That would be a good plan. Silently, of course, so as not to be discovered.

After about fifteen minutes he was getting cramp in his legs so he cautiously shifted position. Just then a light spilled onto the stern of the boat, and figures appeared.

'Alright then, we'll go in the tavern, but it's one quart only, and then we have to get going, we need to be at Lynn by tomorrow well before dark.'

'We ain't a fly boat, boss.'

'We are now, Jake, yer Nick Ninny. Mr Barnes gives the orders, we does what we's told, and we gets paid, right?'

Three men clambered out of the boat, and set off along the path to the promise of ale. Richard waited a few moments, and then relaxed a little. What had the captain called Jake? A Nick Ninny? That didn't sound like bargee cant. It was something he'd taught Edward, after he heard George use the phrase. Had Edward said it in their hearing? Had they picked it up from him? He had to investigate.

The cabin was open and they had left the lamp burning. It only took a few seconds to determine nobody could be concealed within this tiny and rather disgusting little hole, where presumably all three men slept somehow. Where else could he search? Under the tarpaulin? He moved along the bank, calling softly, 'Edward? Are you there?'

Was that a grunt? A very faint grunt? From near the front of the barge? He moved closer. He called again. Yes, definitely, a grunt. He scrabbled at the ropes holding down the canvas, managed to lift one off its hook, and found there was just room to squeeze inside. He slid into the stygian darkness, even blacker than the lightless towpath, and tumbled forward onto something soft. Something soft and dusty. He sneezed, trying to keep it as quiet as he could.

'Edward?'

Grunt.

He reached out, and moved his arm as far as he could. Inched across the boat, searched some more. And then, definitely, that was not a flour sack. It was an arm, in a coat sleeve. How he wished for light. He moved crabwise across the cargo, so he could feel with both arms. It was a man, certainly, tied up tightly, and gagged too. It had to be Edward. Who else could it be? And what could he do?

The knots were far too stiff for him to undo, even with the extra strength he had in his fingers these days. Even the gag was immovable. How could he cut through these cords? All he had with him was his pen knife in his waistcoat pocket, which was fairly sharp, but only designed to cut quills, not thick rope. Still, it would have to do, he would do his best.

It was stuffy under the canvas, but still cold. He wriggled so he could get his penknife out, and then open the blade, all without dropping it. He'd never find it again if he did. Then, to work on the gag. Carefully, sawing away at the thick cloth, fibre by fibre, hoping the blade wouldn't break, and that he wouldn't cut Edward either. It took an age, but eventually he felt something give, and there was a sound of spitting as Edward got the lump of cloth out of his mouth and took some deep breaths.

'Thanks, whoever you are,' he said, voice dry and cracked.

'It's Richard. I'm so glad I found you. Are you well?'

'In the Pink, cub. I really enjoy lying in a cargo hold bound and gagged, it's the way I prefer to spend Saturdays.'

'Sorry. I mean, have they injured you?'

'Not much; but come on, get those ropes cut. I'm dreadfully stiff.'

Richard worked his way around so he could get at the ropes holding Edward's wrists. He chose a section of the cord, and started to work on it. His blade didn't feel as though it was up to the job, but it was making some progress. If only he could go more quickly.

Noises from the bank. Men's voices, heavy footsteps. What should he do? He stopped, holding his breath, keeping as still as he could. Even Edward, not given to silence, became still and quiet.

There was banging, the sound of ropes, the whinny of a horse, splashing of water. The boat began to rock, very gently. Then, gradually, the unmistakeable sensation of movement. They were on their way to King's Lynn, and Edward was still trussed up. Disaster!

There was nothing for it but to keep working at Edward's ropes, and then try and think of a plan once he was free. This one, as far as he could feel, was about half way through. He put his mouth close to where he thought Edward's ear might be and breathed, 'I'm nearly through, but it's slow work. Keep your spirits up.'

The rope fell apart, but Edward's arms still seemed bound together.

It was so difficult in this darkness to know whether he was cutting the right parts, but he just had to do his best. He set to work on the next cord. This one seemed easier: he was nearly through this one, he thought. Then, all of a sudden, the blade of his knife snapped, cutting his finger before it fell somewhere into the darkness. He cursed under his breath.

'Richard, I have a blade in my waistcoat, use that.'

He felt his way over Edward's body, under his coat, to where he thought his pockets might be. It was a most peculiar sensation, handling a man's body like this.

'No, not there, that's my crotch. Higher up, you Nick Ninny.'

Richard pulled his hand back as if stung. Gracious, this was getting out of hand. He didn't like to think what Sir George would say at his unladylike behaviour. Still.

Eventually he retrieved Edward's pen knife and started again on the ropes. This knife was much less sharp but more robust. After about five minutes more work he had the rope cut through and Edward could free his arms. They didn't seem to work very well, he said, so while Edward massaged them as best he could in the confined space Richard set to work on his legs.

His fingers were aching, his hands cramping, but eventually he had the last rope cut and Edward was free. He lay back in relief while Edward tried to get some life back into his leg muscles. What could they do now, though? Must they stay here until King's Lynn? And what would they do then?

'Can you swim?' whispered Edward.

'No, why?'

'Because we have to get off this hulk slap-bang. And we appear to be on a river. Full of water, eh?'

'Oh.'

'Now, the horse is on the port side, right?'

'No, on the left.'

'That's what I said. So, we can slip under the tarpaulin or whatever it is to starboard, and slide silently into the water, and swim across to the other bank. You up for it?'

Richard felt terrified. He'd never even tried to swim, and the water would be freezing in December, and he would drown, and he didn't dare risk it.

'Look, what we'll do is take off our boots, and our coats, because otherwise they'll get full of water and weigh us down, and then we'll undo a bit of the tarp. We'll both go in the water together, and I'll hold you up, and I'll tow you across to the opposite bank in no time. It'll be fine. Well, it'll be icy cold, but it can't be worse than Derwent Water at Christmas. Better than facing Mr Barnes in Lynn, too, whoever he is.'

Richard saw he had no choice. 'Alright. We have no alternative, do we? But be sure not to get your mouth under water, and especially don't swallow any. I knew a man who died from falling in the Cam.'

With the greatest difficulty he tugged and cajoled his boots off his feet, and wriggled out of his coat. Edward had made a gap in the fastenings of the canvas, and they both moved across, slowly so as not to give themselves away by rocking the boat. There was a faint light from outside, such a relief after so long in utter blackness. Perhaps it was houses? Friendly faces? Assistance?

'We ought to let our coats and boots into the water too, so they won't find them once they come to fetch you,' whispered Richard.

'Good idea.'

They lowered their clothes into the water, careful not to make a splash. At the last minute Richard remembered Sir George's letters in his coat pocket and retrieved them, stuffing them down his breeches, before letting the things slide into the river.

It was most tricky, manoeuvring both of them to the gunwales at once, so they could slip silently overboard together. First Edward, and then Richard, slid over the side, until they touched the water. Then at a whispered signal, they both lowered themselves carefully into the dark, rippling stream.

Richard had to stifle a scream. It was unbearably cold, numbing, painful. He was going to drown, he was being pulled down, the water was closing over his head. He clamped his mouth shut, held his breath. And strong arms grasped him around his neck from behind, lifting his chin into the air, towing him. He gasped for breath. He tried to relax, to allow Edward to support him, but it went against all his instincts. He so wanted to struggle, to thrash about. Somehow he held still, trusting in his friend. The barge's shape, a darker shade of black against the sky, moved on past them, then the light in the cabin, and then it was gone, except for the sound of the horse's harness, and the swish of the wash.

Richard felt himself being tugged across to the opposite bank. Slowly, it seemed, so slowly. He would die of cold before they got to safety. And then, there was something solid. Edward had him grab hold of a pole of some sort, told him to hold on while he got out of the water. He tried to grab on to Edward at first, and then as Edward forced his hands off his shirt, held on to the pole for dear life. There was a lot of splashing, and then Edward's hands reaching down and hauling Richard up and onto what seemed to be some kind of jetty. They had made it.

CHAPTER 26

WET, SHIVERING AND EXHAUSTED, THE two of them struggled across a field and onto the road where there were houses, at least some of which were lit. One had a lamp burning above the door, it looked like an inn. They headed for it.

Once in the saloon they saw a great fire and dripped across to it, turning their backs to it so their clothes steamed. There was a clock on the wall, it said nine o'clock. Surely it could not be still so early? Richard felt he had been out all night.

The landlord, not to mention the habitués, stared at them. 'A pint of old ale, and a whisky for my friend here,' said Edward, between chattering teeth.

Needless to say, the man did not serve them. Instead he called his wife, who took them through to a back parlour and fetched towels, and instructed them to take off their wet things immediately, what were they thinking of going for a swim in that nasty dirty water at this time, she'd fetch them some dry things, and where were they from, were they students on a dare, or had somebody pushed them in, and where were their boots, their feet must be cut to ribbons, and so on, and so on.

Richard realised he had escaped one danger only to face another. He had to take off his wet things, but he couldn't strip off in front of Edward, no way could he. But how to escape? He towelled his head while he thought, and then sat down and struggled with his tattered stockings which clung to his legs with tenacity. Edward had his waistcoat and shirt off already, and he was undoing his breeches when the mistress of the house came in, carrying a bundle of clothes.

'Madam, could I trouble you for the use of your privy?' begged Richard. 'It must be the cold water, but I am in sore need.'

He took some breeches, a rough shirt, and a woollen jacket, and disappeared with the woman. Once safely inside the privy he stripped off his other garments with difficulty in the confined space and, shivering even more, dried himself. He put on the loaned clothes, making sure to button up the coat to conceal his chest, and squeezed out the wet one as best he could. The letters in his breeches were pulp: he consigned them with regret into the privy. Holding the wet bundle away from his body, he made his way back to the parlour. Fortunately Edward was now also changed, and standing as close as he could to the fire. He joined him there, and gradually felt the heat seeping through him.

'I told the innkeeper we had been out for a long walk and it had taken far longer than we had expected, so we couldn't get home before nightfall. I said we had missed our footing in the dark, and fallen in the river,' said Edward.

'What about our not having boots or coats?'

'Well yes, I said we had pulled them off once we fell in, so as not to be dragged down by them. It was the best I could do.'

'So what now?'

'I don't know.'

'And where are we?'

'The sign said the inn is the King's Head. I'm afraid I don't know how far we had got before we jumped ship.'

The landlady came back in, and fussed around them, giving them stockings and feeling their hands for warmth. She also had a selection of old boots to try. It seemed they were in Fen Ditton, which seemed impossible. Surely they had been in the barge for hours? But the clock had said otherwise, and they had not passed through Baits Bite lock. It must be true.

'Madam, how may we return to Cambridge?' asked Richard. We shall of course repay you for your kindness, and return the clothes and boots as soon as we can.'

'Well, I don't know about that,' she replied. 'Are you at the university, then?'

'We are. Emmanuel College. We'd very much like to get back there tonight, if we can.'

'Well, it's getting very late. I don't know but what you ought to stay here for the night, till you've got properly warm, like.'

'We really would like to get back to college, madam. It's quite important.'

'Hmmm. I'll see if Jem could hitch up a horse to the dogcart, if you like. You won't want to be walking far in those old boots.'

'That would be most kind. Really. We are so grateful. We will be able to pay Jem once we get back to college. I have only a few coins in my pocket at the moment.'

'Be away with you. That's nothing, it isn't every day we get half-drowned travellers walk into our bar, it'll be talked about for weeks here I'll be bound.'

So, in a short while, Jem helped them load their wet bundles of clothes and climb up onto the elderly vehicle, and they drove the three miles into town at a sedate pace suitable to the great age of the horse. The porter on duty, Mr Chapman, answered their knock, and was to put it mildly so surprised at their appearance that he forgot to comment on their lack of gowns, or to put them in the late book. He was able to pay Jem from the supply of ready money kept in the lodge for such things as receiving post, and Jem drove off most satisfied, with their promise to return the clothes as soon as possible.

'I am so looking forward to my bed,' said Edward.

'No, wait a minute, we can't go to bed yet. We need to . . .' Richard paused. Peter ought to be back in college by now. They really ought to go and see him. Even if that meant letting Edward know about his real job. Yes, he had to do this. Also, he couldn't let Edward go back to his rooms where James Smith might be. And he needed to hear Edward's story himself.

'Come with me. It won't take too long. You need to meet someone. He needs to talk to you as well.'

Peter was in his rooms. He was dumbfounded by their picturesque appearance, and after getting them to set their damp bundles in his basin, and providing a large glass of wine for both of them, by their story.

It seemed Edward had gone with James to meet a friend in a coffee house, and then the three of them had gone to a tavern across the Small Bridges, where he had tried at their suggestion a special type of ale, notwithstanding the early hour. The next thing he knew he was sitting tied up in the Black Prince's cabin, and being questioned by the bargees and by the other man. He had told them they were grannies, and noddies, and so on, and that he knew nothing about anything, and they should let him go forthwith, but all that happened was that they gagged him, and carried on moving down river.

The barge had presumably been moored by the King's Mill because he had heard them cursing as they took the boat along past the colleges while he was being questioned, and he could hear the splashing as the horse made its way through the water. He had overheard the bargees saying to someone, maybe to Smith, that they were set for King's Lynn, and they were to deliver him to a Mr Barnes, but apart from saying he still had a sore head he had no more to add.

'Barnes?' said Peter. 'Are you sure of the name?'

'As sure as I can be of anything just now.'

Richard chipped in. 'The men mentioned him when I was hiding by the Pike and Eel too.'

'Oh, yes. They moved me out of the cabin into the cargo hold once we had moored at the tavern, I think they must have waited till it was dark and they were out of the way to do it.'

Peter considered for a long while. Richard and Edward drank their wine, and scratched from time to time. Their borrowed clothes were somewhat itchy.

'Right,' he said at length. 'This is what we will do. Or rather, what I and my colleagues will do. You two will get some rest, and attend the University sermon tomorrow, and try and behave normally.'

'But,' began Richard.

'But nothing. You have been amazing tonight, and Edward must be extremely grateful to you, but now we just have to round up the conspirators.'

Edward must have looked confused, because Peter broke off and gave him a very abbreviated version of the events at the ball, and the situation he had stumbled into.

'And by the way, did you mention your visit to the Pink Houses with Richard to anyone?'

'No, not at all.' He paused, looked shamefaced. 'Well, maybe. Only to James, we'd had a few ales one night and I may have said something about having had quite a lark looking for spies by the river with Richard here. Perhaps.'

'Hence why you were kidnapped and being taken for questioning to Mr Barnes of King's Lynn. Who I suspect is Lord John Barnes, one of our agents, who may well be in fact a double agent. Well, well, well. In this game you can't trust anybody.'

'Might he be the man I saw talking to Noakes and Smith at the . . .' Richard broke off, realising he was about to give away his secret.

'Indeed. Did he have a somewhat plethoric face?'

'He did.'

'Right. Now, I am sure Smith will have made himself scarce, but just in case, I shall go with you to the Brick building and make sure.' He went into his study and after some sounds of metal on metal came back with a pistol in one hand, and some rope in the other.

'Come with me, you two.'

Richard made sure he took his wet clothes with him as he did not want the cloth he used to bind his breasts to be discovered by Edward. They descended the stair into Chapel Court and made their way around to the lads' staircase. Ascending as quietly as possible,

Peter tried the door to Edward's room. It was locked. Edward opened it (once he had retrieved his key from his sodden waistcoat) and Peter entered first, gun at the ready.

James Smith was in his room, putting something into his box. He looked around wildly as Peter entered, made a dart for the window, then presumably remembered the long drop and raised his hands.

'I arrest you, James Smith, on a charge of treason against His Majesty King George,' said Peter. 'Edward, perhaps you would like to do the honours with this rope?'

'With the greatest of pleasure, Mr Winton.'

Being careful to keep out of the line of Peter's gun he tied James' arms, and pulled the knots extra tight. 'The boot is on the other foot, now, eh, bacon-brain?' he said. He looked down at the floor. 'Although in my case, my footwear does need some attention still.'

'Sit Mr Smith on the floor, please, Edward, and have him cross his legs. And then I think you should go and change into a more conventional costume. We still have a few things to do tonight, it seems.'

Edward did as he was ordered, none too gently, and then disappeared into his room. Richard likewise went upstairs and found his second pair of breeches, and a less itchy shirt. Glad that Sir George had insisted on him having a second coat and another waistcoat, which he had thought unnecessary, he completed his outfit with clean stockings and his low shoes, omitting his stock at this late and unusual hour. He went back down to Peter and his prisoner.

Peter had been interrogating Smith the while. The threat of the gallows looming with the charge of treason had loosened his tongue remarkably. Unfortunately the lad seemed not to know anything much that they had not worked out themselves, beyond that he had carried out instructions from Mr Cork, in exchange for much-needed funds, as his father could barely support him at the University, and he wanted to help his brothers make their ways in the world, and be able to afford some amusements at college, and so on.

He did not know the identity of the older man he had talked with at the ball. He was there simply to take messages between Cork and anyone he did not wish to be seen with. He had been instructed to tell the older man that all was ready, and that was all. He didn't know who the younger man was either, but he thought he was an undergraduate. No, he didn't know which college, but it wasn't Emmanuel. No, the name Noakes meant nothing to him. Cork didn't tell him people's names as a matter of principle, unless he had to. The older man had been very angry when some chit of a girl had chopped at the cake with a sword and foiled his plans, and he had given him a message to take to Cork to say he had to go to King's Lynn after the ball, and to make sure he was kept informed.

He knew nothing of the damage to Richard's room. He had been ordered to take Edward to meet someone in the coffee house, and to stay with him until he was dismissed. Because of this commission he been out all day until just before dark, the other man had kept him by his side until then in case he needed messages taking, and then he had attended evening chapel, and been in Wilks' rooms until supper trying to learn some Greek verbs, although he hadn't been able to concentrate, before coming back here. Might he be treated leniently if he turned nose?

Peter told Edward to fetch the poker from the fireplace and to stand guard over his prisoner, and lam him on the head if he tried to move. Edward took up his position with alacrity, and stood, weapon raised, as if he hoped Smith would give him an excuse to use it. Peter went with Richard down to Cork's rooms. The door was locked, there was no answer to his knock. He handed the pistol to Richard, who held it as though it was a baby bird that might break in his hands, while he worked on the lock with picks. The door swung open and they entered, once Richard had gladly given up the pistol to Peter.

Cork was gone. The rooms were emptied of his belongings, just the furniture and the pictures remained.

'As I thought,' said Peter. 'He's got the wind up, not sure how. Maybe because of the debacle at the ball, or perhaps once he'd wrecked your room, Richard, yet found nothing. Very well, I shall convey Smith to the town lockup, and instruct the porters to detain Mr Cork if he were to show himself in college. I need to send men to King's Lynn to arrest Barnes, and put out an alert for Cork in this whole neighbourhood. It will be a busy night.'

Locking the door behind him, (as he said, there was no point advertising his skills), he returned to Edward's room and disappeared off with Edward and his prisoner. Richard climbed wearily up to his room, looked once at his wet bundle, and lay on his bed fully clothed. In a moment he was asleep.

CHAPTER 27
EPILOGUE

ONLY FIVE DAYS REMAINED UNTIL the end of term. Richard learned that Cork had been caught together with Barnes at his lordship's estate in Norfolk, and that the crew of the Black Prince had been arrested once they moored in Lynn harbour later on Sunday. Mr Noakes had been let be for the time being, at the request of a colleague of Winton's in Trinity, whose identity Peter wouldn't disclose, but who Richard deduced must be the man Sir George had visited when they first arrived in Cambridge. It seemed so long ago now that he had come here. The idea was that Noakes might lead them to other conspirators, and he had a man assigned to shadow him. His correspondence would be read, and his contacts monitored.

Mr Chapman, the porter who had let them into college the previous night had been sworn to absolute secrecy, under the laws about the defence of the kingdom, both about their unconventional entrance to college and the subsequent departure of Winton with his prisoner, and his interest in Mr Cork. He was able to tell them that Mr Cork had departed hurriedly that afternoon, without stating his destination. Nobody else seemed to have become aware of their comings and goings, so Winton's secret appeared safe, at least for now, not to mention Edward's and Richard's involvement.

The gunpowder remaining at the Pink Houses was impounded, the tenant arrested, and the explanation of the failure of the watcher to detect the removal of the powder became apparent. It had gone in several small flour bags, supposedly destined for market. The actual destination of the powder and the place of the bomb's manufacture remained unknown, however.

As for Richard, returning to normal college life seemed rather flat after all the excitement. Not exactly boring, or leading to him feeling irritable or tetchy, just lacking in something. He hoped it wasn't only that he wished he could see Mr Blackburn once more, in his person of Rose, of course. He had heard with sorrow that he had suffered a head injury in the melee, which had not been immediately apparent, but that as soon as he had recovered he was to leave for the North, to investigate problems besetting a cavalry regiment there. He, if he was truthful, suspected strongly that that gentleman was a major cause of his unsettled state. But there was always the Christmas vacation, though, when he might be able to be Rose again, and perhaps have him visit?

On the other hand, he had nearly worked through Euclid, much to Mr Laughton's surprise and pleasure, and could look forward to perhaps starting the Principia next term? Not to mention, his future now looked in quite a different direction from how it had nine months previously, at the start of his Season. He intended to be an intelligencer. Perhaps not one of the conventional type, to be sure. However he had certain, shall we say, advantages that other men did not have. Rose might have to make another appearance in the service of her country, he thought.

In the meantime, there was something else he needed to learn from Peter. It seemed a very necessary skill, however unladylike it might be. He wanted to learn how to pick locks.